CATFISH
CHARLIE

**Look for these exciting Western series
from bestselling authors
William W. Johnstone and J.A. Johnstone**

The Mountain Man

Luke Jensen: Bounty Hunter

Brannigan's Land

The Jensen Brand

Smoke Jensen: The Early Years

Preacher and MacCallister

Fort Misery

The Fighting O'Neils

Perley Gates

MacCoole and Boone

Guns of the Vigilantes

Shotgun Johnny

The Chuckwagon Trail

The Jackals

The Slash and Pecos Westerns

The Texas Moonshiners

Stoneface Finnegan Westerns

Ben Savage: Saloon Ranger

The Buck Trammel Westerns

The Death and Texas Westerns

The Hunter Buchanon Westerns

Will Tanner, Deputy US Marshal

Old Cowboys Never Die

Go West, Young Man

WILLIAM W. JOHNSTONE

AND J. A. JOHNSTONE

CATFISH CHARLIE

PINNACLE BOOKS
Kensington Publishing Corp.
www.kensingtonbooks.com

PINNACLE BOOKS are published by

Kensington Publishing Corp.
900 Third Avenue
New York, NY 10022

Copyright © 2023 by J.A. Johnstone

PUBLISHER'S NOTE
Following the death of William W. Johnstone, the Johnstone family is working with a carefully selected writer to organize and complete Mr. Johnstone's outlines and many unfinished manuscripts to create additional novels in all of his series like The Last Gunfighter, Mountain Man, and Eagles, among others. This novel was inspired by Mr. Johnstone's superb storytelling.

All Kensington titles, imprints, and distributed lines are available at special quantity discounts for bulk purchases for sales promotion, premiums, fundraising, educational, or institutional use. Special book excerpts or customized printings can also be created to fit specific needs. For details, write or phone the office of the Kensington Special Sales Manager: Attn. Special Sales Department. Kensington Publishing Corp, 900 Third Ave., New York, NY 10022. Phone: 1-800-221-2647.

PINNACLE BOOKS and the Pinnacle logo Reg. U.S. Pat. & TM Off.

ISBN: 978-0-7860-5046-8
First Kensington Hardcover Edition: December 2023
First Kensington Mass Market Edition: April 2024

ISBN: 978-0-7860-5047-5 (ebook)

10 9 8 7 6 5 4 3 2 1

Printed in the United States of America

Chapter 1

May 2, 1891

"**B**ushwhack" Wilbur Aimes, Deputy Town Marshal of Wolfwater, in West Texas, looked up from the report he'd been scribbling, sounding out the words semi-aloud as he'd written them and pressing his tongue down hard against his bottom lip in concentration. He knew his letters and numbers well enough, but that didn't mean he had an easy time stringing them together.

He almost welcomed the sudden, uneasy feeling climbing his spine, stealthy as a brown recluse spider.

He frowned at the brick wall before him, below the flour sack–curtained window, the drawn curtains still bearing the words PIONEER FLOUR MILLS, SAN ANTONIO, TX, though the Texas sun angling through the window every day had badly faded them.

The sound came again—distant hoof thuds, a horse's whicker.

Silence.

A bridle chain rattled.

Bushwhack, a big, broad-shouldered, rawboned man, and former bushwhacker from Missouri's backwoods, rose from his chair. The creaky Windsor was mostly Marshal Abel Wilkes's chair, but Bushwhack got to sit in it when he was on duty—usually night duty as he was on tonight—and the marshal was off, home in bed sleeping within only a few feet of the marshal's pretty schoolteacher daughter, Miss Bethany.

Bushwhack shook his head as though to rid it of thoughts of the pretty girl. Thinking about her always made his cheeks warm and his throat grow tight. Prettiest girl in Wolfwater, for sure. If only he could work up the courage to ask the marshal if he could . . .

Oh, stop thinking about that, you damn fool! Bushwhack castigated himself. The marshal's holding off on letting any man step out with his daughter until the right one came along. And that sure as holy blazes wasn't going to be the big, awkward, bearded, former defender of the ol' Stars an' Bars, as well as a horse-breaker-until-a-wild-stallion-had-broken *him*—his left hip, at least. No, Miss Bethany Wilkes wasn't for him, Bushwhack thought, half pouting as he grabbed his old Remington and cartridge belt off the wall peg, right of the door, the uneasy feeling staying with him even beneath his forbidden thoughts of the marshal's daughter.

He glanced at his lone prisoner in the second of the four cells lined up along the office's back wall.

"Skinny" Thorson was sound asleep on his cot, legs crossed at the ankles, funnel-brimmed, weather-beaten hat pulled down over his eyes.

Skinny was the leader of a local outlaw gang, though he didn't look like much. Just a kid on the downhill side of twenty, but not by much. Skinny wore his clothes next to rags. His boots were so worn that Bushwhack could see his socks through the soles.

The deputy chuffed his distaste as he encircled his waist with the belt and soft leather holster from which his old, walnut-gripped Remington jutted, its butt scratched from all the times it had been used to pulverize coffee beans around remote Texas camp-fires during the years—a good dozen. Bushwhack had punched cattle around the Red River country and into the Panhandle—when he hadn't been fight-ing Injuns or bluebellies and minding his topknot, of course.

You always had to mind your scalp in Comanche country.

Or breaking broncs for Johnny Sturges, until that one particularly nasty blue roan had bucked him off onto the point of his left hip, then rolled on him and gave him a stomp to punctuate the "ride" and to set-tle finally the argument over who was boss.

That had ended Bushwhack's punching and break-ing days.

Fortunately, Abel Wilkes had needed a deputy and hadn't minded overmuch that Bushwhack had lost the giddyup in his step. Bushwhack was still sturdy, al-beit with a bit of a paunch these days, and he was right handy with a hide-wrapped bung starter, a sawed-off twelve gauge, and his old Remington. Now he grabbed the battered Stetson off the peg to the right of the one his gun had been hanging from, set it on his head, slid the Remington from its holster and, holding the long-barreled popper straight down against his right leg, opened the door and poked his head out, taking a cautious look around.

As he did, he felt his heart quicken. He wasn't sure

why, but he was nervous. He worried the old Remy's hammer with his right thumb, ready to draw it back to full cock if needed.

Not seeing anything amiss out front of the marshal's office and the jailhouse, he glanced over his shoulder at Skinny Thorson once more. The outlaw was still sawing logs beneath his hat. Bushwhack swung his scowling gaze back to the street, then stepped out onto the jailhouse's rickety front stoop to take a better look around.

The night was dark, the sky sprinkled with clear, pointed stars. Around Bushwhack, Wolfwater slouched, quiet and dark in these early-morning hours—one thirty, if the marshal's banjo clock on the wall over the large, framed map of western Texas could be trusted. The clock seemed to lose about three minutes every week, so Bushwhack or Wilkes or Maggie Cruz, who cleaned the place once a week, had to consult their pocket watches and turn it ahead.

Bushwhack trailed his gaze around the broad, pale street to his left; it was abutted on both sides by mud brick, Spanish-style adobe, or wood frame, false-fronted business buildings, all slouching with age and the relentless Texas heat and hot, dry wind. He continued shuttling his scrutinizing gaze along the broad street to his right, another block of which remained before the sotol-stippled, bone-dry, cactus-carpeted desert continued unabated dang near all the way to the Rawhide Buttes and Wichita Falls beyond.

The relatively recently laid railroad tracks of the Brazos, San Antonio & Rio Grande Line ran right through the middle of the main drag, gleaming faintly now in the starlight. Most businessmen and cattlemen in the area had welcomed the railroad for connecting San Antonio, in the southeast, with El Paso, in the northwest, and parts beyond.

Celebrated by some, maligned by others, including Marshal Abel Wilkes.

The San Antonio & Rio Grande Line might have brought so-called progress and a means for local cattlemen to ship their beef-on-the-hoof out from Wolfwater, but it had also brought trouble in the forms of men and even some women—oh, its share of troublesome women, as well, don't kid yourself!—in all shapes, sizes, colors, and creeds. However, it being a weeknight, the town was dark and quiet. On weekends, several saloons, hurdy-gurdies, and gambling parlors remained open, as long as they had customers, or until Marshal Wilkes, backed by Bushwhack himself, tired of breaking up fights and even some shootouts right out on the main drag, Wolfwater Street. Marshal and deputy would shut them down and would send the cowboys, vaqueros, sodbusters, and prospectors back to their ranches, haciendas, soddies, and diggings, respectively.

The road ranches stippling the desert outside of Abel Wilkes's jurisdiction stayed open all night, however. There was nothing Wilkes and Bushwhack could do about them. What perditions they were, too! When he'd heard all the trouble that took place out there, Bushwhack was secretly glad his and the marshal's jurisdiction stopped just outside of Wolfwater. Too many lawmen—deputy U.S. marshals, deputy sheriffs from the county seat over in Heraklion, and even some Texas Rangers and Pinkertons—had ridden into such places, between town and the Rawhide Buttes, to the west, or between town and the Stalwart Mountains, to the south, never to be seen or heard from again.

In fact, only last year, Sheriff Ed Wilcox from Heraklion had sent two deputies out to the road ranch on Jawbone Creek. Only part of them had returned home—their heads in gunnysacks tied to their saddle horns!

As far as Bushwhack knew, no one had ever learned what had become of the rest of their bodies. He didn't care to know, and he had a suspicion that Sheriff Ed Wilcox didn't, either. The road ranch on Jawbone Creek continued to this day, unmolested— at least by the law, ha-ha. (That was the joke going around.)

Bushwhack shoved his hat down on his forehead to scratch the back of his head with his left index finger. All was quiet, save the snores sounding from Skinny Thorson's cell in the office behind him. No sign of anyone out and about. Not even a cat. Not even a coyote, in from the desert, hunting cats.

So, who or what had made the sounds Bushwhack had heard just a minute ago?

He yawned. He was tired. Trouble in town had kept him from getting his nap earlier. His beauty sleep, the marshal liked to joke. Maybe he'd nodded off without realizing it and had only dreamt of the hoof thud and the bridle chain rattle.

Bushwhack yawned again, turned, stepped back inside the office, and closed the door. Just then, he realized that the snores had stopped. He swung his head around to see Skinny Thorson lying as before, only he'd poked his hat brim up on his forehead and was gazing at Bushwhack, grinning, blue eyes twinkling.

"What's the matter, Bushwhack?" the kid said. "A mite nervous, are we?"

Bushwhack sauntered across the office and stood

at the door of Skinny's cell, scowling beneath the brim of his own Stetson. He poked the Remington's barrel through the bars and said, "Shut up, you little rat-faced tinhorn, or I'll pulverize your head."

Skinny turned his head to one side and a jeeringly warning light came to his eyes. "My big brother, Frank, wouldn't like that—now, would he?"

"No, the hangman wouldn't like it, neither. He gets twenty dollars for every neck he stretches. He's probably halfway between Heraklion an' here, and he wouldn't like it if he got here an' didn't have a job to do, money to make." Bushwhack grinned. "Of course, he'd likely get one of Miss Claire's girls to soothe his disappointment. And every man around knows how good Miss Claire's girls are at soothing disappointments."

It was true. Miss Julia Claire's sporting parlor was one of the best around—some said the best hurdy-gurdy house between El Paso and San Antonio, along the San Antonio, and Rio Grande Line. And Miss Julia Claire herself was quite the lady. A fella could listen to her speak English in that beguiling British accent of hers all day long.

All *night* long, for that matter.

Only, Miss Claire herself didn't work the line. That fact—her chasteness and accent and the obscurity of her past, which she'd remained tight-lipped about for all of the five years she'd lived and worked here in Wolfwater—gave her an alluring air of mystery.

Skinny Thorson now pressed his face up close to the bars, squeezing a bar to either side of his face in his hands, until his knuckles turned white, and said, "'The Reaper' ain't gonna have no job to do once he gets here, because by the time he gets here, I won't be here anymore. You got it, Bushwhack?"

The Reaper was what everyone around called the executioner from the county seat, Lorenzo Snow.

The prisoner widened his eyes and slackened his lower jaws and made a hideous face of mockery, sticking his long tongue out at Bushwhack.

Bushwhack was about to grab that tongue with his fingers and pull it through the bars, pull it all the way out of the kid's mouth—by God!—but stopped when he heard something out in the street again.

"What was that?" asked Skinny with mock trepidation, cocking an ear to listen. "Think that was Frank, Bushwhack?" He grinned sidelong through the bars once more. "You know what? I think it was!"

Outside, a horse whinnied shrilly.

Outside, men spoke, but it was too soft for Bushwhack to make out what they were saying.

The hooves of several horses thudded and then the thuds dwindled away to silence.

Bushwhack turned to face the door, scowling angrily. "What in holy blazes is going on out there?"

"It's Frank, Bushwhack. My big brother, Frank, is here, just like I knew he would be! He got the word I sent him!" Skinny tipped his head back and whooped loudly. Squeezing the cell bars, he yelled, "I'm here, Frank. Come an' fetch me out of here, big brother!"

Bushwhack had holstered the Remington, but he had not snapped the keeper thong home over the hammer. He grabbed his sawed-off twelve gauge off a peg in the wall to his left and looped the lanyard over his head and right shoulder. He broke open the gun to make sure it was loaded, then snapped it closed and whipped around to Skinny and said tightly, "One more peep out of you, you little scoundrel, an' I'll blast you all over that wall behind you. If Frank came to fetch you, he'd best've brought a bucket an' a mop!"

Skinny narrowed his eyes in warning and returned in his own tight voice, "Frank won't like it, Bushwhack. You know Frank. Everybody around the whole county knows Frank. You an' they know how Frank can be when he's riled!"

Bushwhack strode quickly up to the cell, clicking the twelve gauge's hammers back to full cock. "You don't hear too good, Skinny. Liable to get you killed. Best dig the dirt out'n your ears."

Skinny looked down at the heavy, cocked hammers of the savage-looking gut shredder. He took two halting steps back away from the cell door, raising his hands, palms out, in supplication. "All . . . all right, now, Bushwhack," he trilled. "Calm down. Just funnin' you's all." He smiled suddenly with mock equanimity. "Prob'ly not Frank out there at all. Nah. Prob'ly just some thirty-a-month-and-found cow nurses lookin' fer some coffin varnish to cut the day's dust with. Yeah, that's prob'ly who it is."

His smile turned wolfish.

Grimacing, anger burning through him, Bushwhack swung around to the door. Holding the twelve gauge straight out from his right side, right index finger curled over both eyelash triggers, he pulled the door open wide.

His big frame filled the doorway as he stared out into the night.

Again, the dark street was empty.

"All right—who's there?" he said, trying to ignore the insistent beating of his heart against his breastbone.

Silence, save for crickets and the distant cry of a

wildcat on the hunt out in the desert in the direction of the Stalwarts.

He called again, louder: "Who's there?" A pause. "That you, Frank?"

Bushwhack and Marshal Wilkes had known there was the possibility that Skinny's older brother, Frank, might journey to Wolfwater to bust his brother out. But they'd heard Frank had been last seen up in the Indian Nations, and they didn't think that even if Frank got word that Wilkes and Bushwhack had jailed his younger brother for killing a half-breed whore in one of the lesser parlor houses in Wolfwater, he'd make it here before the hangman would.

There were a total of six houses of ill repute in Wolfwater—not bad for a population of sixty-five hundred, though that didn't include all of the cowboys, vaqueros, miners, and sodbusters who frequented the town nearly every night and on weekends, and the mostly unseemly visitors, including gamblers, confidence men and women, which the railroad brought to town. It was in one of these lesser houses, only identified as GIRLS by the big gaudy sign over its front door, that Skinny had gone loco on busthead and thrown the girl out a second-story window.

The girl, a half-Comanche known as "Raven," had lived a few days before succumbing to her injuries caused when she'd landed on a hitchrack, which had busted all her ribs and cracked her spine. Infection had been the final cause of death, as reported by the lone local medico, Doc Overholser.

Anger at being toyed with was growing in Bushwhack. Fear, too, he had to admit. He stepped out onto the stoop, swinging his gaze from right to left, and back again, and yelled, "Who's out there? If it's you, Frank—show yourself, now!"

Bushwhack heard the sudden thud of hooves to his right and his left.

Riders were moving up around him now, booting their horses ahead at slow, casual walks, coming out from around the two front corners of the jailhouse flanking him on his right and left. They were ominous silhouettes in the starlight. As Bushwhack turned to his left, where three riders were just then swinging their horses around the right front corner of the jailhouse stoop and into the street in front of it, a gun flashed.

At the same time the gun's loud bark slammed against Bushwhack's ears, the bullet plundered his left leg, just above the knee. The bullet burned like a branding iron laid against his flesh.

Bushwhack yelped and shuffled to his right, clutching the bloody wound in misery. He released the twelve gauge to hang free against his belly and struck the porch floor in a grunting, agonized heap.

He cursed through gritted teeth, feeling warm blood ooze out of his leg from beneath his fingers. As he did, slow hoof clomps sounded ahead of him. He peered up to see a tall, rangy man in a black vest, black hat, and black denim trousers ride out of the street's darkness on a tall gray horse and into the light from the window and the open door behind Bushwhack.

The guttering lamplight shone in cold gray eyes above a long, slender nose and thick blond mustache. The lips beneath the mustache quirked a wry grin as Frank Thorson said, "Hello, there, Bushwhack. Been a while. You miss me?"

The smile grew. But the gray eyes remained flat and hard and filled with malicious portent.

Chapter 2

Marshal Abel Wilkes snapped his eyes open, instantly awake.

"Oh, fer Pete's sake!"

Almost as quickly, though not as quickly as it used to be, the Colt hanging from the bedpost to his right was in his hand. Aiming the barrel up at the ceiling, Abel clicked the hammer back and lay his head back against his pillow, listening.

What he'd heard before, he heard again. A man outside breathing hard. Running in a shambling fashion. The sounds were growing louder as Wilkes—fifty-six years old, bald but with a strap of steel-gray hair running in a band around his large head, above his ears, and with a poorly trimmed, soup-strainer gray mustache—lay there listening.

What in blazes . . . ?

Abel tossed his covers back and dropped his pajama-clad legs over the side of the bed. He'd grabbed his ratty, old plaid robe off a wall peg and shrugged into it and was sliding his feet into his wool-lined slippers, as ratty as the robe, when his daughter's voice rose from the lower story. "Dad? Dad? You'd better come down he—"

She stopped abruptly when Abel heard muffled thuds on the floor of the porch beneath his room, here in the second story of the house he owned and in which he lived with his daughter, Bethany. The muffled thuds were followed by a loud hammering on the house's front door.

"Marshal Wilkes!" a man yelled.

More thundering knocks, then Bushwhack Aimes's plaintive wail: *"Marshal Wilkes!"*

What in tarnation is going on now? Wilkes wondered.

Probably had to do with the railroad. That damned railroad . . . bringin' vermin of every stripe into—

"Dad, do you hear that?" Beth's voice came again from the first story.

"Coming, honey!" Abel said as he opened his bedroom door and strode quickly into the hall, a little breathless and dizzy from rising so fast. He wasn't as young as he used to be, and he had to admit his gut wasn't as flat as it used to be, either. Too many roast beef platters at Grace Hasting's café for noon lunch, followed up by steak and potatoes cooked by Beth for supper.

Holding the Colt down low against his right leg, Abel hurried as quickly as he could, without stumbling down the stairs, just as Beth opened the front door at the bottom of the stairs and slightly right, in the parlor part of the house. The willowy brunette was as pretty as her mother had been, but she was on the borderline of being considered an old maid, since she was not yet married at twenty-four. The young woman gasped and stepped back quickly as a big man tumbled inside the Wilkes parlor, striking the floor with a loud *bang*.

Not normally a screaming girl, Beth stepped back quickly, shrieked, and closed her hands over her mouth as she stared down in horror at her father's deputy, who lay just inside the front door, gasping like a landed fish.

Abel knew it was Bushwhack Aimes because he'd recognized his deputy's voice. The face of the man, however, only vaguely resembled Bushwhack. He'd been beaten bad, mouth smashed, both eyes swelling, various sundry scrapes and bruises further disfiguring the big man's face. He wore only long-handles, and the top hung from his nearly bare shoulders in tattered rags.

"Oh, my God!" Beth exclaimed, turning to her father as Abel brushed past her.

Like Abel, she was clad in a robe and slippers. Lamps burned in the parlor, as well as in the kitchen, indicating she'd been up late grading papers again or preparing lessons for tomorrow.

"Good God," Abel said, dropping to a knee beside his bloody deputy, who lay clutching his left leg with both hands and groaning loudly against the pain that must be hammering all through him. "What the hell happened, Bushwhack? Who did this to you?"

He couldn't imagine the tenacity it had taken for Bushwhack in his condition to have made it here from the jailhouse—a good four-block trek, blood pouring out of him. The man already had a bum hip, to boot!

"Marshal!" Aimes grated out, spitting blood from his lips.

Abel turned to his daughter, who stood crouched forward over Aimes, looking horrified. "Beth, heat some water and fetch some cloths, will you?"

As Beth wheeled and hurried across the parlor and into the kitchen, Abel placed a placating hand on his deputy's right shoulder. "Easy, Bushwhack. Easy. I'll fetch the sawbones in a minute. What happened? Who did this to you?"

Aimes shifted his gaze from his bloody leg to the marshal. "Thor . . . Thorson. Frank Thorson . . . an' his men! Shot me. Beat me. Stripped me. Left me in the street . . . laughin' at me!" The deputy sucked a sharp breath through gritted teeth and added, "They busted Skinny out of jail!"

"Are they still in town?"

"They broke into one of the saloons—the Wolfwater Inn! Still . . . still there, far as I know . . . Oh . . . oh, *Lordy*!" Bushwhack reached up and wrapped both of his own bloody hands around one of Abel's. "They're killers, Marshal! Don't go after 'em alone." He wagged his head and showed his teeth between stretched-back lips. "Or . . . you'll . . ." He was weakening fast, eyelids growing heavy, barely able to get the words out. ". . . you'll end up like me—*dead!*"

With that, Bushwhack's hands fell away from Abel's. His head fell back against the floor with a loud *thump*. He rolled onto his back and his head sort of wobbled back and forth, until it and the rest of the man's big body fell still. The eyes slightly crossed and halfway closed as they stared up at Abel Wilkes, glassy with death.

Footsteps sounded behind Abel, and he turned to see Beth striding through the parlor behind him. "I have water heating, Pa! Want I should fetch the doc . . . ?" She stopped suddenly as she gazed down at Bushwhack. Again, she raised her hands to her mouth, her brown eyes widening in shock.

"No need for the doc, honey," Abel said, slowly

straightening, gazing down at his deputy. Anger burned in him. "I reckon he's done for, Bushwhack is."

Beth moved slowly forward, dropped to her knees, and gently set her hand on the deputy's head, smoothing his thick, curly, salt-and-pepper hair back from his forehead. "I'm so sorry, Bushwhack," she said in a voice hushed with sorrow.

"Stay with him, take care of him as best you can, honey," Abel said, reaching down to squeeze his daughter's shoulder comfortingly. "On my way into town, I'll send for the undertaker."

Beth looked up at her father, tears of sorrow and anger in her eyes. "Who did this to Bushwhack, Pa?"

"Frank Thorson."

Beth sort of winced and grimaced at the same time. Most people did that when they heard the name. "Oh, God," she said.

"Don't you worry, honey," Abel said, squeezing her shoulder once more. "Thorson will pay for what he did here tonight."

Abel gave a reassuring dip of his chin, then turned to start back up the stairs to get dressed.

"Pa!" Beth cried.

Abel stopped and turned back to his daughter, on her knees now and leaning back against the slipper-clad heels of her feet. Beth gazed up at him with deep concern. "You're not thinking about confronting Frank Thorson alone—are you?"

Abel didn't like the lack of confidence he saw in his daughter's eyes. "I don't have any choice, honey."

Aimes was his only deputy, and there was little time to deputize more men. He needed to throw a loop around Frank Thorson and the men riding with him before they could leave town. This was his town, Abel Wilkes's town, and he'd be dogged if anyone, including Frank Thorson, would just ride in, shoot and beat his deputy to death, spring a prisoner, then belly up to a bar for drinks in celebration.

Oh, no. Wilkes might not be the lawman he once was, but Wolfwater was still his town, gallblastit. He would not, could not, let the notorious firebrand Frank Thorson, whom he'd had run-ins with before, turn him into a laughingstock.

Trying to ignore his deputy's final warning, which echoed inside his head, Wilkes returned to his room and quickly dressed in his usual work garb—blue wool shirt under a brown vest, black twill pants, and his Colt's six-gun strapped around his bulging waist. He grabbed his flat-brimmed black hat off a wall peg and, holding the hat in one hand, crouched to peer into the mirror over his dresser.

He winced at what he saw there.

An old man . . .

His dear wife's death two years ago had aged him considerably. Abel Wilkes, former soldier in the War Against Northern Aggression, former stockman, former stage driver, former stagecoach messenger, and, more recently, former Pinkerton agent, was not the man he'd been before Ethel Wilkes had contracted bone cancer, which they'd had diagnosed by special doctors up in Abilene. Abel's face was paler than it used to be; heavy blue pouches sagged beneath his eyes, and deep lines spoked out from their corners.

There was something else about that face staring back from the mirror that gave Wilkes an unsettled feeling. He tried not to think about it, but now as he set the low-crowned hat on his head, shucked his Colt from its holster, opened the loading gate, and drew the hammer back to half cock, he realized the cause of his unsettlement. The eyes that had stared back at him a moment ago were no longer as bold and as certain as they once had been.

They'd turned a paler blue in recent months, and there was no longer in them the glint of bravado, the easy confidence that had once curled one corner of his mustached upper lip as he'd made his rounds up and down Wolfwater's dusty main drag. Now, as he stared down at the wheel of his six-gun as he poked a live cartridge into the chamber he usually left empty beneath the hammer, his eyes looked downright uncertain. Maybe even a little afraid.

Maybe more than *a little* afraid.

"Don't do it, Pa. Don't confront those men alone," Beth urged from where she continued to kneel beside Bushwhack as Abel descended the stairs, feeling heavy and fearful and generally out of sorts.

Beth wasn't helping any. Anger rose in him and he shifted his gaze to her now, deep lines corrugating his broad, sun-leathered forehead beneath the brim of his hat. "You sit tight and don't worry," he said, stepping around her and Bushwhack, his Winchester in his right hand now. "I'll send the undertak—"

She grabbed his left hand with both of her own and squeezed. "Pa, don't! Not alone!"

Not turning to her, but keeping his eyes on the night ahead of him, the suddenly awful night, Abel pulled his hand out from between Beth's and headed through the door and onto the porch. "I'll be back soon."

Feeling his daughter's terrified gaze on his back, Abel crossed the porch, descended the three steps to the cinder-paved path that led out through the gate in the white picket fence. He strode through the gate and did not bother closing it behind him. His nerves were too jangled to trifle with such matters as closing gates in picket fences.

As he strode down the willow-lined lane toward the heart of town, which lay ominously dark and silent straight ahead, Abel shook his head as though to rid it of the fear he'd seen in his daughter's eyes . . . in his own eyes. Beth's fear had somehow validated his own.

"Darn that girl, anyway," he muttered as he walked, holding the Winchester down low in his right hand. *She knows me better than I do. She knows my nerves have gone to hell.*

Fear.

Call it what it is, Abel, he remonstrated himself.

You've grown fearful in your later years.

There'd been something unnerving about watching Ethel die so slowly, gradually. That had been the start of his deterioration. And then, after Ethel had passed and they'd buried her in the cemetery at the east end of town, that darn whore had had to go and save his hide in the Do Drop Inn. The gambler had had Wilkes dead to rights. The marshal had called the man out on his cheating after hearing a string of complaints from other men the gambler had been playing cards with between mattress dances upstairs in the inn.

So Abel had gone over to the inn, intending to throw the man out of town. The gambler had dropped his cards, kicked his chair back, rose, and raised his hands above the butts of his twin six-shooters.

Open challenge.

Let the faster man live.

Abel remembered the fear he'd felt. He had a reputation as a fast gun—one of the fastest in West Texas at one time. "Capable Abel" Wilkes, they'd called him. His dirty little secret, however, was that when he'd started creeping into his later forties, he'd lost some of that speed. His reputation for being fast had preceded him, though. So he hadn't had to entertain many challengers. Just drunks who hadn't known any better or, because of the who-hit-John coursing through their veins, had thrown caution to the wind.

And had paid the price.

The gambler had been different. He'd been one cool customer, as most good gamblers were. As Abel himself once had been. Cool and confident in his speed. That night, however, the gambler had sized Wilkes up, sensed that the aging lawman was no longer as fast as he once had been. Abel hadn't been sure how the man had known that.

Maybe he'd seen the doubt in Abel's own eyes.

The fear. That fear.

Abel had let the gambler make the first move, of course. Over the years, the lawman had been so fast that he'd been able to make up for his opponents' lightning-fast starts. That night, however, Abel would have been wolf bait if the drunk doxie hadn't stumbled against him in her haste to leave the table and not risk taking a ricochet.

She had nudged his shooting arm just as the man had swept his pearl-handled Colt from its black leather holster thonged low on his right thigh. Abel's own Colt Lightning had cleared leather after the gambler's gun had drilled a round into the table before him, between him and his opponent. Abel's bullet had plunked through the man's brisket and instantly trimmed his wick.

Abel had left the saloon after the undertaker had hauled the gambler out feet first. He'd tried to maintain an air of grim confidence, of a job well done, but the other gamblers and the saloon's other customers all knew it to be as phony as he did. If that drunk, little doxie hadn't nudged the gambler's arm at just the right time, the undertaker would have planted Abel in the Wolfwater bone orchard, beside his dearly departed Ethel.

Leaving their old-maid daughter alone in the cold, cruel, West Texas world.

Now he swung onto Wolfwater's broad main drag, dark except for up at the Wolfwater Inn, half a block ahead and on the street's right side.

Abel felt his boots turn to lead. He wanted to do anything this night, except confront Frank Thorson and Thorson's men. Abel didn't know whom Frank was running with now, but for them to do what they had done to Bushwhack, they all had to be every bit as bad as Frank.

No, Wilkes wanted nothing to do with them. But he couldn't very well ignore them. He wanted to turn tail and run home and hide. Wait for the Thorson storm to pass. That's why he did what he did now. He quickened his pace.

There was only one thing worse than being dead.

That thing was being a laughingstock in front of your whole dang town.

Chapter 3

As Abel stepped onto one of the boardwalks fronting the businesses on the main street's north side, a gun cracked and a girl screamed from the direction of the Wolfwater Inn, dead ahead of him now, two buildings away.

He increased his pace, hardening his jaws and quietly jacking a live round into his carbine's action. The large plate glass window of the Wolfwater Inn was aglow with guttering umber lamplight. The watery light angled down onto the boardwalk fronting the place. As Abel stepped up onto the boardwalk, six feet from the orange glow, he stopped and pressed his right shoulder against the building's adobe brick wall.

Doffing his hat, he edged a look through the dirty glass.

"I said *Dance!*" a man's voice yelled.

There was a flash and a loud *pop* and the little dove, who stood in front of the table where six rough-looking men in dusty trail garb yelped, began to shuffle her bare feet, dancing, as the boisterous men lifted the hem of her gauzy cream nightgown above her bare ankles. Well, it wasn't really dancing. She was just moving her pale, delicate bare feet to keep them from getting shot off.

Sleep ribbons jounced in her hair.

The man who'd fired the shot was none other than Frank Thorson himself. He sat with his knees spread wide, another little doxie perched on the right one, her arms around Thorson's neck. She was a dark-eyed brunette who looked about as thrilled at the doings in the Wolfwater Inn as the little doxie doing the dancing while she stared down at her feet and sobbed.

The other men, including Skinny, sat around the same table as Frank, laughing as they swilled whiskey from shot glasses and beer from soapy mugs.

Abel could see several other girls poking their heads out from the dark mouth of a hall straight out across the room from him. Abel knew that down that dark hall was where Jed Timmerman's girls plied their trade. Now they watched in horror as Frank Thorson continued to fire his six-gun at the feet of the girl the other girls likely considered as close as any sister. One of them, a tall Mexican with Indian-dark skin, was sobbing into the hand that a pretty blonde held over her mouth.

Timmerman himself stood behind the bar on the room's far left side, looking ghostly pale, uncertain, and weary, clad in a pale cotton nightgown and with a pale cotton night sock on his head.

"That tears it!"

Anger overriding his reticence, Abel set his hat on his head and, holding his Winchester up high across his chest, pulled away from the window and tramped straight ahead along the boardwalk. He pushed through the batwings, took two long steps inside, and stopped, the louvered doors clattering back into place behind him.

He fired a warning round into the ceiling above his head, causing dust and plaster and bits of pressed tin to sift onto the floor around his boots, and yelled, "Hold it right there, Thorson!"

As the thunder of his shot continued to echo around the cavelike room, Abel jerked the cocking lever down, ejecting the spent, smoking cartridge, which clattered onto the floor over his right shoulder. He slammed the lever up against the gun's frame, seating a fresh round in the chamber, and said, "You've had enough fun for one evening. Toss that hogleg away and have your boys, including Skinny, do the same with theirs. You're all coming with me!"

His back to Abel, Thorson froze in his chair, holding his smoking six-gun straight up in his right hand, behind the back of the girl sitting on his right knee. The other men, including Skinny, had jerked their gazes toward the big, potbellied lawman standing in front of the batwings, tracking each of them with his carbine, narrowing one eye as he gazed down the barrel.

Silence hung over the saloon.

Thorson's men, including Skinny, suddenly all looked sober as judges.

Yeah, Abel thought, trying not to smile. *Yeah, yeah, see? You still got it. This ain't as hard as you thought it would be, is it? You got 'em all dead to rights!*

It helped, of course, that Thorson's men were all distracted by the girl. Still . . . pride made Abel stand a little straighter, squaring his shoulders, and made him spread his feet a little wider.

There were six in Thorson's bunch; Abel's carbine held fourteen rounds. Thirteen remained. Six men against thirteen rounds. Let Frank do the math.

Maybe that was what the outlaw leader was doing now as he stared straight ahead at the little doxie who'd stopped dancing and stood with her head down, one pale foot resting atop the other. She held two fistfuls of her nightgown just above her hips. Maybe Frank was going over the odds, wondering how fast Abel was with the carbine.

Whatever he was thinking, the back of his neck above the collar of his gray shirt was beet red, and Abel didn't think that was from sunburn alone.

Inwardly the lawman smiled.

"Drop it, Frank." Abel kept his voice low, but hard. "I won't tell you again!"

Suddenly, too quickly for Abel to follow or realize what was happening, Frank lurched up out of his chair. At the same time, he closed his right hand, his gun hand, around the girl's waist, picking her up off his knee. As he swung toward Abel, a shrewd grin on his savage, mustached face, and a deadly glitter in his gray eyes, he held the girl in front of him, her bare feet dangling two feet above the floor. Quick as an eye blink, he'd switched his .45 Colt to his left hand and, holding the girl with his right arm, he raised the Colt to her left temple, and ratcheted back the hammer.

"Tell me one more time, Marshal!" Frank barked. "Tell me one more time how it's gonna be!"

He chuckled as he dipped his chin and drilled Abel with his evil-eyed gaze. "Toss yours down or the girl gets her head blown off!"

Just as suddenly as Frank Thorson had gained his feet and swung toward Abel, using the girl as a shield, the confidence in Abel softened into an embarrassing mush he could feel in his knees.

No! he silently railed against it. *You still have the upper hand here, Wilkes! Don't forget who you are! You're the man you've always been! Only your confidence has waned, that's all!*

He steadied the carbine in his hands, kept aiming down the barrel, this time at Frank Thorson's left eye, above and to the right of the girl's head. "Kill her and you die."

Frank glanced at Skinny and the men to his right as he faced Abel. All looked a little constipated as they sat in their chairs, hands on their pistol grips, but leaving the hoglegs in their holsters. They were just drunk enough that they were having trouble figuring out what they ought to do.

"Kill me an' they kill you!"

"Dead is dead, Frank! Think it over, Frank!" Abel hooked his own hard smile, staring coldly down the barrel of the carbine at Thorson's left eye. "You ready to die here tonight?" He cut his gaze quickly toward the appropriately named Skinny sitting on the far side of the table from where Frank had been sitting and was now standing. "Are you ready to die here tonight for that little whore-killing punk you call a brother?"

Yeah, yeah. You still got it, Capable Abel Wilkes!

Skinny leaped to his feet and leaned over the table before him, yelling, "You go to hell, Wilkes. You kill my brother an'—"

"Sit down, Skinny," Frank said through gritted teeth. "Sit down an' pour yourself another drink. The marshal an' me—we're just havin' a little understandin', that's all."

"Drop the gun, Frank," Abel insisted, keeping his

hands and the Winchester steady, and mighty impressed with himself for doing so, his confidence continuing to grow. "Drop the gun. Have your boys drop theirs, and we'll all live to see another bright, clear West Texas morning." He smiled, enjoying himself now, already seeing in his mind's eye himself hazing Frank Thorson and his worthless brother and the four other men over to the hoosegow.

Don't go ridin' into Wolfwater thinkin' Capable Abel Wilkes is all used up, they'll say. *Hell no! Why, just the other night he filed Frank Thorson's horns for him, locked him up with Skinny in the same cell Frank done broke Skinny out of! Ha!*

"Drop the gun, Frank," he said again, even quieter this time.

He could see the doubt in Frank's eyes. The fear.

Yeah, he had Thorson on the run. Frank Thorson feared death, same as any man.

The saloon was so quiet that Abel thought he could hear a mouse ratcheting around under one of the floorboards near the room's rear. He could hear the quick, raspy breaths old Jed Timmerman was raking in and out of his lungs behind the bar.

Meanwhile, Capable Abel Wilkes held the carbine steady in his hands. If he could have seen his own eyes now, they'd appear steely. Yeah. No fear in his eyes now. None of the fear he and Bethany had seen in them only a few minutes ago.

He stared into Frank's eyes. They were cast with both anger and . . . fear. Abel took great satisfaction in that. He still had it, by God! He could still take down even an owlhoot of Frank Thorson's caliber!

Finally the outlaw leader pulled his gun away from the whore's head in disgust and said, "All right, fellas, drop your gu—"

"*Dad!*" came a cry from the night outside the Wolf-water Inn. It was Beth's voice. *No, couldn't be. Beth is home.* But then, the familiar, female voice came again, shriller this time, sort of gasping, sobbing. "*Dad!* Oh, God, no. Please! You're *hurting* me!"

Abel's heart thumped against his breastbone.

His hands holding the carbine shook a little.

Still, he kept the Winchester aimed at Frank Thorson's head.

Only, the fear had suddenly left the outlaw leader's eyes. Now the man shaped a slow smile beneath his blond mustache.

Abel could hear several sets of footsteps out on the street. They were growing louder.

Beth's voice again: "Dad!" A man laughed and there was the sharp crack of an open hand laid against a face.

Beth screamed.

More laughter from out on the street, growing louder as the men and Beth approached the Wolf-water Inn.

"Dad," Beth sobbed. "I'm so sorry, Dad! I didn't . . . I didn't hear them until . . . they were already in the *house*!"

Abel clenched his jaws as he continued to stare down his carbine's barrel at Frank Thorson's head. His grinning head.

"Thorson, you demon!" he bit out.

Thorson laughed. His snake eyes drew up at the corners as he said, "Sent two men after your deputy, Wilkes. Figured they'd lead us to you . . . to your daughter. Was expectin' you, ya see." He clucked and shook his head. "Darn fool."

Outside, Beth screamed again. There was the thud of a body hitting the street.

Beth wailed, "*Please*... why are you doing *this*?"

Frank raised his .45 to the doxie's head again, clicked the hammer back. "Drop the carbine, Wilkes," he said through an oily grin. "Or this girl gets kicked out with a cold shovel. That girl out there, though," he added, speaking slowly, raw menace in his evil eyes, "is going to die oh ... so ... very ... *slooooww*!"

Outside, there was another sharp *crack*. Beth screamed again. There was the unmistakable sound of cloth being torn.

"No!" Beth sobbed.

Abel turned his head slightly to his right to shout through the window, "Let her go, you devils!"

Outside two men—the two men who'd followed Bushwhack to the Wilkes house—laughed. Beth sobbed.

When Abel returned his gaze to Frank Thorson, the man's .45 was no longer aimed at the doxie's head. It was aimed at him.

Thorson grinned, cheeks dimpling to either side of his thick blond mustache. The .45 blossomed smoke and fire. The bullet ripped into Abel's right shoulder.

It was a large, hot fist ripping the carbine out of his hands and throwing him straight back onto a table. Groaning, clutching his bloody right shoulder with his right hand, he rolled off the table and onto the floor. The table came down on top of him. Lying on his back, raking breaths in and out of his lungs, he gritted his teeth against the searing pain in his shoulder as well as against the screams and cries of his daughter on the street beyond the big plate glass window.

Hearing the slow thump of footsteps growing

louder, watching a long shadow slide toward him, Abel groaned as he slid his right hand to the old Colt holstered on his right hip. He groaned again as he began to slide the .44 from the holster. Then the long, tall shadow slid over him, the table was kicked away, and he looked up to see Frank Thorson standing over him, grinning, his devil's eyes flashing beneath the flat brim of his low-crowned black hat.

The outlaw leader held the cocked .45 straight down along his right leg.

Abel froze in horror, watching the .45 slowly rise, hearing his daughter sobbing and groaning and complaining in the street to his right.

Abel grimaced up at Thorson as the grinning outlaw aimed the cocked .45 at Abel's head.

"Please," Abel begged, hating the fear he heard in his own voice. The desperation. "Let her . . . go! She . . . she . . . she's a *schoolteacher*, for Pete's sake!"

Thorson chuckled. Beneath the man's malicious laughter, Abel could hear the drumming of the footsteps of the outlaw's men and his brother, Skinny, most likely, striding quickly toward the batwings and out onto the street.

They were whooping and hollering and laughing in goatish celebration.

"No!" Abel said through a strangled wail. "Please . . . for the love of all that's merciful—*noo*!"

Thorson laughed. "All that's merciful don't include me!"

Abel watched in frozen terror as the outlaw's right index finger drew back against the .45's trigger.

That was the last thing he saw before everything went dark.

Chapter 4

The great fish—at least in its own mind, it was great—moved silently through the muddy water.

It stopped and pulled something dead and scrumptious-looking out from under a tree root protruding from the underwater bank of the large, dark pond that formed an oak-shaded backwater of Wolfwater Creek. The stream, slow this time of the year, early August, trickled down out of the Stalwart Mountains and traced a course not far from where the tracks of the Brazos, San Antonio & Rio Grande Railroad Line angled up around the range's eastern bastions from the south.

The fish pulled part of the dead thing out from under the log with a great jerk of its flat head. The dead thing was a half-grown javelina, or wild pig, that had foolishly tried to cross the stream earlier that spring, upstream from the pond. It had been swept away and drowned by the chill spring water, and the haphazard spring currents had sucked it into the pond and lodged it under the root. The pig was a bloated, ugly black mess as the great fish—thirty pounds, if it was an ounce, and as long from stem to stern as a leg of your average-sized man—jerked another part of it out from beneath the root and consumed it greedily. Its dark, crescent eyes half closing dreamily as it chomped, finding the morsel every bit as delicious as it had looked and smelled there in the murky, muddy water further obscured by long, hairlike weeds jutting up from the bottom.

The weeds waved this way and that in the gentle current, as did the great fish's long whiskers, as the fish swallowed the tender morsel, then started swimming back under the root for more. It was afternoon, judging by the sun's slant on the water overhead, and the fish was hungry. The last thing it had eaten was the meat out of the shell of a tortoise that had not been dead nearly long enough.

The fish—named Bubba Jones by the one man who both loved and hated him, though mostly saw him as a dozen nice-sized, meaty filets fried in a cast-iron skillet with butter, salt, and pepper over an open fire—spied movement in the corner of his right eye. He turned to see something splash into the stream, sending air bubbles foaming up around it. The thing was a cork, to which string was attached at both bottom and top. A hook was attached to the end of the lower, two-foot stretch of string. It was a sail hook that had been bent to form a U, with one side longer than the other, the end of the short side sharp as a razor's edge. If you looked closely, you could see the irregular marks in the hook made by the pliers that had bent it.

Bloody guts had been impaled to the sharp end of the hook.

Bubba Jones's practiced, discriminating sniffer detected chicken guts.

But such a slight snack did not compare to the full meal Bubba had left under the root.

Bubba smiled to himself. He chuckled.

Foolish man with his foolish hook and bobber!

(Bubba felt far superior to the man who both loved and hated him, though he did not know that he'd been named by the man after the man's fattest cousin, "Bubba" Clarence Jones, of Tivoli, Texas, who'd been so fat he'd once pulled his single-hole privy over just by trying to exit it.)

Bubba Jones turned back to the remaining meal under the root, the edges of torn flesh beckoning, when he spied even more movement out of the corner of his right eye. The water was so murky he couldn't see the object clearly. But he was curious enough—something even tastier and stinkier than the dead pig?—that he'd decided to hold off on the meal at hand and swim up along the side of the bank to investigate. Bubba was not worried that one of the other, lesser, and unnamed catfish in this neck of the pond would poach his meal.

The other, lesser, unnamed catfish in this neck of the pond, and even the lowly carp, knew who the biggest fish in this neck of the pond was. By now, they all knew whose meal the pig was—they all kept at least one eye skinned on the biggest fish in the pond—and would not be foolish enough to intrude on Bubba's territory at the risk of becoming the biggest fish in this neck of the pond's meal.

Finger food for Bubba.

So Bubba swam up a ways, to the left of where the cork and the baited hook lolled in the pond, maybe eight feet out from the bank. This other thing Bubba had detected was much nearer the bank than the cork and hook—maybe only a foot, if that much, out away from the shore.

Bubba swam closer to the object in question until he recognized what he was looking at from only three feet away.

A man's thick, pale foot with a bulbous big toe.

A bulbous big toe with a nail as thick as a snail shell. In fact, the nail *resembled* a snail's shell—a mottled yellow color with tiny corrugations running across it from left to right.

The foot that the toe belonged to hung down two feet beneath the surface of the water, the toes sticking straight out in front of it. The fish-belly white ankle and shin and calf above the foot were matted with fine brown hairs that gently waved, like the grass at the pond's bottom and the fish's whiskers in the pond's current. As Bubba looked up through the water, he could see the man's other foot and part of his leg, bent inward to rest against the bank just above the water.

The man's faded red longhandle legs were rolled up to nearly his knees.

Bubba couldn't see much more of the man above the surface of the pond. But he knew who he was. Just as the man knew who Bubba was. They'd been together out here, day after day, for a long time. The man who both loved and hated Bubba, and who had given Bubba the less than complimentary nickname, appeared to be resting back against the roots of the same tree he usually rested back against, his cane pole held loosely in his right hand on the ground by his side.

Bubba turned to the bated hook lolling in the water to his right.

He looked at the big, swollen toe with the discolored nail. Bubba knew what the man's feet looked like. This wasn't its first rodeo with the man. That big toe was oddly swollen, the nail even more discolored than it usually was.

The man, whom Bubba both loved and hated, had injured the toe recently. That toe probably ached like the blazes. Of course, not having toes, Bubba really didn't know, but Bubba, unlike other catfish, had a good imagination. That had come from so many times studying the man and his methods and outfoxing him. The man had been angling for Bubba, day after day, for a very long time. The man was no doubt resting back against the tree, taking pulls from a large stone jug, as he usually did when he came out here to fish the pond, occasionally pulling up one of the usual, lesser fish whose wits were far too dim to avoid the man's so-called trickery—the obvious baited hook and the cork that had been pried out of a whiskey jug and smelled so bad that even Bubba wouldn't take a nibble out of it.

Studying the swollen toe, Bubba smiled. He moved his jaws around, filing his razor-edged white teeth against each other. Then, with a flick of his tail, he swam straight up and over to the foot to which the big, swollen, probably very tender toe protruded. Hovering there in the murky water, Bubba opened his mouth wide, then clamped it over the swollen appendage of topic, chomping down hard.

A bellowing wail rose from outside Bubba's watery world as the big, tender toe was wrenched out of Bubba's mouth and shot straight up out of the water. The pole dropped into the water and floated down . . . down . . . down to the bottom of the pond.

* * *

"AHHH-OOOOO-AHHHHH-OOOOO-AHHHHH!

"OW! OW! OW! OHH! OWWW!

"YOU DEVIL OF A LUNATIC FISH!" cried "Catfish" Charlie Tuttle, jumping up and down on his right foot while holding his left foot with its throbbing toe across his right knee. "CUSSED DEMON SPAWN, BUBBA!" he bellowed at the deceptively placid, sun-glinting surface of the pond reflecting the oaks, cedars, cottonwoods, and mesquites peppering the shoreline around him.

He dropped the painful foot and looked at it.

Little pinpricks of blood bubbled up around the nail.

Oh, how it hurt!

HAD hurt! Now, being trifled at it by a fish—the very SAME fish he'd been stalking for the past two summers—it hurt even WORSE!

"Consarned gilled vermin think it's funny, eh?" Catfish bellowed at the placid pond, at the semi-shaded part of it where the assault had been affected. He'd been leaning up against a cottonwood stump standing roughly four feet back from the shore. His jug lay there, his own homemade mustang grape wine still dribbling from the lip, near a large wet patch in the sand and gravel and short grass, where a goodly portion had already spilled. "Ah, no—and I even lost a goodly portion of my special recipe. I cuss you, Bubba! I cuss you and I cuss your *entire bloodline!*"

Catfish unholstered his bone-gripped Colt Army .44, clicked the hammer back, and emptied all five chambers into the pool he usually fished, on the east side of the pond, a long stone's throw from his mud brick cabin sitting back a hundred yards, in a clearing in the creek-side trees. He always kept the one under the .44's hammer empty, lest he should accidentally shoot something off his person that would have him cussing his watery nemesis in soprano.

Catfish raised the smoking Colt straight up by his shoulder in his right hand as pale smoke slithered from the barrel. The big, swarthy man, in his early sixties, with long, salt-and-pepper hair and matching, dragoon-style mustache and tangled beard, ground his molars as he scowled down at the water with his piercing, frosty gray eyes. "Laughin' at me—ain't ya? Sure, sure," Catfish said, spatting a wad of chaw to one side, then wiping his lips with the left grimy sleeve of his balbriggan top.

He was clad only in wash-worn balbriggans, gun belt and holster on the left side of which was sheathed his bowie knife, and his high-crowned, badly weathered Stetson. "You go ahead an' laugh. Sure, sure. Laugh. Just know, my blood enemy, you'll soon be in a salt barrel in my keeper shed, and who'll be laughin' then, Bubba Jones? *Ha!*"

Catfish raised his left knee and slapped it with his left hand.

That only kicked up the throbbing pain in his swollen purple toe—the very one he'd dropped an iron shod wagon wheel on not two days ago, and which had kept him up for the past two nights, trying to dull the agony with his mustang grape wine plucked from the slopes of the nearby Stalwart Mountains, and considering plans to travel to Wolfwater for something a little stronger, though he wasn't sure that was possible. If ever a wine could rival whiskey in the skull pop category, it would be Catfish Charlie Tuttle's.

From behind Catfish came a delicate, tentative "Ahem."

Catfish froze.

He looked down at the Colt in his hand. Empty.

He'd let himself get caught out here, half-naked and with an empty hogleg!

Catfish Charlie, he remonstrated himself silently, *don't you know that with all your years of lawdoggin' behind you, you got more enemies in Texas than the Great Arsonist himself, William T. Sherman, has in all the Rebel South?*

Not only had he popped off all his ammo, and not only was he standing around out here clad in only wash-worn long-handles, he'd just made a fool out of himself, emptying his trusty Colt at a fish!

He swiveled his head and turned around slowly, stretching his lips back from his teeth, half expecting to find a passel of hollow-eyed human jackals behind him, each one with a bone to pick with former Texas Ranger, as well as Oklahoma and Texas town tamer, Catfish Charlie Tuttle.

Good Lord—it was even worse than he'd thought!

It was so bad that he glanced down at the turned-over jug near his throbbing big toe and wondered if he hadn't overdone it with the last batch of mustang grape wine. Could he be *hallucinating*?

Was he actually seeing the two-seater surrey owned by Mayor Derwood Booth sitting on the two-track trail behind him, where the trees parted to accept the trail that jogged the hundred or so yards back to his shack? If not, then the mayor himself—young and small and well-groomed and wearing a three-piece suit and little, round, steel-framed spectacles—was seated on the buggy's front seat, on the left side, the driver's side, the reins of the harnessed black Morgan in his hands.

If not, then the Reverend Ezekiel Elmwood, minister of the First Presbyterian Church in Wolfwater, sat beside him, looking as grim as a pallbearer.

If not, then the founding mother and matriarch of the Wolfwater Women's Sobriety League sat in the back seat directly behind the mayor, while Wolfwater's primary madam—yes *madam*, as in a woman in the business of running a brothel and procuring prostitutes—sat beside the Widow Kotzwinkle, looking no less sober than the widow, though a whole lot more ravishing.

Miss Julia Claire, with her emerald-green eyes, flawless skin, ruby-red lips, and chestnut hair flowing down about her shoulders, was a whole lot younger, prettier, and better filled out than not only Mrs. Kotzwinkle but most, if not all, other women not only in Wolfwater, but in all West Texas. The fact was highlighted to best effect by the low-cut bodice of the spruce-green velveteen gown she wore. Like all her gowns, it had been sewn on her exquisite body by Wolfwater's own master tailor, Ezra Kantor, formerly of somewhere in New Jersey, wherever that was, exactly—the far end of the earth, as far as Catfish knew. He'd rarely left Texas other than to fight against the rabid bluebellies in the Civil War.

The madam's shoulders were bare beneath a gauzy silk cream shawl, likely also sewn by the fussy Mr. Kantor. On her head was a green picture hat with faux flowers being nudged this way and that in the breeze whispering off the pond in which the granddaddy of all catfish in Wolfwater Creek, Bubba Jones, lolled at the muddy bottom, chuckling with unabashed self-satisfaction.

"Good Lord, man," said the long-faced, gray-headed,

gray-bearded, black-suited pastor, knobby hands clutching the head of the carved cherrywood walking stick before him. "Have you gone *mad*, Catfish?"

The dapper, young, bearded, bespectacled mayor turned to the pastor, then turned his grave, wide-eyed gaze back to the big, potbellied, longhandle-clad, barefoot man holding the empty six-shooter down beside him. "I certainly hope not. For I do believe . . . we *all here* believe . . . or *did believe* . . . that you, Catfish Charlie, are the only thing standing between us and well"—he shrugged his thin shoulders and glanced once more at the reverend before returning his anxious gaze again to Catfish Charlie—"well . . . *hell*."

They all said "heck" at the same time.

Then the lovely Julia Claire glanced at the pond behind Charlie and arched one pretty brow. "That said, Catfish, I do believe you're going to need a bigger gun!"

Chapter 5

"He's going to need a bigger gun, and we're going to need a better man!" intoned the Widow Kotzwinkle. "Look at him. Just *look* at him. He's half-naked and drunk in the middle of the day!"

She closed her white-gloved hands over the back of the seat in front of her, to either side of the tall, slender Reverend Elmwood, who clucked and shook his head at Catfish distastefully. "Good Lord, Catfish! You've really let yourself go, man!"

He pulled his mouth corners down and wagged his craggy head.

The dandified mayor, Derwood Booth, held his right hand up, palm out. He wore prissy-looking black gloves. "Don't judge him too harshly, good people. Besides," the bearded man added, making a sour expression, "we're desperate."

"We are, we are desperate," said the lovely Julia Claire in her haunting British accent. She turned her doe-eyed brown gaze on Catfish and beseeched, "Oh, won't you help us, Catfish? After the demise of Marshal Wilkes and Bushwhack Aimes, Wolfwater has regressed to its old lawless ways. The way it was before you tamed it almost ten years ago!"

Feeling more than a little self-conscious, clad in only his longhandles, battered hat, and unloaded gun, Catfish scowled incredulously at his uninvited guests. He'd been called Catfish ever since he was a kid, who had, as he still did now, snuck off with his cane pole to his favorite catfish hole every chance he got. Now that he was retired, he had a whole lot more chances.

There was just something so soothing about being alone at some quiet little catfish hole—just him and his pole and chicken or frog guts for bait, and, these days, a stone jug of his home-brewed mustang grape wine. It would have been more soothing, however, if he could ever catch the biggest catfish in his current hole in the backwater pond here on Wolfwater Creek, instead of being outfoxed by the fish Bubba Jones at every turn!

Oh, well, he still caught plenty of catfish. Nothing better than a pan of the mud bulls and fried potatoes and a few—well, maybe more than a few—slugs from his jug while sitting out on his porch and watching the West Texas sun drop slowly into the prickly West Texas desert.

"Hold on, hold on," Catfish said now, ignoring the insults fired at him by his uninvited guests. "What's this about the 'demise' of Abel Wilkes and Bush-whack Aimes? Are you tellin' me those fellas are *dead*?"

All four just stared at him, blank-faced.

They exchanged dubious looks before returning their gazes to Catfish once more. The mayor said, "You mean . . . you haven't heard?"

"No, hell—er, heck, I mean," Catfish added for the benefit of the reverend and the widow. "I haven't heard anything."

He felt suddenly disoriented and out of sorts. He had a queasy feeling in his guts. Part alcohol. Part shock at the news that the alcohol was making it hard for him to wrap his mind around.

He and Abel Wilkes had been friends. Best friends at one time. He and Abel had fought in the war together, and Wilkes had been his deputy. This was when Catfish, having been forced to retire from the Texas Rangers because of the precarious position of a bullet in his back, had taken the town marshal's job in Wolfwater, back when Wolfwater had been a hellish place still attacked a few times every month by renegade Comanche. The bullet had been placed there—too close to his spine to remove without the risk of making him a cripple—by a regulator known as "Black" Taggart.

A man whom Catfish had seen neither hide nor hair of ever since.

Between Comanche attacks, Wolfwater had been overrun by border toughs of every stripe—gringos, Mexicans, and everything in between. Hide hunters as well, of course, back in those wild postwar days on the Texas frontier. Even with that bullet in his back that often caused violent spasms—sometimes for hours or days at a time—Catfish Charlie had cleaned up the town.

With the help of his old pal Abel Wilkes and Brazos McQueen, of course. Yeah, ol' Brazos was there, too. Good ol' Brazos. Catfish and Abel and Brazos had been the three amigos back in those wild old days—days with the bark on, for sure!

Catfish had no idea where the former old buffalo soldier was now. He hadn't seen Brazos since ... well, since ...

No, don't think about that tragedy now, too, on top of Abel Wilkes's demise. Stay focused, Catfish!

"It happened over a week ago," Mayor Booth said, his voice reaching through Catfish's cluttered mind, like the words of someone speaking at the end of a long, dark tunnel. "I thought for sure you would have heard."

Suddenly unsteady on his feet, Catfish took one stumbling step backward. He got both feet beneath him again and felt the burn of embarrassment in his bearded cheeks.

"You should come to town more often, Catfish," Julia Claire said, a concerned expression on her nearly flawlessly beautiful china doll's face. She had to be pushing forty, but she didn't look a day over thirty. That was part of the mystery about her. No one knew where she'd come from before she'd arrived in Wolfwater with three steamer trunks and two carpetbags, one of which, it was said, had been stuffed to brimming with cold, hard cash.

She'd used the money, as mysterious as the lovely, obviously educated and cultivated lady herself, to buy "Beaver" Thorn's tumbledown saloon, the Buffalo Wallow, and turn it into Miss Julia Claire's Lone Star Outpost—a house of liquor, gambling, fine music, and the charms of her dozen or so well-trained doves.

Yeah, there were many mysteries surrounding Miss Julia Claire, none more than her seemingly ageless beauty. Some said she wasn't human, but a ghost. Some said she was "teched," likely by some Comanche shaman who'd been part of a band of warriors who'd attacked Miss Claire's wagon train from back east—if such a wagon train there had been, that was. All speculation, of course. The shaman, according to the possibly entirely made-up story, had fallen in love with her and gifted her with eternal beauty.

Yeah, lots of mysteries, lots of stories.

Regarding Catfish now, she winced and shook her head. Her lustrous brown eyes, with their long, even darker brown lashes, contrasting the fine ivory of her complexion, traveled Catfish's six-foot-four-inch body from the top of his long-haired head and tangled beard down past his fat belly stretching out his thread-bare longhandle top, to his knock-kneed legs and grimy, bare feet with one swollen toe with its yellow-colored nail.

"Come to town on occasion, Catfish. You need to . . . to get away from here. You're too isolated. Not good for a man. Stop by the Lone Star. A hot, sudsy bath and the prettiest girl in the house on me."

"Really, Miss Claire!" intoned the widow, her craggy, fleshy face mottling red with exasperation beneath the broad brim of her red velvet picture hat. "We did not ride all the way out here to this . . . this"—the widow looked around at the pond and the fat, ragged man before her and the less than humble cabin slouched in the clearing behind her, and said, "*perdition* for you to further despoil this . . . this . . . catfish-fishing drunkard!"

Catfish flinched again, this time at the widow's attack. He took another stumbling step backward, shook his head again to clarify his thoughts, and turned to the mayor. "What happened? To Abel, I mean. Who . . . who killed him?"

He felt anger rise in him at the thought of his dear friend's demise. At the same time, he felt helpless to do anything about it. The ladies had told him that, in so many words, if he hadn't known it already.

Still, he needed to know who . . .

"Frank Thorson," the reverend said. "Abel and Bush-whack had his kid brother, Skinny, locked up for killing a whore."

"Threw the poor girl out a window," Mayor Booth added, his little, round spectacles glinting in the sunlight that was acquiring a softer edge now as the afternoon drew on.

"My God," Julia Claire said, shaking her head. "Animals. The filth. The evil!"

"Purely, purely," agreed Reverend Elmwood, turning his mouth corners down and shaking his head.

"Well, we all get what comes to us—don't we?" the widow said, turning her pious, judgmental gaze to the beautiful woman sitting beside her. "That wouldn't have happened, and we wouldn't have felt we had to drive out here—on a wasted mission, it turns out," she snapped in disgust at Catfish Charlie, "if, as my organization has been calling for, we'd banned the sins of drink, gambling, and—"

"All right, all right," said Julia Claire, raising her hands to her temples. "Let's save *that* conversation for the council meetings—shall we, Widow?"

"Harrumph!" said the widow, settling herself in her seat and turning her face away from them all in profound disgust, not only at her fellow townsfolk and Catfish, but at all humanity.

The mayor looked at the former lawman. "We thought we'd let you know, anyway, Catfish. Knew you'd want to know. Thought maybe . . . thought maybe . . . well . . ."

"That I had it in me to do anything about it," Catfish finished for him wearily.

"Yes," the reverend replied, halfheartedly, dropping his gaze to the tips of his polished brogans and opening and closing his clawlike hands around the handle of his walking stick. "Yes. Be that as it may, it's obvious we made a mistake."

Catfish looked away then, too, stretching his lips back from his teeth in deep shame and frustration. He'd never felt as low as he did right here, right now in his life. He used the barrel of his empty Colt to scratch the back of his head, then turned back to the four townsfolk sitting before him in the dusty black carriage. "Where's Thorson now? He still in town?"

"No," the mayor said, shaking his head. "He rode up into the Stalwarts. They say he has a hideout up there. He took . . ."

The mayor stopped, then tried to continue again, but before he could get any more words out, Julia Claire continued for him: "He and his bunch took Bethany Wilkes with them. After they killed her father, they took her . . ."

She didn't bother finishing. Her pursed lips and pain-racked eyes said the rest.

The unspeakable rest.

Bethany Wilkes, Abel's daughter. The town's teacher.

For God's sake . . .

"Without law," the reverend said with a deep, fateful sigh, turning again to Catfish, "well, you can imagine what Wolfwater has become."

"Lawless," the widow said, flaring her nostrils. "Just *lawless*!" She turned her castigating glare to the mayor. "And the railroad hasn't helped a bit. Why, the devils are flocking in droves to stomp with their tails raised high!"

Derwood Booth flinched. Of course, as a city

booster and businessman himself—he owned a brickyard at the edge of Wolfwater—he was one of those responsible for bringing the iron horse to their fair city.

"All right, all right, gentlemen . . . ladies," he said with a grim air of finality and futility, releasing the carriage's brake and casting a grim, pitying look at Catfish once more. "I think we've done about all we can for Wolfwater out here. We'll be on our way." He reined the Morgan around, clucked to the horse, and turned to glance over his shoulder as he called back to the former town marshal, "Good day to you, Catfish. Do take care of yourself!"

He clucked louder and tossed the reins against the Morgan's back, urging the horse into a lope back toward Catfish Charlie's humble cabin, which slouched in the afternoon heat as much as Catfish himself slouched here on the shore of the backwater pond and the home of Bubba Jones, who'd skunked him once more.

And bit his consarned toe.

Catfish gave a deep, ragged sigh, then holstered his empty Colt.

He stooped to pick up his jug. He sloshed it around. Or tried to. There was nothing in it to slosh.

He cussed, glanced at the backwater pond once more, then began his slouching, barefoot trek back to his shack, feeling as low-down as a pig's belly in a mud wallow.

Chapter 6

Catfish wasn't so low that he forgot to reload his Colt .44.

At least he remembered to do that. Well, actually, it was automatic as he walked barefoot back to his shack in the lush grass growing in the center of the two-track trail. He limped along, wincing at the pain in his big toe.

The magic had been taken out of the day. First by Bubba Jones and then by the two harpies and the two popinjays from town. Ah, heck, Miss Julia wasn't a harpy. She was just concerned about Catfish Charlie. He might have been a head-breaking town tamer in his day, but there was a softer side to him, and the non-criminals had quickly found that out. They liked that about him. The contrast between his dark side and his light side.

A few years back, when he was better-looking and in better shape—a good fifteen, twenty pounds lighter—he and Miss Julia had come close to being an item, despite the twenty-year difference in their ages. Back then, she'd never looked at him as she'd looked at him just now. Back then, she'd looked at him with warmth and admiration. A few times, she'd even kissed him on the lips.

It had never gone further than that, however. Catfish Charlie had been wedded to his job, just as Miss Julia had been—and still was—wedded to hers. Besides, it hadn't seemed right to either one of them.

Being in love and all that.

Oh, Catfish had been in love a few times, but nothing had ever come of it. He wasn't the settling-down kind. At least he wasn't the settling-down-with-a-woman kind. He was more the kind to settle down to fish and to drink himself pie-eyed every afternoon and continue through the evening while frying up his catfish and potatoes on a cookfire in his yard.

Something really stuck in his craw now as he climbed the three steps to his rickety front porch, looking down to see his mouser, Hooligan Hank, staring up at him to the right of the hemp rug fronting the rickety front door, a dead, half-eaten mouse between Hank's paws.

"Ah, Hank," he said, setting the empty jug down beside the hide-bottom chair to the left of the door. The hide sagged deeply from all the time his considerable bulk had spent in the chair. He sank into the chair now, the chair and his old bones creaking wearily and in unison. He leaned forward, elbows on his knees, and entwined his hands together. "Ol' Abel Wilkes is dead, and Frank Thorson has Abel's daughter. He's doing God only knows what to poor Beth right now. And I'm too dang old and fat and just plain too no-good-anymore to do a blame thing about it. What do you think about that, Hank?"

The cat regarded him dubiously, canting his head

a little to one side. Hank gave his tail a single whip. Then he seemed to shake his head.

"You too, eh?" Catfish said with a dry chuckle. "Ah, heck—you too." He placed his hands on his knees and heaved himself up out of the chair—the chair and his own ancient bones creaking as one again. "Stay there. I'm gonna fetch me a fresh jug." He turned to the door. "When you're down this low, you can't get any lower."

He went inside and tramped over to the shelves he'd built into the cabin's back wall, beyond his crude, knife-scarred eating table and to the left of his sheet-iron stove and dry sink. He still had five stone jugs lined up there.

He dragged one down off the shelf, chewed the cork out of it, spit it onto the floor, and caught sight of himself in the mirror hanging over the washstand.

Nah. That's not me.

He moved closer, slowly crouched, until a grizzled old man stared back at him through drink-bleary eyes. Long, unkempt salt-and-pepper hair hung down past his collar. His beard was long and scraggly; crumbs from both breakfast and lunch clung to it.

He stretched his lips back from his teeth and scrunched up his face as rage climbed up from behind him like some spectral, sharp-fanged bear to give him a big, brutal hug. He clenched his fist and shouted, "You haggard old fool!" He smashed his fist into the mirror; the glass broke into a hundred shards and dropped to the floor.

He hooked the jug over his right shoulder and took a deep gulp . . . another . . . another . . . and another.

He lowered the jug. A slow smile spread across his face.

"There. Now that's better."

Hating himself, but still feeling better, he tramped back out onto the porch, sat himself back down in his chair, and planted the jug on his thigh. Nothing like a pretty, sun-dappled afternoon spent with a jug of his own good wine.

He stared at the dusty mesquites, the cedars, the sotol cactus sprinkled in among them, and tried not to think about Abel Wilkes. It was impossible not to, of course, but the more liberal pulls he took from the jug, the duller the teeth of those memories became.

The more he hated himself as well.

He wasn't sure how much time had passed when distant thunder rumbled, and a chill breeze rose. A meow sounded out in the brush to his left and Hooligan Hank came running out, meowing softly, anxiously, the noise deep in his throat. Catfish hadn't realized the cat was gone until he reappeared, thumping up the porch steps and then sitting in front of the door, turning to Catfish and giving another commanding meow as he shifted his weight from one right front paw to another.

"Storm blowin' up," Catfish said, glancing at the northern sky. "A West Texas corker. Ol' Hank knows one, for certain-sure. He's more Texas than I am!"

He hauled himself up out of his chair and opened the door for Hank. The cat ran inside.

Catfish closed the door and sank back down in his chair.

The storm came, lashing rain, thunderclaps that sounded like detonated powder kegs, lightning that would light up the whole sky, and then, three or four seconds later, jagged streaks of the stuff like glowing giant bowie knives rending the sky from the outside.

Catfish usually enjoyed a good summer storm. He even enjoyed the start of this one. But then, the longer the storm wore on, the rain cutting straight down from the porch roof's overhang to cut a deep trough in the West Texas caliche . . . and the more chugs he took from the jug . . . the darker his mood grew.

"You're sixty-two years old, Catfish, you old scudder," he sobbed at the intermittently lit-up sky. "You're six-four, an' you're fat, you're lazy, you're a drunkard, and you ain't even all that great of a catfish fisherman despite you're bein' called CATFISH!"

He sobbed, took another pull from the jug, and sobbed some more, until he was sitting there in the chair, the jug almost empty, head down, bawling like a three-year-old toddler wanting his blanket. He didn't know it, but ol' Hooligan Hank was sitting on the shelf in the window flanking him, peering out from between the open flour sack curtains, regarding his lord and master—if any cat can have a lord and master—bewilderedly, Hank's eyes glowing like molten copper in the storm's dimming light.

"Hang it all, anyway!" Catfish raged, pushing up out of his chair and throwing the nearly empty jug out into the night. It crashed faintly to the ground, the sound nearly drowned by another peal of window-rattling, ground-jarring thunder. "One of your best friends is dead and his daughter's bein' molested by one of the blackest devils this side of Hell, an' all you can do is sit here and chug your busthead and simper like a whining child. Just a gallblasted whining child!"

Catfish stepped up to the front of the porch and bellowed loudly into the storm, shaking his fists at the unseen gods in the stormy firmament who had allowed him to become such a low-down, dirty, drunken, catfish-fishing dog.

Lightning flashed to his right—a wicked crash of thunder and jagged, razor-edged blue light that struck a big cedar not thirty feet away.

KA-BOOOOMMMMM!

The entire cedar was lit up like a Christmas tree. It seemed to swell and pulsate inside the halo of smoking blue light. Suddenly it exploded and broke in half, the top half jackknifing over the bottom half. Bright blue and red sparks shot out from the jagged break.

The concussion hammered against Catfish with the force of a runaway lumber dray. He was hurled straight back against the cabin, between the window and the door. Badly dazed, he dropped straight down the worn adobe bricks to the rotting porch floor. He sat there for a second or two, blinking his eyes, trying to clear them, to no avail, bells tolling in his head.

Then he gave a fateful sigh and slid down the wall to fold up on his left shoulder and hip, out like a doused flame.

His head and back ached, but he was hardly aware of it for most of the night.

He woke only when he felt the morning's warm light bathe his face. He jerked with a start, staring at the sun-silvered floor of his stoop. He groaned at the ache in his head and shoulders and in the small of his back.

He'd slept a good six or seven hours in that uncompromising position, twisted over on his left side, the bulk of his weight on that shoulder and hip. The position of a passed-out old sot. He tried to move, but felt as though his limbs had hardened into that ungodly arrangement.

Ungodly for a man his age and in the shabby shape he was in.

He groaned, dug his fingers into the porch floor, and tried to heave himself onto his back. It took several tries, and by the time he'd rolled onto his backside, sort of half sitting up with his head and shoulders resting against the shack's front wall, he thought he'd broken his neck.

He canted it slowly to each side, gritting his teeth, feeling the bones in the back of his neck grinding together.

"Dang," he said. "Dang, dang, dangit, anyway. Why do I have to be such a blasted drunk?"

When he was satisfied that neither his neck nor back was broken, just aching like the devil, he turned onto his right side, planted his hands and knee beneath him, and heaved himself slowly to his feet, feeling as though rusty railroad spikes had been driven into every joint in his body. Breathing hard and still flexing his neck, shoulders, and spine, he peered into the window before him.

Hooligan Hank stared back at him, looking not one bit happy. He was an early riser, Hooligan Hank was. It was a nice, clear morning after the storm, the air smelling clean. Puddles dotted the yard fronting the cabin, but they'd dry out fast. Everything dried out fast in West Texas.

Walking like a man a good ten years older than he was, his feet and ankles aching right along with the rest of him, Catfish made his way to the front door, threw it open. Hank bolted out with an indignant meow, thumped across the porch, down the steps, and made a wild dash into the brush around the side of the cabin, tail raised angrily.

He was late for the hunt.

A horse's whinny rose from the stable and small corral flanking the cabin. That would be Jasper wanting his oats and hay. Good Lord—how late was it, anyway? Catfish glanced at the sky. The sun was well up.

"I'll be hanged if it ain't almost midmorning."

He sighed and moved on into the cabin.

He filled his speckled black pot from his rain barrel on the stoop. The pot still had the bullet crease across its side, near the handle, compliments of the bullet that had been hurled through a window of his office when he'd manned a Texas Ranger's station in Abilene. He'd snuffed the wick of the jasper who'd fired the bullet—Arniss "Hog" Tatum, who'd done some time in the pen for selling whiskey and rifles to the Comanches, compliments of Catfish himself.

"I've had a helluva life," Catfish grumbled as he built a fire in his stove, moving around stiffly on his sore feet and ankles. "There's only so much that can be expected of a fella . . . Heck, I've taken over a half-dozen bullets to my ugly hide, and I still got one in my consarned back! You know it's true, Abel!" he said as though his old friend were sitting at the table like they all three used to do—Catfish, Abel, and ol' Brazos, before heading out in the morning to keep the lid on the churning, bubbling pot that had been Wolfwater ten years ago. "When I was a much younger man!" Catfish added, sitting down now to the coffee he'd brewed and which sent up several curls of aromatic steam.

He looked at Abel sitting across from him. His old friend didn't say anything. Just regarded him dubiously, turning his own stone mug around in his big, Texas-weathered hands.

"Oh, hell," Catfish said, rising suddenly and shuffling over to the door, holding his cup and staring out.

He felt as bound up as a mountain lion trapped in a hay barn.

He couldn't look at Abel anymore. There was cold, bitter accusing in his old friend's eyes, and it had every right to be there. But then Catfish, trying to look at his old friend—surely the man's spirit come to plague him, to chide him for his uselessness, his drunkenness, his cowardice—became aware of young Bethany staring up at Catfish from where she sat on the hide-bottom chair just a few feet to his right.

Staring at him with those large, round, dark brown eyes.

Her mother's eyes.

"Oh, for the love of God's bitter brown earth," Catfish complained, not able to hold the girl's gaze any longer than he'd been able to hold her father's. "Not you, too!"

He glanced at her once more.

He glanced away.

He glanced at her again, and she was no longer in the chair. He turned to stare into the kitchen, at his battered, square, wooden table. Abel was gone now, too.

It was only Catfish here now. Just Catfish and his consarned conscience.

He turned again and stared into the sunbathed yard fronting the cabin and down the two-track trail that cleaved the trees as it rolled off down toward the backwater pond in whose depths Catfish's nemesis lolled, fat and satisfied.

Everything was an affront to Catfish this bright, fresh, new day: his cat, his horse, Bubba Jones, his dead friend, and Abel's daughter, who was by now likely dead as well. None of them, however, were as much of an affront to Catfish as Catfish himself.

He held his cup up in front of him, the elbow of the hand holding it propped against the doorframe. He stared out hard toward the pond. "You're gonna do it, aren't you, you old reprobate." He chuckled dryly. "I'll be hanged if you ain't really gonna do it."

He stared along the two-track toward the pond and nodded. "Yep, you're gonna do it. Because, even though you're a low-down, drunken, dirty, shaggy-headed, pale shadow of your former self, you're not dead. And as long as you're not dead, you have to kill Frank Thorson and that little coyote firebrand brother of his, Skinny. Yep, you have to kick 'em both out with a cold shovel or die tryin'."

Catfish sighed fatefully, took another deep sip of his coffee.

"Best get started, you old scudder," he told himself, and tossed the rest of his mud out over the porch steps into the yard. "You're burnin' daylight."

He returned to the kitchen, heated water, stripped down, and washed himself at the washstand over which there was no longer a mirror. That was all right. He'd had enough of that old fool staring back at him.

Once he was relatively clean, he combed his hair, his beard, and mustache. He knew he probably didn't look much better than before—he needed a visit to a proper tonsorial parlor—but he was beginning to feel better, anyway.

At least part human now.

Once clean and groomed, he started the process of rummaging around for his old duds. Soon he was wearing a fresh pair of balbriggans, butterscotch corduroy pants, a red shirt with a bib-front top boasting a gold button, his worn brown leather vest, and his high-crowned brown Stetson, which, like him, had seen better days.

He pulled on wool socks and his brown leather boots into the tops of which he tucked his trouser cuffs.

He put the cabin in order, stuffed trail supplies, including two boxes of .44 cartridges, into his war bag and saddlebags, slung both over his left shoulder, and pulled his prized 1866 Winchester "Yellowboy" repeater down from the hooks above the mantel of his small brick fireplace.

He froze when the rataplan of horse hooves sounded outside, growing louder.

One rider coming fast.

Catfish frowned. "Now who in holy blazes . . . ?"

Friend or foe? he asked himself, then gave another bitter laugh. Who was he kidding? He didn't have any friends left. Not on this side of the sod.

He pumped a live round into the Yellowboy's breech and clomped to the door. Holding the rifle's brass butt plate against his cartridge belt slanting down over his right hip, he jerked the door open quickly and took one long step onto the porch. He tightened his hand around the Winchester's neck, aiming it straight out in front of him.

The rider was just then reining in a fine, long-legged, chestnut gelding to a skidding stop in front of the stoop. The man, clad in a long black duster and a billowy red neckerchief, lifted his head so that the broad brim of his black hat pulled up to reveal his face—as black as mahogany and carpeted in a thick, curly black beard peppered with a whole lot more gray than when Catfish had last seen his old friend.

Once his friend.

His foe now?

As the dust settled around the newcomer, that handsomely chiseled face, with broad, high-tapering cheekbones and coal-black eyes, regarded Catfish without expression.

Catfish's heart hiccupped. For a minute he couldn't catch his breath, he was so taken aback. Then, finding his voice, he exclaimed:

"Brazos!"

Chapter 7

Julia Claire had been a nervous wreck ever since she, the mayor, the reverend, and the pious Widow Kotzwinkle had returned to town just ahead of the storm, which had now passed. Julia had gone to bed in her suite of rooms on the third floor of her multifaceted establishment—the Lone Star Outpost—at her usual time, which was midnight. After most of her customers, save a few die-hard gamblers, had left for the night.

Since Marshal Abel Wilkes had been so mercilessly killed, leaving the town essentially lawless, she'd been closing off her third-floor brothel area after eleven. The jakes, or paying customers, had grown more and more brazen in the days since, so out of concern for the safety of her girls, Julia closed the brothel down before midnight, ushered the customers out, and sent the girls to bed for the night—to sleep.

She herself had gone to bed at midnight, but slumber had eluded her. So she'd crawled out of bed, donned her thick pink wrap against the penetrating chill after the storm, and gone down to her office, which was located off the storage area at the back, in the original part of the rustic, rambling log building, which she'd purchased from the old hide hunter Beaver Thorn.

Now she sat nursing a snifter of Spanish brandy and tapping a small card against the blotter on her large oak desk lit by a green-shaded lamp. Most of the office was in shadow, adding to Julia's unease. She hadn't been afraid of monsters in years, but she suddenly felt as though monsters lurked in the shadows behind the large, well-appointed office's heavy brocade and leather furniture, which was arranged around the large stone fireplace in the wall to her right.

She could fairly see the yellow of the creatures' occasionally blinking, menacing eyes!

The card.

She held it between the thumb and index finger of her left hand, tapping it against the blotter. She held it so that the writing on it—scripted in a large, flatly looping, decidedly male, educated hand—faced her.

It read: *I know your secret.*

The small ivory envelope lay beside it, her name written in the same hand as the note. She'd found the envelope under her office door after she'd returned from her and her fellow townsfolk's desperate but futile visit to the shack of the washed-up lawman, Catfish Charlie Tuttle. Poor Catfish—he'd deteriorated just awfully since he'd drawered his badge . . .

I know your secret.

Anxiousness throbbed in Julia.

Who'd left the card, and what did it mean?

Well, there is really only one thing it could mean, isn't there?

She'd been dreading this for years.

Her mind raced. The harder she tried to keep the thoughts . . . the old fears . . . from coming, the faster they came.

Was all she had built here—one of the finest establishments in West Texas—about to be taken away from her? Was the life she'd made for herself, a life she herself had dictated the terms of, not some *man*, about to turn to ashes?

Again, she tapped the note on the blotter.

She jerked with a start when something scraped across the window behind her. Frowning, puzzled, she turned and studied the curtained window.

Silence.

Probably just a branch of the shrub back there scratching across the glass.

She turned back to face her desk and the note lying face-up on top of it, the heavy, inked letters boldly accusing, taunting . . . threatening.

Again, something scraped across the window behind her.

She gasped, jerking again with a start, and hipped around in the chair to study the curtained window. The scrape had sounded louder that time. Her heart fluttered as she studied the green velvet drapes.

The scrape had increased her anxiousness.

Trying to suppress her fear of what she might see out there, she rose from the chair, slowly raised her hands, and used the back of each to slide the curtains roughly a foot apart. The window faced the alley running behind the Lone Star Outpost. It was too dark in the alley to see much of anything except the lumpy, dark shapes of some cedar and cottonwood trees, a few storage sheds, and one old, unused stock pen facing the Lone Star on the alley's opposite side.

She pressed her face up close to the glass, blocking the reflection of the lamp behind her. As far as she could tell, there was no one back there. On the other hand, the shaggy shrub abutting the back wall, its branches rising a few inches above the bottom of the window, was not moving. There seemed to be little or no breeze after the rain.

What, if not one of the branches, had scraped the window?

She studied the branches of the scrub cedar. Suddenly a couple of them moved down low on her right. She gasped and stepped back, almost falling into the chair flanking her. Then a shadow bounded out away from the shrubs—in the dim starlight, a small, cat-shaped shadow, with tail raised, bounded across the alley and into the darkness between the stock pen and a tumbledown shed.

Julia chuckled, then let the curtains fall back into place.

"A cat, Julia," she said to herself with dry self-mockery. "Only a cat." She sat back down in the chair. "Don't let your nerves—"

Again, something scraped against the glass, louder than both previous times. It was followed by a soft crunching sound—maybe the stealthy tread of a foot?

Anger rising inside her, she rose again from the chair and slid the curtains apart once more. "All right—who's out there?" she said to the dark alley beyond the window.

Still, she could see nothing. No movement whatever.

Anger and fear made her heart flutter.

"Only one way to get to the bottom of this!" she said tightly, turning and opening the top right-hand drawer of her desk.

She pulled out a leather-covered box a little smaller than a shoebox. She tripped the hasp and opened the lid, revealing a .38-caliber pocket pistol resting on a molded bed of red velvet—a pretty, snub-nosed, silver-chased revolver with pearl grips that glinted in the light of the oil lamp.

She clicked open the loading gate, pulled back the hammer, and turned the cylinder, making sure that all six chambers showed brass. Then she eased the hammer back into its cradle, clicked the loading gate home, and, holding the revolver barrel up beside her right shoulder, walked out from around the desk and across the carpeted office to the door.

She opened the door and stepped out into the storage room. The dark shapes of crates, barrels, filled gunnysacks, and large sausages, which were hanging from the rafters, were revealed in the light from the lamp behind her. Leaving her office door open, she stepped out into the large, mostly dark room, swung right, and made her way through the clutter to the heavy back door.

The locking bar rested in its steel cradle across it.

She removed it with a grunt, leaned it against the wall on her left, then placed her hand on the steel handle. She paused, drawing a couple of deep breaths, steeling herself against her fear.

She should call Howard Richter, the bouncer on duty in the gambling parlor, but she would handle this herself. What if whoever was trying to scare her was the same man or men who'd left the note under her door? No one else could know.

She was alone in this.

And if whoever was out in the alley was the same man who'd penned the note, she might as well know sooner rather than later. The possibility that she could shoot him or them fluttered across her anxious brain. If the law became involved, though there was no longer any law in Wolfwater—which worked both for and against her—she could say whoever was in the alley was trying to accost her or to break into the storage room. With the storage room so close to her office and her safe, in which she stored large quantities of cash between runs to the bank, she either needed to post a guard back here or get a more substantial door.

Tucking her bottom lip under her upper teeth, Julia drew the door slowly open, wincing against the groan of the two large steel hinges.

She took one step into the alley and slid her gaze slowly from her left to her right. "Who's out here?" she said, keeping her voice low.

It still sounded loud in the alley's dark, eerie silence, which was broken only by the distant yipping of a coyote somewhere out in the rocky desert. She took another step into the alley, turned right, and walked toward the window beneath which the murky black shapes of the shrubs sat. As she did, she clicked the pocket pistol's hammer back to full cock and aimed it out straight ahead of her.

"Who's here?" she said, hearing both anger and anxiety in her voice. "I know you're out here. Who are you and what do you want?"

Her slippered feet crunched in the sand and gravel.

The shrubs slipped up on her right now. She stopped at the near edge of the window and peered behind the shrubs.

Nothing. Just prickly desert branches.

She turned to carefully study the alley around her.

Still seeing nothing, she walked on, past the shrubs to the building's rear corner. Ten feet beyond lay a mercantile, the window in the wall facing Julia dark at this hour. She peered up the alley between the mercantile and the Lone Star Outpost toward the main street, a hundred feet away.

Nothing there, either.

No human shapes. Nothing moving.

Hmm.

Julia frowned as she again looked around her.

Could her anxiousness about the note have made her imagine the scraping against the window? Or at least have blown it out of proportion?

Again, she looked around.

Nothing.

That must be it. Just her imagination. Her nerves.

Gently setting the pistol's hammer back into its cradle, she lowered the gun, turned, and retraced her steps back to the storage room's back door, which she'd left open in her haste and nervousness. She stepped back into the cluttered room, the light showing through her open office door.

She'd just turned to shut the door when a floorboard squawked and someone grabbed her from behind. A thick, smelly hand closed over her mouth, muffling her scream. More footsteps sounded and then another hand ripped the .38 out of her grip. As the man who'd grabbed her from behind lifted her up off the ground, keeping his hand clamped tight over her mouth, he said, "Get that bag over her head *fast!*"

Someone stepped up from her right, and in a blur of murky, dark motion, a bag was thrust down over her head just as the man behind her removed his hand from her mouth.

"No!" she yelled inside the smelly, dark bag. She tried to yell again, but then a gag closed tightly around the bag and over her mouth. It was jerked back taut behind her head, and as she struggled in vain against the big man holding her from behind, the gag was quickly knotted painfully tight against the back of her neck.

Then, moaning against the gag, she was brusquely thrown to the floor. A man's heavy knee was thrust down against her back, and both her arms were pulled back behind her.

"No good strugglin', dearie," a deep, breathless voice said into her right ear as her hands were tied behind her back. "You're not goin' anywhere, an' no one's comin' to save you!"

She heard the clomping of hooves and the rattle of wheels in the alley.

Terror a racing stallion inside her, Julia groaned against the gag and struggled against the ropes—in vain. She was picked up like a sack of grain, carried into the alley—she could feel the change in the air around her—and then hurled as equally unceremoniously into the back of the wagon with a loud *thump*.

Her meeting with the splintery floor of the wagon dazed her, taking some of the fight out of her.

Two more thumps as her assailants leaped into the wagon on either side of her.

"Get goin', Gannon!" said the man on her left, his voice furtively low. "We ain't got all night!"

Then hooves clomped, a horse whickered, the wagon lurched forward, and Julia was carted off to only God knew where!

Chapter 8

"Stop fightin' it, dearie, or I'll put a bullet in your head," said the throaty, grotesquely resonant voice of one of the two men riding in the back of the wagon with Julia.

She felt the hard, round maw of a pistol pressed against her temple as she lay on her side, bound, gagged, and with a smelly canvas sack over her head. There was the ratcheting click of a gun being cocked.

Another man near Julia laughed.

They didn't feel the need to keep their voices down now. They were in the desert outside of Wolfwater. Blinded as she was by the bag, Julia had no idea what direction they were heading, but, judging by the violent pitching of the wagon's wheels over rocks and chuckholes, they were not on a main trail. They'd been on the secondary trail for a good fifteen, twenty minutes; though to Julia, whom the jarring was making sick, as was the nasty taste of the canvas bag in her mouth, it felt as though it had been hours.

Oh, God—when will the jarring stop?

Rage and terror had kept her trying to work her hands free of the rope binding them together at the wrists, trying to spit the awful, musty, coarse sack out of her mouth, though the rope and gag held fast. No give in them at all.

She could barely breathe, and she felt her hands swelling, tingling, and aching from the restriction of the blood. This was pure torture. Part of her wished the man with the repellently resonant—almost feminine—voice would just pull the trigger and put her out of her misery.

But no. She may have been terrified, but she had enough spleen in her to want to survive so that sometime she could give these fools—whoever they were— their just deserts.

She chomped down on the gunnysack in her mouth, seething and gritting her teeth. She lay as still as was possible with each strike of a rock or hole bouncing her clear up off the wagon floor and slamming her back down again. The pistol was pulled back from her temple. She heard the soft click of the hammer being depressed.

"Not far now, lady," said another man, who had a deeper, more guttural voice than the man who'd held the gun to her head.

Both men smelled like whiskey and sour sweat. She'd smelled it when they'd first jumped her, and she smelled it now, even through the awful-tasting and smelly gunnysack.

The lowest of men, both. The one driving, too, she knew. Gannon.

Someone must have sent them on this errand, this taking of her out of her own establishment.

Who?

The man who'd sent the note. Who else?

The front of the wagon slanted down and then it bounced through what she assumed was a rocky wash. She heard branches raking against the sides of the wagon. The deep-voiced man cursed, as though one of those branches had scraped him as well.

The man with the odd, resonant, almost-feminine voice laughed.

The scraped man cursed.

The wagon slowed, bounced a few more times, then turned sharply to the left and stopped.

"Let's get her out," said the deep-voiced man.

Arms slid beneath Julia and then one of the men grunted in her ear as she was lifted off the wagon floor.

"Take her," said the man with the deep voice.

And then Julia was half dropped and half laid in another man's arms—the odd-voiced man's arms as he stood on the ground at the end of the wagon. She heard the deep-voiced man give another grunt and then a thump as he leaped out of the wagon into sand that sounded wet from the recent storm. She was transferred to his arms and then she was being carried somewhere, the big man leading the other two, who clomped along behind him and his cargo.

Boots clomped on wood, there was a click followed by the whine of hinges.

Julia was carried apparently through a door and into a building. She could vaguely see the wan yellow glow of a light through the coarse canvas of the gunnysack. She was plunked down into a chair, which creaked beneath her, and she gave a startled "Oh!" at her rump's sudden meeting with the hard seat of the chair. Behind her, the door was closed with a wooden thud. She felt the relief of pressure against her mouth as the gag was unknotted behind her head.

Suddenly the sack was pulled off, and her hair danced into place around her shoulders. Some fell into her face, and she shook it back behind her, blinking and looking around, ears still ringing, hips and shoulders still aching from the violent ride.

She was in a large, barren, low-ceilinged, earthen-floored room.

An abandoned saloon? Or maybe the bunkhouse of a ranch? To her left, a couple of boards were laid across two barrels. Dusty bottles were cluttered on shelves on the wall behind the makeshift bar. There were three tables, one of which had only two legs and was slanted over onto the floor. One of the tables had a couple whiskey bottles, three glasses, and playing cards on it, as well as an overfilled ashtray.

There were a few dusty, sooty chairs in various states of disrepair. Cobwebs were everywhere. A pot-belly stove hunched in the room's middle, just ahead and to Julia's right. A single wagon-wheel chandelier hung down over the table that held the bottles, glasses, and playing cards. There were only two lamps attached to it, both with soot-blackened glass shades, which caused the weakness of the room's light. One of the glass shades had a jagged crack running down its side.

A man walked up from behind Julia. He walked to a door on the room's opposite side. He was big and lumbering, with thick, shaggy hair hanging down from his high-crowned cream hat. He was dressed in ragged trail garb, including a dark gray wool coat hanging down to his hips. A pistol was holstered on his broad right thigh.

Julia glanced over her shoulder.

Two more men stood behind her. They locked gazes with her, leered at her, one nudging the other with his elbow. The elbow nudger was likely the man with the repellently feminine voice. He was short, round-faced, and with off-puttingly bright blue-green eyes. He was dressed as motley as the big man, who probably owned that deep, guttural voice. The other man, standing beside the round-faced man, was tall, horse-faced, dark-haired under his weather-beaten Stetson, and slump-shouldered, with a weak cast to his gaze betraying an extreme weakness of character.

He'd been the wagon driver. Gannon.

Julia hooked her upper lip angrily at the two behind her and then turned her head forward as the big man stopped at the door and rapped the knuckles of his gloved left hand on it.

"She's here, boss."

"Untie my hands," Julia said. "I can't feel them. The ropes are too tight."

The big man had just opened his mouth to respond, then closed it when the door suddenly opened with a click. The big man stepped aside as a tall, pale man stepped out. Handsome in a city kind of way, but with the odd features—long, hooked nose, eyes set too far apart—of inbreeding, he wore a monocle in his left eye, a slender length of black silk dangling from it. In his right hand was a walking stick with a silver horse head handle.

He was dressed in an impeccable three-piece black suit, with a white silk shirt, metallic green waistcoat with gilt flowering, and a thick silk-ribbon black tie.

"Oh, my God," Julia heard herself say through a gasp. She drew a deep breath, trying to calm her nerves and assuage her shock. "Sergei . . ." She paused, drew another breath, her heart racing.

Of course—it had to be him.

When she found her voice again, she said, "How . . . on *earth* . . . did you find me?"

The tall, overdressed man with the monocle smiled as he walked toward her, hardly able to bend his right knee. Mostly, he dragged the heel of that square-toed boot along, making long gouges in the earthen floor, adding to the others Julia had seen there, but had assumed had been made by chair legs.

No, they'd been made by the crippled right leg of her former husband, Sergei Zhukovsky . . .

"Not a very warm greeting—would you say, my dear?" the tall, extremely thin, and hollow-cheeked man said in his faint Russian accent. He'd done a good job of learning English in the years since he'd left his homeland. He'd graduated Harvard Law School, after all. Yes, a learned man. A cultured, well-read man.

Also, a low-down, dirty . . .

"After what you did to me . . . ?" he finished now as he stood over her, looming over her, all of the impeccably dressed six feet four inches of him, while his wavy gray-streaked auburn hair, parted on the right side, fell down over his right ear. He'd said this last with no trace of his previous, phony smile, and his voice had hardened to the packed ice of a Russian winter.

He knocked the cane against his right leg.

"Nerve damage," he said, glowering down at her. "But that was nothing compared to the knife in the neck!" He reached up with his ringed right hand to jerk down the paper collar of his shirt and his string tie to reveal a nasty-looking, knotted, six-inch pink scar.

Julia gasped, winced.

"Ugly, isn't it?"

Julia didn't know what to say. Her heart was racing.

Yes, of course, it would have to be him who'd sent the note. She should have recognized his handwriting. But she hadn't seen him in twelve years. Had thought—my God, she'd *hoped*!—she never would again.

"Gentlemen," Sergei Zhukovsky said loudly, glancing at the man behind him and the two still standing behind Julia, his voice acquiring that phonily pleasant tone again, "meet my darling wife—Mrs. Sylvia Zhukovsky, the former Miss Sylvia Jones, of Baltimore, Maryland!"

"Jones?" said the big man, frowning. "I thought the name was Ju—"

"Julia Claire?" said Zhukovsky. Glaring down at Julia, he shook his head and pursed his lips. "Made up the name. No, she's sweet little Sylvia Jones from Baltimore. The English accent is as phony as the rest of her. Sylvia, I'd like you to meet my friends." He inclined his head to indicate the big, sloppy, broad-hipped man behind him. "That's Gunther Gross. The little man behind you is Mick Staggerford. The tall drink of water is Kurt Gannon."

"Some friends you have, Serg," Julia said. "You had no right to send them for me. To sic them on me and to treat me so . . . so"—she cast each man a hard-eyed glare, in turn, before turning back to the tall, monocled man standing over her—"disrespectfully!" She pulled violently against the ropes binding her wrists. "Untie me. I can't feel my hands!"

Zhukovsky glanced at one of the men behind Julia and nodded.

"You sure, boss?" asked Mick Staggerford in his repellent voice.

"What can she do?"

True. Even untied, she was powerless against these four men. Zhukovsky's lackeys were all armed with both pistols and knives of the bowie variety. There'd be no escaping them, either, of course.

Staggerford moved up behind her. She heard the snicking sound of the man unsheathing his knife. As he cut the ropes, Julia's former husband—well, she supposed they were *still officially* married, God help her soul!—limped his way over to the table on which the bottles, glasses, and playing cards lay. He glanced at the appropriately named Gunther Gross and jerked his chin toward his office. As Gross nodded and disappeared into it, Julia sucked air through her teeth as the ropes were suddenly released and the blood rushed into her hands.

They burned as though she'd tried to pick up a hot skillet.

She leaned forward in her chair, rubbing them together and groaning.

Gross brought a square, labeled bottle and two goblets out from the office and placed each on the table, one before Zhukovsky and one in front of a chair on the other side of the table from the Russian. He plucked the cork out of the bottle and half filled each goblet with the amber liquid.

"Stop fussing, Sylvia, and come over here and enjoy a glass of brandy with me. We've much to catch up on—don't you think?" Zhukovsky sat sideways in his chair, facing her, the cane leaning against the table. He held his goblet in his bejeweled right hand, smiled at her, the monocle glinting in the dim light from the lamps above his head, and swirled the brandy around in his glass.

"I'm not Sylvia anymore," Julia said, curling her

upper lip and flaring her nostrils at the insufferable man. She refused to lose the made-up accent. "I'm Julia Claire."

"Hmm, yes." Zhukovsky sipped from his glass, swallowed, and the tip of his tongue came out of his broad mouth and ran across the underside of his upper lip. "We'll see for how much longer."

Julia glared at him fiercely, desperately. "Why didn't you die? I left you for *dead* . . . after you all but *mauled* me!"

She'd meant to kill him, but she'd read in a newspaper when she'd fled him and the scene of their fight that he'd been hanging on by a thread. Ever since, she'd worried about just such a meeting as this one.

"You were stealing from me, my dear. Don't you remember?" Zhukovsky glanced at the glass on the other side of the table from him. "Come, come. Let's have a civilized conversation." He looked at the two men by the door, then glanced over his shoulder at Gunther Gross. "You men—outside. I'll call you if I need you."

"You got it, boss," Gross said, and tramped across the room, following behind the other two men, who were going out the door.

"Make sure you weren't followed out from town!" Zhukovsky yelled behind them.

"Oh, we weren't, boss." Gross glanced over his shoulder as he stepped through the door, then smiled. "We're professionals." He drew the door closed behind him.

"Professionals, eh?" Julia said coldly, rising from her chair and walking stiffly toward the empty chair across the table from Zhukovsky. "More like vermin dressed like ragamuffins."

"They got the job done—didn't they? Besides, they came highly recommended. Sometimes it's best to hire men who blend in with a crowd. They've been in Wolfwater for days, following you around, learning your habits. They slipped my note under your door." Zhukovsky took another sip of his brandy.

Julia sat in the chair, but left her own glass on the table. "Why are you alive?"

"You failed to sever the jugular, my dear. Still, I lost a lot of blood there on my study floor. It took me almost a year to recover. Still can't walk like a man should walk." He showed his small white teeth at her, like an angry dog. A dog with a monocle that glinted again in the lamplight from above. "Thanks to you, my thieving, long-lost wife!"

"I took nothing that didn't belong to me. The seventy thousand I took out of your safe you embezzled from my father. Nearly ruined him. His heart finally did him in—thanks to you, my *thieving, long-lost husband*! Then my mother followed only a few months later!" Julia nodded slowly. "That money was mine. Once Mother passed, I was determined to get it back and to get away from you. I knew that you'd never give me a divorce. You'd have killed me first, which is what you tried to do!"

"Only after I walked into my office that night and discovered that you'd found the combination and opened my safe!"

"You were going to ravage me, Serg. Your own wife!"

Zhukovsky raised his shoulders and chuckled. He lifted his glass, smiled into it, and added, "What can I say—you did look ravishing amongst all those greenbacks . . . looking so uppity . . . and angry. I've always loved the way you look angry."

He chuckled, sipped.

Enraged, Julia slammed her still-tender hand down on the table, kicking up the burning pain once more. "How did you find me! I thought I'd taken such great care to cover my tracks!"

Chapter 9

Catfish Charlie Tuttle reined in his steeldust gelding on the shoulder of a bald, craggy rampart
high in the Stalwart Mountains, forty hard miles
south of Wolfwater. He swung down from the saddle
with a heavy grunt. Before he'd left his cabin, he
hadn't been in the saddle for days, and his weary old
behind wasn't as molded to the leather as it once had
been.

He'd be hanged if he'd let on to Brazos how hard
the two-day ride had been on him. He turned now to
see his old friend—still a friend?—rein in his fine
chestnut named Abe and swing down from the
leather. Brazos's face was as expressionless as when
Catfish had first seen the man back at his cabin.

Like Catfish himself, Brazos McQueen dug cased
field glasses out of his saddlebags, and trudged up to
within six feet of the crest of the ridge they were on.
Then they dropped and crawled, doffed their hats,
set them aside, and raised the binoculars to peer
through them.

Catfish tightened the focus on his own glasses

until five riders swam into clear view, just then making their way out from behind a thumb of a rock on the next ridge beyond a barren, boulder-strewn canyon in which the lens-clear, high-country sun fairly hammered down. Catfish couldn't tell much about the riders, only that none of them resembled the tall, slender, blond-mustached Frank Thorson, who was said to still ride a gray stallion.

"It's not them," Catfish said to his old partner now, lowering the glasses. "Frank's bunch. Not them."

"Nah, I don't think so, either. Maybe bounty hunters, maybe banditos. These crags have always crawled with both."

"Neither might give us a warm reception, Brazos. Both might have long memories."

"That's all right. I don't much care for either stripe, my ownself, an' my memory is just fine." Lying belly-down to Catfish's left, he returned his glasses to his baize-lined leather case. He was a few years younger than Catfish's sixty-two, but not by much. Still, he hadn't let himself go to seed the way Catfish had. Brazos was a little over six feet, broad-shouldered, flat-bellied, and he still owned the long-legged, ambling stride of a lifelong horseman. He'd been raised in slavery in Kentucky and had joined the Union Army after the Emancipation Proclamation.

After the war, he'd headed west.

Catfish often wondered, as he knew Brazos likely had, too, if they'd fought against each other in one of those long, bloody, chaotic skirmishes they'd both been involved in. Neither one had ever talked about the war.

Catfish scrutinized his old friend and partner closely. They'd let their horses rest a while. They'd been pushing hard for two days. Only a few minutes ago, they'd seen the curl of dust of the riders on the next ridge and had, in wordless agreement, just like old times—they knew each other well enough they didn't have need for much jabber—decided to investigate.

Now as their mounts cropped the tough, sparse brown grass thirty feet down the slope behind them, occasionally stomping a hoof and blowing, Catfish said, "You know, we been together now for two whole days, and you haven't mentioned one word about Vonetta."

Brazos turned to him, face still bland, though the brows a little ridged now over the molasses-black eyes. Finally he turned onto his back, sat up, and dug into his shirt pocket for his makin's sack. "I got nothin' to say on the subject."

"It's there between us. You know it is."

Brazos cast him a hard, grave look. "Of course, it is." He gave a dry chuckle. "I'm here to go after Abel's killers and to get Beth'ny back. After that, I'll ride on out of this country one more time . . . for good."

He twisted the quirley closed and struck a match to life on his thumbnail.

Brazos was the only one who'd never called Charlie by his nickname. He'd always called him Cha'les—from the first time they'd met when renegade Union soldiers had burned the farm of a Black family in the Panhandle, killing them all, including three sons, and raping and killing two younger daughters. Catfish had been Captain Charlie Tuttle, Texas Ranger, while Brazos had been a sergeant in the same service—one of the first Black men to ride for the Rangers until the organization became the State Police Force and had banned the hiring of

Blacks. Until that day, when they'd both been hunting outlaws solo, they'd never before crossed paths.

Together, they'd hunted down the soldiers, killing four, taking two to Amarillo for hanging, and were together for roughly the next twenty years, off and on . . . until that crazy, sad afternoon four years ago at the stage relay station in Wolfwater and Brazos had ridden out, not to be seen or heard from again by Catfish until two days ago.

"It wasn't what you thought it was, Brazos."

Brazos drew deep on the quirley and blew the smoke straight out before him. "Don't wanna talk about her." He paused, then turned a harsh look at his partner. "Don't make water in my boot an' tell me it's rainin'. You both betrayed me. I saw what I saw."

"What you saw wasn't what you thought . . . *think* . . . it was!"

Brazos snapped his head toward him once more, his black eyes wide and white-ringed. "Like I said— I'm only here to avenge Abel an' get his daughter back!" He took another drag from the quirley, disassembled it, and let the hot, dry breeze take the bits of tobacco and paper. He rose, pushing off his knees. "Come on if you're comin'. We got a job to do. Let's quit chinnin' like a coupla toothless old fools on a loafer's bench!"

Catfish heaved himself up with a curse and a grunt. "I still got a *few* teeth left in my head, you stubborn old ringtail!"

Brazos took up his chestnut's reins and turned to Catfish. "Maybe so, but I saw you puttin' salve on them cankers on your big, old, white behind last night." He looked down at the older man's bulging, jiggling belly as Catfish trudged down the slope, kicking stones and gravel in his wake, wincing with every step. "Look at you. You done gone to seed, you worthless old grayback. If I woulda known, I wouldn't have stopped at your place. I'd have kept ridin' up into the Stalwarts to avenge Abel an' Beth my ownself!"

The leaner man shook his head in disgust and pulled himself with relative litheness into the saddle.

Catfish looked up at him, red-faced, breathless. "You know what, Brazos?"

"What's that?" the former buffalo soldier fired back.

"You can go to hell!"

"Ha—that's a laugh!" Brazos reined his gelding around and rode out. "Ridin' with you, I done *have*!"

They didn't talk for nearly an hour, but rode higher and deeper into the bald, rocky, up-and-down country of the Stalwarts.

Then, just as they were entering a deep canyon between church steeple spirals of rock jutting from anvil-like shoulders on either side, Catfish raised his gloved right hand while drawing back on Jasper's reins with his left.

"Hold up."

Brazos checked his chestnut down and sat staring into the shaded canyon before them, sliding his gaze from the steeplelike rock jutting skyward on his left to that on his right. A slight wind blew, lifting dust from the canyon floor just ahead. That slight *whirring* and the ratcheting cry of a hawk turning slow circles over the canyon were the only sounds.

"I don't see nothin'," Brazos said in his low, musically resonant voice.

"Me neither," Catfish said, equally as quietly. "But I sure *feel* it."

"What do you feel?"

"Trouble."

Brazos looked at him, one brow arched. "Trouble?"

Catfish dipped his chin and raised his eyes to gaze up from beneath the broad brim of his hat, holding his right hand just above his thigh and extending his index finger nearly straight up. "I think I seen a shadow move amongst them rocks up there."

About forty feet up above the canyon floor, and on its right side, was a niche in the rock wall, an opening between the wall itself and a twenty-foot-high column of rock jutting out from it and up. In fact, there were several niches in the walls on each side of the canyon, plenty of places for a man or men to affect a bushwhack.

Brazos followed Catfish's pointing finger to the niche, studied it for a time, and then said, "I seen it, too. Just the shadow of that hawk's all."

He nudged his horse ahead.

"Hold on. I feel somethin', blameit!"

Brazos stopped the chestnut and curveted the mount, scowling back at his partner. "You've gone as soft in your thinker box as you have in your old behind. My senses are still as sharp as yours ever was, an' I don't sense a thing. All I see is that lone hawk up there!"

Catfish stared at the rocks rising above both sides of the canyon.

He scowled, deeply confounded. He felt a witch's cold finger of warning prodding the back of his neck, just below his collar. But he couldn't see a blame thing. Also, there were no hoof or man prints in the inch or so of soft clay sand paving the canyon floor. If men and horses had been about, that soft sand would hold prints.

Were his senses letting him down, just as his old behind was?

Was he just jumpy?

After all, he hadn't hunted owlhoots in years.

Yeah, that must be it. He was getting jumpy. *Scared.*

He felt the flush of embarrassment rise in his craggy cheeks, above his unruly beard, and ordered Jasper on ahead with a soft nudge of his spurs. He and Brazos dropped down the slight rise they were on and into the canyon, the steep walls closing around them. Catfish removed his Yellowboy from the sheath jutting up from under his right thigh. He quietly levered a round in the action and lowered the hammer to half cock—just in case.

Brazos gave him an arch-browed, dubious look.

Catfish ignored him, though he did see his old lawdog partner hook one hand over the walnut grips of his long-barreled .45 Peacemaker positioned for the cross-draw high on his left hip. Catfish gave a wry snort at that.

They rode slowly, each man looking around warily. Catfish kept an especially sharp eye out. That witch's finger would just not stop bedeviling him.

On, they rode, gazing up at the crenelated stone walls around them, at a boulder supported precariously by a stone pedestal high on their left, at a natural arch over a cave high on their right. From behind that pedestal rock or from inside the cave would both be good places for a man or men to shoot down at the trail.

No shots came.

And then both formations slipped away behind them . . . farther and farther back.

The cliff walls lowered gradually, spread farther apart. They found themselves traversing a shallower canyon with a boulder-choked, cedar- and cactus-studded dry wash curving toward them from their right side. They rode in the open sunlight now, the shadows of the steeper walls having slipped away behind them.

The old witch pulled her finger away from the back of Catfish's neck.

He heaved a heavy sigh of relief and depressed his Winchester's hammer.

"There!" Brazos suddenly bellowed, thrusting up his right arm and pointing finger. "Sun flash!"

At the same time, a rattlesnake hissed off the trail's left side, about ten feet ahead of Jasper, who pitched suddenly and whinnied shrilly, rising high and curling his front hooves at the cobalt mountain sky. Catfish heard the screech of a bullet just above his head a wink before he found himself plunging down Jasper's left hip, the reins ripped out of his left hand. By sheer instinct, he managed to keep his right hand closed around the Yellowboy.

He gave a wailing curse as he kicked free of his stirrups and saw the ground coming up around him fast. The bark of the rifle that had hurled that bullet reached his ears an eye wink before he struck the ground on his back and shoulders. As Jasper bounded up the trail, buck-kicking and avoiding the diamond head of the striking rattler by only inches, Brazos leaped off his own horse's back, his repeater in his hands.

He slammed the butt of the rifle against the chestnut's rump. As the horse ran up the trail after Jasper, Brazos dropped to a knee, jacked a round into the Henry's chamber and fired.

A man screamed.

The rattlesnake rattled.

As Catfish tried to suck air back into his battered lungs after the ground had beat it out of him, he glanced ahead to see the rattler, its coils as big as a man's arm, staring at him, forked tongue darting in and out of its mouth, its small, hard crescent eyes glinting copper as they bore down on its prey.

Chapter 10

Catfish rose to his knees, pulled the Yellowboy's hammer back, aimed hastily, and blew the viper's head off. It landed six feet beyond the leaping rest of it, mouth still opening and closing, the bloody back of its head caked with clay-colored sand.

The headless body dropped and coiled again, only three feet in front of Catfish.

In the corner of Catfish's left eye, he saw a man step out from behind a cottonwood growing up around a high boulder forming the shape of a half-tipped-over cabin. Brazos's Henry spoke twice quickly, each whip-cracking report preceded by the rasping of the cocking lever. The would-be shooter jerked back, dropped his rifle, slapped both hands to his chest, then stepped forward and over the edge of the boulder, turning a somersault before dropping out of sight.

A muffled thud rose as the would-be shooter struck the ground.

Catfish looked around, ready for another attack. At least he thought he was ready. He was sore as hell.

He hadn't taken a tumble like that in years. That was two tumbles within days of each other. At least this one he'd taken when sober.

When no shooters or would-be shooters appeared, he turned to Brazos, just as Brazos turned to him, a look of disgust on his old partner's face. "You all right?"

Anger rose in Catfish. "Don't 'all right' me." He used his rifle to hoist him to his feet. "I've hurt myself worse fallin' out of bed!"

"Don't doubt that a bit," Brazos said, brushing a gloved hand across his nose. He looked over to where the first shooter had fallen, then turned back to Catfish. "You check that one. I'll check this one over here."

The anger and indignation grew in Catfish. "Stop givin' the orders!"

Brazos shook his head, then heaved himself to his feet and went running all too nimbly into the rocks and brush where the first man he'd shot lay.

"Show-off," Catfish carped, then flexed his neck and back and hips and knees and ankles, just to make sure once more, for the second time in two days, that nothing was broken. Then he bit off a glove, stuck two fingers between his lips, and whistled.

When he'd retrieved his hat, reshaped it, and set it on his head, he ambled up into the rocks toward the boulder from which the second shooter had fallen. By the time he'd returned to the trail, Jasper was waiting for him, reins dangling, having answered the whistle, though he hadn't answered that whistle in a while. Mostly, Catfish only rode the horse now and then—and mostly just to town for supplies—just to keep the stable green out of him.

Catfish stood in the trail, bent over, hands on his knees, huffing and puffing. The fall from Jasper's back and the trek into the rocks had all but killed him. When he heard Brazos approach, he straightened, brushed a sleeve across his mouth, and tried to look all-business, not one bit winded, though he knew his swollen red face and rising and falling chest likely gave him away.

Brazos didn't miss a consarned thing.

"Who was yours?" Catfish asked his old partner.

"What do you mean?" Brazos said, scowling at him incredulously. "I shot 'em both."

"You know what I mean!"

Brazos gave a dry chuckle. "Mosby Carlisle. Yours? Er . . . I mean, the *other* one?" he said with a wry arch of a brow.

"'Kettle' McPherson."

"Ah."

Two known cattle rustlers. They'd probably glassed Catfish and Brazos on their back trail and figured they were shadowing them, likely having stayed away from Wolfwater long enough to not know the two had retired several years ago.

"Yeah, well, I figured it wasn't Thorson's men," Catfish said, spatting to one side. He brushed the dust off his Yellowboy and slid it into its sheath. "They're likely holed up in that cabin beyond that next peak, Bear Lodge Ridge. They hole up there for weeks at a time, I've heard. If they still have Beth with 'em, well . . ."

Brazos cast his bleak gaze up the trail to a low rocky pass. "They might be holed up a mite longer."

Catfish reached into the saddlebag pouch on the near side of Jasper's back and pulled out a small, flat, hide-wrapped flask. He glanced at Brazos, who drew his mouth corners down in disgust, as well as in reproof.

Catfish unscrewed the cap on the flask. "For medicinal purposes."

He took a deep pull, then one more, and raised the flask toward Brazos. "Nip?"

Brazos shook his head as he stared toward where his chestnut was coming back from up the trail, answering its own rider's whistle. Brazos turned back to Catfish, a forked vein in his forehead just beneath the brim of his hat—a vein that Catfish knew too well—swollen in anger. "I'm not here to drink with you, Cha'les. I'm here only to avenge Abel and get Beth back . . . if there's anything of her to get back, that is."

"All right, all right, you surly bluebelly cuss!" Catfish leaned against Jasper and scowled incredulously toward his partner. "How've you stayed in such good shape?"

"I haven't been spendin' these past five years drinkin' like you obviously have! While fishin' that backwater pond of yours, no doubt!"

"Where've you been?"

Brazos grabbed the chestnut's reins. "Just mount your horse, Cha'les!"

Catfish sighed. "Wherever it's been, it sure hasn't done your spleen any good." He returned the flask to his saddlebags, then grabbed Jasper's reins and heaved himself into his saddle. By the time he got the steeldust turned around, Brazos was already trotting up the trail toward the pass. "Owly cuss," Catfish grouched, and nudged Jasper into a lope.

Two hours later, they were both lying belly-down again, near the top of a ridge, their hats on the ground beside them. The high Bear Lodge Pass lay behind them. The valley they were now in, fed by Bear Lodge Ridge, was unusually verdant for the Stalwarts, with pines and cottonwoods all around them, and peppering the valley into which they both gazed with their field glasses.

They couldn't see well through the pines following the ridge down toward the valley floor, but they could see the small shake-shingled shack sitting down there, on the other side of Bear Lodge Ridge, which was liberally sheathed in willows. A couple of ranchers had at one time run cattle in this neck of the range, until they realized it was too far back down the mountains to send them to market. The ranchers had gone in together and built the shack at the bottom of the valley, which they'd called the Bear Lodge Creek Cabin, of course.

Cowmen in general had very little imagination.

It had been a jointly owned line shack in which three to four cowboys from both ranches would all settle in for a few weeks at a time. Their intent had been to watch the cattle and to watch for the Bear Lodge Creek bears, after whom the creek and valley had been named, changing it from the original Comanche name meaning "cool running water." Those grizzlies were hell on cattle, especially late in the summer when they were paunching up, so to speak.

After two groups of cowpunchers, one from each spread, had gotten into a disagreement over a poker match late one night, and shot the beans out of each other and had caused the cattle to stampede over a nearby cliff, the two ranchers decided Bear Lodge Creek was just too dang much of a nuisance to deal with anymore. So they ran their cattle back to their home ranges and left the line shack to whoever wanted to move in.

Which had been . . . and still was, mostly . . . owlhoots on the run from bank, stagecoach, train, and mine robberies.

It had been said that Frank Thorson holed up here from time to time, when he was on the run as well. Catfish had never doubted it, though by the time Frank had started his own infamous depredations around the country and farther south, Catfish had been retired. Likely, the reason Abel Wilkes hadn't done anything about Frank Thorson was because Frank had quit the area around Wolfwater—Abel having kept the lid on the town after Catfish had left it in his former deputy's capable hands. Besides, the so-called "line shack" was just too far away from Wolfwater to contend with, since his jurisdiction only extended as far as the Wolfwater city limits, same as Catfish's had.

Of course, little matters like jurisdiction never kept any lawdog worth his beans from running down owlhoots who preyed on his town.

Catfish didn't know if Frank and Skinny and the four other tough nuts were holed up there now, of course. But the cabin was a hot spot for outlaws on the run. Especially those who'd done especially dastardly deeds and likely would be chased. The Bear Lodge shack was remote and hard to get to, and there weren't a whole lot of other places in the mostly bald, craggy Stalwarts to repair to.

Catfish was betting Frank was here.

Of course, Catfish hadn't been in the game for a while, so whether his thinking was in any better shape than the rest of him was anyone's guess . . .

At the moment, he was hopeful.

A good nine or ten horses were in the corral flanking the place, which meant *someone* was holed up here. Possibly ol' Frank and his weasel brother, Skinny.

Yeah, he was hopeful.

And feeling a little desperate at the moment.

For he knew that his old trail partner . . . former friend . . . was doubtful and probably wishing he'd ridden up into the Stalwarts alone without his old, gone-to-seed former partner—his former friend bogging him down and dang near getting himself shot out of his saddle. That's what would have happened if that viper hadn't saved his bacon.

"How do you want to play it?"

Catfish turned to Brazos lying belly-down to his right, field glasses in one gloved hand, Henry repeater in the other hand.

Catfish blinked, surprised. "You askin' me?"

"You used to know how to play it, Cha'les!"

"All right, all right, you surly cuss!" Catfish returned his gaze to the low-slung cabin on the other side of the creek at the bottom of the valley.

He stared bare-eyed, chin just above the ground, running his right index finger over his lips, making faint blubbering sounds. He ran his eyeballs across the creek and over the cabin and then back to the corral and log stable, in which the horses milled. Two ran around the others, chasing each other in play, causing dust to rise.

The others regarded them dubiously.

One of the runners was a stallion. A gray stallion with a wind-buffeted, coal-black mane.

That would be Frank Thorson's horse.

Just then, the gray stopped suddenly and tried to mount one of the geldings standing in the middle of the corral. The gray gave a jeering whinny. The gelding, a zebra dun, jerked its head back to try and nip the gray's left wither, but missed. It bolted away from the gray. The gray dropped back down to all fours, shook its head, gave another mocking whinny, and continued running around the outside of the group amassed in the middle.

Catfish gave a wry laugh and shook his head.

"What's funny?"

"I do believe we tracked Frank down, Brazos."

"How can you be sure?"

"See that gray—the rapscallion mocking the geldings?"

"Seen him. He needs a bullet."

"So does his owner."

Catfish chuckled, satisfied with himself. The Thorson brothers were here, by God. He crabbed down the slope, away from the crest, and set his hat back on his head. He gained his feet and cast his bright-eyed, confident gaze to his partner. "You take the front door—you bein' the front-door sorta fella, an' all. I'll take the back door—me bein' the back-door sort of fella, an' all . . ."

"That's a good way to shoot each other!" Brazos said, also crabbing down the slope and casting an incredulous glance over his left shoulder at his former partner, former friend.

"You don't shoot me; I won't shoot you." Catfish grinned.

Brazos gained his feet. "You're askin' for a lot of restraint, Cha'les."

Catfish turned to him, gave him a grave, level look. "It wasn't me. It was Dick Gleeson. I convinced her to leave town so the fool little hellion wouldn't break your heart. Besides, she'd come between us. The money I gave her was stage fare."

"She was carryin' my baby, Cha'les."

"No, she wasn't. It was Dick Gleeson's child. That's what she came to tell me that night at the hotel, when you found us together."

Brazos stared at him darkly, his large, dark eyes growing larger. He was pondering it all; it was a lot to swallow. Especially after so many years had passed.

"For what it's worth, she felt bad about what she did. Steppin' out on you with that popinjay gambler, Gleeson." Catfish shrugged. "It was just her nature. Just like some men, she couldn't help herself."

Brazos opened and closed his hands around the Henry. A flush rose behind the natural darkness of his cheeks.

He looked away and then he said, "What do we do once we're in the cabin?"

"What we usually do . . . er, *did*. Just don't shoot the girl." Catfish extended his right hand. "What do you say, partner?"

Brazos gazed down at the cabin. "Lawdie, Cha'les. Two of us against nine, ten of them. And we're gettin' a mite long in the tooth." He glanced at Catfish's bulging belly, then shook the proffered hand. "Not to mention thick in the waist."

"Yeah, well." Catfish laughed, patted his steeldust's rump, silently ordering the ground-reined horse to stay, and tramped off, up along the crest of the ridge to the east, with lighter feet than he'd felt for a while. It was good to be back hunting outlaws with Brazos, just like the old days.

He just wished that Abel hadn't had to die, and Bethany kidnapped, to bring them back together.

Chapter 11

"Oh, you took great care to cover your tracks, my dear," Sergei Zhukovsky told his long-estranged wife. "Great care, indeed. It's not every day a person just drops off the face of the earth. But that's what you did."

"How did you find me?"

"I've had Pinkerton agents on your trail for the past ten years. I would have gone out looking for you myself but"—Zhukovsky rubbed his right thigh—"travel isn't as easy as it once was." He sipped his brandy. "An agent found you purely by accident. He was passing through Wolfwater a month ago and found this beautiful, elegant woman running her own saloon. In Wolfwater. Texas. Suspicious, he asked around about you and found out that no one—not a single person he spoke to in Wolfwater—knew where you'd come from or anything about your previous life. You see, my dear, sometimes mysteries alone attract attention."

Julia heaved a ragged sigh. She lifted her brandy

and swallowed a goodly portion to take the edge off her nerves. When she'd set the glass back down, she scowled across the table at her former husband. Yes, *former.* She could not, would not, call him her husband. Not after what he, in his savagery and greed, had done to her family. What he'd tried to do to *her* when in her fury and desperation she'd snuck into his office to rob back the money he'd stolen from her father.

Julia had no doubt that in Zhukovsky's own rage he would have murdered her after he'd had his way with her. She'd known too well that reckless, killing glint in his eyes.

"What do you want from me?"

"Money," Zhukovsky said. "Every last dime you stole from me . . . times two." He grinned coldly.

"What?" Julia scowled. "I don't have that kind of cash. Most of my money is tied up in my business!"

"Get it. If I don't have one hundred forty thousand dollars by the end of the month, I will reveal the secret of who you truly are, my dear. Not only that"—again, that wolfish smile—"I'll have you arrested and imprisoned for common thievery and attempted murder."

Julia hardened her jaws and slammed her open right hand down on the table. "Damn you, Serg! That money belonged to my family. I had every right to it!"

The smile on the Russian's mustached face broadened. Again, the monocle glinted in the sheen from the wan overhead lamps. "Prove it. You see, you might have done a good job of covering your tracks, Sylvia, but when I embezzled that money from your father, I did a rather supreme job of covering my own tracks. Neither you nor anyone else could prove that money came from your father's business."

Julia stared across the table at the sick, jaded creature before her, who felt supremely self-satisfied with the vise he had her in. She'd never loved him. She'd only married him because her father had wanted that. Howard Jones, suffering from the bad effects of smoking too many cigars, and having had a previous bout with rheumatic fever, had thought the dashing, young foreigner he'd brought in to manage his business dealings would be an ideal mate for his only daughter, Miss Sylvia Jones, fresh out of finishing school.

At the time, Sergei Zhukovsky had been charming and deferring. He'd shown little of the man he really was until after he and Sylvia were married. Then, little by little, the oafish, irritable, self-centered, and greedy man had begun to appear . . . until Sylvia's father had realized only too late that Zhukovsky had been stealing from him, while pretending to invest with Jones's best interests in mind.

After her father's long, painful death, followed closely by that of her mother, Sylvia had decided to take matters into her own hands . . . to take back what rightfully belonged to her, to disappear and start another life for herself in the West.

She'd vowed that never again would she hitch her star to a man. After what Zhukovsky had done, she could never trust another man again.

She looked down at her hands wrapped around the brandy glass. They were shaking so hard that brandy threatened to slop over the sides.

"Oh, come now, my dear," Zhukovsky said. "Stiff upper lip!"

Julia drew another deep breath and glared across the table at him. "You're really enjoying this."

"Oh, yes. Yes, I am. You see, I've waited years for this! To see the comeuppance of the slattern that crippled me, almost killed me . . . ruined my health for the rest of my life."

"You had it coming!"

"Be that as it may . . ."

"I told you—I can't afford your price, Serg. I don't have that kind of cash on hand."

"You have a month. Get a loan. I'm sure you have plenty of collateral in your little establishment. I hear it's quite the success." Zhukovsky raked his goatish eyes across her robe. "And I'd also speculate that there is a man or two in or around Wolfwater who might float you a note. For a certain price."

He cackled out a girlish laugh.

Julia felt hot blood rise in her face.

It was his turn to slap the table . . . in victory. "Oh, this is priceless!" When his raking laughter settled, he sat back in his chair, raised his cane above the table, and poked it at her as though aiming a rifle. "One hundred forty thousand dollars by the end of the month. I'll send my men for you, as I did this evening. You will bring it to me here, and then you will be free to carry on with your charlatan ways."

"But—"

"*Gentlemen!*" Zhukovsky yelled at the door. "Please return my guest to town. Don't forget the bag!"

He laughed as the men filed into the room and gave the former Sylvia Jones the same brutish treatment they had before. She struggled as futilely as she had before, hearing beneath her own gag-muffled curses the insane laughter of the man she'd been foolish enough to marry.

* * *

Catfish moved out from around a boulder and used the barrel of his Yellowboy to shove a pine bough aside. Here he had a clear view of the cabin's back wall. The stabled horses were maybe forty yards ahead and off to his right.

The big gray had winded Catfish.

That was all right. He'd expected the horses to wind him. Women, dogs, and horses were the bane of a lawman's existence. As in poker, you played the cards you were dealt.

Catfish smiled to himself. Here he was, already back seeing himself as a lawman again.

Don't get ahead of yourself, old son. Like Brazos said, neither one of you is a spring chicken, and you haven't taken down any outlaw . . . much less an outlaw of Frank Thorson's desperate caliber . . . in a good many years. Heck, you can't even catch your arch catfish enemy, Bubba Jones.

Still, he'd be hanged if he didn't feel the excitement. That urge for vengeance was a good feeling, too. He hadn't felt that for a while. Now he was here, and he was going to avenge Abel and do what he could to pry Bethany away from these desperadoes."

He released the pine bough, turned to his right, and strode as quietly as he could toward the stable and corral. Several of the other horses had winded him now and were moving uneasily toward the near fence, lifting their snouts high, working their noses. Likely, Thorson and whoever else was in the cabin with him had not posted pickets. If they had, Catfish would have known it by now.

They were confident in the cabin's isolation . . . and in their own cunning . . . to believe they'd not been trailed. They'd shot both lawmen in Wolfwater, and most of the good citizens had obviously been too afraid of Thorson's reputation to form or join a posse.

Good, good. Let the scoundrels rest easy . . .

Catfish stepped up beside another pine and looked at the horses again. They were about twenty feet between him and the gate. He brushed his fist across his nose and grinned.

Catfish, you old son of a devil.

What're you gonna do?

He knew exactly what he was going to do. He'd done it before, and it had confused his quarry enough before that they'd been fairly easy pickin's. Of course, they hadn't been Frank Thorson, but . . .

Catfish, you old devil . . .

He just hoped Brazos was still patient enough to follow his lead, as he had in years gone by.

Keeping a cautious eye skinned on the cabin's two rear windows, Catfish moved slowly up to the corral gate. Quickly but quietly, he slid the wire loop up over the corral's end post, then kicked the gate open wide. The horses were milling around edgily.

Stepping back from the gate opening, Catfish removed his hat and waved it. "Come on, you cayuses—get movin'!" he whispered.

Frank Thorson's big gray put his head down and shook it, then gave a shrill whinny and bounded forward and out the open gate. The others, whickering and prancing and lifting dust, followed suit, keeping a wary eye on Catfish, who kept waving his hat.

The thunder of the horses rose.

Men's incredulous voices sounded inside the cabin. Catfish dropped to a knee, raised the Yellowboy to his shoulder, and clicked the hammer back. He gazed down the Winchester's barrel through the dust wafting around him.

Boots pounded inside the cabin, and just as the last two horses galloped past him, heading into the tall-and-uncut east end of the shack, the back door opened. A man stuck his hatless head out, then turned to yell into the cabin behind him, "The horses are out an' on the run!"

He grabbed a hat and rifle, then ran out into the yard and into the dust kicked up by the horses. Catfish recognized him as the outlaw Wade Cormorant—longtime horse-and-cattle rustler, when he wasn't jumping mine claims.

"Hold it, Wade!" Catfish bellowed, tracking the man with the Yellowboy. "It's your old pal Catfish Charlie Tuttle!"

The man stopped suddenly, boots skidding in the sand and dirt. He hadn't seen Catfish yet, but he saw him now. As three others ran out of the cabin, some with holsters and shell belts hooked over their shoulders, Cormorant shouted, "It's Catfish Charlie! *Kill him!*"

Catfish dropped the man instantly, then dropped one of the others, while the third man fell to a knee and raised an old Spencer repeater to his shoulder. Catfish recognized the man as another bottom-feeder—Henry Winterthorn, a fellow owlhoot of the recently departed Cormorant.

More shouts rose from the cabin.

There was a loud crash and then Brazos shouted, "Put 'em down, fellas—it's Brazos McQueen and I got one helluva chip on my shoulder for the Thorson brothers!"

More loud stomping from inside the cabin, as well as cursing and shouting.

Then a veritable fusillade arose and two more men ran out of the cabin, crouching and shooting six-shooters toward Catfish, lips stretched back from their teeth. The one on the right was Frank Thorson. Catfish would have recognized the tall blond man anywhere. Just as one of Thorson's bullets screeched through the air, two inches off Catfish's right cheek, before plunking into a corral post behind the old lawdog, Catfish drilled one into Frank's left knee.

Frank screamed, fell, and rolled, clutching the ruined limb.

Catfish dropped the man Frank had run out of the cabin with, sending him stumbling backward and into the cabin's rear wall, triggering both six-shooters in his hands straight above his head. Meanwhile, another man ran out, clutching his arm and swinging around to shoot his lone hogleg back into the cabin.

Catfish saw a flash inside the cabin, heard the roar of Brazos's Henry. His target stumbled straight backward. Catfish shot him between the shoulder blades. The man stumbled forward and dropped to his knees before twisting around and rolling onto his right shoulder and hip, shaking as he expired.

"No!" came a cry from inside the cabin. "Don't shoot me! Ah, hell—don't shoot me!"

The thunder of footsteps grew louder until Catfish saw Skinny Thorson come running out of the cabin and into the yard. He took three long running strides, then fell to his knees, dropping the gun in his right hand and raising both hands high above his head.

"Don't shoot me, Catfish!" Skinny cried, his ferret face twisted grotesquely with fear. "I'm too young to die!"

Slow footsteps sounded behind the cowardly kid.

Then Brazos stood in the doorway behind him, his Henry repeater now resting on his shoulder. Gray smoke curled from the barrel. He stared over the kid's head at Catfish.

"What do you think?" he asked.

"Have you seen Beth?"

Brazos nodded, inclined his head back and to one side.

"How is she?"

"Not good."

Catfish turned to Frank. Frank looked up at him, wide-eyed. "Now you just wait, Catfish. You just wai—"

The thunder of Catfish's Yellowboy cut him off. He flopped over on his back, a neat round hole in the middle of his forehead.

Chapter 12

Catfish and Brazos each whistled for their horses, then Catfish left Brazos with Skinny Thorson and moved slowly into the cabin, his guts tied in knots. There wasn't much furniture in the place—just a long table, some chairs, a potbelly stove, and an old tarnished-brass bed in one corner.

There were three dead men in the place, lying in pools of their own blood. Brazos could still clean up with the Henry. Catfish would give him that.

Beth lay on the bed, wrapped in what appeared to be a single sheet.

She lay on her side, curled in a tight ball, shivering. Her hair was a tangled mess. A nightgown, robe, and slippers lay on the floor by the bed. The room stank with what these animals had done to the poor girl.

"Beth . . ."

She turned to him. She had a nasty cut on her lower lip, and her right eye was puffing up. There were welts on her cheeks and on her forehead.

"Don't look at me, Catfish," she said in a thin little

voice, and lay her head back down on the stained mattress. The only bedding was the one thin sheet. One small pink foot stuck out from beneath it. It appeared heartbreakingly fragile here in this fetid hell of a cabin.

Catfish sat down on the bed. It sagged deeply with his weight. "They're all dead, darlin'. Except Skinny. He'll hang. There's nothin' more they can do to you."

"Please, Catfish," Beth said, voice quavering with emotion. "Just go. You an' Brazos, go. I just want to be alone. I want to die here . . . *alone!*"

She sniffed and sobbed. The bed shook with her sorrow.

Catfish chewed off his right-hand glove and slid wet curls of her brown hair back from her cheek—a gentle caress. Still, she gave a start at his touch. At his *man's* touch, after she'd been treated so terribly by men. If you could call what lay outside men.

They were lower than the lowest vermin.

"We can't let you do that, Beth—Brazos an' me. We're gonna get you back to town, get you to Doc Overholser. He'll take good care of you."

Catfish paused. She just stared down at the bed— her big, jovial, intelligent spirit drained out of her.

"Think you can ride?" Catfish asked her.

She shook her head.

"We'll rig a travois for you, then. We'll stay here tonight, ride out tomorrow. We'll keep Skinny outside. You won't even have to look at him. We'll get these dead men out of here."

Tears welled in her eyes and dribbled down her cheeks to the blue mattress ticking.

"You rest easy, darlin'," Catfish said. "We'll be right outside." He wanted to give her shoulder an affectionate squeeze, but decided not to touch her again. She'd been touched enough.

Outside, the thud of oncoming horses sounded.

Catfish walked back out through the rear door. His horse and Brazos's chestnut each stood with their reins dangling, sniffing and disapproving of the smell of fresh blood. Brazos's chestnut, Abe, whickered deep in his chest and stomped a rear hoof. Jasper shook his head.

Skinny knelt where he'd been kneeling before, near his dead brother. His arms hung straight down at his sides. Brazos was pulling a rope out of his saddlebags. Skinny glared up at Catfish and said, "I thought you two old devils was retired!"

Brazos turned to him, holding the rope.

Catfish raised a hand to his partner. "Don't tie him yet."

Brazos lowered the rope to his side.

Catfish prodded the kid with his boot toe. "Get up, Skinny."

"What? No!"

"I said get up!" Catfish reached down and jerked the kid to his feet. Then he rammed his fist into the kid's belly.

Skinny yelped as Catfish's fist jerked him up off the ground. The scoundrel jackknifed forward, dropping to his knees. Catfish jerked him to his feet once more, then punched him once with his right fist and once with his left fist. Skinny moaned and went flying. He lay in the dirt on his side, glaring up at Catfish, brushing blood from his lips with his shirtsleeve.

"That's against the rules," Skinny said. "I know it's against the rules!"

"No rules out here, kid," Brazos told him. He looked at Catfish. "How's Beth doing now?"

"In no condition to ride," Catfish said. "We'll stay here overnight, build her a travois in the morning."

Brazos looked at Skinny. "How're we gonna get him to town?" He glowered at Catfish. "You ran off all their hosses, Cha'les!"

Catfish winced. "I reckon I didn't think it all the way through."

Catfish had just checked on Beth once more, and now he stepped out the cabin's back door. It was good dark now. He and Brazos had a small fire going, just off the cabin's back stoop. They'd dragged two chairs out there, and Brazos sat in one now, slowly sipping the coffee they'd brewed on an iron spider.

Skinny Thorson sat to the left of the stoop.

Catfish and Brazos had dragged his dead brother and the rest of Thorson's gang off into the brush.

Brazos had tied Skinny to a roof support post, hands behind his back, ankles tied straight out in front of him. The kid hadn't said two words since Catfish had taken him to the woodshed, so to speak.

He and Catfish and Brazos would sleep out here tonight, leaving the cabin to Beth.

"How is she feeling?" Brazos asked.

"Same. Hasn't moved. Refuses food, even coffee."

Brazos sighed and sipped his java. "I sure hate what those animals did to that poor girl, Cha'les."

Catfish used a leather swatch to remove the coffee-pot from the iron spider and refilled his cup with the steaming brew. "Yep, to her and her father. Abel didn't deserve to be gunned down like that, neither. He was just tryin' to keep the lid on the town."

"I hope they can find another pair of lawmen."

"Me too." Catfish eased his weight into the chair to

Brazos's left. "I hear it's gone to hell in a handbasket all over again . . . since Abel's been gone. What, with the railroad an' all."

Brazos was leaning forward in his chair, elbows on his knees, running his thumbs along the rim of his cup. "Maybe we oughta pin the badges back on again, Cha'les."

He glanced at his old partner.

Catfish frowned skeptically. "You serious?"

Brazos smiled and wagged his head. "Nah. Them days are long over for me."

"Yeah. Me too." Catfish sipped his coffee. "I'll hang around the office long enough for the judge to come and play cat's cradle with Skinny's head, though."

Skinny glared up at him, curling one half of his torn, bloody upper lip.

"Then I'll head back to my shack. I got me a catfish been makin' a bloody fool out'n me."

Brazos chuckled. "You always did like a platter of greasy catfish, Cha'les."

"Always have, always will."

Brazos looked at him sidelong. "Dick Gleeson, eh?"

Catfish looked at his old partner.

"Vonetta," Brazos said. "She was really steppin' out with that fancy gambler?"

"Sure enough." Again, Catfish sipped his mud. "Sorry, Brazos. I didn't want you to know . . . about whose the baby really was. I just wanted to get her out of town. She agreed, took the ticket I bought for her, and then she was gone."

"Hmm." Brazos tapped his thumbs on the rim of his cup. "I reckon I fell flat on that one." He glanced at Catfish again.

"Forget about it." Catfish stared at his coffee, then said, "You got a woman now?"

"Nah." Brazos sipped his coffee. "Figure I'm done."

"Where you been, partner?"

"Here an' there. Driftin'. Rode shotgun on a stagecoach up in Colorado. Did some mule-skinnin' in the Rockies. Worked as a gold guard on a train up in Dakota country. Just driftin'."

"Yeah. Well, you look good."

"Thanks. You don't."

Catfish snorted.

"The years," Brazos said. "They pile up on a fellow."

"Sure 'nough," Catfish said with a sigh. He was about to add something more, but Brazos raised his left hand abruptly, leaning his head to one side, listening, frowning.

In the corral, the horses whickered uneasily and turned their heads to peer eastward. They lifted their heads and worked their noses. Jasper gave his tail an owly switch.

"Company, sounds like," Catfish said as the clomping of hooves rose in the distance beyond the corral. He reached back for the Yellowboy leaning up against the cabin and set it across his knees.

Brazos grabbed his own repeater. "Sounds like."

"Popular place."

"Yep."

At the same time, both men jacked live rounds into their rifles' actions and lowered the hammers to half cock. They waited as the hooves grew louder. Shadows moved in the brush beyond the corral. Jasper whinnied, pranced. His greeting . . . or warning . . . was answered in kind by one of the newcomers' horses.

The hoof thuds stopped.

A man called, "Halloo the cabin!"

"Ride in slow," Catfish returned.

A man clucked; the thudding resumed. Catfish watched three riders silhouetted against the starlight ride up to within forty yards of the cabin and stop. They were just at the edge of the firelight, so Catfish couldn't see much about them, except that one was larger, bulkier than the other two. He sat to the right end of the group. All three looked around, the orange light of the fire reflected in their eyes beneath their hat brims and in their horses' eyes as well.

Their gazes seemed to catch on the bodies humped in the brush to the right of the fire. Earlier, Catfish had heard sniffing and snorting over there. Wolves, coyotes, or wildcats.

"Trouble here, maybe, eh?" called the big man, sitting up straight, one fist on his hip.

Catfish and Brazos sat in silence, tapping their thumbs on their rifles.

The three men looked at each other, and then the big one turned to Catfish and Brazos once more. "We'll ride on."

"Do that," Brazos said.

The three men sat staring toward the two men on the porch, and Skinny sitting on the ground to Catfish's left, hang-headed, none too pleased with his sorry lot.

"Say," said the big man, canting his head to one side and riding up closer to the fire. He stopped just on the other side of the flames and, sliding his gaze from Catfish to Brazos and back again, said, "Ain't you Catfish Charlie Tuttle an' Brazos McQueen?"

Catfish and Brazos stared at him.

The big man gave a dry chuckle and glanced over his shoulder at the other two, who remained at the edge of the firelight. Turning back to Catfish and

Brazos, he said, "I thought you two was finished. Years ago, now . . ."

"We got a little left in us," Catfish said.

The big man glanced into the brush. "I see that."

Brazos scowled beneath the brim of his black Stetson. "Ain't you Merwin Carlisle?"

"What if I was?"

Catfish and Brazos looked at each other and chuckled.

Then Catfish turned to the big man and said, "Why don't you haul your fat behind out of here, Merwin? You done already worn out your welcome."

Carlisle blinked. He had a big, round, bearded face with deep-set eyes. In the firelight, Catfish saw a long, sickle-shaped scar running through his beard, down his left cheek. Compliments of a fellow boarder in the Texas State Pen, most likely.

"Still impolite as ever—eh, Catfish?" Carlisle said.

"You heard me," Catfish said.

He could see anger building in the old outlaw's eyes. Carlisle reined his beefy dun around and rode back the way he'd come. "We may meet again one day, Catfish . . . Brazos."

The other two sat staring at Catfish and Brazos and then reined their mounts around and followed Carlisle into the night's deep shadows beyond the corral. Their hoof thuds dwindled to silence.

Brazos said, "Did you notice the saddlebags on Merwin's hoss?"

"They looked a mite swollen."

Catfish stared into the darkness beyond the fire, listening, tapping his gloved right thumb against the off-cocked hammer of his Winchester.

The fire burned low.

The two horses in the corral stared off into the darkness. Jasper had his tail arched.

Finally there was a sudden fast clomping of hooves and three shadows moved, the three horseback riders coming fast—one from Catfish's left, one from straight out in the trees, the other to the right of the fire.

Guns flashed in the darkness and Merwin Carlisle shouted, "Get them old dogs, boys!"

Moving faster than he'd thought himself able, Catfish slid down off his chair, drew the Yellowboy's hammer back to full cock, pressed the butt plate to his shoulder, and returned fire at the man on his left, who, judging by his size growing in the darkness beyond the cabin, was Carlisle himself. Catfish fired three times, jacking and firing.

Merwin screamed, threw his arms straight out from his shoulders, and flew backward off his galloping mount.

Brazos had been blasting away to Catfish's right, evoking a scream from over there as well. He and Catfish each fired two rounds at the rider approaching quickly from the fire's far side. That man threw his rifle up high above his head and rolled straight back over his horse's arched tail. He turned a single somersault, then lay flat on his face and belly, unmoving.

Catfish pushed off his knees, standing.

Brazos did the same.

"Well," Catfish said, drawing a deep breath, the smell of powder smoke strong in his nose, "I reckon we have a hoss for Skinny."

Skinny cursed.

Brazos chuckled.

Chapter 13

Julia Claire was still seething.

It had been two nights since she'd been kidnapped from her own establishment in Wolfwater, but every second of that torturous debacle lived on in her mind, as well as in her body. Her joints still ached from the rough ride out to wherever her former husband had taken her. The nerve of the arrogant Russian!

Sergei Zhukovsky didn't need her money. He *came* from money. He was just enjoying terrifying her. And for what?

Revenge.

Because she'd merely defended herself against his vicious attack. Yes, her retaliating with her own brand of rage had crippled him, weakened him—she'd noticed the hollows in his cheeks, the sickly yellow in the skin around his eyes, the streaks of gray in his hair—but he'd deserved what he'd gotten. Now he was trying to give back as good as he'd received. And Julia Claire—yes, she would forevermore continue to see herself as her alias Julia Claire rather than as Serg's former wife—had no idea what she could do about it.

Well, she had *some* idea. An inkling, anyway.

That's why her chief bouncer and footman, George McGrath, was just then driving her down a desert trail along the bank of Wolfwater Creek. They were rounding a bend as they followed the trace between a bullet-shaped butte on the trail's left side and the creek itself on the right. Julia rode in the rear seat, stylish picture hat shading her face, holding a parasol above her head for extra shade. McGrath was a big man, as were all of Julia's bouncers. But he, like all her other bouncers, was mostly hired muscle, trained to be more defensive than offensive.

That's why Julia hadn't considered George or any of her other bouncers for the task she had in mind.

Also, she wanted a true professional, and she did not want the task to have any association at all with her business. At least, not more than necessary, given that she owned the place.

As the carriage rolled out from around the butte and crossed Wolfwater Creek via a wooden bridge, a large, majestic house of wood frame and white clapboards spread out before her. Several large barns, stables, and corrals lay to the left, down a slight, wooded hill from the house. Cowboys were working cattle in one of the corrals, while a handful of others were sitting on a corral fence, watching another man—tall and lean and wearing a black Stetson and billowy red neckerchief—attempt to break a bucking bronc. Dust rose around the violently pitching horse and the rider, who, while tossed this way and that in the saddle, appeared to be doing a most expert job of maintaining his precarious perch.

The drovers on the fence yelled and whistled encouragement.

As the carriage passed through post oaks and cottonwoods on the far side of the creek, one of the men in the yard turned toward the house and yelled up the hill, "Visitor, Mr. Dragoman!"

McGrath clucked the fine gelding in the carriage's traces up the path lined with decorative white stones. There were three wrought-iron hitchrails fronting the house's broad front porch, the end of each rack forming the shape of the Dragoman brand, which was a simple circle *D*.

A tall, broad-shouldered man stood atop the porch, clad in customary drover's garb and looking all-business beneath the brim of his brown Stetson, while cradling a Winchester repeating rifle in his brawny arms. One of Dragoman's customary pickets.

Grant Dragoman had many business holdings, including both the Circle D and the San Antonio & Rio Grande Railroad. Any man as successful as he was in this uncouth country had his share of enemies. Recognizing her, and no doubt expecting her arrival, the picket merely dipped his chin and pinched his hat brim to Julia. As the big oak front door opened behind him, the picket turned and sat back down in the rocking chair he'd been sitting in when Julia's carriage had first pulled up to the house.

Grant Dragoman himself stepped out of the big house, his large, sun-reddened face aglow with a delighted smile.

"Why, Julia—to what do I owe the honor? The note you sent from town mentioned you'd like to visit, but there was nothing about the business you wished to discuss." The big, regal-looking man, in a black vest over a red shirt and turquoise-studded necklace, stepped forward and entwined his big hands before him. "Not that you need a reason, of course. A visit from you is always more than welcome. You must know that. Perhaps this is a social call . . . ?"

His gray eyes glinted hopefully.

Julia gave a wan smile of her own as McGrath took her hand to help her down out of the red-wheeled carriage. When she had both feet on the ground, she looked up at the rancher once more—an old lion now in his early sixties, but still owning the bull shoulders, relatively flat belly, and slender legs of the seasoned frontiersman. Grant had established the Circle D with his father over twenty years before, fighting the land away from the wildcats, grizzlies, rustlers, nesters, miners, and, of course, Indians.

No small feat in western Texas.

His gray-laced dark brown hair was combed straight back from a pronounced widow's peak.

"Oh, Grant, you flatter me!"

The bouncer/footman hitched the carriage horse, a fine Appaloosa, one of two Julia had bought from Dragoman himself several years ago. Julia returned the parasol to the carriage, then climbed the broad porch steps, holding the hem of her long, metallic orange traveling gown above her ankles.

"How good to see you, my dear," the rancher said, taking both of Julia's hands in his own as she gained the top of the porch.

She turned her cheek as he leaned forward to offer a friendly peck. Maybe not so friendly, Julia sometimes thought. The man's wife had died several years ago. His three sons had all run off to professional lives back east, while one daughter practiced medicine in Denver. They were an accomplished bunch. Dragoman lived alone out here, but not by choice. He'd proposed to Julia on several occasions. He'd also offered to buy the Lone Star Outpost from her.

"Why should a beautiful woman like you work so hard?" he'd said over dinner one night at the Lone Star. "I could take this over for you, put all the worries of such a business on my own plate, while you rode my blooded horses all around the Circle D— not a care in the world." His smile had softened, turned more intimate. "Aside from pleasing me, of course, dear Julia."

She hadn't accepted, of course. Her life was her own. She'd told him as much over drinks. Now, however, she welcomed his fawning gaze, though she couldn't help feeling some shame for doing so. After the unwelcome appearance of her ex-husband, and his assault on her out at some remote road ranch whose whereabouts he obviously wanted to keep secret, she felt desperate enough to take advantage of Dragoman's flattery.

"Come on inside," the rancher said, offering his arm. "Is it too early for a drink? I know I'd like one."

He gave her a dry chuckle as he ushered her inside his sprawling, well-appointed house decorated in a decidedly manly fashion, with animal rugs and skins and trophy heads on the walls. As he led her inside his spacious parlor, just off the main living area and kitchen, he called for his half-Indian, half-Chinese servant, Xavier, to bring cheese, sausages, and a fresh bottle of bourbon, which Julia knew Dragoman regularly had shipped here from a distillery in Kentucky he owned a part interest in.

When he and Julia were seated on two short, separate sofas on either side of a stout, square coffee table, with drinks in thick goblets and the cheese,

bread, and sausages on fine plates on the table between them, Dragoman sipped his bourbon, then
sighed and leaned back in his sofa, stretching his
arms out on the deeply cushioned back of it.

He said, "Well, now, Julia—it's the weekend.
Knowing how wild tigers couldn't drag you away
from the Lone Star during such a ripe time for business, unless for something very important, I must
confess you have me more than a little curious." He
smiled and lowered his eyelids about one-quarter
way. "Decide to accept one of my many, most hum-
bling proposals?"

"I do apologize, Grant." Julia unpinned her hat
from her hair and set it down on the sofa beside her.
"And you're quite right. It is terribly important."

She sipped her bourbon, crossed her legs, and
gave him a long, grave stare. "It is also quite embarrassing. Quite tawdry, I might add."

Dragoman gave her another toothy, openly admir-
ing smile. "If it involves you, I doubt very much
there's anything tawdry about it."

"Oh?" She arched a brow. "Well, then . . . try this."
She glanced at the door and then the windows, all of
which were closed. Good. "I need a man killed for me."

She thought for a moment the rancher's eyes were
going to pop out of his head. He looked as though
he'd swallowed something he couldn't get past his
vocal cords.

"Well," he said, lowering his arms from the back of
the sofa, "I must admit this is . . . well"—he chuckled—
"somewhat of a surprise."

"I'm sorry to speak so bluntly, but I saw no reason
to beat around the bush. I need a man killed for me,
Grant. Yes. A staunch antagonist. Of course, I don't
expect you to accomplish the task yourself. Or any of

your men, for that matter. I wouldn't even want that. I need a man—well, a professional. A *quiet* professional."

Dragoman gazed back at her from across the table, obviously still having trouble digesting what he'd just heard. Finally he crossed his arms on his broad chest and nodded slowly. "I know such men."

"I figured you would." No man who'd attained the rancher's status, and had acquired all that he'd amassed so far, hadn't had dealings with such men in the past. Julia had heard rumors—some more than rumors—about Dragoman himself. Stubborn nesters and miners had a way of mysteriously disappearing from graze that Grant considered his own, even if it was officially open range.

He cleared his throat. "Um . . . Julia, if I am to have a man killed, I'll need the man's name."

"God, that sounds so terrible! I never thought I'd be having such a conversation."

Dragoman smiled. "Getting cold feet?"

"No." Julia shook her head, convincing herself. "None at all. I'll need you to keep what I tell you secret."

"I wouldn't have it any other way."

"I need my former husband killed."

"Oh . . ." The rancher gave a slow nod. "I thought you might have been married before. Never wanted to ask, of course. You were never forthcoming about your past."

"For good reason, Grant."

"I don't doubt it. Tell me what you can . . . what you feel comfortable telling me."

She gave a few sketchy details and then told him about the other night, when Zhukovsky had sent the three brigands to kidnap her and take her for the wagon ride in the desert.

"They put a bag over my head. Sergei didn't want me to know where he'd taken me."

"Any idea?"

"None. It was too disorienting. I don't even know the direction we left town."

"I see."

"Not much to go on, I know."

"Tell me what this Sergei Zhukovksy looks like."

She did.

"With that limp and his accent, he'd stand out in a crowd."

"That's why I don't think he'll come to town. I think he intends to stay where he had me taken the other night—wherever that is."

"And he's sending his men for the money . . . in a month."

"That's what he said."

"What did the inside of this remote building look like?"

She told him.

"Hmm," Dragoman said. He leaned forward and took a slow, thoughtful sip of his whiskey, rolling the glass around between his big hands that were as red as his Texas-weathered face.

"Does it sound familiar?"

Dragoman took another sip of whiskey, set the glass down on the table, and leaned back in the sofa. "No. All kinds of abandoned cattle ranches and road ranches out here, tucked away in these spiny hills. I'll put a man on it. I'll have him track this Zhukovsky down for you, Julia." He smiled, gave her a reassuring wink. "Don't worry. He'll never be heard or seen from again."

A chill crawled up Julia's spine, and she shuddered. Her breath grew heavy, anxious for a time, and then she took a sip of her whiskey, set the glass back down, and said, "How much will you be needing . . . ?"

Dragoman frowned as though puzzled by the question. "Nothing, of course. We're friends. Friends help friends, Julia." He shrugged, smiled. "You never know—maybe someday I'll need a favor from you sometime."

Julia felt that chill crawl up her spine again. She leaned forward to reach again for her glass, suddenly wondering if she hadn't just made a deal with the devil. She sipped the whiskey, looked across the table at her accomplice.

No. Grant Dragoman was not the devil. He was just a friend helping a friend. She drew a deep, calming breath, then leaned back in the sofa, crossing her long legs beneath her skirt again. She was very much aware of the affect such a simple movement had on men.

"Who is this . . . man . . . you intend to put on it, Grant?"

"As little as you know, the better. Probably the same for both of us. Rest assured, he knows these hills—every hollow and wash. Wherever Zhukovsky is holed up, he'll find him."

Dragoman leaned forward, stretched his hands across the table, and wrapped them around Julia's, gently squeezing. He was so close that Julia could smell the bourbon and a recent cigar on his breath. "He won't bother you again. Whatever he is blackmailing you for"—the rancher pursed his lips and shook his head—"will never be known."

Suddenly Julia felt her throat constrict with emotion. With relief. "Thank you so much, Grant. Thank you so much."

"Nonsense. We'll make no more mention of it." He smiled again and sat back in the sofa. "Well, maybe one more time. When this thuggish ex-husband of yours has been kicked out with a cold shovel."

Dragoman chuckled, slitting his gray eyes, his broad chest rising and falling sharply, making his necklace jerk.

Just as suddenly as Julia had felt the ill-omened chill replaced by relief, it switched back to the chill again . . . crawling up her spine to the back of her neck and remaining there—a scorpion about to sink its stinger into her.

Chapter 14

That uneasy feeling stayed with Julia even after she and George McGrath had started back to town.

The stocky, bull-necked man, who wore a handlebar mustache and long, curving muttonchops down to his jawline, must have sensed her unease. When they'd been roughly twenty minutes on the trail—the ride was a good hour and a half through some rugged terrain including a badlands near Wolfwater Creek—he glanced over his right shoulder at her. Blinking against the dust kicked up by the horse and powdering his bowler hat, he asked, "Everything all right, Miss Claire? You seem a mite troubled."

He spoke in a thick Irish brogue.

The question startled Julia out of the trance she'd been in. She felt a warm rush of blood rise in her cheeks, suddenly feeling self-conscious, guilty . . . paranoid?

As with most aspects of her life, especially after having fought her way out of that big, oppressive mansion in which she'd resided with Sergei, after leaving him lying unconscious in his office and washing his blood from her hands and face, no one must know about the favor she'd asked Dragoman to do for her.

"Me? Oh, no, no—I'm fine, George. Just tired. The drive out here always wearies me, that's all." She offered a phony smile.

McGrath offered a genuine smile in return. "I see, ma'am. Just checking." He winked and turned his head back forward as the horse followed a bend in the trail around several cottonwoods that stood along a dry tributary of Wolfwater Creek. As the carriage rounded the bend and began to straighten out, three riders rode out from behind the trees and onto the trail, checking their horses down and turning them to face the carriage.

"Whoa, there!" McGrath said to the horse, drawing suddenly back on the reins.

Julia had just started to fall into another trance and didn't see the riders until the carriage rocked to a sudden stop; then McGrath said loudly, "And just what in bloody hell is *this* all about? This is Miss Claire and she's been given free passage on Circle D range!"

Only, the three riders facing the carriage, stoic-faced, weren't Circle D riders. They were Sergei Zhukovsky's men—the big, savage-faced Gunther Gross, the small and vaguely effeminate-looking Mick Staggerford, and the tall, gangly Kurt Gannon. Each held a rifle across his saddle pommel.

Staggerford spread his lips back from his small, dark, crooked teeth and said in his oddly repellent voice, "Hello again, dearie. Nice day for a ride, eh?"

Julia sat frozen in her seat, a fresh wave of terror washing over her. It was a tidal wave.

McGrath glanced over his shoulder at her, this

time frowning with red-faced incredulity. "You know these . . . um . . . *gentlemen*, Miss Claire?"

"She knows us, all right," said the tall, droopy-eyed Gannon. "Knows us far better than she'd like to—don't ya, ma'am?"

Gunther Gross piped up, "Boss wants to see you again. You see, we been ordered to keep an eye on you. Your little jaunt out to the Circle D to see your friend Dragoman is gonna make him mighty curious." He bunched his lips and shook his head dramatically.

Again, McGrath glanced over his shoulder at Julia. Then he whipped his head forward. Sylvia saw the back of his neck turn red as he leaped to his feet, causing the Appaloosa to jerk with a start. He pulled the .45 Colt from the holster on his right hip, aimed it straight up from his shoulder, and ratcheted the hammer back.

"I don't think she wants to see you or anyone else of your ilk at all, buckos. Now kindly clear the trai—"

Before he could get the last word out, Gunther Gross jerked his rifle to his shoulder, jacked a round into the action, and aimed at McGrath. The rifle bucked and roared, flames lapping from the barrel.

Julia heard herself scream beneath the rifle's thunder as she watched a fist-sized hole open between McGrath's beefy shoulders. Blood and white bits of bone spewed from the ugly wound onto the seat back, to Julia's left. The big man screamed and triggered his Colt into the air as the Appy gave a shrill whinny and lunged forward. McGrath flew straight back over his seat and landed on the seat beside Julia. He groaned, shuddered, and slid over to rest his now-hatless head on her shoulder. He and Julia both bounced violently as the Appaloosa bounded straight up the trail. Shouting, Zhukovsky's men reined their own mounts quickly out of the whinnying mare's way.

Julia looked at McGrath in shock, and then, realizing she was aboard a runaway, slid the footman off the seat and onto the floor. She held the seat before her in both hands, knowing she could be swept from the carriage at any time, for the horse . . . and the carriage right along with it . . . was fairly flying up the trail!

She rose from the rear seat and hurled herself straight forward and into the front seat. The horse and carriage lurched sharply to the left. Julia screamed as she was nearly hurled over the door on the carriage's right side. Heaving herself forward and dropping to her knees, clutching the carriage's front panel now for support, she looked for the reins.

Thank God, McGrath had thought to wrap them around the brake handle. Only, he'd wrapped them merely once around the handle; Julia watched in horror as the leather ribbons quickly slid from around the handle toward the ground racing past between the carriage and the horse's quickly scissoring hooves!

She cried out anxiously as she threw herself forward across the narrow gap between the seat and the front panel. The reins were uncoiling quickly . . . only about a foot of leather left!

"No!" she cried as she reached for the handle, grabbing the ends of both ribbons just an eye blink before the reins would have been lost and trailing along the ground.

"Thank God!" she said, breathless, taking both the ribbons in her right hand and heaving herself up onto the seat. The wind had already taken her hat and her hair blew out behind her.

She leaned back in the seat, tugging on the reins.

"Whoa, girl! Whooooa, now! *Stop!*" she screamed into the wind.

To no avail. The badly frightened horse merely laid her ears back all the flatter against her head and lunged into an even faster all-out run.

The runaway horse was only part of Julia's problems, she realized as guns popped behind her. She glanced over her shoulder to see Zhukovsky's three thugs galloping after her, one of them, Gunther Gross, just then jacking a round into his rifle's action and raising the gun to his shoulder. Smoke and flames spat from the barrel. The report's sharp *whip-crack* reached Julia's ears just after the bullet had screeched past her, so close she could feel the hot curl of air against her left ear.

She ducked her head, flinching, then hauled back on the reins once more. But it did no good. As the trail, winding through and up and over low hills peppered with sotol, scrub oaks, and cedars, curved sharply to the left, the mare kept going straight, heading straight up-country. A low hill lay just ahead.

"Oh, my God!" Julia cried again, flinching as another bullet screeched only inches above her head to blow a leaf off a cedar just ahead and to the right of the galloping mare.

The horse flinched, climbing the low hill—the carriage and Julia just behind. As the mare plunged down the hill's other side, the carriage went airborne, Julia along with it, her rump leaving her seat and her heart flying into her throat. When the front wheels struck the hill's far, sloping side, Julia slammed back down into her seat so hard that the reins went flying out of her hands.

Again, she cried out in terror and desperation . . . both of which grew inside her when she saw one of the deep canyons of the badlands area along Wolfwater Creek yawning wider and wider straight ahead of her as guns continued to crackle behind her.

The canyon was roughly a hundred yards straight ahead across the desert—a giant, toothy mouth opening wider and wider to accept her.

Eighty . . .

Sixty . . .

Forty . . .

"Whoa! Whoa, girl!" a man's voice shouted beneath the thunder of the mare's hooves and the rattling and banging of the carriage.

Julia's lower jaw sagged in surprise when she saw a lean Black man in a high-crowned, broad-brimmed black hat, black duster, and red neckerchief gallop seemingly out of nowhere—from ahead and to her right.

"Whoa! Whoa! Whoa!" he yelled as he leaned out over his fine chestnut horse's left wither to grab the cheek strap of the horse's bridle. Gradually he turned his own galloping horse to the left, easing the mare left as well, so that the gaping mouth of the red canyon slid off to the right and was no longer coming up so fast.

Deathly fast.

When the mare and the carriage were parallel with the canyon, and only about twenty feet away from the edge, Julia's savior drew back on his chestnut's reins with his right hand while pulling back on the horse's bridle with his left hand.

"Whoa! Whoa, girl! Whooooa!"

Relief was a cool wash of air blowing over Julia as the rider gradually slowed the horse, maintaining a firm grip on the bridle until the mare gave an anxious whinny and, grinding her rear hooves into the sandy, gravelly soil stippled with buckbrush and cactus, stopped abruptly, rocking back on her haunches and giving another whinny.

The man and the chestnut stopped as well. Blinking against the dust rushing over him from behind, and keeping a firm hold on the runaway's bridle, the man turned to Julia and said in a vaguely familiar voice—a voice out of the wavering mists of the distant past—"You'll want to set the brake now, Miss Claire!"

She gazed at her savior incredulously, her heart still racing, mind spinning. "Oh . . . yes, yes." She reached for the brake handle and rocked it forward until the wooden blocks clicked down against the wheels.

She looked at the canyon opening perilously close on her right, shuddered, and heaved a ragged breath. "My God," she said, panic slow to die inside her, beneath the relief. She shook her head, jostling her hair, which hung in messy, dusty tangles down over her shoulders. "I was . . . I was . . . so close . . ."

She looked at the man again, frowned, puzzled, slow to comprehend all that had happened, her recognition of the man building slowly inside her, but tempered with the improbability of them meeting way out here and at such an opportune time.

Final recognition swept through her to mix with the other tangled feelings. "Brazos?" she said. "Brazos *McQueen?*"

She just then realized that guns were still cracking behind her, albeit more distantly than before. She

turned to see three riders—the men who'd been
chasing the carriage—gallop up a hogback bluff a
couple of hundred yards away, horses and riders obscured by scattered cedars and oaks. A fourth, thick-
set rider in a tan hat and butterscotch vest galloped a
beefy steeldust up the bluff behind them, triggering
a pistol in his right hand, the crackling reports reaching Julia's ears a good two seconds after smoke
puffed from the barrel. Julia could hear the pursuing
rider's angry shouts mixing with the rataplan of his
and the horses of the three men he was chasing.

He, too, looked familiar, even from a distance . . .
as did his voice. Yes, this wasn't the first time she'd
heard the distinctive, hoarse baritone raised in exasperated anger.

Julia raised a hand to shield the sun from her eyes,
again beetling her brows with incredulity. "Is that . . .
is that . . . ?"

"Keep a tight rein on your hoss, Miss Claire," said
Brazos McQueen.

She glanced at the slender Black man—yes, he was
Brazos McQueen, all right, a man she hadn't seen in
a good many years, since he'd disappeared so suddenly and mysteriously from Wolfwater. He swung
the chestnut around and booted it after the four riders just then cresting the hogback, the first three disappearing down the far side, the man behind them
still shouting and shooting.

"Be back shortly. Cha'les has 'em on the run!"

Julia frowned as she turned to watch him gallop
the chestnut toward the hogback. Disbelievingly, she
heard herself mutter, as though to fully comprehend
the information with her mind, which was such a
wreck after her near-death experience, "'Cha'les . . .
has 'em on . . . the . . . run . . . ?"

Chapter 15

Catfish and Brazos had spotted what looked like trouble from their perch on a hilltop a couple of hundred yards east of the trail where the trouble appeared to be occurring—three horseback riders appearing to block the passage of a chaise pulled by an Appaloosa that Catfish had recognized through his field glasses as one of the two fine animals owned by Miss Julia Claire.

Further scrutiny through the glasses, peering through the screen of dusty cottonwoods lining the trail, told him that Miss Claire was, indeed, in the back of the carriage, while one of her beefy bouncers/footmen was in the front seat, driving. It so much appeared that the three horsebackers were confronting Miss Claire and her driver that Catfish had unhitched the travois carrying Beth Wilkes even *before* one of the three horsebackers shot Miss Claire's driver.

Beth was still in so much shock after what had happened to her that Catfish didn't think she even knew when he and Brazos took off at dead gallops down toward the cottonwoods from which the carriage had just then bounded off behind the startled Appaloosa. The two old-timers left their prisoner, Skinny Thorson, gagged and tied to the saddle of the horse that they had appropriated from one of the three scalawags they'd shot the night before.

The three obvious owlhoots wheeled their mounts and took off after Miss Claire's driverless carriage, throwing lead as they did.

"Brazos, you try to stop that chaise!" Catfish had shouted, crouched low in his saddle and giving Jasper his head. "I'll try to scour them miscreants from her trail!"

That's how Catfish found himself now galloping up and over the hogback butte, rage causing him to cuss up a storm and throw lead at the three brigands just as they'd thrown lead at a defenseless woman aboard a runaway carriage. He'd just started down the butte's opposite side when he checked Jasper down abruptly and scowled into the canyon beyond as the three men he'd been pursuing separated and continued galloping through a broken country of scrub oaks, cedars, and cacti.

Their horses were obviously fresher than Catfish's. Jasper had pulled Beth's travois through the up-and-down Stalwarts for a good thirty miles. He and Brazos had taken a shortcut both Catfish and Brazos knew about from their earlier days hunting rustlers and claim jumpers out this way. That's how they'd found themselves on Circle D graze, in the first front of the Stalwarts, just in time to interrupt the dustup on the two-track trail below.

Catfish cursed as he stared after the three cowardly devils as they disappeared in that broken country below. He flicked open his still-smoking Colt's loading gate and began punching out the spent loads and replacing them with fresh from his cartridge belt. That's when he heard the horse coming fast up the butte behind him.

He'd just shoved his freshly loaded hogleg back into the holster thonged on his right thigh and turned to see Brazos rein his fine chestnut to a stop at the top of the bluff a few yards up from Catfish. Dust rose high behind and around them.

Brazos scowled at Catfish, then peered into the canyon before turning his incredulous gaze on his partner again. "Where'd they go?"

"To hell, for all I care!" Catfish said. "They split up down there. Jasper's blown."

Sure, blame it on Jasper. As if your hairy old behind don't feel like three layers of skin have been plumb scraped off by a rusty bowie knife!

"Recognize 'em?"

Catfish shook his head, removed his hat, brushed his right shirtsleeve across his sweaty forehead, and returned the battered topper to his grizzled head—his face and big, pitted nose red from fresh sunburn.

He looked at Brazos. "Miss Claire?"

"Spooked."

"What's she doin' out here?"

"We didn't exactly have time to sit down for a long palaver about it, Cha'les."

Catfish chuckled. "You're just as ornery as you ever was."

"We'd best get back to Miss Claire and Miss Beth. We did leave Beth alone with one of the men who molested her, you know, Cha'les."

Catfish winced. "I didn't see no other way. But you're right. Let's get back."

"Yeah," Brazos said, poking a gloved index finger

at the sky. "Before that settles in an' we're swimmin' for it."

Catfish followed the man's troubled gaze. In all the foofaraw with the road agents or whoever they were, he hadn't noticed big purple clouds rolling in, piling up on top of each other, looking like several castles, with ominous-looking steeples, turrets, and spires.

Cloud shadows were rolling quickly across the sage, thickening.

"Holy moly—I didn't even notice!"

"Yeah, well, you will soon!" Brazos said as they both reined their mounts back up and over the crest of the bluff.

"You fetch Miss Claire! I'll get back to Beth and Skinny. I got me a feelin' we're gonna have to hole up out here less'n we wanna get soaked to the gills and fried by that lightnin'!" Catfish said, glancing at a sharp flicker inside a particularly large, plum-colored cloud.

The flash was followed about three seconds later by an ominous rumble.

"We'll head up that ridge," he added, glancing at a cedar- and boulder-peppered rise on their right. "There's a cave not too far away, if my memory isn't as sorry as the rest of me!"

Brazos yelled above the wind and the thunder of their horses' hooves, "We holed up there during a storm after we ran down those Cartman brothers— Billy an' Pete!"

"Yeah, an' left 'em feeding the worms!"

Catfish laughed as he and Brazos separated, Brazos heading toward where Miss Claire stood by her wagon, running a hand down her mare's long snout, soothingly, while the building wind lifted the horse's tail and the woman's long, badly mussed hair. She stared toward the two men with a long-faced, pale, anxious expression.

Catfish couldn't blame her a bit, but he also couldn't help wondering what she was doing way out here on a weekend, when business at the Lone Star would be booming. As he galloped Jasper up the knoll on which he'd left Skinny tied to his horse and Beth in the travois, he saw that Beth didn't even react to his reappearance. Poor gal was in a bad, bad way and she didn't even have her pa, Abel, to go home to.

Skinny sat his own mount, looking indignant at having been left tied to the horse, with a storm brewing.

"Don't even say it, Skinny," Catfish said as he reined Jasper to a skidding halt. "Don't give me any more reason than I already have to stick my pistol in your mouth and feed you a pill you won't digest!"

He swung his tired, old carcass down from Jasper's back and dropped to a knee beside Beth, who only just now turned her expressionless eyes to him. The wind was blowing her hair around her face. Catfish had wrapped her in a striped blanket he'd found in the shack the Thorson brothers had been holed up in with the rest of their motley gang.

"How you doin', honey? I'm so sorry for leavin' you, but I didn't see any other way."

Beth just turned her head away and gave a feeble nod.

It was already spitting rain.

"We're gonna have to take cover real soon, honey," Catfish said, tying the leather thongs he'd attached to the makeshift, quickly-knocked-together travois to Jasper's saddle. "That storm's movin' in fast. I know a cave up the ridge yonder. We'll meet Brazos and Miss Claire."

He glanced toward where Brazos was driving the woman's carriage toward him, Beth, and Skinny, heading for the ridge beyond.

"If you don't hurry, you old scudder," Skinny carped after a quick glance at the fast-building clouds, "we're all gonna . . ." When he saw the owly look on Catfish's craggy face, and saw the older man's hand close down over the bone grips of his .44, he let his voice trail off and looked away with a wince, a flush rising in his pale, pimply cheeks.

"Keep it closed now," Catfish said, "or I *will* make good on my promise."

He untied Skinny's horse from a cottonwood branch, then mounted up, saying to Beth, "Hold on now, honey. We'll be to shelter in just a few minutes."

Catfish just hoped the cave he had in mind wasn't currently occupied. Rustlers had been known to hole up in the cave while bleeding off Dragoman's herd. Also, the place had been home to wildcats . . .

Catfish was just pulling out when Brazos approached in the chaise, Miss Claire sitting beside him, her face long and paler than usual, her long hair blowing back in the wind, which was spitting cold rain now. As the carriage passed, Brazos's chestnut tied behind, Catfish saw the body of the lady's bouncer, George McGrath, slumped on the floor, a bloody hole in his chest. The man rocked from side to side as the chaise climbed the hill behind the still-wide-eyed mare.

"I'll follow you," Catfish said, and pulled in behind the chaise, trailing Skinny's horse on a lead halter rope, the travois making a raw scraping sound as it followed along behind Jasper. He didn't want to put

Beth inside the carriage with the dead man. Besides, it was a short jaunt up to the cave.

He was mildly surprised the carriage hadn't suffered a cracked wheel or axle, deadheading over such rough terrain, but it appeared to roll reasonably well behind the horse.

The grade was relatively gentle. Presently they followed a slanting game trail up into cedars, small pines, and boulders that had tumbled down from higher on the ridge. Catfish saw the notch cave carved into the stony ridge just ahead of them, beyond a pocket of boulders that would serve as a shelter for the horses.

Now the wind was howling and the trees were thrashing and dancing. The rain started in earnest, coming down at a hard slant, just as they reined the chaise and the horses up inside the boulders. The cave was just above them and on their right. Catfish clambered down from his saddle and made the short hike up to the cave, unsheathing his hogleg in case he saw yellow cat eyes glowing in the dark.

He did not. Just some fur-tufted rabbit bones and the tracks of coyotes. The cave smelled gamily sour, but it would serve.

He hurried back down to his horse, lifted Beth out of the travois, and carried her up the hill. As he did, Miss Claire hurried up beside him. She was carrying a blanket she'd taken out of the chaise. "My God, what did they do to that poor girl?"

"What do you think?"

"Animals! We'll need a fire and some water for coffee. We need to get her warm."

"I'll find both," Catfish said as he stepped into the cave and gentled Beth down against the right-side wall.

He hurried back down to the horses, tipping his hat down against the cold, slanting rain that was rife with the smell of desert cedars and sage. He pulled Skinny down from his saddle, led him into the cave, and pushed him down against the wall opposite where Beth was being administered to by Miss Claire, securing the kid's hands behind his back and tying his ankles together.

When he got back down to the horses and the carriage, Brazos already had his own, Miss Claire's, and Catfish's horses unsaddled and was pulling hobbles out of his and Catfish's saddlebags.

Catfish yelled above the wind and lashing rain, "I'm gonna see if I can find dry wood for a fire!"

"Good luck!"

He found some relatively dry tinder and branches on the lee sides of boulders and under an overhang of the ridge wall. He carried the wood into the cave, where Brazos was just then piling his and Catfish's gear, all of it wet from the rain. Miss Claire sat beside Beth, holding the girl's hand in her own. She'd draped the blanket from the chaise around the girl's shoulders.

Beth just sat staring.

Some of the color had returned to Miss Claire's cheeks. She'd gotten it back by caring for the girl. Catfish knew she was waiting for him to get a fire going, so he got started on it. When he'd coaxed a few small flames to life, and then had some larger ones building and feeding themselves, he filled his and Brazos's canteens by holding them out the cave entrance and into the rain pouring down off the ridge wall. When he had a fire going, he set his coffeepot to boil on a flat rock in the smoky flames.

While the water heated, Brazos helped Miss Claire

build a bed out of his and Catfish's soogans and one of their saddles. They got her snuggled in good, near enough to the fire that the dancing flames, filling the cave with the smell of fresh coffee, kept her warm against the chill air blowing in from outside. When the coffee was done, Catfish filled four cups and passed them around.

Skinny didn't even ask for one. He knew he'd be going without.

Catfish settled in beside Brazos, leaning back against the cave's rear wall. He was soaked, and the fire's warmth felt good. He just hoped he had enough wood to keep the flames built up. Otherwise, it would be a long, cool, damp night. He and Brazos were used to such nights. Miss Claire and Beth were not.

Miss Claire held Beth's hand until the poor girl drifted asleep. Then she came over and sat down beside Catfish and Brazos. Brazos had tipped his hat down over his forehead and crossed his arms on his chest, catching a few winks. Catfish had always been amazed how his taciturn partner could sleep at will.

"How did you two get back together?" Miss Claire asked Catfish.

"Showed up out of the blue." Catfish sipped his coffee, smacked his lips. "Ain't that just like him? Came to go after Abel's killers and get Beth back. Don't know how he heard about it."

Julia turned to Catfish and smiled. She gave his cheek a quick, affectionate peck. "And you went, too."

Catfish sighed. "Well, there are parts of me still stuck to that saddle, so it ain't like I ain't worse for the wear."

"You two must've cleaned up right well." Julia looked at where Skinny sat scowling at them both, looking like a beaver caught in a trap. "Is that scrawny little devil the only one alive?"

Skinny flared a nostril at her, but kept his mouth shut. He knew Catfish was good for his word about feeding him a pill from the wheel of his trusty six-shooter.

"Yep."

"Why?" Julia asked dryly.

"He gave himself up. Don't worry—he'll hang."

"He shouldn't be in here . . . with the girl he and his brother abused so wretchedly."

"No, he shouldn't. I should drill a hole through his head, but it would only disturb Beth, and she's been through enough."

Skinny gritted his teeth and turned to stare out into the rain that continued to pour down off the boulders and thrash the trees like scarecrows in a wind-lashed cornfield.

"Yes. You're right," the woman said. She turned to gaze out at the carriage in which her bouncer, George McGrath, lay dead. Catfish and Brazos had discussed hauling the man inside the cave, but decided that seeing another dead body might be too much for Beth.

Besides, McGrath was done caring about how wet he got.

"Poor George," the woman said thinly. She sighed.

"Who were those men, ma'am?" Catfish asked her. Even though they'd once been somewhat close, or had danced around becoming close, he still felt strangely formal around her. It was the respect she commanded.

She stared out into the rain, appearing to ponder the question, her cheeks turning a little pale once more. She looked down, then turned back to Catfish and shrugged. "Just road agents, Catfish. Common road agents. Nothing more."

"What are you doing out here?"

"I was . . . I was visiting my friend Grant Dragoman, if you must know."

"Figured as much." It was widely known that the rancher fawned after her, that she'd rebuffed his requests for her hand, as well as her business. That made her visit to the Circle D all the more curious. Catfish frowned. "On a weekend?"

She merely hiked her shoulder, looked down at her coffee, and stared out at the storm again.

Again, Catfish frowned, puzzled, incredulous. "Are you sure they were road agents, ma'am?"

"Of course, Catfish." It was her turn to frown, looking a little miffed. "Who else would they be?"

Catfish supposed they could have been road agents. They might have seen her, recognized her, knew of her wealth, decided to shake her down.

Still, something seemed blamed odd about her demeanor.

Oh, well. He wasn't going to get anything more out of her, he could tell. He sighed, doffed his hat, and rested his head back against the cave wall.

In the corner of his eye, he saw her give him a cautious look.

Mysterious woman.

"Long night ahead," Catfish said.

"Yes," Miss Claire said.

Chapter 16

Catfish opened one eye. Then he opened the other eye.

For a few seconds, he wasn't sure where he was. In fact, he was surprised and disoriented not to find himself in his little cabin near his catfish pond with Hooligan Hank on the prowl for mice outside, and Bubba Jones lolling in the muddy pond water, silently taunting him, his nemesis. Then he saw, to his left, the fire that had burned down to just a few barely glowing coals, as he'd run out of dry fuel an hour ago.

He saw Miss Claire—yes, even in his mind, even despite their history, he still referred to the regal woman by her formal surname—curled up in his soogan, her head on his saddle, on the other side of the near-dead fire, near where Beth slumbered, curled on her side. Brazos sat beside Catfish, leaning his head back against the cave's rear wall, black hat pulled down over his eyes.

Now Catfish thumbed his own hat up on his forehead and lifted his chin from where it had sagged nearly to his chest as he'd slept.

He stared out into the dark night beyond the low, crescent-shaped opening. The storm's raw fury had stopped hours ago, but it had continued to rain until after dark. Now the rain had stopped, and Catfish thought he could see a few wan stars. The rain continued to drip from the rocks and trees, making a near-musical ticking sound.

What had awakened him?

It came again—a horse's very low, barely audible whicker.

Soft as it was, Catfish recognized it as Jasper's.

Brazos heard it, too. He'd been snoring softly, but now the snores stopped and the former buffalo soldier drew a deep breath, lifted his chin, and poked his hat up onto his forehead.

He turned to Catfish, who sat staring out into the night, his hand automatically closing over the bone grips of the .44 holstered on his right thigh.

Very quietly so not to awaken the women, Brazos said, "Jasper?"

"Uh-huh?"

Then another horse gave a snort and shifted its hooves on the damp ground.

"That was Abe," Brazos said.

"Uh-huh." Catfish had ridden long enough with Brazos to recognize the whicker of his former partner's horse, as well as his own. "Somethin's got 'em spooked."

Both men pushed to their feet, Brazos moving annoyingly more fleetly than Catfish, Catfish noted with a miffed flare of a nostril. They both grabbed the rifles leaning against the cave wall beside them and, crouching low beneath the cave's shallow ceiling, stepped very quietly across the cave. They headed outside, where, standing side by side, they straightened to their full heights, Catfish a few inches taller than his former partner. But also considerably thicker in the waist, gallblastit.

The horses continued to stir, stomping around, whickering quietly. Through the murky darkness—it was nearing false dawn—Catfish could see all three mounts staring through the gaps between the boulders, down the gentle grade through the pines to the desert valley below.

Jasper flicked his ears.

"Somethin's movin' around down there," Brazos said, again very quietly.

"Uh-huh."

Catfish glanced at Brazos, canted his head to their right, then to their left. The message having been well practiced and clear, Brazos understood immediately. He moved down the grade before them, quartering right. Catfish moved down the grade as well, quartering left, holding his Yellowboy straight out from his right hip.

He walked slowly around a boulder and then straight down the slope, taking one slow step at a time, scowling into the night's thick shadows just now being relieved by a slow-approaching sunrise.

A quiet sound rose from the darkness ahead of him and on his left—a very slight snapping sound, as though the tread of a stealthy foot coming down on a twig.

Yep, something or someone's moving around down there, all right.

Catfish thought of the three men who'd accosted Miss Claire on the trail. Had they come calling again?

He continued moving slowly down the slope, angling gradually left, toward a ravine cutting around the shoulder of the bluff. He moved as quietly as he could, wincing when his own foot crunched pine needles and old leaves. He used to be able to move more quietly, but that was a good thirty, forty pounds ago . . .

Scattered rocks and boulders lay ahead.

He moved into them, the large rocks rising around him.

He paused to very quietly pump a live round into his Yellowboy's action, then continued moving into a jagged corridor formed by the rocks.

A *thump* sounded behind him. He swung around with a start, tightening his gloved right index finger around the Yellowboy's trigger. A fist-sized stone rolled down the grade for about four feet, then stopped.

Catfish's heart quickened.

Where had that come from?

"All right," he said quietly. "Who goes there?"

He moved forward, back the way he'd come, looking from left to right, scanning the tops of the rocks around him, where he had the uneasy feeling someone was about to take a shot at him.

He came to a break in the rocks on his right. Stepping into the break, he drew back a little more firmly on his Winchester's trigger, expecting a gun flash at any second. He moved deeper into the rocks. The brush and cactus lining the ravine lay ahead of him.

He stopped suddenly, lifted his nose, sniffed the air.

There was the sickly sweet smell of something wild.

"Look out, Cha'les!" came Brazos's raised voice from behind him.

Catfish swung around.

A large, wailing snarl sounded a quarter second before flames stabbed from a rifle barrel before him, maybe ten feet away and angled up toward his left. Another snarling wail and something large, silhouetted against the lightening sky, appeared above and before him. Catfish raised the Yellowboy and fired just before the rifle was knocked out of his hands and something big and furry slammed into him hard, knocking him flat on his back, smashing the breath from his lungs.

He looked down toward his waist to see two yellow eyes glowing before him. The big cat, lying half on top of him and feeling as heavy as a horse, blinked twice, opened its mouth, filling Catfish's nostrils with a rancid smell like that of something dead that had lain too long in the sun.

Catfish's guts recoiled at the stench, as well as at the two long yellow fangs curving down from the cat's upper jaw. He expected the cat to lunge up at him and tear out his throat.

But then the mouth closed, the large, square head lay down on his chest and turned to one side with a long, deep-throated groan, as though the puma had decided, instead of dining on him, to take a nap on him.

"Good God!" Catfish grunted, trying to suck air back into his lungs and having little luck.

He looked up over the beast's head to see Brazos step up out of the shadows. Brazos leaned his rifle against a rock, then crouched to grab both of the animal's rear legs and pulled the beast off Catfish with a loud grunt of his own. When the beast's head had slid off Catfish's feet, Brazos released the cat's rear legs.

"I told you to look out."

Catfish sucked a breath into his battered lungs and glared up at his partner. "You try lookin' out when you're as old and fat as me." He rolled onto his belly, pushed up onto his hands and knees, then climbed to his feet. He picked up his hat, reshaped it, and set it on his head.

"Ha!" he said. "You still got my back—don't you, partner?"

"Obviously, someone has to. Just like old times." Suddenly Brazos gave a rare smile, his white teeth showing in the lightening darkness.

Catfish stepped around the beast, which had nearly had him for an early-morning snack. He rested his forearm on Brazos's shoulder and said, "What do you think? Should we clean up Wolfwater again . . . once more?" He grinned. "For old times' sake?"

Brazos pushed Catfish's arm off his shoulder and gave a sour expression. "Good Lord, you stink!" He brushed off his shoulder with the back of his hand.

"Ha!" Catfish picked up his rifle and brushed it off. He scowled down at the dead mountain lion. "You think *I* do? That panther ain't had a bath in a lot longer than me!"

Both men strode back up the hill to where the hobbled horses were still snorting and stomping. Miss Claire stood just outside the cave, her slender, buxom figure limned by the growing dawn light slanting through the trees and around the rocks. She had her hands entwined before her.

"Good Lord," she said, "I was so worried!" She dropped her voice and pitched it dreadfully. "Did . . . did they . . . those men . . . return?"

"No," Catfish said, shaking his head. "It was a mountain lion."

Miss Claire heaved a sigh, as though relieved the shot had meant a cat and not her three assailants. Again, Catfish wondered at the woman's curious behavior. A shadow moved behind the woman, and then Beth Wilkes ducked out through the cave, the blanket wrapped around her. She stepped up beside Julia and gazed down at Catfish and Brazos.

"I heard," she said, her voice small and thin and barely audible above the morning piping of birds. "It was . . . it wasn't *them*, was it?"

"They're all dead, except that tied-up polecat in there, honey," Brazos said. "You don't have to worry about them anymore."

She frowned curiously, scrutinizing the lean man standing beside Catfish. "Brazos," she said. "What . . . what . . . are you doing here?"

Catfish and Brazos shared a curious glance.

The girl must have been so dazed she hadn't realized that Brazos had been one of the two men who'd rescued her. She was just now coming out of her trancelike state. Miss Claire reached over and took Beth's hand.

"He came to help, dear," she told the girl. "Both he and Catfish are here to help."

Again, Beth stared down the grade at the two men. "Just me an' Pa? Or the town?"

"The town," both men said at the same time.

Miss Claire smiled.

They broke camp as the murky gray light of dawn washed over the ridge.

Catfish was tired and hungry and thirsty for coffee, but a meal would have to wait until they reached Wolfwater. The wood was too wet for a fire. Besides, he wanted to get Beth to Doc Overholser as soon as possible.

Her life had changed drastically over the past several days. Her father had been killed and she'd been kidnapped and badly abused. It would take her a while to accept her new life, as well as to heal her soul, but Catfish was buoyed by the fact that she elected to ride back to town with Miss Claire in the chaise rather than continue on the travois.

She sat up front beside Julia, the body of George McGrath lay on the seat behind her. If the dead man's presence affected her, she didn't show it. Catfish thought she'd probably seen so much death and destruction, not to mention endured her own torture, over the past few days that she'd become numb to almost everything.

Catfish and Brazos, with Catfish trailing Skinny Thorson's horse by its lead rope, followed the carriage down off the ridge, then picked up the trail back to Wolfwater. The lemon orb of the sun rose, and the air warmed quickly, humid from the damp ground. The sky had been scoured fresh and clear by the storm. There wasn't a cloud in sight during the procession's slow ride back to town, which they entered just after midday, the motley group with the dead man lying in the back of the carriage merging with Wolfwater's rollicking midday horse-and-wagon traffic. They rode down the broad main street, to the right of the El Paso & Rio Grande tracks, which had been laid straight through the heart of the town.

Catfish was surprised by all the commotion on a Sunday. Then again, he wasn't all that surprised. The silver rails were the cause of all the men and painted ladies gathered on the boardwalks of the town's many saloons and hurdy-gurdy houses. Many of the faces he'd never seen before.

As they passed along the street, loud voices rose from a break between the Continental Saloon and a Chinese bathhouse. Brazos stopped his chestnut and glanced at Catfish.

"Look there."

Catfish followed his gaze into the break, where a good dozen men were gathered around two other men fighting bare-chested inside the circle of revelers, knives in their fists, slashing and cutting as they bobbed, feinted, and sidestepped, yelling curses at each other. The crowd around them was passing greenbacks around, placing bets on the fight's outcome.

"Well, I'll be," Catfish said as the carriage continued along the street ahead of them. "Abel and Bushwhack never would've allowed that."

"Don't take long for the mice to play," Brazos said, "when the cat's away. No, it sure as heck don't, Cha'les."

"Hey, look there," Catfish said as they gigged their horses ahead. He'd fastened his gaze on a man standing with a crowd of other men outside the One-Eyed Pig Saloon, on the street's right side. "Isn't that the regulator, 'Texas Jack' Silver? The tall, well-dressed drink of water with the pearl-handled six-shooter in the cross-draw position?"

"Do believe it is," Brazos said as they rode on past the Pig, as the saloon was locally known. "Didn't we throw him out of this country about six years ago?"

"He was picking off nesters with a Sharps Big Fifty. We couldn't prove it, but we threw him out, anyway."

"Well, he's back," Brazos said. He cast his gaze toward the left side of the street and added, "And I do believe I just saw 'Blue' Murphy walk into the Red Lantern."

Blue Murphy was a gunfighting card sharp out of Abilene.

"Do believe we put him away for a few years—didn't we?"

"Well, he's out," Brazos said. "And he's back."

Catfish sighed as he watched Miss Claire check her carriage down in front of the largest building on the main drag—her very own Lone Star Outpost, which was three brick stories with the name painted across the top of the upper story in large green letters. It boasted a wide, broad wooden front stoop, on which yet another crowd of men and girls had gathered, over a dozen horses tied to the three hitchracks out in front of the place—on a Sunday!

"I do believe we got our work cut out for us, Brazos," Catfish said.

"Looks like it, Cha'les," Brazos said darkly. He glanced at Catfish. "We up to this? It's been a good many years for both of us. You're what—sixty-two? An' I'm fifty-eight!"

"Oh, stop braggin'!"

"Just sayin'."

Catfish tipped his head back and scratched his neck. "I reckon we'll find out what we got left." He glanced at Brazos as they both slowed their mounts in front of the Lone Star Outpost, behind Miss Claire's chaise. "You havin' second thoughts, partner?"

"Yep."

"Yeah—me too," Catfish said with a dry laugh.

Miss Claire had stopped her carriage, and several bouncers had emerged from the saloon's batwing doors. Several onlookers had announced the lady's long-delayed arrival; another man yelled in surprise, "An' she's got Miss Beth with her!"

As the bouncers and the customers spilled down the porch steps, Miss Claire yelled for someone to fetch the doctor to her suite.

"Well, I'll be hanged if it ain't Catfish and Brazos McQueen their ownselves!" another man said, pointing at where Catfish and Brazos had halted their horses behind the chaise.

"And Skinny Thorson!" exclaimed another man.

"Did you two bring down ol' Frank?" This question came from the mayor, Derwood Booth, moving quickly out through the batwings as well. Astonishment shone on his face as the dandy stood at the top of the wooden steps, looking with relieved surprise from Miss Claire to Beth, who was now being helped out of the carriage by two brawny bouncers, to the two former lawmen.

Catfish didn't feel like shouting above the din. He didn't much care for the popinjay, anyway.

He turned to Brazos and said, "Looks like Miss Beth will be well taken care of. Miss Claire too. Let's go air out our old office and throw this skunk in the clink."

He glanced at Skinny, tied to his saddle behind him and Brazos. The kid's nervous gaze was on the crowd fronting the Lone Star, all giving him the wooly eyeball. He turned to Catfish and glared.

They continued down the street, neither Catfish nor Brazos noticing the dark pair of eyes staring after them from atop the Lone Star's veranda.

Chapter 17

Catfish opened one of the four cell cages lined up along the back wall of the little jailhouse office, uncuffed his prisoner, then grabbed a handful of Skinny's collar and tossed the termite inside.

"Get in there, you little ringtail. This is where you're gonna reside until I can get the circuit court judge up here from Heraklion. Until then, you'll be livin' on bread and water. But only if you're good and keep your mouth shut!"

Skinny bounced off the back wall with an indignant yowl and collapsed onto the cell's single cot. He cast Catfish a hard glare, screwing up his pimply little weasel face, and said, "You're abusin' me, an' that's against the law. I got rights, you old mossyhorn!"

Catfish returned the glare as he shucked his bone-handled .44 from its holster. "What'd you call me?" he asked, holding the hogleg down low against his right leg and clicking the hammer back.

Skinny's eyes dropped to the cocked revolver. They returned to Catfish's face with considerably less venom than a moment ago. He winced, averted his gaze, and said with deep chagrin, and no small amount of spine-lessness, "Uh . . . all right . . . all right . . ."

"All right, all right, Mr. . . . ."

Skinny's gaze darted back to Catfish with deep in-credulity. "Huh?"

"'I'm sorry, Mr. Tuttle, for addressing you so disre-spectfully,'" Catfish said through the barred cell door, tapping his thumb against the Colt's cocked hammer. "That's the response I'm lookin' for."

Brazos glanced at Catfish, his lips beneath his mustache quirking a bemused grin. He turned to Skinny, who glanced back at him as though for help. Brazos was giving none of it. He shaped his own hard, commanding look through the bars and dipped his chin expectantly.

Skinny sighed as he sagged back on his cot, resting his back against the wall and crossing his arms on his chest in defeat. He said poutingly, looking toward his lap, "I'm, uh . . . I'm sorry, Mr."—he sighed again—"Mr. *Tuttle* for addressing you so dis . . . disrespect-fully."

Catfish cackled a delighted, self-satisfied laugh and turned to Brazos. "You know, old partner, if it weren't for the little matter of him to get his neck stretched by ol' Judge Hiram Farnwright, known throughout West Texas for bein' as uncompromisin' as a rattlesnake, I think our prisoner here might be prime material for finishing school—one o' them rich ones back east. You know—one o' them the rob-ber barons send their offspring to!"

Brazos chuckled and shook his head. "Cha'les, Cha'les, Cha'les." He gave a rare smile of genuine warmth. "It is fine bein' back together, old friend." He didn't add it in words, but his eyes told Catfish he was sorry for their misunderstanding regarding the showgirl. It was rare that between the two of them Brazos would make a mistake like that. To Catfish, it just meant his old friend had a much deeper well of feeling than he'd ever given him credit for.

"Let bygones be bygones," Catfish said. "How 'bout we drink on it?"

Brazos shrugged. "Why not?"

Catfish walked over to his old desk abutting the jailhouse's front wall, to the right of the door. He crouched to open a bottom drawer. "Ol' Abel must've kept a bot—"

He'd pulled the door only half open when hard-galloping hooves thundered on the street outside the office. They were cut off abruptly, then replaced by loud boot thuds on the stoop outside the front door. Two hard, insistent knocks, rattling the door in its frame, the glass in the window.

The knocks were still echoing around the cavelike room as both Catfish and Brazos slapped leather and drew cold steel from their holsters, clicking the hammers back. They'd been out of the badge-toting profession for a good while, but the old instincts for danger and survival were still sharp.

They shared an incredulous glance; then Charlie walked over to the door, clicked the latch, jerked on the handle, and stepped into the doorway, thrusting his cocked Colt out in front of his bulging paunch. A handsome young man, with either Mexican or Indian blood, stood facing him. He wore a fringed buckskin shirt and black charro-style trousers, with hammered silver conchas running down the outsides of the legs. His shirt was fancily stitched in the old Spanish style. On his head was a crisp, cream, low-crowned Stetson trimmed with a rattlesnake band. Thick dark brown hair curled down over his ears.

Jutting up from his right hip was an ivory-gripped, silver-chased Colt .44.

Catfish blinked. For a few seconds, he thought he was looking at a player from a Wild West show having come to town on the consarned train. From three feet away, he could smell liquor on the kid's breath. He appeared in his early to midtwenties, with dark, grimly purposeful eyes staring directly at Catfish, who had a few inches on the kid's five-ten or so.

Catfish said, "Uh . . . can I . . . can I . . . help you, sonny?"

"Don't 'sonny' me, mister. I heard that low-down vermin you just dragged into town was the man who murdered my sister!"

Catfish lowered his own Colt slightly and glanced skeptically at Brazos, who returned the look.

Catfish turned back to the kid. "What's that?"

The kid stepped forward abruptly, catching Catfish by surprise. He gave Catfish a shove back and to one side as he stepped past him into the jailhouse. Brazos, still standing by the desk, raised his own hogleg a little higher, though the kid still hadn't unpouched his own.

He stopped between Catfish and Brazos.

The kid thrust out an arm and pointed a coldly accusing finger at Skinny Thorson, who was just then climbing warily up off his cot. "That's him—isn't it? The low-down dirty dog you hauled into town. The one who killed my sister, Helena, by throwing her out a window and onto a hitchrack, breaking her back!"

He snapped his head toward Catfish. "That him?"

Catfish turned toward him, took two steps forward. "You're . . . ? You're . . . ?"

"Helena's brother. Folks around here knew her as Raven. That was her so-called 'professional' name."

"Yeah," Catfish muttered, nodding his head slowly, pondering the surprising information. "Yeah . . . that's him."

"I knew it!" Slick as lightning, the kid's hand dropped to the Colt and in a blur of fast movement he raised the pretty hogleg and cocked it as he thrust it toward Skinny's cell at the rear of the jail office. "You're going to die, mister!"

Skinny yelped and threw himself facedown against his cot, then rolled onto his side, raising his hands to his face and casting his terrified, beseeching gaze toward Catfish and Brazos, screeching, "Don't let him shoot me! Don't let him shoot me! The bean eater's plumb *nuts*!"

At the same time, Catfish and Brazos raised and aimed their own six-shooters at the kid's head. "Hold on, hold on!" Catfish bellowed. "Don't cheat the hangman, boy!"

"My sister is *dead*!" the kid said, keeping his livid glare on the cowering Skinny. "And he is still alive! But not for *long*!"

"*No!*" Skinny yelped, and rolled onto his belly to bury his face in the cot's wool blanket.

"Oh, fer chrissake!" Brazos said, stepping forward, and smashing the barrel of his .44 across the kid's head, putting a deep dent in his hat.

The kid's .44 barked. The bullet squealed off a bar in the door of Skinny's cell, evoking yet another scream from the office's sole prisoner. The kid grunted, lowered the Colt in his hand, and sagged sideways. Brazos caught him in both arms and eased him into the chair by the room's main desk abutting the front wall.

Though he was at least halfway unconscious,

somehow the kid managed to hold on to his pistol. The hat remained on his head, dent and all.

Brazos grabbed the pretty Colt out of the kid's hand and turned his incredulous gaze, black brows ridged over his black eyes, to Catfish, and stuffed the hogleg behind his cartridge belt. "Now, ain't this a fine kettle of fish, Cha'les?"

"I know, I know," Catfish said, holstering his Colt. "I never said it was gonna be easy, partner. Poor kid done lost his sister to that little snake," he added, jerking his chin to indicate the cell and its inhabitant. Skinny was peeking cautiously out from behind the arms he'd crossed over his head, as though he thought the insignificant appendages would somehow keep him from swallowing a pill he could not digest.

Catfish and Brazos stared down at their unexpected guest, who appeared to be coming around, fluttering his eyelids, grimacing, and rocking his head slowly from side to side.

Brazos said to Catfish, "Maybe we oughta just let him shoot him."

"No!" Skinny cried. "You two old duffers keep that bean eater away from me. I got rights. I know my rights."

Catfish gave a caustic grunt and glanced at Brazos. "Sure is tempting, ain't it?"

"Sure is."

"You know we can't do that, partner. We have to abide by the law again, now that we're sort of unofficially wearing the badges."

"Yeah, but we ain't officially wearing them yet, Cha'les."

Catfish sighed and stepped over to the desk. He opened the top drawer. There both badges—TOWN

MARSHAL and DEPUTY TOWN MARSHAL—lay faceup on a large strip of red velvet. Someone, probably the mayor, had been anticipating the hiring of two new lawdogs, and wanted to make the badges, which appeared recently, carefully buffed, as enticing as possible.

In contrast to the head-breaking job itself.

Catfish gave another wary sigh and pinned the town marshal's badge to his shirt, near the bottom left corner of his breast pocket. There it would be partially concealed by his vest, reducing the chances of the sun flashing off it and making him an overly compelling target for one of his old enemies, of which there were plenty in these parts.

He turned and handed Brazos the deputy town marshal's badge. "There you go, partner. Might as well make it all official. There should be some ceremony and maybe some Mescins blowin' horns in our honor, kids sellin' tacos in the street, but I reckon Wolfwater's too desperate for such foofaraw."

Brazos looked at the badge in his hand, made a distasteful expression, as though conflicted about pinning it to his shirt again. But pin it to his shirt, he did.

By now, the kid had come around. He removed his dented hat and rubbed the side of his head, glaring up at Catfish. "You have no right to keep me from killin' that gutless cur who killed my sister." He held his hand out to Brazos. "I'll have my gun back!"

"I'm gonna hold it for safekeeping." Brazos hiked a hip on the edge of the desk and closed his hand around the pistol wedged behind his cartridge belt.

The kid looked at the badge pinned to his shirt, behind his duster. Then he looked at the badge on Catfish's shirt as well. "What're you two old mossy-horns doing—playing like you're law? Can't this town find anybody younger?" He glared at Skinny, sitting up on his cot now, staring warily toward the newcomer. "Someone with guts enough to let a grieving brother avenge his sister?"

Catfish stood in front of him, his beefy arms crossed on his chest. He glanced at his deputy. "You know, partner, I'm already gettin' a mite tired of being talked down to by yonkers."

"I got a feelin' it's just beginnin', Cha'les."

"Just means I'm gonna have to dent a few hats, is all." Catfish plucked the hat off the kid's lap, re-shaped it, and set it down on its owner's head. "What's your name, kid? Where you from?"

The kid reached up to adjust the set of the topper on his head, giving it a slight tilt to one side in front. "I am Juan Montana. I was working at the B-Bar-8 outfit, outside San Antonio, when a friend got word to me about Helena. About what happened to her"—he glanced at Skinny again, causing the outlaw to wince and look at the floor—"and who did it. When I got to town, I heard his brother broke him out of jail. You two couldn't hold him!"

"Yeah, well, that wasn't us," Brazos said. "It was a good friend of ours, who is no longer with us, compliments of Skinny's older brother, Frank Thorson. Abel Wilkes was a good lawman. He was outnumbered and he had his daughter to worry about. You'd best hold your tongue, or I'll put a crease in your hat my ownself. One that'll go all the way through!"

Skinny rose from his cot, walked up to his cell door, and wrapped each hand around a bar. "You gonna arrest him? He tried to kill me!"

Catfish and Brazos shared a conferring look. Juan

Montana looked up at them each in turn, awaiting a response.

Catfish ignored him. He turned to Montana. "How'd your sister get into the . . . well, the world's oldest profession, anyway?"

"She and I were raised by our father. Little shotgun ranch outside of Mesilla, in the New Mexico territory. Our father was a bad, rough man. A drunk. He whipped us both and treated my sister—well, let's just say he treated her miserably. After one such time, I killed him with my own hands in a Mesilla saloon."

Montana held his hands together as though around the man's neck, hardening his jaws and bunching his lips furiously. "There were witnesses. Someone summoned the sheriff. I ran. I learned later that my sister, feeling as though she was worth nothing better, began working at a whorehouse in Las Cruces. I visited her many times, begged her, pleaded with her to stop desecrating her body in such a way." He shook his head, sighed. "She wouldn't listen. She didn't feel she was good for anything more than . . ."

Tears glittered in the kid's dark brown eyes. He choked off a sob, sniffed, shook his head, and regained his composure. "She didn't think she was good for anything more than that. I don't know how she ended up here. I haven't seen her in years." He cast another fierce glare at Skinny. "Now I never will again . . . thanks to him!"

"Don't worry," Brazos told Montana. "He'll hang. Judge Farnwright from Heraklion will see to that."

"No," Montana said, bitterly, keeping that branding-iron glare on his sister's killer. "It has to be family.

I have to avenge her. I owe her that much. She deserves the respect in death she never saw in life."

"See?" Skinny said, pointing through the bars of his cell door. "He's pur-dee crazier'n a tree full of owls!"

"Shut up and sit down, Skinny," Brazos said. "Or I'll give him his gun back."

Skinny grimaced, backed away from the cell door, and slacked down on his cot.

"Juan," Catfish said, "I know how you feel. I'd feel the same way. Anybody would. But I'm 'Catfish' Charlie Tuttle, and me and my partner, Brazos McQueen, are the law here in Wolfwater. We can't let you kill that son of Satan. You can't play judge, jury, and executioner. That's not how the law works. I know it ain't fair, but that's the law, and these badges me an' Brazos have on our shirts mean we have to uphold the law or we might as well take these badges off and join the outlaws."

"We're not gonna do that," Brazos said. He glanced at Catfish. "Can't do that."

"You have to leave him up to us. I'm gonna go over and cable the judge in a few minutes. He'll be here in a week or two, perhaps."

Juan Montana looked at Catfish. He looked at Brazos. Then he looked at Skinny, sitting on the edge of his cot, staring back at the Mexican, looking a little green around the gills. His expression remained hard, implacable, and uncompromising.

He held his hat out to Brazos, palm up. "I'll have my gun back."

Catfish and Brazos shared another darkly conferring look. Then Brazos pulled the silver-chased Colt out from behind his cartridge belt, opened the loading gate, held the pistol barrel up, and slowly turned the wheel. The cartridges dropped, one by one, from their chambers to fall with tinny *pings* to the wooden floor.

Brazos flicked the loading gate closed and extended the hogleg to Montana, butt first. The kid reached for it.

Brazos pulled the gun back toward him and narrowed an admonishing eye. "Don't you come around here again with this thing loaded, fixin' to drill our prisoner—hear? You do, you'll join him!"

Montana just stared at him.

Brazos gave him the gun.

Montana rose from his chair, holstered the hogleg, looked once more at Skinny, then sauntered out the open door. Hoof thuds dwindled to silence.

Skinny rose from the cot, ran up to his cell door. His eyes were as large and round as silver dollars. "He's gonna kill me for sure!"

Ignoring him, Catfish turned to Brazos. "Why'd you give him his gun back, partner?"

"Hell, I don't know," Brazos said in frustration. "I reckon . . . I reckon I felt sorry for him."

Catfish sighed. He glowered at Skinny, who looked even more drawn and pale than before. Then the recently reinstated Catfish Charles Tuttle, Town Marshal of Wolfwater, Texas, turned to his deputy and said, "You ready for that drink now, partner."

"I sure as hell am . . . partner." Brazos gave a dry laugh and shook his head. "Heckuva first day back on the job, Cha'les."

Digging out the bottle, Catfish laughed dryly in return. "Sure is!"

Chapter 18

Brazos woke with a start, jerked his head up off his pillow.

Instantly his long-barreled Peacemaker was in his hand, his thumb ratcheting the hammer back. His heart thudded. He looked around the dark room before him—all brown mist and blurred edges in the first light of dawn that barely touched the room's single window.

He'd heard something.

He drew a breath to calm his heart and the sudden rush of blood in his ears. Then he heard it again—a very soft thudding, rustling sound.

Again, his heart thudded.

Brazos swept the bedcovers back with his right hand, dropped his bare feet to the floor. Clad in only his wash-worn longhandles, he crossed the small bedroom to the door, twisted the knob, and drew the door open quickly. He peered around the tiny cabin. A shadow flickered across the curtained window to his left.

Someone was out there, all right.

Holding the Peacemaker barrel up near his right shoulder, Brazos padded across the cabin's scarred puncheon floor. A footstep sounded outside, then another. Someone was approaching the door. Just then, the interloper stepped up onto the small front stoop. Brazos heard the soft thud of a stealthy foot, the creak of a wooden floorboard. Gritting his teeth, he placed his left hand on the porcelain knob. He turned it and, just like he'd done with the bedroom door, he drew it open quickly and thrust the Russian straight out before him.

"Oh!" The person before him stumbled straight backward, dropping the load of split stove wood in his arms.

No. *Her* arms . . .

She got her ankle-booted feet set beneath her and closed her hands over her mouth, staring at the cocked Peacemaker in Brazos's hand. He could see the dim light of the dawn glinting fearfully in her round, dark eyes, over the hands clamped across her mouth to quell another scream.

"Mrs. Rose!"

"Mr. McQueen!"

Brazos depressed the Peacemaker's hammer and holstered the gun. "I'm so sorry . . . I didn't . . . I didn't know it was you." He crouched to pick up the wood she'd dropped—six or seven sticks of split pine and cedar. "What're you doin' out here? You know I can fetch my own wood!"

Mrs. Rose rented the cabin behind her own humble shack, a hundred feet at the end of a meandering, well-worn path that connected the two hovels. She lowered her hands from her face to cross her arms beneath her breasts, over the humble flower-printed cambric dress she wore. She was a handsome

Black woman, a few years younger than Brazos himself. She'd lost her husband two years before, gunned down by a drunken gambler who objected to the presence of a Black man in the saloon they were both drinking and gambling in.

Mrs. Rose hadn't shared too much about her husband, but Brazos had been able to tell by her demeanor, in the four days since he'd taken a room here in the shack she rented out to help with her own paltry income, that Mr. Rose had not been a man she'd been proud of. Now she lived alone in her own ancient log cabin, originally built and owned by a prospector, one of the first few on Wolfwater Creek, and took in laundry and sewing.

"You've been working so hard," Mrs. Rose said. "I saw last night when I fetched water from the creek to fill the bucket in your kitchen that you had no wood for this morning. I heard you return . . . not all that long ago—you've been keeping late nights, Mr. McQueen—and knew you were likely too tired to fetch your own wood. Not that I'm keeping tabs on you, Mr. McQueen. And not that I didn't think that—oh!" she intoned, laughing quietly and shaking her head. "How I do go on!"

"Thank you, Mrs. Rose. I do apologize for . . . well . . ."

"Were you expecting someone, Mr. McQueen?" She frowned questioningly up at him. "I've seen you . . . seen you walking around your cabin after you've returned from work, as though you're afraid that someone might . . ."

She clapped a slender, work-callused hand to her mouth, her dark eyes flashing lustrously, with a wry intelligence and humor that belied the hardness of her life—living alone with a small child and working her mahogany hands nearly to the bone every day and night. Still, she'd retained her beauty, as well as her figure. Brazos had not been too busy or too distracted with laying down the law in Wolfwater to notice.

"There I go again," she said.

"An old lawman's habit," Brazos said. "A lawman, you know . . . we tend to make a lot of enemies. I do believe Cha'les and I have done made our share already in just the week we've been back on the job together."

It was true. They'd broken up enough fights and laid down the law in enough saloons, just sort of introducing themselves to the town, and locking up a few miners for fighting, that both men knew they had targets on their backs. It was also true, however, that when Brazos circled his cabin every evening once returning home, he wasn't just looking for men whose feelings he might have hurt, or whose jaws he might have cracked earlier that day.

"Old friends, you and Mr. Tuttle?"

"Yes." Brazos smiled. "Old friends . . . me an' Cha'les."

"Nice to be back working with him again."

"You could say that." It was. He'd missed being around the at-once surly and amusing legendary lawman. Again, he felt a pang of guilt and foolishness for his mistake about Catfish and Vonetta. He should have known Catfish would never have betrayed him in the way Brazos thought he had. "Anyway," he said, turning with the load of wood in his arms and stepping back into the cabin, "let me set this wood down by the stove."

"I tell you what, Mr. McQueen," Mrs. Rose said, stepping into the doorway and placing one hand on the frame, "no need for you to start a fire. I already have breakfast started at my place. Fresh coffee on the stove . . ."

Brazos dropped the wood in the corrugated tin washtub he used for a wood box, and turned back to the woman. Mrs. Rose had suddenly, self-consciously, adjusted the wide red bandanna tied around the top of her head to hold her long, curly black hair back from her face. Her visage was still smooth and supple, despite her age and all her long years of hardship—both emotional and physical.

It was the way of most people, but the way of people like his people, most of all. He knew from personal experience, having been born on a plantation back in Alabama several years before the war freed him, had made it legal for him to travel around, free, to more or less choose his own future, like other men. Like white men.

Though most Black men knew that no Black man was ever really free. Maybe on paper, but there were other ways—many various and sundry other ways—to enslave a man. Half the saloons in Wolfwater still didn't allow Black men to cross their thresholds or to mingle with their working girls.

"I believe I won't take time for breakfast," Brazos said, striding slowly back toward her. "But, perhaps coffee . . . if you don't think it'd be improper. You know—a man in your cabin . . . ?"

"Oh, I don't care what's proper, Mr. McQueen," she said, adjusting the bandanna with the index finger of her left hand, tucking a stray lock of hair under it. She glanced around the yard, touched now with the milky light of dawn. "Besides . . . who's going to know?"

Her home and the cabin she rented were set back

off the main trail into Wolfwater, in some scraggly desert trees on the opposite side of the creek from the town, with buttes shelving around it, concealing it from the trail, as well as the town itself.

"All right, then," Brazos said, and hooked a wry half smile. "But only if you stop with the 'Mr. McQueen,' Mrs. Rose. I'm Brazos."

"I'm Hettie." She flashed a white-toothed smile of her own.

"All right, then." Brazos was about to extend his hand to indicate her cabin, but then he suddenly realized he'd been standing here in his longhandles, talking to this woman. "Oh, Lordy!" he intoned, looking down at himself. "I didn't . . . I didn't realize . . . !"

She laughed into her hand. "It's all right, Mr., er, I mean, Brazos." She laughed huskily. "I was wondering when you were going to notice!" Still laughing, she swung around and began striding toward the back door of her cabin at the end of the curving path. "I'll have that coffee good and hot when you get here!"

Brazos closed the door, opened it, and called, "All right. I'll be there in five minutes," then closed the door again.

He sighed and chuckled, then headed for his bedroom to dress.

Fifteen minutes later, he was seated at the lady's kitchen table. She filled the two cups she'd set on her oilcloth-covered table, and Brazos felt his stomach grumble and his mouth water as the smoking coal-black liquid tumbled from the spout of the large white-speckled black pot into the thick white mug.

"That smells fine, Mrs. Rose."

She gave him an admonishing look from beneath her brows.

He chuckled, then said, "Old habits do die hard . . . Hettie." He glanced at the bowl and the small burlap pouches of flour and sugar and the two brown eggs that also sat on the table, near a porcelain mixing bowl, in which a long-handled wooden spoon rested. "I don't want to interrupt your cooking, Hettie."

She set the pot back on the warming rack on the range, then returned to the table, rubbing her hands on the white apron she wore around her waist. She sat down in the hide-bottom chair across the table from Brazos. She tucked one leg under her, sitting sort of sideways, one arm hooked over a spool jutting up from the chair back.

"I'm in no rush. Peter won't be up for another hour, I'm sure. He wasn't feeling well last . . ."

She let her voice trail off when a latch clicked behind her. Both she and Brazos turned to see one of the two doors in the rear wall, in the parlor side of the cabin, open slowly. A boy's small, round face under a cap of tight, black hair appeared. He was dressed in a white cotton gown that hung nearly to his small brown feet.

"Peter . . ."

"Momma." The boy's chocolate eyes slid to Brazos. He reacted hopefully. "Is it Poppa . . . ?"

Hettie glanced at Brazos, coloring behind her natural tan, then returned her gaze to the boy. "No, Peter. It's our neighbor, Mr. McQueen," she said, glancing at Brazos with a smile. "You remember him. He's the nice man renting the other cabin."

"Oh," Peter said, his eyes remaining on Brazos.

"How do you feel, child?" Hettie asked him.

"Better."

"Maybe you'd better go back to bed and sleep another hour. I'll call you when breakfast is ready."

"All right," the boy said. Keeping his vaguely curious gaze on the man wearing the black duster, where behind its left lapel the deputy marshal's badge shone, he slowly closed the door until the latch clicked.

Hettie turned back to Brazos, gave a somewhat sheepish smile, and lifted her steaming mug to her lips.

"His pa?" Brazos asked, frowning curiously across the table at the woman.

She sipped the coffee, swallowed, and hesitated, again a flush rising behind the natural dark coffee color of her nicely tapered cheeks. She set the coffee cup down, averted her gaze to it, then lifted her eyes to Brazos. "I'm afraid I wasn't able to tell him that his father died," she said, keeping her voice low. She ran a hand in a small circle on the oilcloth. "If I had, I would have had to tell him *how* Samuel died. In a common saloon brawl with other men as drunk as he."

She frowned, heaving a weary sigh.

"I'll have to eventually, of course," she said, glancing again at the closed door behind her. "I thought I'd put it off until . . ." She shrugged a shoulder. "Until he might be able to understand, though something like that will be hard for him to understand at any age, I'm afraid. Peter is a sensitive child. His stomach often bothers him. That was the problem last night."

"Poor child," Brazos said. "I'm sorry, Hettie. Life hasn't been good to you. It's not fair. You're a good lady."

"No, but who is life fair to, Brazos?" She arched one brow. "You?"

Brazos shrugged and took another sip of his coffee. "I can't complain."

"Can't you? Or maybe you won't."

"What good would it do?"

"You were here before, I'm told. A few years ago."

"Yes."

"You came back to avenge your friend Marshal Wilkes."

"That's right. And to fetch his daughter back from those jackals."

"You're a brave, honorable man, Mr."—she smiled again—"Brazos."

Brazos shrugged again. "Any man would have done it, if he was close enough. I was close enough. I figured Cha'les would go after her . . . an' them. He'd need help."

"And you're staying."

"For now, yes, ma'am. Until we can get the town's wolf back on its leash." Brazos gave an ironic grin over the steaming rim of his cup. "Might take a while."

Hettie gazed across the table at him, chin down, demurely. "Would I be too forward if I said I was glad?"

Brazos felt the blood rise in his cheeks. He shared a shy, crooked smile. "No, ma'am."

"Would I also be too forward in asking you if you'd like to have supper with me and my son some night, Brazos?"

Brazos's smile was still on his face. "No, ma'am. It might be a while, though. Cha'les an' I got our hands full, especially around the supper hour, even during the week these days, with the train having come to town." He paused, kept his direct gaze on her own, feeling an intimacy growing between him and this kind, hardworking, still-comely woman. It felt good, that feeling. Warm, gentle—unlike anything else he'd felt after his return to Wolfwater, aside from his easy friendship and camaraderie with Catfish Charlie

Tuttle. "As folks do in the ritzy hotels, can I pencil my name on your register? Ink it in later?"

"Well, this humble cabin is far from a ritzy hotel, Brazos."

"Not to me, Hettie."

"Then you can do just that."

Brazos tipped back the last of his coffee, set his cup back down on the table. "I best head into town, get to work," he said with a sigh. He himself hadn't gotten much sleep. He could do with another hour or two, but, like he'd told Hettie, he and Catfish were badly understaffed. So far, they'd hired two night deputies to act mainly as jailers, to keep an eye on the several prisoners he and Catfish had arrested over the past several days. "Thank you for the coffee."

"I enjoyed our talk."

"I did, too."

Brazos rose and walked over to the door. He removed his hat from a peg to the right of the door and set it on his head.

"Oh, wait." Hettie rose from her chair. "I have your clothes. Freshly washed just yesterday."

She walked into the parlor, where several sets of neatly folded clothes were stacked on a horsehide sofa. She returned them to Brazos, who dug several coins out of his pants pocket.

"Much obliged, Hettie," he said, extending his hand to the woman, over the small pile of clothes in her own hands.

"Oh, no," she said, placing her left hand on his right one. "You already paid me—remember?"

"Oh." Brazos looked down at the woman's hand on his own. How warm her hand was. Soft, despite all her hard work. Feminine.

She looked down at her hand on his. Again, a flush rose in her cheeks, and she pulled her hand back quickly, self-consciously. Brazos accepted the clothes, still feeling another, not unpleasant, flush in his cheeks behind his beard.

"Maybe I'll stop in for coffee again," he blurted out, wanting to say one more thing before he had to leave, which he discovered he was reluctant to do.

My God—was he tumbling for this woman?!

"I would like that," she said.

He pinched his hat brim to her, fumbled with the door, awkward in his self-consciousness, then pulled the door closed behind him, knocking it against his heels, almost tripping. He stood on the small porch fronting the woman's cabin, staring out at the dawn building in the willows screening the creek. He grinned, chuckled, shook his head.

He'd be damned if he didn't feel seventeen years old.

Not a bad feeling.

He chuckled again, then turned and strode down off the porch, walking back around Hettie's cabin, to leave the clothes in his own before heading back into the Wolfwater fray.

Chapter 19

Catfish Charlie studied the surface of the catfish pool in the gray dawn light.

As he did, he stroked the big, liver-colored tabby in his arms. Hooligan Hank purred luxuriously, resting his chin on Catfish's left forearm. Hank had been alone for several days. Not that Hank couldn't handle being alone. There were few cats as independent as Hank, and that was saying something.

Still, Charlie had returned to his and Hank's remote cabin the previous night, the first time since he'd ridden out with Brazos to avenge Abel Wilkes and Bushwhack Aimes. Truth be told, he'd missed ol' Hooligan Hank, and he'd missed his cabin. After returning to Wolfwater with Bethany Wilkes, he'd spent several nights in town, taking brief naps in the jailhouse and working in close tandem with Brazos.

The town needed taming in a bad, bad way. There were stabbings and shootings almost every day and night, and it was going to take a while for the dunderheaded miners, prospectors, cowboys, gamblers, traveling drummers, con artists, and everyone else to get accustomed to the idea that Wolfwater was no longer wide open. Catfish and Brazos intended to button it up fast. They each had the aches and pains to show for it as well. Catfish himself had sore ribs, compliments of the pickax handle swung by a laborer working on yet another infernal railroad, who'd come to town and gotten hammered and in the mood for a fight.

Catfish also had scraped and bruised knuckles, which he looked down at now as he stroked Hooligan Hank. He gave a dry chuff. He had the hands of a working lawman again. He'd be galldanged. He hadn't figured on toting the five-pointed badge again, but now that he had, he'd kind of taken to the idea. Aside from the job taking him away from his cabin, that was. And despite the possibility of him getting beaten up and/or shot in the back. But that was why he and Brazos had been working closely together—so they could watch each other's backs.

Just like old times.

To that end, Catfish needed to haul his battered, aching carcass back up onto Jasper's back and get started on the eight-mile journey to Wolfwater. He'd considered getting a room in town, as Brazos had done, but he couldn't sleep in town anymore. Not since he'd moved out here and had experienced all this peace and quiet near the catfish pool on Wolfwater Creek.

Peaceful, despite the frustration of the one catfish he hadn't been able to land.

Bubba Jones.

The one thing Catfish didn't like about working in town again was, he couldn't continue his hunt for the elusive fish. He had a feeling Bubba was under the delusion he'd won the war. *No, no, no. The war ain't over, Bubba Jones.*

The catfish might have won a few battles, but the war was far from over. Soon Catfish and Brazos would have Wolfwater back purring contentedly and quietly, just like Hooligan Hank was doing in Catfish's arms. After that, Catfish could take an afternoon and an entire Saturday off and drown some more frog guts in another attempt to finally hook his nemesis, filet Bubba up, and fry him with a light dusting of cornmeal with salt, pepper, and a few heaping dollops of fresh butter.

The thought made the recently reinstated lawman's mouth water.

Catfish stopped petting Hank. He frowned at the dark pool before him, which was gradually acquiring a gray sheen as the sun climbed closer to the eastern horizon. He thought he'd spied movement in the pool, a flickering shadow roughly five feet out from the very spot on the shore where Bubba had chomped his toe—a lingering injury that still grieved him from time to time, especially when he first stomped into his boots in the morning.

"Hmm," Catfish said, moving slowly to his right along the shoreline. "Wonder . . . wonder . . ."

He stopped suddenly and drew a sharp, startled breath as the big fish exploded out of the dawn-gray water. It curved its body into a glinting eyelash as it rose a good three feet above the water turned silver by Bubba Jones's exploding out of it. The fish twisted around, turning his big head and snout toward the man who'd been trying to catch him for the past two years.

"Oh, you wicked cuss!" Catfish growled, anger burning in him. "Makin' fun of this ol' fox, are you?"

He would have sworn that just then ol' Bubba Jones opened his mouth and narrowed his eyes, silently snickering at him just before he flipped himself upside down to plunge headfirst back into the water. His nemesis slapped his tail fin against the pond's surface, lifting another white splash that turned another spot in the otherwise-smooth surface silver and sent the morning cool water up over Catfish's boots and trouser legs. Catfish saw the big fish's dark shape dwindle down . . . down . . . down into the pond's murky depths, fading quickly from view.

"Sissified coward!" Catfish yelled.

The aggrieved angler stared at the water, grinding his back teeth, imagining the big fish hovering down there, just above the muddy bottom, laughing as he remembered how badly he'd humiliated the old devil who'd spent—wasted?—so much time gunning for him.

Literally gunning for him the last time they'd met, to Catfish's even further humiliation when he'd realized a carriage filled with Wolfwater's primary mucky-mucks had witnessed the entire humiliating episode. The lovely Miss Julia Claire had even made the not-so-vaguely jeering comment that Catfish was going to need—what was it she'd said again?

"A bigger gun," he said now, glowering into the pond. "Hmm. I'd use dynamite if it wouldn't blow that mocking cuss to uneatable smithereens. Nah, nah . . . I'm gonna eat you, Bubba Jones . . . if you're the last meal on this earth I ever eat!"

Catfish just then realized Hooligan Hank had stopped purring.

He looked down to see the cat staring up at him skeptically.

A flush rose in Catfish's cheeks. Hank's gaze said it all.

Catfish was making a dang fool of himself.

He gave a dry laugh and shook his head. So he was. So he was . . .

Still, though, he was gonna catch that fish and eat him . . . when he got the time.

Sure as tootin'.

"Well, Hank," Catfish said, crouching to set the cat on the ground, "I'd best get my neck out of its hump over ol' Bubba and get my fat behind to town. Brazos will be at work soon, an' he's gonna need my help. I'll meet you back at the cabin . . ."

Hank gave a low moan and ran off, tail high, toward the mouth of the trail that led through the woods to his and Catfish's cabin. Catfish cast one more indignant glance at the watery home of the mocking fish, then swung around, hitching his .44 and his trousers higher on his hips. Giving another frustrated sigh, he ambled off along the trail behind the cat.

Back at the cabin, he poured a bowl of the fresh cream he'd toted out from town and set it on the porch. He'd already saddled Jasper and tied him to the hitchrack fronting the shabby but tight and comfortable hovel. Now he retrieved his Yellowboy from the cabin, closed the door, locked it, and slid the rifle into its saddle scabbard.

He turned to Hooligan Hank, hungrily lapping cream.

"I hope to be back tonight, Hank," he told the cat. "If I'm not . . . well, you got a nice, comfortable hideout under the porch and I know you won't go hungry." He chuckled as he unlooped the reins from the hitchrack and hauled his aching carcass into the saddle. Hank was a good mouser; his broad back, thick shiny fur, and sagging belly sang the story of many successful hunts.

Catfish wished he could sing such tales of success as the cat.

"Later, my friend," he said, and reined Jasper out away from the porch.

The cat paused in his lapping to give Catfish a quick glance and a tail flick before returning to the thick, rich cream.

Catfish rode out through the rocks, greasewood, prickly pear, and sotol cactus to the main trail that curved off through the rocky desert just as the sun lifted its head above the horizon and spread a lemony light across the terrain spiking up around him. The sun chased shadows out from the sides of the low hills, rocky haystack buttes scored with ravines, red sandstone dikes, and shelving mesas.

He followed the old freight road that trailed down from the ranches, mining camps, and outlaw lairs in the Stalwarts rising behind him, to the south, toward the town of Wolfwater, hunkered in a bowl between bluffs and stony ridges ahead of him, to the north. The Wolfwater Rocks rose redly behind a blue mist of morning distance, twenty miles away, ahead and on his right. The trail generally followed the curving course of Wolfwater Creek, on his left. He couldn't see the creek because of the brush and desert maples spiking its banks, but he did see a sleek gray coyote wander up out of it and start on a course that would take it across Catfish's trail. But then, the coyote stopped suddenly, turned to see the horse and rider, crouched down slightly, changed course immediately, and slinked off into the rocks lining the base of a red dike off the trail's right side, fifty yards ahead.

"Good morning to you, too, Mr. Coyote," Catfish hailed, waving his hat and chuckling. He didn't know why he felt so good despite his sundry aches and pains. It must be because he had a job of work ahead of him, and maybe that was what a man really needed—a job of work to do.

Otherwise, he went a little soft in his thinker box and spent too much time drinking mustang grape wine and obsessing about catfish . . .

Charlie was roughly halfway to town and riding through a canyon between tall red-stone ridges spiked with barrel cactus and tufts of Mormon tea, when he reined up suddenly. He'd seen the morning sun flash off something in some rocks on the ridge ahead of him, off the trail's right side. Just beyond a bend that followed a large bulge in the belly of the ridge wall, and about a hundred feet up from the trail.

"Hmm," Catfish pondered, feeling a chill, despite the morning's warmth. Chicken flesh rose along both sides of his spine. He frowned at the rocks in which he'd seen the flash, only to see the flash again. "Someone drawin' a bead on ol' Catfish?" he asked himself aloud.

Then the trail dipped and drew up close to the base of the ridge, taking those rocks in which he'd seen the glint out of view. They were too far above him and masked by the bulge in the wall. The trail wound around the base of the wall, however, and if he stayed on it, he'd likely be right in the line of fire of whoever was gunning for him, hunkered down in those rocks.

Leastways, he figured, someone was gunning for him up there.

He had to assume so, anyway.

"Tell you what, pard," Catfish said as he and the steeldust approached a natural flue crawling up the side of the ridge and through the bulge, tracing a serpentine route up toward the top of the ridge, "why don't you go on ahead?" He wrapped his reins around his saddle horn and slid the Yellowboy from its boot. "We'll meet up again, once I've figured out if someone's layin' for me up there or not . . ."

Ten feet ahead, a stout but twisted cedar root poked out from the natural flue in the ridge wall on his right. Roughly fifteen feet up from the ridge's base. Taking the Winchester in his left hand, Catfish stood in his stirrups and raised his right arm high above his head, hooking it around the root. Jasper kept moving at a slow walk, and Catfish, holding fast to the cedar root firmly lodged against the inside of his elbow, slid back off his saddle and over Jasper's tail, swinging his lower body sharply left, toward the flue.

The root made a crunching sound.

Catfish looked up in keen dismay to see the root break off roughly four feet from the end. Catfish gave a groan as he watched that crack in the ridge wall slide toward his dangling feet, until his feet were no longer dangling over it, but were in the flue itself, along with the rest of him, landing hard, then falling sideways to the floor of the flue. The pain drove up from his ankles through his knees and into his hips.

Somehow he managed to hold on to his rifle.

"Oh, you damn fat fool!" Catfish silently scolded himself, suppressing the added grievances to his old carcass and heaving himself to his feet, though both ankles felt as though rusty railroad spikes had been hammered into them. "Did you forget you're not twenty-two years old anymore, and you're damn near a hundred pounds heavier than when you *were*?!"

Despite his obvious age and depleted physical resources, he scrambled up the flue, which cut deeper into the ridge as it rose to the crest far above. He had no time to lick his wounds, for Jasper would likely be rounding the broad curve in the bend of the trail, which followed the base of the ridge wall, in just a minute or so. He held the Yellowboy in his right hand and used his left hand to push off rocks as he climbed the meandering crack, finding plenty of handholds in the form of rocks and stone thumbs bulging out of the floor of the flue, as well as from its sides.

His would-be bushwhacker—now possibly lying in wait for Catfish in the rocks just above him, to his left—had likely taken this same route up to his own position.

As he scrambled up the shallow chasm, Catfish watched an imaginary timepiece clicking away inside his head. Then suddenly he climbed two rocks up, out of the flue, and there the son of a devil was. The bushwhacker was hunkered down in rocks nearly straight across from Catfish's position, facing away from Catfish, aiming a Winchester rifle down toward the trail on which Jasper was just then appearing, saddle empty, reins tied to his horn.

The ambusher aimed his rifle down, cheek snugged up against his rifle stock. Then suddenly realizing that he had no target but an empty saddle, he jerked his head up from his rifle.

"You blame fool!" Catfish shouted, dropping to one knee on a flat slab of rock protruding from the ridge fall. "You think this is Catfish Charlie's first rodeo?"

The man jerked his cream-hatted head around. He swung his rifle around, too, stretching his lips back from his mustached mouth in exasperation.

"Drop it or I'll blow you back to the devil who spawned you!" Catfish bellowed.

The gunman did not heed the order.

He kept swinging that Winchester around, the sun glinting again off the barrel.

The Yellowboy spoke the language of death, bucking and roaring. The bullet plowed through the bushwhacker's right shoulder, knocking the man back and to one side. He dropped the Winchester, which clattered onto the boulders, and then the man himself fell out of the nest of rocks he was in, giving a terrified scream.

"No, no, no!" Catfish yelled.

He'd shot the man in the shoulder because he wanted him alive, to explain just why in blue blazes he'd wanted to shoot Catfish. Not that plenty of men didn't have their reasons, but Catfish wanted to learn the nature of this man's. Instead, Catfish heard the thuds and groans of the man tumbling down the ridge toward the trail below.

There was one resolute groan and final thud as the falling man's fall reached completion.

"Galldangit!" Catfish bellowed, pounding his gloved left fist against his thigh. "If you're dead, you dry-gulchin' devil, I'm gonna shoot ya *again*!"

Chapter 20

When Brazos had returned his clothes to his cabin—he'd taken the time to consciously note that they'd acquired the scent of the woman who'd so thoroughly washed, dried, and ironed them—he went back to the small stable to saddle Abe. He rode into Wolfwater as the sun was just climbing above the horizon. The dust was roiling up behind lumber and mining drays, and ranch wagons were already clattering here and there in the first industry of a bright, soon-to-be-hotter-than-the-hobs-of-Hell West Texas day.

He checked in at the jailhouse first.

He and Catfish had arrested a good dozen men over the past few days, but only seven remained. Seven men besides Skinny, that was. If you could call Skinny a man, which Brazos thought was entirely negotiable. The eight prisoners were being guarded by the old horse breaker, Waldrick Henricks. These days, Henricks, with two bad hips and two bad shoulders, had little else to do but sit in a chair, with a double-barreled, sawed-off, twelve-gauge Parker resting across his knees, while he sipped coffee "sweetened" with un-labeled who-hit-John.

An old friend of both Brazos's and Catfish's, he was a small, skinny, arthritic man, similar to a goblin, with a face resembling a topographic map of the West Texas desert. It was so craggy and dark, he could have been mistaken for one of Brazos's folks of African descent—if not for his piercing sky-blue eyes and a long, straight blue-white mustache, side-whiskers, and a spade beard hanging off his chin.

According to Henricks, the night had been rela-tively quiet, save the prisoners' snoring and sporadic demands for better treatment. There were only four cells, with two cots in two and only one in the other two. So some of the prisoners had to sleep on horse blankets on the floor. Henricks said none com-plained long, though, and he grinned at Brazos while raising the stout sawed-off in his gnarled, claw-like hands.

Brazos glanced at the disgruntled, motley collec-tion of men lounging around in the four cells lined up at the back of the room, most smoking and drink-ing coffee Henricks had shoved through the slots in their cell doors. The place was as smoky as a saloon at one o'clock on a Saturday morning. They all gave him the wooly eyeball; one man—a wheelwright named Driscoll—blew a smoke plume at him and flared an angry nostril.

Brazos gave a dry chuckle and turned to Henricks. "I'm gonna take a look around, make sure no stores have been broken into an' the bank ain't been robbed. Then I'll head over to Mrs. Conover's place for breakfast. I'll have her send some beans and bacon over, though none of them 'scallions deserve anything but bread and water. When I get back, I'll take over till midnight. Cha'les will likely be back to town soon."

"No hurry, Brazos," Henricks said. "I'm so stove up, I can't sleep, anyways, an' if I go home, I'll just have to listen to Gert complain about how worthless I am and how much whiskey I drink." He gave a slow wag of his head, grimacing, and sipped his spiked coffee.

Brazos smiled, pinched his hat brim to the jailer, and was about to go out, when Henricks said quickly, "Say . . . you know that good-lookin' young Mex you was tellin' me to watch out for? The brother of the whore Skinny broke like a toothpick over a hitching post."

He cast a quick glance at Skinny sitting on the edge of his cot, holding a cigarette in one hand, a cup of coffee in the other. The doxie killer was in his stocking feet and his hair was spiked from sleep. He appeared no happier than when Catfish and Brazos had first brought him in. He quickly lowered his gaze, sheepish. He was not a favorite of the men around him, since he'd killed a young lady they'd taken pleasure in patronizing. That's why Brazos and Catfish had jailed him with only one other man—a docile, corpulent drunk still asleep on the floor and snoring on his back, smiling serenely, hands entwined on his considerable paunch.

"Seen him?" Brazos asked the jailer.

"He walks by the jailhouse from time to time. I see him out the window or when I'm smokin' on the stoop. Gives me the evil eye, like he's fixin' to cause some trouble. Once, he just stood outside the barber shop, by that oil pot over there, just starin' toward the jailhouse." Henricks gave his head another slow wag. "Just starin' like he's fixin' to set fire to the place."

"Seen him myself a few times," Brazos said. "Watch yourself, Waldo. He might be trouble. Cha'les an' I might have to read to him from the book again."

Henricks raised the Parker. "Don't worry."

Brazos went out, mounted Abe, and took a thorough tour of the town, making sure no trouble had erupted in the few hours since he'd retreated to his cabin for too-little, too-light sleep. Amazingly, he spied no broken windows or busted-down doors, and no men lying dead in the street. That was a first since he and Brazos had pinned the stars to their shirts the second time around.

Maybe he and his partner were starting to get a toehold.

Pleased with the way the lid had seemed to stay on the town for the past few hours, he turned the chestnut in the direction of Ida Conover's Good Food, a favorite little eatery situated in a mud brick shack on a side street, not far from the creek. He hadn't visited the place since he'd returned to Wolfwater, but he'd been meaning to. As he headed that way, he spied a man standing at the front corner of the post office, staring toward him. He was a short, swarthy man in a broadcloth black coat and bullet-crowned black hat.

As Brazos started to draw back on Abe's reins, the man lowered the hands he had crossed on his chest, turned, and slipped stealthily into the twelve-foot break between the post office and a haberdashery. Brazos nudged the chestnut ahead and gazed down the break just as the short, swarthy gent—maybe owning some Mexican blood—gained the rear of the alley. The man cast a quick, cautious glance over his shoulder, then disappeared behind the haberdashery.

"Hmm," Brazos said, staring into the break and pensively fingering his beard.

He booted Abe ahead and turned him around a corner, heading west. He reined up again sharply. He'd just seen the front of a tightly funneled hat and part of a man's face pull back behind yet another building corner—this one a harness shop sitting directly across the street from Ida Conover's.

"Lawdy," Brazos exclaimed softly under his breath. "I'll be hanged if that, too, don't look suspicious." He hipped around in his saddle, half expecting to see the first man he'd seen earlier flanking him, maybe leveling pistol sights on his back. "Wouldn't it be nice if a fella could grow eyes in the back of his head?" Brazos muttered as he pulled Abe up to one of the two hitchracks fronting the two-story eatery, which had a long, slightly sagging porch running along its front wall. A plate glass window was in the front wall, to the left of the door, the name of the place stenciled in gold-leaf lettering in a broad arch.

Brazos dismounted and looped his reins over the hitchrack. No other horses but Abe were tied at the rack, but there was plenty of fresh horse plop in the street. As Brazos mounted the front porch, he glanced around him, making sure he wasn't about to get drilled a third eye—one he couldn't see out of. When he turned his head forward, he saw the shadow of movement in the big window.

He paused, apprehension touching him once more.

Was he about to walk into a whipsaw of flying lead?

In Wolfwater of this day and age, he wouldn't doubt it a bit.

He unsnapped the keeper thong from over the

Russian that was thonged on his thigh, continued up the steps, and loosened the big popper in its holster. He crossed the porch, tripped the door's string and leather latch, pushed the door open, took one cautious step inside, and stopped.

Fast movement to his left made him close his hand over the Russian's grips.

A loud, husky female voice, raspy from whiskey and cigarettes, exclaimed, "Brazos McQueen, about time you made an appearance, you handsome son of Satan!"

Brazos turned to his right just as a short, skinny woman dressed in a man's checked wool shirt, with sleeves rolled to her elbows, and skintight blue denim pants, the cuffs of which were tucked into the tops of her boy-sized, hand-tooled leather cowboy boots, leaped into his arms and wrapped her skinny arms, deeply tanned and seasoned to the color of ancient saddle leather, around his neck. As she did, she used one hand to pluck the loosely rolled, ash-dripping quirley from between her thin lips before planting a dry kiss on his cheek.

"Where you been hidin' your skinny behind? Ol' Henricks said you was in town, but I ain't seen hide or hair of you till now!"

Brazos laughed, gave the lady a hug, then set her back down on the floor. "I do apologize, Miss Ida, but we been busy, me an' Cha'les. Tryin' to get this town back on its leash after Abel and Bushwhack were killed has been a job of work. A full-time job, at that."

"You an' Catfish—back together again," Ida said with a delighted smile, the wheat paper quirley between her lips leaking more ash. "Just like old times."

"I reckon. Speakin' of old times, you still cookin' that chili omelet?" Again, Brazos grinned, this time in delight of remembered meals he'd taken right here in the appropriately named Ida Conover's Good Food.

"Couldn't let a local favorite like that one go." Ida turned toward the counter on the room's right side, shoving her sleeves a little higher up on her arms. "You have a seat and I'll rustle it up with all the surroundin's." She glanced over her shoulder. "Coffee?"

"Please. Hot an' black—just like me!" Brazos grinned as he headed for a table in the shadowy corner of the room opposite the front door.

"Just like you, darlin'. Comin' right up!"

Ida disappeared through a door behind the counter and returned a minute later with a brown stone mug of steaming coffee. "Back at your old table," Ida noted, and set the mug down before Brazos. "Back to the wall."

Brazos doffed his hat and turned it crown down on the table. "Can't be too careful."

Ida chuckled and started back to the kitchen, but stopped suddenly when two men, whom Brazos had seen through the window rein up in front of the café, walked in through the front door. They were a couple of rugged-looking characters in worn range gear. One was tall and slender, with yellow hair and blue eyes, while the other was of average height, burly and round-faced, with a dark brown beard. Both men were somewhere in their late twenties, Brazos thought, eyeing them over the steaming rim of his coffee mug.

Neither man so much as glanced at either Brazos or Ida as they grimly, expressionlessly kicked chairs out from a table in the eatery's front corner, on the opposite side of the room from Brazos. They both sat facing Brazos. Ida glanced at the deputy, shrugged a skinny shoulder, and turned to the newcomers.

"Coffee, gents?" she jovially asked in her nasal-raspy voice.

The yellow-haired man merely nodded, leaning forward in his chair to adjust the bone-handled six-shooter thonged low on his right thigh.

Neither man had yet looked at Brazos.

Ida was walking around behind the counter when two more riders rode up to the eatery, dismounted, and tied their horses to the same hitchrack as the one Brazos's chestnut was tethered to. Brazos recognized both men. At least he recognized one of them and thought he'd seen the other one before as well—out on the street as he'd been riding over here. One was the short, swarthy man in the black broadcloth coat and bullet-crowned black hat. He was thick around the middle, and he wore two pistols on his broad hips in shiny black leather holsters.

A walrus mustache mantled his broad, thick-lipped mouth.

The other man wore a light tan Stetson, with a tightly funneled brim. He had a hawklike face and his long, sandy mustache hung down around his mouth to jostle against his chin. Now as he and the other man entered the café, he rolled a matchstick around between his lips. These two headed for a table up near the counter. The stocky man sighed as he removed his hat, ran a thick hand through his brown hair, then pulled out a chair and sat in it.

They both sat facing Brazos, though these two hadn't yet looked at him, either.

Ida fired another dubious glance at Brazos, then addressed the newcomers, "Coffee, gents?"

"Coffee for me," said the swarthy man. He glanced at his flinty-eyed, hawk-faced partner and gave a snide smile. "He don't drink coffee. Just milk."

"Milk for me, coffee for him," said the hawk-faced man. "That's all we'll be having."

"Just two coffees for us," said the yellow-haired man sitting with the bearded man at the table in the corner near the door. "We won't be eating anything, either."

"All righty, then," Ida said with skeptically arched brows. Her eyes slid to Brazos once more, and then she pushed through the door to the kitchen.

Her tone wasn't quite as jovial as it had been before.

She sensed trouble. Brazos sensed it, too.

Of course, these four could be here just to drink coffee and milk, but the way all four sat partially facing Brazos, he doubted it. He hadn't liked the evil eyes he'd been given out on the street earlier, either.

He sipped his coffee and regarded the four men before him.

They were pointedly avoiding his gaze.

His sipped his coffee with his left hand, leaving his right hand resting under the table on his right thigh, ready to reach for the big Peacemaker holstered for the cross-draw on his left hip.

None of the four other customers said anything. A clock ticked on the wall to the left of the door, near the yellow-haired man and the bearded gent. Beneath the clock's monotonous beat, Brazos could hear Ida singing softly, nervously, in the kitchen while she prepared his omelet and fried his potatoes. Suddenly he wasn't nearly as hungry as he'd been before.

These men were here to kill him, all right.

He didn't know why, but that's what they were here for.

Four against one. Tall odds. And something told him that all four were right handy with their six-shooters, too. He found himself wishing Catfish was here to back his play. The older lawman had gone to seed, but he'd proven himself up in the Stalwarts.

Brazos had just finished his coffee—and what a nervous cup it had been, too—when Ida pushed through the door behind the counter and came out from behind the counter with a tray bearing two steaming platters. She glanced at the four other customers, cast Brazos another tense look, and then set the tray down on his table, saying too cheerfully, "Here we are, my dear. The chili omelet, just the way you like, with a half a bushel of fried potatoes!"

She swung around and headed back toward the kitchen, announcing, "I'll fetch the pot and refresh your cup!"

"I'm good, Ida," Brazos said, eyeing the four wolves seated before him, staring a little too intently at their tables. "Just stay back there."

Again, Ida cast her nervous gaze around the room.

Then she winced a little, turned, and disappeared into the kitchen.

The door hadn't swung shut behind her before the four men glanced around at each other.

The bearded man by the door nodded.

And then all hell broke loose.

Chapter 21

All four men leaped out of their chairs, snatching cold steel from leather holsters.

As much as he hated to do it, Brazos grabbed the end of his table with his left hand and leaped to his own feet, raising the table in front of him, shieldlike. The chili omelet and fried potatoes struck the floor with a crash. At the same time, Brazos shucked his big Peacemaker and commenced returning fire at the two men crouched over their own table, near the counter, triggering lead at him.

As bullets tore into his table, smashing against it with loud pounding sounds, he shot the swarthy, stocky gent through the chest, then triggered a round at the man's hawk-faced partner, blowing the hat off the man's head. Brazos heaved his table toward the hawk-faced man and his partner, who was just then falling back over his own chair, screaming.

Brazos leaped to his feet, triggered a round at the two men at the front of the room, then ran forward and dove atop a table, striking the table on its right side, tipping it over so it, too, became a shield of sorts. Two bullets ripped into the edge of it, and then Brazos raised his head and gun hand over the top of the table and shot the yellow-haired man. The man screamed and flew backward, triggering his bone-gripped Colt into the ceiling, then flying back through the window behind him in a shrill screech of breaking glass.

"You done used up all your lives, Black man!" yelled the hawk-faced man, triggering a round that sliced across the nub of Brazos's right cheek.

Brazos returned fire, but missed as the man dove to the floor himself, bringing a table down with him. A gun continued thundering from the front of the room, two more bullets plowing into the floor near Brazos's left elbow. Brazos raised the Russian again, just as the lone survivor at the front of the room flung a chair at him, running toward him. Brazos deflected the chair with his left arm and shot the man through the forehead.

Brazos turned to his right, just as the hawk-faced man gained his feet, grinning and extending his Remington straight at Brazos. The deputy's spine turned to jelly. The grinning man had him dead to rights.

Just then, the door to the kitchen opened behind him.

Ida came striding out, raising a long, double-barreled Greener in her small hands. She aimed down the double bores, and screamed, "No shootin' up my place, you ringtail varmint!"

Both the Greener's barrels erupted in smoke and flames.

The thunder was like that of a keg of dynamite being detonated.

The hawk-faced man triggered his Remington

wide as he screamed, and the force of the double load of double-ought buck lifted him two feet off the ground and hurled him across the room. His boot glanced off Brazos's right temple before he hit the floor to lie facedown in the mess of the deputy's spilled breakfast.

The man shook, sighed, and lay still.

The two-bore had carved two holes the size of pumpkins in the man's back. Blood oozed through the shreds of his torn brown vest.

"Ha-haaaa!" Ida cackled wildly. "We sent all four back to the demon that spawned 'em!" Laughing, she pounded her boots on the scarred puncheons and did a little dance.

Then she looked around the bloody room and at her shattered window. The smile left her face. "Darn!" she intoned, smashing a boot down on the floor and punching her thigh with her clenched left fist in bereavement. "Look what they done to my place!"

"Sorry, Ida," Brazos said, pushing off a knee as he climbed to his feet, brushing his fist across his bullet-grazed cheek.

Galloping hooves sounded on the street outside the restaurant. Brazos swung around, raising the still-smoking Colt in his hand. He lowered the piece when he saw Catfish rein Jasper up in front of the restaurant, shucking his Yellowboy from its scabbard and swinging down from the leather. The big, potbellied man pushed through the door, levering a round into the Winchester's action.

"Stand down, Cha'les," Brazos said, flicking his Peacemaker's loading gate open to begin reloading. Obviously, no man—especially a lawman—wanted to

be carrying around an empty gun in these danger-
ous environs. "You're late to the dance!"

"Yeah, well, I been deflecting lead my ownself,"
Catfish said, lowering his Yellowboy and stepping
into the room, looking around at the fresh beef piled
on the floor.

"You have?" asked Brazos.

"North of town. Haskell Benson."

"The gunfighter out of Kansas?"

"One an' the same." Catfish looked out the window
at the yellow-haired man lying dead on the stoop.
"That's Casper Finnegan."

"Thought I recognized him from his wanted
dodger," Brazos said, letting his empty .45 shells fall
onto the floor around his boots.

Catfish looked at the shorter man resting back
against the wall near the door, head tipped to his
right shoulder, hair hanging in his face. "That's the
bank robber Chester Fordheim. I've tangled with
him before, a couple years back. I thought he was
casing the bank, so I ran him out of town on a long,
greased rail."

He moved around the saloon, checking out the
other two dead men. "Don't recognize these two, but
they have the look of the devil about 'em—that's for
sure."

"Coordinated effort, eh, Cha'les?" Brazos said, replacing his spent rounds with fresh from his shell
belt.

"Sure seems that way." Catfish shouldered his rifle.
"I wanted to take Benson alive, but he gave up the
ghost before I could shake out of him just what his beef
with me . . . er, *us* . . . was." He looked at the dead man
with his face planted in Brazos's omelet.

"Waste of a good omelet," Ida complained. She turned to Brazos. "You sit down, honey. I'll fetch a cloth for that cheek and rustle you up a whole new omelet."

"No, thanks, Ida," the deputy said. "I seem to have lost my appetite."

"I know what you mean, partner," Catfish said. He placed his hand on Brazos's shoulder. "Until we can get to the bottom of why these fellas had it in for us, we best assume there's more of their ilk out there." He hooked his thumb over his shoulder to indicate the street outside the café. "Prowlin' around. Gunnin' for us. I got me a feelin' these fellas are part of a larger gang."

"I do believe you're right, Cha'les."

"You let Ida clean up that cheek for you," Catfish told his deputy. "I'll send for the undertaker and head out on my rounds."

Catfish was making his rounds an hour later when a bell rung over a door and a familiar voice said behind him, "Catfish, may I have a word with you, please?"

"Oh, of course," the lawman said, turning to see the lovely Miss Julia Claire step out of a ladies' hat shop onto the boardwalk fronting the place. As usual, she was elegantly attired. Today she wore a lime-green velveteen frock, with a lace-edged bodice that highlighted the comeliness of her figure to great degree. A large, matching hat was pinned to the hair piled atop her head, and Catfish suspected another hat resided in the large brown paper sack she held down low in her right hand.

Catfish pinched his hat brim to her and winced a

little as he self-consciously tried to suck in his gut a little. "What can I do for you, ma'am?"

Miss Claire used a white-gloved hand to slide a lock of her dark brown tresses back from her cheek. "Well, you see . . . you see"—she glanced at the board-walk and gave a troubled wince of her own—"this is difficult. It's about Miss Wilkes. Beth Wilkes."

"Oh," Catfish said. "How is Miss Bethany, anyway? I keep meaning to stop over to the Lone Star to see how she's doing, but Brazos an' me have been busy of late."

"Oh, I know you have, Catfish. And I would like to reiterate how grateful I and the rest of the towns-people are to have you and Brazos back on the job."

"Truth be told," Catfish said with a smile, "I think we both needed it. Me more so than my partner." He patted his gut. "I was going to wine fat out there. Back to Bethany . . . she still at your place, I take it?"

"Yes, that's the problem."

"Oh, well, if you need—"

"It's not a matter of my needing compensation. It's just that . . . well . . . she's refused to entertain the notion of going home. You see, Catfish, she wants to work for me. She wants to work the line."

"Bethany?"

The lady sighed. "It's quite astonishing, I know. She's a schoolteacher, for mercy sake. But after what happened . . . with the Thorsons . . . she thinks she is sullied. She is too ashamed to return to school. She insists that the only thing she's good for is . . . well—"

"Working upstairs at your place," Catfish finished for her with a deeply troubled tone in his voice.

"Exactly. Look, Catfish, you know I love my girls. They all came from very humble circumstances, and I fear that if they weren't working for me, they'd be—well, far worse off. Working for someone who treated them with far less respect and care than I do. Most of them are orphans. But Bethany came from a good home. She's just ashamed, afraid to show her face in public, and she is deeply, deeply heartbroken over the death of her father. I've urged her to ride out to the cemetery with me, in my carriage, to visit his grave. She's refused."

"Oh, boy." Catfish thumbed his hat brim up higher on his forehead. "Do you think I should talk to her? Abel was like a brother to me, and Beth is like a niece."

"I was hoping you'd suggest that. It certainly can't hurt. She's very stubborn, but maybe you can convince her to return to her and Abel's home, and to start teaching again. The doctor has said she's fine now . . . physically."

"Yeah, that's a far cry from up here, I know," Catfish said, tapping an index finger to his temple. "Well, no time like the present. I haven't heard any shooting within the past hour or so."

Though when he had last heard it, it had been a pip, he did not add to the woman.

"Thank you, Catfish," Miss Claire said. "Shall we?" She began walking along the street, heading back in the direction of her establishment.

With men having drawn targets on his and Brazos's backs, the lawman was reluctant to walk to the hotel and saloon with her. She might take a bullet meant for him. He decided to go ahead after a brief hesitation. Doubtful anyone would try anything right out on Wolfwater's busy main street. He hitched his pants and gun and shell belt up higher on his hips and followed in the woman's footsteps, arriving safely at the Lone Star Outpost a few minutes later.

Already, the place was busy. Not surprising. It was usually at least somewhat busy from sunup to sundown. Miss Claire led Catfish through the saloon, where businessmen in three-piece suits and sleepy-eyed gamblers were cracking eggs into beer schooners or finishing up platters of steak and eggs, and up the stairs to her third-floor suite.

"I'll let you speak to her privately," Miss Claire said, poking a key into the lock on her door and turning it. "She's probably still in bed, but I'm sure she'll feel comfortable with you. She probably won't feel comfortable with any other man ever again . . . except for you, and Brazos, of course."

"I know. That's why it's so surprising she wants to work for you."

"Some things just don't make sense."

"I'll go in and have a palaver with her," Catfish said.

He twisted the doorknob, eased open the door, and, removing his hat, stepped into the lady's nattily, tastefully appointed suite of rooms, which included the parlor area he was stepping into now, outfitted with elegant furniture, including a red scroll-back fainting couch, velvet drapes closed over the windows, and a large piano. Bethany lay on the couch, beneath a blanket with a floral pattern. She lay curled on one side, her brown hair sprayed across a green silk pillow.

"Hello, Catfish," she said quietly in the room's shadows abated by bright Texas sunlight angling in around the edges of the drapes. "I heard you and Miss Claire in the hall."

"Hello, honey," Catfish said, standing somewhat awkwardly by the door, kneading his hat brim as he held the topper down in front of his belly. "I'm sorry I haven't come callin' till now."

"I've heard you've been busy—you an' Brazos. Working to haze the coyotes back into their lairs after they killed my father."

"Well . . . yes . . ."

There was a small writing desk near the fainting couch. A plush-covered wooden chair, with a high, fancily scrolled back, fronted it. Catfish moved into the room, drew the chair up to the couch, and sat in it, setting his hat on his lap.

"I understand you don't want to go home," he said, reaching forward and tenderly sliding a few stray locks of the girl's hair back from her pale cheek.

"Papa's not there," she replied in a little girl's thin voice. "He'll never be there again. I don't want to return there . . . not if he's not there." She rolled her eyes to look up at Catfish for the first time since he'd entered the room. "I want to stay here. I want to work for Miss Claire. I can earn my keep."

"Oh, I don't think that'd be necessary, honey."

"I want to. It's all I'm good for," she added, choking back a small sob.

"Ah, that's not true. That's not true at all. You need to go home, honey. The doctor said you're ready to go back to school."

Bethany shook her head. "I can't."

"Why not?"

"Everyone knows. I'm sure even the children know."

"No one judges you for what happened, sweetheart. That wasn't your fault."

"Still . . ."

Catfish drew a deep breath, released it slowly. The

poor girl was in a bad way. The Thorsons had robbed her of her honor, her dignity. Leastways, that's how she saw it. Catfish had the almost undeniable urge to go back over to the jailhouse and blow Skinny's kneecaps off.

But he'd rather watch the little viper hang. That would be even more satisfying. He wished the circuit judge would get here soon.

"I think it's just gonna take you a little more time to get comfortable with going out again. You take your time. I'll check back on you in a few days. We'll ride out to the cemetery and visit your father's grave. Put some flowers on it. I'll rent a carriage, and we'll have us a nice ride, maybe even a picnic."

"I don't think so, Catfish," she said thinly. "I want to stay here. I want to work for Miss Claire. It's all I'm good—"

"No, no, no," Catfish said, putting some steel in his voice. "That's not true, and I don't want to hear you say it again. I want to get you out of here. Just for an hour or two. Just you an' me. I'll give you a few days. Will you promise to think about it?"

Bethany rolled her eyes up, to look at him again, wrinkling the skin above the bridge of her nose with incredulity. "Why, Catfish?"

"Why? Because I love you, honey. Don't you know that?"

She stared up at him. A vague light seemed to grow in her eyes, but she said nothing.

"Promise me you'll think about it? Just you an' me. A ride out to your father's grave. We'll pay our respects, say a prayer."

She continued to stare up at him. Then she turned her head sideways to the pillow again and stared down at the floor.

Catfish sighed. That appeared to be all the response he was going to get out of the poor girl.

He rose from the chair, returned the chair to the desk, then strode slowly to the door. He'd just reached the door and was setting his hat on his head and reaching for the knob, when she said very faintly, "Okay."

Catfish glanced back at her.

He smiled, opened the door, and went out.

Chapter 22

Several days later, Break o' Day Livery Barn manager Russell McCormick said, "Here you are, Miss Claire. Best mare in my barn!"

Julia laughed and caressed the Appaloosa's long, fine snout. "I don't doubt it a bit," she said, accepting the reins from the tall, lean man in pin-striped overalls, who was somewhere in his late sixties and looked every day of it. He stabled both of Julia's prized mares and took great care of them both. "Lilly's wonderful and so is Henrietta." Julia planted an affectionate kiss on the Appy's snout, which had a white blaze in the shape of Florida running down it. "Thank you so much. I hope to have Lilly back in an hour or so."

"Takin' a ride in the country, ma'am?"

"No, no!" Julia flushed a little at the passionate way she'd blurted that out. She had no interest in riding far from town with her ex-husband still in the area. At least she assumed he was still in the area, though she hadn't seen him or the three reprobates in his employ since they'd accosted her and killed

George McGrath on her way back from Grant Drago-man's ranch. "No," she said again, with less vigor this time. "I'm just going to ride out to the cemetery and place some flowers on Abel Wilkes's and Bushwhack Aimes's graves."

If and when Bethany accompanied Catfish to the cemetery, Julia didn't want the girl to see that the graves had not been decorated. Of course, Julia didn't know if anyone had placed flowers on them, but she doubted it. Family usually did that. Bushwhack had no surviving family, and Bethany was the former town marshal's only family, and she still hadn't stepped foot outside of the saloon since she'd returned to town nearly two weeks ago now.

"I see—that's nice of you, Miss Claire," said the livery manager. "Someone should tend them. They were good men. Anyway, enjoy your ride, miss."

"Thank you, Russell, I appreciate—" Julia cut herself off abruptly. For just then, she'd seen a tall, darkly dressed man, with one glinting monocle and holding a walking stick, standing beside a cream horse on the opposite side of the street from her. He was leaning on the walking stick, as though he had a bum leg.

Which her ex-husband certainly did, compliments of Julia herself.

Sergei Zhukovsky, sure enough!

Her heart thumped as the tall, thin, very pale man smiled at her. Then a long train of mules pulling large ore drays rocked and rattled past the Lone Star Outpost, out front of which Julia and Russell McCormick stood; the big Pittsburgh wagons obliterated Julia's view of the man.

"What's the matter, Miss Claire?" the liveryman said. "You see someone you know over there?" He was squinting at the passing ore train that was lifting an enormous cloud of tan dust on the other side of the newly laid train rails.

"Uh . . . no . . . no," Julia said, heart thudding again when she thought she'd seen Zhukovsky's three kidnapping brigands standing on the boardwalk behind him, looking as unshaven and seedy as she remembered the last time she'd seen them. She turned back to McCormick and feigned a smile as she said, "I thought so, but . . . but I was wrong, I'm sure."

No, she wasn't wrong. Zhukovsky and his three brigands were keeping a close eye on her.

Where is Dragoman's assassin, anyway?

"I see, ma'am," McCormick said. "Well, good day, then."

The liveryman mounted his own horse and rode off.

A few seconds later, the last wagon in the ore train rumbled on past Julia, giving her another clear view of the street's opposite side. Only, Zhukovsky and his seedy henchmen were no longer there. Julia looked around, shading her eyes with her hand, frowning nervously.

Then she saw them riding out of town to the west, two blocks away, and just then booting their horses into trots at the western edge of town. The tall Zhukovsky crouched low and pulled his bowler hat down lower on his head, his black frock winging out around him like a crow's wings in the wind. They rounded a bend, following the curve of the rails, obscured by the dust still kicked up by the ore train.

And then they were gone.

Julia felt weak in the knees, faint.

Then another figure caught her attention on the other side of the street. He'd just walked out of the

Occidental Saloon. He was very tall, broad-shouldered, and with three or four days' worth of beard stubble. He wore a high-crowned black Stetson and a long, dark brown duster. Held a rifle on his right shoulder, gloved right hand wrapped around the neck. He stepped up to a chestnut horse tied to a hitchrack fronting the Occidental and shoved the rifle into the scabbard strapped to the chestnut's saddle. He untied the reins from the hitchrack, swung up into the leather, and neck-reined the mount into the street.

As he did, he glanced toward Julia, gave a queer little smile, and pinched his hat brim to her.

He touched his spurs to the chestnut's flanks and trotted off down the street to the west.

Julia frowned after him, curious.

Dragoman's assassin?

Julia's fear was tempered by curiosity, a deep need to know if he was the assassin Grant Dragoman had called in. She needed to know if she would have to continue to keep looking over her shoulder or if she could rest easy in the knowledge that Zhukovsky and his henchmen were dead, rotting in a wash somewhere out in the desert. Constant worry had rendered her sleepless, so exhaustion weighed heavy on her.

She pulled her felt hat down lower on her head, stepped forward, and swung up onto the mare's back. She booted the horse west, but held her to a walk, not wanting to get too close to the men she was pursuing. She knew what she was doing was foolish, but she couldn't quell the impulse. She was a hunted woman, and she needed to know if she would be hunted no more.

She kept the assassin—if he was the assassin—just barely in sight ahead of her, a mere jostling speck on the horizon. Soon after leaving town, he swung to the southwest, traveling cross-country. She followed him for a good half hour. Then he disappeared. Julia reined in the mare on a low rise. Ahead, and below her, lay a rocky red canyon abutted on its south side by a tall ridge of jagged rock. She lowered her gaze to the ground and saw several sets of fresh hoofprints. The assassin and those he was pursuing had dropped down into that twisting canyon.

Julia's heart quickened. Hope rose in her. Yes, he was Dragoman's assassin, all right. He'd appeared a right capable man as well.

A crackle of gunfire rose from that jagged cut ahead of her.

Julia gasped.

A man shouted shrilly. There was another short crackle of gunfire, and then silence, save for the rustle of the breeze brushing against that rocky ridge.

Anxiety rose in Julia once more. Had the assassin accomplished his task?

She booted the mare down off the ridge, stopped her at the edge of the canyon, led her into the concealment of large rocks, and tied her to a small cottonwood. She found the trail the men ahead of her had taken down into the canyon and followed it on foot. She was more likely to be seen atop the mare, and she didn't think the gunfire had come from more than maybe a hundred yards ahead.

She followed the canyon's twisting course for half that distance and stopped suddenly. Ahead of her were rocks and willows lining yet another, smaller wash inside the larger one. A thrashing sounded. Labored breathing, faint grunting. Frozen in place, fear turning her knees to stone, Julia stared straight ahead until the willows moved and the assassin appeared, pushing through the branches and stumbling forward on the toes of his boots.

He'd lost his hat. He held his rifle in his right hand, dangling low against his leg.

His face was dirty and streaked with sweat, his eyes bright with pain.

He held his free hand against his belly. Blood oozed through his bullet-torn shirt and between his splayed fingers. His eyes found Julia and he stopped suddenly, then staggered toward her for three more steps. Then he stopped, groaned, looked down at his ruined belly, and dropped to his knees.

He dropped from his knees to the ground and lay still.

Julia closed her hands over her mouth in shock.

Distant footsteps sounded ahead of her.

Fear made her heart lurch. She swung around and ran back along the ravine. She scrambled up out of it, mounted the mare, and booted her into a ground-churning gallop back in the direction she'd come.

She'd ridden hell for leather for three hundred yards before she passed the niche in the rocks and cactus in which Catfish waited, fully concealed.

Catfish had witnessed the entire curious display in town.

He'd seen the four odd-looking strangers staring at Julia before riding west out of Wolfwater. He'd seen Julia staring back at them, obviously troubled. He'd seen the tall man with the rifle exit the Occidental, pinch his hat brim to the woman, and put his mount on the trail of the four odd-looking strangers—one impeccably dressed, very thin and pale and wearing a monocle; the other four as lowly-looking as any raggedy-heeled, southwestern-border tough.

He'd seen Julia anxiously mount her fine mare and take off after the man trailing the first four.

Catfish's curiosity had been piqued. He'd seen the four strangers in town before, loitering around Julia's Lone Star Outpost, as though they were keeping an eye on the place. They had the look of trouble about them. He'd seen the tall hard case, always toting the Winchester, also lingering around Julia's.

They were trouble or had come to trouble, all right.

A few minutes ago, Catfish had heard the crackle of distant gunfire.

Now, glancing behind him to see Miss Claire galloping the mare around a high escarpment and fading from sight, Catfish booted Jasper out of the rocks and swung him southwest, heading in the direction from which the shots had been fired. One more shot gave him pause and then he continued forward until he came to a twisting arroyo with a steep red rock ridge jutting up from its southern bank.

He stopped Jasper, ground-reined him, and shucked his Yellowboy from its scabbard. He jacked a round into the action, lowered the hammer to half cock, and followed the prints of several sets of horses, as well as a lady's riding boots, into the ravine. A few minutes later, he came to where the man with the rifle, the man who'd followed the first four out of town, lay belly-down, atop his rifle.

He'd been shot in the belly. The bullet had exited his lower back.

The last shot Catfish had heard had likely been the one that had drilled a round through the man's head. It had likely been meant to finish him, but the way the man lay told Catfish the man had already been dead.

Catfish kicked the body over. He hadn't gotten close enough to the man in town to recognize him. Now he saw he was the hired regulator Eldon Ring. Catfish had seen the man before, passing through Wolfwater, but he'd never had reason to arrest him. As far as he knew, the man—a known killer—had never had charges brought up against him.

Now he never would.

Catfish returned to Jasper, mounted up, and tried to follow the first four men, but lost their trail along the stone-floored ravine. He swung Jasper around and headed back in the direction of town, shaking his head in perplexity.

Just what in blue blazes kind of trouble had Miss Claire gotten herself involved in?

He booted the steeldust into a hard run, wanting to catch up to Julia and find out why she'd followed Ring out of town, who'd obviously been following the men who'd spied him on their back trail and bushwhacked him. Judging by the tracks, the woman was riding hard, though. If she kept up that pace, he wasn't sure he'd catch up to her. That was all right. He knew where he could find her in town.

No point in killing Jasper.

He'd just eased the gelding into a trot when something screeched through the air past his right side. The bullet spanged shrilly off a rock behind him.

Jasper whinnied, tried to pitch. Catfish drew sharply back on the reins as the crack of the rifle that had flung the bullet at him reached his ears. Another bullet came whistling eerily toward him from a red sandstone ridge ahead, and on his right. He didn't have the luck he'd had with the first bullet. This one punched hotly across his right temple and ripped his hat off his head to send it flying into the air behind him. Catfish's gloved hands slipped off the reins. Knowing from experience what was going to happen next—and because Jasper was already starting to buck again—Catfish kicked his feet free of the stirrups so he didn't get caught up and dragged, turned to his right, and let himself roll gently from his saddle.

He hit the ground with a vision-blurring jar, the air punched out of him with a loud *"oaff"!*

Again, the report of the rifle reached his ears from that damnable ridge.

As Jasper ran off hard, dragging the reins along the ground to either side of him, kicking dust and gravel over Catfish, the lawman scrambled to his feet and ran to a low dike off the trail's right side, one whose ridge was spiked with rocks and prickly pear. One of those spiked pears went flying over Catfish's head when another bullet came hurling in from that ridge, followed a few seconds later by the rifle's bark.

"Son of a buck!" Catfish groused, brushing his fist across his temple and seeing the thick smear of blood on his glove. "Who could *that* be?"

Had Catfish been followed from town by someone wanting to eliminate him just as badly as Eldon Ring, and the four others preceding him, had wanted to vanquish one another?

Catfish racked a round into the Yellowboy he'd managed to hold on to in his tumble from Jasper's back. He lifted his bloody, hatless head just enough to edge a look over the lip of the dike. He drew it down quickly when he saw the stab of flames and smoke from a niche about halfway up the red sandstone ridge. The bullet slammed into the top of the dike, and gravel and another prickly pear went flying off over Catfish's head.

Catfish lifted his head once more, bringing the barrel of the rifle up as well, and sent two rounds of his own hurling toward that niche in the rocks. He saw a hatted head just then jerk down behind rocks, and both of Catfish's slugs slammed into the side of the ridge where the hatted head had been a quarter second earlier.

"Damn!" Catfish said, angrily pumping another round into the Winchester's chamber. "Does *anyone* fight *fair* in Texas anymore? Used to be when a man had it out for you, he stood before you, went ahead and said so, and unsnapped the keeper thong from over the hammer of his hogleg."

Men in Texas used to confront each other like adults!

When another round slammed into a rock on the ridge above Catfish's head, he jerked up quickly, scrambled up and over the ridge, and ran toward another, higher dike ahead on his left. Just before he reached cover, he sensed a bead being drawn on him. He hurled himself up and off of his spurred boots, and his aching two-hundred-plus pounds went arcing through the air before he slammed belly-down on the ground and rolled up quickly against the base of his new covering dike.

As he did, a bullet slammed into the red sand and gravel just inches off the heel of his right boot, making a cold stone of dread drop in his belly. He leaned up close against the dike and squeezed the Yellowboy in his hands, holding the rifle before him.

Galloping hoofbeats sounded behind him, growing louder.

Catfish cast an anxious look behind him. "Now who in hell could *this one* be? There a *second* man out here fixin' to perforate my wretched hide?"

Was he being surrounded?

Another bullet caromed toward Catfish, clearing the higher crest of his current covering dike and plowing into the ground several feet behind him. The gun crash came a half second later.

The hooves' thudding grew louder as the rider approached.

And there he . . . er, *she* . . . was—riding out from between two low hills roughly thirty yards behind him.

She turned her lovely, hatted head toward him and, pulling back on the mare's reins, yelled, *"Catfish?!"*

Chapter 23

"Good Lord A'mighty, lady!" Catfish yelled, gesturing anxiously with his free hand. "Get down! Can't you hear the—"

Just then, her green felt hat, with a low, boxlike crown, went flying off her head.

"Oh!" she said as the mare whinnied and lifted its front hooves off the ground. Miss Claire lost the reins and, dark eyes wide and round as billiard balls, somersaulted over the mare's arched tail. She hit the ground on her belly and lay there, stunned, her long, brown hair hanging loosely about her head, having come free of the French braid she'd had it in.

"Oh, for pity's sake!"

Catfish leaped up and ran over to her. He dropped to a knee beside her, sent three shots caroming into the rocks where he knew the dry-gulcher was hunkered, then jerked her to her feet by one arm and half dragged her back toward the dike. She ran wildly, black wool riding skirt swinging about her scissoring legs. She cried, "Oh, oh, oh!" then "OHHH!" as another bullet caromed off the far ridge, tore through the wildly buffeting side of her skirt before spanging loudly off a rock.

Catfish heaved himself forward, pulling the lady along with him, and together, in a tangle of arms and legs, rolled up behind the dike he'd been hunkered behind before the appearance of his second unexpected guest. The report of the rifle that had sent the last bullet flying through her skirt barked angrily from the ridge.

Catfish got himself untangled from the woman, though he had to admit the entanglement hadn't been all *that* uncomfortable. Just the same, exasperation exploded in him as he said, "What in holy blazes are you *doin'* here? I figured you'd be halfway back to town by now, the way you were gallopin' away from that ravine! Are you just purely *addicted* to gettin' your purty self *killed* . . . uh, ma'am?"

She shook her tangled hair back out of her face, poked a finger through the hole in her skirt, then looked up at Catfish leaning a little higher against the dike. Her eyes were as wide as a deer's that knew a rifle's sights were on her, and her perfectly sculpted cheeks were pale. "I . . . honestly . . . don't . . . I heard the shooting behind me and I . . . I just had to know *who* was shooting at *whom* . . . this time around!" Tears glistened in her eyes and her face crumpled in a sob as she said, "Oh, my God—the trouble my life has come to!"

"If I may make a suggestion, Miss Claire, your life might not come to such trouble if you didn't ride out *lookin'* for it!"

"Well, why are *you* out here, Catfish?" she returned, eyes bright now with her own brand of exasperation, nudging aside her terror and befuddlement. "Is there not enough trouble for you in *town?*"

"When I see trouble bleedin' out from town, I fig-

ure it's my job to follow it. An' if you didn't look trouble followin' two sets of trouble! Just what were those
four characters doin' lurkin' around your—"

Just then a bullet tore into the lip of the bridge,
spraying more prickly pear thorns down on Catfish's
head. A few of those thorns found the bullet crease
on his right temple, and he jerked his head down,
gritting his teeth against the pain, cupping his hand
over the bloody notch.

"Jumpin' Jehosophat!" he exclaimed. "I'm gonna
kill that jasper if it's the last thing I do before I myself
expire!"

"Which does not look all that unlikely." Miss Claire
unknotted the red bandanna from around her neck.
"Given the nature of that wound and how much blood
you appear to be losing from it. Pull your hand away."

"No, it hurts!"

"Don't be a child, Catfish!"

"How *dare* you! You're the one who rode back
here *toward* gunfire, young lady! An' you ain't even
gettin' *paid* for it!"

"Remove your hand!"

Catfish removed his hand, but said, "We got no
time to fool with this scratch. I gotta kick that bush-
whackin' devil out with a cold shovel before he can
do it to both of us—*owww!* Dangit, that *hurts!*"

She just plucked a prickly pear thorn from the
notch on his head.

"*Child!*" she said, and wrapped and knotted the
bandanna around his head, positioning a wide point
she'd made in it directly over the wound.

Gritting his teeth in anger, Catfish raked a fresh
round into his Winchester's breech and said, "You
just watch this child! I'm gonna blow that bugger to
smithereens, before—"

"Who is this bugger, Catfish?"

"I thought maybe you'd know, since you seem acquainted with everyone else out here, includin' the notorious Eldon Ring, who followed them four devils out of town."

"That was his name—Ring?"

"Who're the other four? Never mind. Let me kill this scurvy swine before the sun goes down an' he works around us an' fills us so full of lead we'll rattle when we walk!"

He started to lift his head again, to take another gander at the nest of rocks on the ridge, but stopped when she reached up and placed a tender hand over his bullet-notched temple. "Do be careful, Marshal. I don't want you to die because of me."

Catfish couldn't help giving the pretty lady a warm smile. "Ah, heck, there's a lot less purtier'n you I could die for, Miss Claire. But don't worry. I ain't figurin' on givin' up the ghost until I've found out just exactly what I'd be givin' it up *for*!"

"Good luck!"

"From your lips to God's ears!"

He leaped to his feet, sent two quick shots into the niche in the rocks where he could see the crown of the hat of the devil slinging lead at him, making the man pull his head lower and out of sight. Then he leaped out from behind the dike, up a slight slope, then swerved sharply left between two boulders, just as another bullet plowed into the ground nearby, the report echoing shortly afterward. He ran out from between the boulders then, knowing the man in the rocks couldn't see him from here, because there were thumbs and fingers of rock and more boulders blocking him from view, ran as fast as he could up the face of the escarpment.

It wasn't very fast, but he was mildly surprised to see how quickly he could move, given his bullet-notched temple and the amount of blood he'd lost. He wasn't breathing too hard, either, which was also surprising. But then, maybe he'd lost weight over the past couple of weeks, and maybe his lungs were healthier, since he hadn't had a whole lot of time to indulge his vices—mainly, food and liquor.

Maybe this job was actually good for him—if it didn't kill him, that was, which was entirely possible. Given the head wound, he might even be a dead man running right now . . .

No point in dwelling on that.

He stopped now to the left of a rock slab halfway up the dike. From here, he could see up around the slab to the nest of rocks from which the shooter had fired on him. He couldn't see the shooter from this angle—he was too low. If he kept climbing another twenty feet, however, he should be able to look down on his right and into the niche.

He drew a deep breath, took the Yellowboy in both hands, and continued climbing, moving carefully but quickly from rock to rock, breathing hard now and sweating, but his heart pumped excitedly. He gained another rock slab, smaller than the one before, and knelt down behind it. He poked up his head and rifle and aimed down into the niche, which was a relatively flat area, six by six feet, the rocks fronting it maybe three feet high, a solid rock slab of ridge jutting straight above it from behind.

"Tarnation," Catfish said, pressing his cheek up close against the rear stock.

The man was gone.

"Chicken-livered devil," Catfish said.

He climbed up and over the rock before him,

then down fifteen feet and straight across the belly of the ridge, until he found himself stepping over more rocks and into the niche itself. Holding the Yellowboy up high across his chest, he looked around. The man had left one cigarette butt and about ten spent shell casings. Catfish could see the impression of one knee, showing where the man had knelt and fired over the rocks on the outside of the niche down the slope before him.

At Catfish, and then at Catfish and Julia Claire.

Catfish saw the boot prints where the man had left the niche. He followed them, stepping cautiously into a five-foot gap in the mountain wall. Holding the Yellowboy straight out before him, the butt plate pressed against his hip, he moved through the dim, natural corridor. It opened onto a rocky, well-shaded slope.

Hooves clattered on rock somewhere ahead and below him. A saddle squawked; bridle chains rattled. Catfish hurried forward and dropped to a knee as he saw a horse and rider trot to the bottom of the ridge. The rider slowed and turned the horse sharply left. The man turned a look over his left shoulder and up the slope at Catfish.

The lawman's jaw dropped.

The man with the round, doughy, pockmarked face and deep-set lunatic eyes set beneath colorless brows was none other than the son of Lucifer who'd put that pesky bullet in Catfish's back—the bullet that caused him to go limp from time to time, the one that had cost him his commission in the Texas Rangers.

Black Taggart!

Taggart turned his head forward, and then he and the horse were gone, the mount's galloping hooves clacking away to silence. Then there was only the breeze and the piping of the night birds flashing silver as they winged through the mountainside's shadows into the light lingering at the crest of the ridge.

Catfish blinked his incredulity. He rubbed his eyes as though to clear them of the phantom they had spied.

Nah, nah. Couldn't be.

Black Taggart still after him after all these years?

He'd figured the man to be dead by now. He was, after all, a few years older than Catfish himself, and by rights, after the life he'd lived . . . after the lives he'd gone through . . . Catfish should have been six feet under years ago. If that really had been Black Taggart, the old Texas regulator and cold-blooded, cowardly, back-shooting devil who'd given Catfish that pill he couldn't digest, what in holy blazes was he doing here?

Well, Catfish thought, still scowling his disbelief down toward the bottom of the slope, the old killer was obviously still trying to scour Catfish from this side of the sod.

Long memory, ol' Taggart had. But no longer than that of Catfish himself.

Catfish cursed, seated a fresh round in the Yellowboy's action, off cocked the rifle, and rested it on his shoulder. He retraced his steps down the ridge to find Miss Claire standing where he'd left her, looking at him with concern in the quickly dying light, hands entwined before her.

"My God, Catfish," she said, "you look as though you've seen a ghost!"

Just then, Catfish's vision blurred. His knees weakened. The world spun around him. "I . . . I think . . . I did . . . !"

He fell and was out like a snuffed wick.

Chapter 24

Catfish's next fully realized sensation—aside from the throbbing pain in his temple—was of warmth from a fire. He could smell woodsmoke, hear the popping of flames, feel a cool cloth competing with the warmth from the fire on his cheeks.

A woman's soothing voice said, "Too much blood, Catfish. Lost too much blood. We're going to have to sew that wound closed . . ."

Catfish groaned, opened his eyes. The lovely woman stared down at him, the flames of a small fire dancing across her cheeks, glinting in her bottomless brown eyes. He lifted his head a little, looked behind him, and realized he was resting against his saddle. He vaguely remembered hearing the clomp of hooves. Just as vaguely, he remembered Miss Claire unsaddling Jasper, who had apparently returned sometime between Catfish passing out and the lady gathering wood and building a fire near where he'd fallen. It was a good place, sheltered by rocks and sotol cactus, a few dusty cedars.

Catfish's gear was piled around the fire, beyond

which lay near-total darkness. Silence lay over the land. Catfish could see the firelight reflected in the eyes of Jasper standing nearby, untied and unhobbled, apparently, regarding his rider dubiously, maybe a little worriedly. If Black Taggart returned, the loyal mount would alert Catfish.

Miss Claire pulled the cool, damp cloth away from Catfish's head and picked up a worn leather wallet. "I found this in your saddlebags."

"My . . . my sewin' . . . kit," Catfish wheezed out.

"Yes—a needle and catgut. I'm going to stitch that wound closed."

"Aw, heck. No need." Catfish placed his hand over the wound. "It's just a notch."

"It's more than just a notch; I can't get the bleeding stopped. I'm going to sew it closed for you," the lady added, putting some insistent steel in her voice.

Catfish studied her curiously, speculatively, as she removed the needle from the baize-lined kit, as well as a length of catgut thread he used for just such occasions as this—when he was out on his own and needed his hide stitched shut, which used to happen far too often. Looked like it was starting anew again. That's what toting the badge would do for a feller . . .

Maybe he'd been better off retired. Maybe not.

Catfish cleared his throat and asked the question that had been weighing heavy on his mind. At least the one that had been weighing heavy before he'd been distracted by the ambusher's bullet. *Black Taggart.* Imagine that. He almost thought he might have dreamt the man from the foggy, dreamy mists of time.

But no—he'd seen him, all right.

"Why were you followin' Eldon Ring, Miss Claire?"

She sighed as she removed a stick from the fire and turned the needle through a slender red-and-blue flame rising from it, flickering, sending up small cinders that flashed out in the darkness above the fire. "It's a long story, Catfish. Let me sew that wound closed, and then I'll tell you about it." She regarded him with gravity, narrowing one pretty eye. "You're going to be a mite surprised—I warn you."

"At my age, I can't be surprised by much no more."

"Oh, you think not? Wait and see."

She'd been right.

He was more than a little surprised. He took a pull from the bottle he kept in his saddlebags—strictly for medicinal purposes, of course. He needed it not only to assuage the tooth-gnashing ache in his temple, but, after she'd sutured the gash closed, the shock the woman's story had inflicted on him.

He pulled the bottle down and looked at the woman, who was cleaning the needle with a cloth and returning it to the sewing wallet. "So . . . you . . . so your name's not really . . . ?"

"Julia Claire—no." She drew another deep breath as she closed the wallet and returned it to the burlap bag she'd found it in. "It's Sylvia Jones from Baltimore." Suddenly her accent was gone as she added, "My English accent is as fake as the rest of me."

"Well, I'll be . . ." Catfish sat up a little high against his saddle, astonished by the woman's improbable story, as well as by the disappearance of the accent he'd become so accustomed to hearing in her voice.

It was definitely a night for surprises.

"I married Sergei Zhukovsky—a con artist from Russia. He embezzled thousands from my father, sent him to an early grave. My mother followed my father to the grave soon after from heartbreak." Miss Claire . . . or Miss Jones . . . or whoever in blazes she was . . . lifted each hand in turn to brush tears dribbling slowly down her cheeks from eyes shiny with barely bridled emotion. "I was bound and determined to get that money back from that hideous man who'd mocked my rage at him for what he'd done to my family. Then, like I said, he caught me in his office and would have killed me if I hadn't . . . hadn't . . ."

"Yes, I heard," Catfish said. "You laid into him pretty good, sounds like."

"I thought I'd killed him. I *hoped* I'd kill him! Then suddenly I'm kidnapped, hauled into the desert in the dark of night, and there he was!"

"That was him, this Zhukovsky, ridin' out of Wolfwater with them other three jaspers?"

"Yes. They're his henchmen."

"Seen 'em around town," Catfish said musingly. "Always meant to shake 'em down a bit, find out what they were doin' givin' the Lone Star the evil eye, but me an' Brazos . . . we been so busy."

"Yes, your hands have been full, Catfish."

"And Grant Dragoman hired Eldon Ring . . . to sort of rub your husband and his henchmen off your trail, so to speak . . . ?"

"Yes, so to speak. Oh, God!" Miss Claire—Catfish would never know her by any other handle than Julia Claire—bowed her head and placed her hands over her face in shame, sobbing. "What you must think of me!"

"Now, now . . ."

She removed her hands from her face and regarded him in horror and exasperation. "My entire life here in Wolfwater has been a sham!"

"Don't worry," Catfish said, reaching out to give her arm a reassuring squeeze. "No one else in town need ever know."

She frowned at him, incredulous. "You mean . . . you won't tell?"

"Heck no. What folks don't know won't hurt 'em."

"Oh, thank you, Catfish!" She threw her arms around him and buried her face in his neck, hugging him tightly, with great relief and affection.

Catfish was so taken aback by the gesture, he wasn't sure how to react. Should he return the hug? He'd never been so well treated by such a beautiful lady. He'd just started to raise his hand toward her shoulders when she pulled away from him suddenly and gazed into his eyes. "Still . . . you'll know . . . what a charlatan I am. That I sent a killer to murder my husband."

"The way I see it," Catfish said, "you didn't have much choice. Sounds like this Zhukovsky is one powerful feller. Sounds a little"—he pressed an index finger to the side of his head—"messed up in the ol' thinker box as well. One sick feller. Torturing you so. Doin' his best to financially break you and ruin your standing in Wolfwater."

"Oh, God!" she said, placing her hands on her arms in renewed terror and returning her gaze to Catfish. "What about . . . what about him?"

"You leave Zhukovsky up to me," Catfish said, narrowing one eye at her with certainty. "If I see him and his three henchmen in town again, they won't be in town much longer. In fact, they might not even be on this side of the sod much longer."

"This is going to sound awful," Miss Claire said, "but I wonder why Mr. Ring proved to be so . . . so . . ."

"Incompetent?" Catfish finished for her. "He was never in the top tier of frontier regulators."

"I wonder why Grant Dragoman hired him, then?"

Catfish stretched his lips back from his teeth and

nodded slowly, pensively scratching his neck. "Yeah, that's funny, ain't it?"

Miss Claire looked at him speculatively, then cast that questioning gaze into the fire. She narrowed her eyes as she said, "If I don't pay him . . . Sergei . . . he'll ruin me. You can kick him out of town, but he'll spread the word of who I am . . . who the owner of the Lone Star Outpost . . . really is."

"You know what, Miss Claire?"

She sighed. "Oh, please, Catfish—after all we've been through together, don't you think it's time you called me Julia?"

Catfish winced, rubbed his big, thick hands on his trousered thighs. "That'll take some practice, but I reckon I can give it a shot." He gave a dry chuckle.

"Please try."

"All right, then"—again he chuckled, brushed a fist across his nose—"Julia it is. Uh . . . as I was sayin', uh, Julia, I don't really think anyone in this town, includin' good Mayor Booth or Preacher Elmwood or pious Widow Kotzwinkle, is gonna give a good rat's a . . . er, I mean . . . give a good ding dang about who you were before you moved here to Wolfwater. Or what you did to that crazy fool, Zhukovsky. No, sir . . . er, ma'am—I mean, *Julia*—once folks are out west, they're sort of protected by everyone else out here, because most of them come from pasts back east that they ain't totally proud of, neither."

Julia looked at him, incredulous. "Certainly not Reverend Elmwood."

"You'd be surprised."

"I can't imagine."

"Heard he was runnin' from a little trouble involving him and a deacon's wife from Cincinnati."

"No!" Julia paused, her eyes searching his. "Well, but certainly not the widow."

"Kotzwinkle? Heard she once ran a house of ill repute in Leadville, Colorado!"

"Oh, my god!" Julia covered her mouth with both hands, aghast.

Seeing her smile devilishly behind her hands, Catfish chuckled. "See there? You got nothin' to worry about."

Julia had a good laugh behind her hands, then lowered her hands slowly, sobering, a grave cast returning to her eyes. "So I did all that for nothing. Discuss the situation with Grant . . . have him hire that incompetent killer . . ."

"Don't worry about it," Catfish said. "I've done a lot worse for lesser reasons."

Julia smiled at him warmly, almost intimately. "Maybe you could tell me about it some—"

A sudden roar from out in the darkness cut her off.

"What was *that?*"

The cry echoed around the canyon they were in, dwindling as the echoes vaulted toward the stars.

"That, my dear," Catfish said, reaching for his rifle, "was a wildcat."

Julia gasped as she stared fearfully into the outer darkness.

Jasper had turned to stare in the same direction, whickering deep in his chest and giving his tail quick, anxious switches.

Catfish probed the darkness straight west of the camp with his own eyes and pumped a live round into the Yellowboy's action. *Not again*, he thought. *Not another blame panther. If it weren't for bad luck—with pumas, anyway—I'd have no luck at all.*

Haltingly Julia said, "But it's . . . a long ways off . . . isn't it?"

"Oh, yeah, yeah," Catfish said reassuringly, hoping his words didn't ring as hollow to her as they did to his own ears.

The roar came again, a little louder this time.

Again, Jasper whickered and shifted his feet around.

Julia jerked her worried gaze to Catfish. "That sounded closer."

Catfish heaved himself to his feet, wincing against the sting in his noggin. He tossed a stout, knotted branch on the fire. "Not to worry, Julia. The fire will keep him . . . or her . . . away."

Julia edged a little closer to the fire as she returned her gaze into the darkness, in the direction from which the mountain lion's roar had come.

"Do you have a gun?" Catfish asked her.

Julia fumbled for a pocket pistol from a saddlebag pouch and held it a little uncertainly in both hands. "Yes!"

Catfish glanced at the short-barreled .38, then crouched to pull a spare .44 from a pouch of his own saddlebags. He gave it to her, saying, "Take this one, instead . . . just in case."

He turned and began striding slowly off into the darkness.

"Where are you going?" Julia asked, her voice trembling.

"Just gonna look around a bit."

"Catfish, stay by the fire!"

The problem was, he knew that not all wildcats were repelled by fire. Some, especially those who'd acquired a taste for human blood, a rare delicacy for such a beast, would risk the flames for such a succulent meal. The only things wildcats enjoyed more than the taste of man . . . or woman . . . were horses. As though Jasper had just had the same thought, the horse whinnied shrilly, pitching, clawing his hooves at the dark sky, dropped back down to all four, swung around, and galloped off into the darkness, north of the camp.

"Oh, no!" the lady cried.

"That's all right," Catfish said. "I hate to say it, but ol' Jasper might lead the cat away from us." He immediately felt guilty for the notion; no horse had ever been more loyal to Catfish than Jasper. But better the loyal stallion than Catfish himself or the lady.

"Just stay close to the fire, Julia," Catfish said as he strode slowly away from the flames, hearing the clatter of Jasper's hooves dwindle into the starry night.

The roar came again. Again, it was louder than before. Previous roars had issued from the darkness straight out ahead of Catfish, to the west. This roar had come from ahead and slightly left of before.

Catfish stopped and probed the darkness in that direction.

Behind him, he could hear Julia's trembling voice saying, "Oh . . . oh . . . oh . . ."

He continued forward, heading in the direction from which the last roar had come. He walked slowly down a rocky slope, dark boulders rising around him, as well as tufts of spiked desert scrub and cactus. When he'd walked maybe fifty yards from the camp, he found himself in a narrow arroyo.

Again, the roar came.

Catfish's heart leaped in his chest.

The snarling, angry cry had come from just ahead, on his right.

He turned in that direction, aiming into the darkness, and saw the dull yellow glow of two cat eyes staring at him with flat menace from between two large rocks.

Chapter 25

The Winchester bucked and roared in Catfish's hands.

The first bullet hadn't exploded from the chamber, however, before both glowing orbs disappeared in the darkness.

Catfish slid the Yellowboy slightly to the right and sent two more rounds caroming into the darkness, feeling deeply frustrated when he heard no grieving cry that would have told him at least one of his rounds had hit its target. He jacked another round into the rifle's breech, moved forward across the arroyo, and slowly climbed the bank. He moved through the prickly brush and swung to his right, the direction he thought the cat had retreated to, almost as though it had known Catfish had been about to start firing at it.

The cat couldn't have known that.

Could it?

Some cats were savvy. Especially if they'd had run-ins with other men before. An old hunter for the Rangers had once told Catfish he'd believed panthers—the old frontiersmen's name for wildcats—knew the smell of gun oil and took precautions accordingly.

Catfish stole along the curving bank of the arroyo, right index finger curled against the trigger, right thumb worriedly caressing the cocked hammer. His pulse drummed in his ears, aggravating the ache in his head. He could smell the blame thing. It was the sickly sweet stench of something wild. Wildcats carried that stench like no other animal Catfish had ever encountered, save grizzlies, which he'd tangled with a couple of times in his past, ruining a couple pairs of good drawers before he'd finally gotten the better of the beasts. This had been down around the border country, before the Anglo ranchers and hacendados had hunted most of them out of that country along the Rio Grande.

There was a snapping sound ahead and to his left. It was followed by a low, guttural moaning.

Catfish turned sharply and fired into the darkness.

Again, no sign his round, too hastily fired, had hit its mark.

Dang, Catfish thought as he moved slowly in the direction from which the last two sounds had issued, *it's almost like the consarned beast is luring me toward it. As though* it *was hunting* me*!*

He moved slowly through scattered oaks, mesquites, cedars, and cacti of all shapes and sizes. The rocks were smaller here, but they'd still offer cover to a skulking puma. As he moved up and over a low knoll, he pivoted each way on his hips, making sure the beast hadn't worked around behind him. At the bottom of the knoll, he stopped suddenly.

That sickly sweet odor—sort of like the stench of an overfilled thunder mug.

Catfish tightened his finger on the trigger, looking

around wildly, heart tattooing a war rhythm against his aged ticker.

Where in blue blazes . . . ?

Then he saw those two spherical yellow glows again. Up high on his right. Then he saw the rest of the big beast outlined against the starry night—the big head with triangular ears and long, rangy, muscular body lounging on a stout branch of a big post oak. The two yellow glows flickered as the beast blinked. Then its mouth opened, and the ensuing, enraged roar filled Catfish's head as he took two stumbling steps backward and fired once, twice, three times.

He heard the grieved snarl and closed his eyes, waiting for the big beast to land on top of him as the last one had done. Because, regarding wildcats, at least, that was how his luck was going.

But there was only a very loud, ground-jarring thump, one more groan, and silence.

Catfish opened his eyes.

The big cat lay at his feet, sort of curled up on its side.

It opened and closed its powerful jaws, as though with a yawn. Then its mouth closed, the cat gave a deep chuff, rested its head down between its front paws, and lay still, both half-open, glowing eyes staring at the tips of Catfish's worn boots.

Catfish sighed.

"I'll be hanged," he said.

A woman's scream sounded from back in the direction from which he'd come.

Catfish wheeled. "What in the love of Sam—"

Julia screamed again, shrilly, then screamed: "Catfish! Help!"

"Lawdie, Catfish said as another cat's roar cut

through the night. He broke into a heavy-footed run, the jarring making his head ache miserably. "There . . . there must be . . . *two cats!*" he muttered, wheezing, sucking air into his lungs as he urged his overweight old self into more speed, holding the rifle up high across his lumpy chest.

He ran hard, weaving through the rocks and brush. His lungs felt on the verge of exploding as he ran up the slope. Ahead and above him, he could see the fire's pulsating glow.

"Law . . . law . . . law!" he repeated, exasperated at his bad luck with wildcats.

Again, the lady screamed.

The cat lifted a growling, snarling wail.

Catfish's heart leaped into his throat. Rising higher on the slope, bringing his and Julia's camp in the nest of rocks into view ahead of him, he saw between the boulders, silhouetted against the fire beyond them, the lady standing beside the fire, holding a burning branch in each hand. She was fending off the sidestepping, feinting cat with the branches. The cat was maybe eight feet away from her, swatting at her with each paw in turn, curling the end of its upraised tail.

"Hey!" Catfish called, breathless as he continued climbing the rise. "Hey! Hey! Hey! Hey, there, you mangy critter—come an' get me!"

He couldn't take a shot from where he was, lest he should hit the woman, instead of the panther.

As he'd wanted, the cat wheeled and stood gazing at him with its own eyes resembling miniature torches in the fire's flickering red-orange glow.

"Here, kitty-kitty!" Catfish shouted, dropping to one knee. "Come an' get it, kitty-kitty! A treat just for *you!*"

The cat sat up on its rear feet, lifted its head, and gave a deep-throated, snarling roar. Then it dropped down to all fours, sprang off its rear feet, and broke into a lunging run toward Catfish, who grinned as he pumped another round into his Winchester's breech.

Or tried to.

He ejected his last, spent cartridge and there wasn't another one in the magazine to slide into the breech. He'd snapped off all his caps!

The cat, red eyes glowing, grew larger and larger before him. Catfish could hear the thudding of its dinner plate–sized paws on the gravelly ground, the raking of the air in and out of its bellowslike lungs. He froze for just a second. Then his hands opened. The rifle dropped to the ground. Knowing instinctively he had no time to raise and fire a revolver—the cat was only ten feet away and closing fast, both eyes glowing like coals—he left both Russians holstered. It was also instinct that caused him to slide the big bowie from the sheath on his left hip, behind the cross-draw holstered Peacemaker.

As the cat made its final lunge, Catfish held the bowie in both hands, blade pointed straight up. The cat flung itself against him, impaling its thick neck on the razor-edged blade. It snarled loudly, wickedly, and with great agony as it drove Catfish back off his heels onto his back. He winced as he held both his gloved hands fast around the bowie's handle, feeling the hot blood pour from the open artery onto his own neck and his chest and face. He watched the great jaws open, the long, curved, deadly teeth glinting in the fire's glow. The jaws closed, a couple of those teeth grazing Catfish's nose, as he felt the cat go slack on top of him. The flickering eyes held on

Catfish's eyes as, holding the bowie firmly impaled in the beast's neck, Catfish gave a great, atavistic roar of his own, while using every ounce of strength in his body to heave himself onto his side, rolling the cat off him and onto its back.

Catfish scrambled to his knees, pulled the bowie out of the cat's neck, raised the knife high, and, with another unbridled roar caroming out of his throat, plunged the blade deep into the beast's chest, into its heart so deep he could feel through the knife's handle, through his hands and his arms, the pumping muscle shudder, quiver, buck once, and then fall still.

The cat groaned. Its eyes burned up at Catfish; the light of its wild life dwindled until there was only the reflection of the fire in them. A breath rattled up out of the cat's throat. It turned its head to one side and lay slack beneath him, part of its broad tongue hanging from its mouth.

Catfish stared down at the great, dead cat beneath him.

He looked at both his gloved hands wrapped around the bowie's handle as blood washed up around it to soak the beast's white fur.

The night swirled around him.

He drew a breath, trying to regain his senses. He blinked his eyes. He knew in a vague way he was in shock and needed to pull himself out of it.

Running footsteps sounded to his left. They grew louder until Julia slammed into him from that side, driving him off the cat and onto his back, screaming, "Catfish!" The lady lay on top of him, wrapping her arms around his neck and sobbing into his chest. "Oh, Catfish, I swear, you are the bravest, most capable man I've ever known. My God—you've saved my life!" Her body spasmed as she sobbed against his neck. "Saved my miserable, wretched life!"

"Ah, hell," Catfish said, drawing another breath into his lungs, clearing the fog of excitement from his brain, "it weren't . . . aw, hell—er, I mean *heck* . . . it weren't nothin'." He chuckled, patting the lady's back.

He felt her smile against his neck.

She lifted her head and, smiling into his face, jeweled tears dribbling down her cheeks, said, "I suppose you'd like to get up?"

"Ah, well," he said with another dry chuckle, "only if you want to." He had to admit he'd been in worse positions. He could probably lie here all night with Miss Julia Claire's supple body resting atop his own. Then again, while he might know her by her first name, she was a lady clearly well above his station. And even firmly ensconced in his own lowly station, he *was* a gentleman. Albeit one of lowly and questionable breeding—if such a gentleman exists. "Yeah . . . yeah, I suppose we might."

She smiled at him again, lowered her head, and planted an affectionate kiss on his mouth. Yes, on his mouth. Not on his cheek or nose, but right on the mouth. He stared up at her, somewhat aghast. Her cheeks dimpled again, beautifully, as she flashed her white teeth in another affectionate smile, then pushed off him, rising.

"Here," she said, extending one of her hands to him.

"Whoa," Catfish said, shaking his head to clear it.

What a night. What a day and then a night. His mind rolled over all that had happened. The wild day capped off by Black Taggart, Julia Claire, and yet another wildcat attack.

All *that* capped off by Julia Claire kissing him smack on the mouth!

He accepted the lady's hand. She set her boots in the ground and gave a grunt as she helped heave his too many pounds to his feet.

She gave a ragged sigh, used both hands to slide her long, mussed hair back from both cheeks. "What a night, eh?"

Catfish looked down at the great, dead cat. "Yeah," he said, drawing another deep breath of his own. "What—a—night . . ."

She laughed, then thrust herself against him once more, wrapping her arms around his neck. "Oh, Catfi—"

Her body tensed suddenly.

"Oh!" she cried, just as a rifle roared somewhere in the darkness behind her.

"*Julia!*" Catfish yelled, looking down at her as he felt her fall slack against him and sliding down his chest. He grabbed her arms, holding her against him, yelling once more, *"Julia!"*

Hooves thudded behind her.

A man's voice said, "Oh, hell! NO!"

Another man's voice said, shrill with incredulity, "What did you . . . what did you *do?*"

Julia slumped to her knees. Catfish stared down in shock at her, vaguely hearing a man's hoarse voice yell, "Retreat, you fools! *Retreat!*"

Galloping hooves thudded off into the night.

"Julia!" Catfish cried, dropping to his own knees as the lady slipped out of his hands and fell over on her side. He stared down at her in renewed shock. A shock that was too much for him now, after everything else that had happened. "Oh, Julia—*my God*, what have they done to you?"

His voice, shrill with agony, rocketed around the night.

Chapter 26

Brazos's boots thudded along the boardwalk fronting Nielsen's Apothecary, then fell silent.

Brazos had come to the end of the boardwalk and turned his cautious gaze into the break between the drugstore and a small dry goods store run by Homer Lujack. Lujack was an ex-prospector who'd invested early in Wolfwater, first opening a couple of livery barns, then a lumberyard, and, for the past several years, the dry goods store as well. It was said he'd made even more money when the railroad had come to town, for he'd been one of several men, including the town's mayor, Derwood Booth, who'd owned the land that the rails had been laid on.

A light shone faintly at the rear of the break. It came from a window at the rear of the dry goods store. That was strange. Brazos knew that a storeroom was at the rear of the establishment. Like the rest of the store after eight o'clock in the evening, that part of the store was usually dark.

A dull suspicion rose in the deputy. Lujack or one of his clerks had probably forgotten to blow out a lamp before heading home for the night. Still, Brazos would check it out, make sure no one had broken in to pilfer—what? Sausages? Flour? Some wheels of cheese and bags of coffee? There were other, more attractive shops to rob than Lujack's storeroom, for sure. But Brazos would check it out.

Flipping free the keeper thong from over the hammer of the Colt holstered on his right hip, and tucking his duster back behind the revolver's walnut grips, the deputy stepped off the boardwalk and moved slowly down the break. He stuck close to the shadows on the alley's right side, running his hand along the side of the dry goods store and wincing at the soft crunching sounds his boots made on the gravelly ground.

He stopped beside the window and edged a look around the side of the frame. The window was shut-tered, with glass behind the shutters. Wan, guttering lamplight bled out from between the half-inch gaps in the boards comprising the window coverings. Through the gaps, Brazos saw five men sitting around a card table in the shadowy room lumpy with the sil-houettes of barrels and burlap sacks and sausages and hams hanging from rafters. Cigarette and cigar smoke rose from the table around which the five men had gathered.

Not just any five men, either.

Each was a saloon owner right here in town. Not the cream of the saloon-owning crop, for sure. Some were saloon-owning pimps and gamblers. But re-spected businessmen, just the same.

Hmm, Brazos thought. It wasn't yet one o'clock, which was the curfew he and Catfish Charlie had set for the town's drinking and gambling establish-ments, as well as for its pleasure parlors. Of course, the owners of those establishments had squawked to high heaven over such a limitation to their business, but those were the rules Catfish and Brazos had laid down. They'd all grudgingly agreed, knowing that in the end such a curfew would make the town a safer place, and, also in the end, save them money, since they wouldn't have to make repairs to their establishments after the usual fights that tended to break out in the earliest hours of a new day.

But here they'd gathered in the back of Lujack's Dry Goods, even Lujack himself, apparently playing cards.

Or . . .

No, wait.

No cards lay on the table.

All that lay on the table were five shot glasses, a whiskey bottle, and a wooden ashtray in the shape of a horseshoe.

Brazos slid his head up close to the window. He could hear a low rumble of conversation, but could make out only a few words, here and there, not enough to make sense of what the men were saying. They spoke in low, serious tones, however. Then suddenly there was the squawk of chair legs being raked across the floor, and a man bellowed, "Yeah, well, the men you called in ain't doin' much of a job, are they? Them's that's still alive, that is!"

Brazos turned his head to peer through a crack in the shutters. The man who'd spoken was Ellis Lonetree, owner of the Ace of Spades, a little watering hole on the west end of town. He stood now, fists on the table, leaning forward and glaring pugnaciously at Lujack—a small, gray-headed man in a blue-checked wool shirt. Lujack glared back at Lonetree, one eye narrowed, craggy cheeks reddening.

"They'll take care of 'em—don't you worry. Luck just hasn't been in their favor so far. Soon the way'll be paved . . . an' we'll start hittin' her an'"—he slapped the table suddenly, sharply, making the others, as well as Brazos, jerk with starts—"an' hittin' her hard . . . till she leaves town with her tail between her legs!"

One of the other men turned his head to regard the window suspiciously. Brazos drew his head down quickly. Then one of the men inside said, "Now sit back down, Ellis. An' keep your voice down. This is a *private* meetin', you fool!"

The conversation continued, but the men returned to their previously low, quiet tones. Brazos didn't think he was going to get anything more out of the conversation, so he stepped away from the window and began walking back out of the alley to the main street, lit here and there by flickering oil pots.

As he did, he pondered the information he'd overheard.

"Now ain't that somethin'," he said softly to himself as he approached the alley mouth. "Hittin' *who* hard? Her. Who was *she*?"

And which men weren't "doin' much of a job"?

The men who'd been trying to ventilate Brazos and Catfish?

Could that be the men Lonetree had referenced?

Brazos glanced back down the break toward the wan amber light bleeding out through the cracks between the window shutters. He winced, puzzled, continuing to ponder.

Then he began walking along the side of the street, back in the direction of the jailhouse. "Puzzling," he mused aloud, scratching his bearded neck with an index finger. "Dang puzzlin', for sure . . ."

He passed a couple of saloons still doing a brisk business at this as-yet early hour. When he passed the Black Cat, from which the strains of a polka being played with a piano and a push organ bled out over the wood-framed building's Dutch door, he stopped suddenly, his right hand moving to the handle of the big Colt jutting on his right hip.

He had heard someone or something moving around in the break near the rear of the saloon. There was the scuff of gravel and a low but pained grunt.

He turned to face the murky break, lit here and there by umber lamplight pushing through the saloon's two side windows on the alley's left side, darkly striped by the shadows of the window sashes. Brazos thought he spied movement in the darkness just beyond the light of the second window.

"Who's there?" he called softly.

A man's raking breath sounded. Then, weakly, "Hel . . . help me. I'm hur . . . hurt . . . oh, blazes . . . it *hurts!*"

"What happened?" Brazos called into the shadows beyond the light of the two windows.

"Cut . . . been . . . cut. Robbed!"

Brazos looked around. Anxiety rippled through him. He knew he could be facing a trap. He wished Catfish was here to back his play, but he hadn't seen his partner . . . er, *boss*, he reckoned . . . in hours. Cha'les might have run into trouble his ownself, unless he'd decided to take the day off, return to his cabin, and fish for that consarned gilled varmint that preoccupied him so. So much so, that even when he was napping in the jailhouse, sitting at his desk with his arms crossed on his chest, he'd occasionally bellow the fish's name. "Bubba Jones, you old scudder!" he'd call out, waking himself up with a jerk.

"Help me," came the man's weak, plaintive voice from the darkness at the rear of the alley, before Brazos.

"Hold on." Brazos stepped off the boardwalk and into the break. He moved slowly, cautiously, his right hand closed around the grips of his holstered Colt. He glanced into the two windows as he passed them, making sure no one was crouched in either or both, guns drawn, ready to ventilate him from inside the Black Cat.

All he saw were men standing at the bar or sitting at tables, some with garishly outfitted soiled doves hanging on them. Several men and women were dancing, and two obviously very inebriated men— cowboys from a nearby ranch—were dancing to the piano and push organ, hooking elbows and spinning each other, flouncing in exaggerated imitations of drunk doxies.

Brazos glanced behind him.

Nothing.

He stopped just beyond the light of the second window forming a trapezoid on the gravelly ground. Now he could more clearly see a man moving around on the ground beyond a rock, sage shrub, and stunted cedar. The pale oval of a face turned toward him. He could see gritted teeth as the man raked out, "I need a doctor. I'm hurt bad!"

Brazos took one step forward. "How bad?"

He stopped when the man gazing up at him suddenly broke into a snickering laugh, opening his mouth wide and slitting his eyes. He sobered suddenly and glanced to each side of Brazos and yelled, "Get him, boys! Teach this uppity boy a lesson!"

As the man before Brazos scrambled to his feet, hardening his jaws and gritting his teeth, Brazos saw in the corner of both eyes several man-shaped shadows darting toward him from where they'd apparently been concealed in the shadows at the rear of the Black Cat and the shop on the opposite side of the alley. He wheeled to his left, sliding the Colt from its holster, but no sooner had the revolver cleared leather than a man jumped onto him from behind, bulling him forward into several men approaching from the shadows before him. Fists hammered his face, while the man who'd leaped onto his back, whooping and hollering, drove him to the ground.

On the ground, he was helpless to fend off the kicks and punches to his face, ribs, hips, and legs. He managed to roll over amid the onslaught. He rose to his hands and knees, but before he could heave himself up and try to give as good as he was getting, brusque hands grabbed him from behind, jerked him to his feet, and held him, pinning his arms behind his back. The man behind him yelled, "Hammer him, boys. Hammer this blue tongue silly!"

In the darkness, Brazos couldn't see the fists hammering his mouth, nose, cheeks, and eyes, but that didn't make the savage blows any less real—the warm, metallic-tasting blood issuing from his split lips any less real. An especially powerful fist was rammed mercilessly into his belly. He jackknifed forward with a great *gnahhh!* of expelled air. Hands slipped from his arms and he dropped to his knees, groaning, the shadows and light from the Black Cat's side windows pitching around him.

"That's enough, boys. I think we done what we came here to do." A man crouched beside Brazos, shoved his mouth up close to the deputy's right ear.

"The Black Cat stays open, you understand? No more one o'clock curfew, or what you got here tonight will seem like a warm bath in comparison!"

Brazos could smell the raw whiskey on the man's rancid breath.

He tried to get a look at him, but it was too dark back here; his vision was blurry from the walloping his head had taken in the onslaught. The man's face was a mix of dim light and dark shadows.

There was a grunt. Another fist slammed into the side of Brazos's head. It punched him over sideways, and he lay on his side on the gravelly ground, blinking as he watched the silhouetted figures of the ten or so men who'd assaulted him stride off, up the alley, moving through the umber light of the windows, and then they were gone.

Slipping away like rats in the night, apparently having planned out the beating ahead of time.

A trap.

Brazos had walked right into it.

Rage burned inside him. Rage and humiliation.

He'd walked right into it.

A click sounded beneath the off-key music of the piano and push organ still being played inside the Black Cat. There was a scraping sound, the whine of hinges, and for a few seconds, the music grew louder. Brazos could smell tobacco smoke, whiskey, and cheap perfume in the seconds before the door was closed once more.

A female voice said, "Oh, Lord!"

The smell of cheap perfume grew stronger as footsteps sounded somewhere ahead of Brazos. The girl was coming from the rear of the Black Cat. He could hear the swishing of skirts and then the girl was kneeling beside him, placing a warm hand on the side of his head, over his bloody left ear.

"Oh, Lord!" she said again, louder this time. "Look what they've done to you, dear Brazos!"

Brazos grunted.

He recognized the voice. A doxie who worked in the Black Cat. Cindy May. He'd talked to her a few times when he'd gone into the saloon during his rounds, checking the place out, making sure the customers were behaving themselves. Once, just after he and Catfish had retaken their former positions as Wolfwater lawmen, he'd found a couple of ranch hands roughing the strawberry blonde around, and he'd intervened. They'd sort of been friends since then, him and Cindy May. Exchanging a warm word or two when Brazos entered the place for that look around.

He rolled onto his belly and then gave a loud grunt as he heaved himself up onto his knees. It took some doing to lift his chin from his chest—his head seemed to weigh as much as a wheelbarrow full of ore—but he did it, by God. They hadn't killed him. He was still alive. He might have some busted ribs and a whole lot of aches and pains, but he was still alive, by God.

He'd find them. He didn't care how many there were.

"Oh, my God—look at you!" Cindy said, gently taking his face in her hands. Her light brown eyes, dimly reflecting the light from the windows, slid across his battered countenance. She stretched her lips back from her teeth, shook her head. "Oh, Deputy Brazos . . ."

"Who?" he said, reaching up and taking one of her hands in his. "Do you know . . . who?"

The girl glanced up the alley, cautiously, then returned her gaze to the deputy. "The ringleader's name is Scallion. 'Duke' Scallion." She scowled, shook her head. "He gave me a nasty tattoo on my backside, a few weeks back. Awful man." Again, she gave the surroundings a quick, cautious perusal. "He deals faro at the Yellow Rose every Wednesday and Saturday, starting at noon. I heard he's also a guard at one of the mines."

"Yellow Rose," Brazos raked out, nodding. "Thanks." He drew a deep breath. "Can you help me to my feet, Cindy?"

"Are you sure you should stand? I'd best fetch Doc Over—"

"No, no, no," Brazos said. "I'll be all right. Just need . . . to get on home. Get cleaned up." He tried a smile. "Get some sleep."

Cindy sucked a sharp breath through gritted teeth. "I don't know. You look—"

"I'll be fine," Brazos said, gently draping his left arm across her shoulders. "If I can just get to my feet . . . find my . . . hoss . . ."

The girl grunted as she rose from her heels, helping Brazos to his feet.

"Where's your horse?" she asked.

"Tied . . . in front of the jail office." Standing, Brazos removed his arm from around the girl's shoulders. He shifted his weight from one foot to the other, somewhat surprised he didn't keel over. He took a quick appraisal of his condition. What hurt the worst were his ribs. In other places, he was numb, but he knew that would likely pass in a few hours, and he'd be aching like bloody hell.

For now, however, he thought he could make it over to his horse and back to his cabin.

He felt cold. God-awful cold.

He gave a shiver and looked at the girl regarding him with grave concern. "Can you . . . help me find my gun . . . my hat . . . ?"

"Oh . . ."

She looked around, holding her hair back behind her cheek with one hand.

"Here," she said, and crouched. She surveyed the ground again. "Here's your hat." She crouched once more, straightened, and handed Brazos both his battered hat and his gun.

"Obliged," the deputy said, dropping the Colt in its holster.

He set his hat on his head, gave the girl another grim smile. "Obliged."

He turned and took one step before she grabbed his arm.

"Are you sure you don't want me to help you to your horse, Deputy Brazos?" she asked, frowning worriedly up at him.

He ran his tongue across his cut, swelling lips, then shook his head.

"Nah," he said. "I've hurt myself worse than this falling out of bed."

He chuckled. It was a joke Catfish would have made. He pinched his hat brim to the girl, then made his way slowly up the alley toward its mouth, staggering as though he'd consumed several bottles of Taos Lightning, the notion of which—the painkilling properties of which—seemed right welcoming at the moment.

He hoped he still had a bottle back at the cabin.

Chapter 27

Catfish stared down in shock at the woman lying prostrate before him.

Blood glistened darkly in the starlight on the lower right side of her back.

"Oh, Julia, my lady," Catfish said, placing his hand on the back of her head. "Don't die, lady. Please don't die on ol' Catfish . . ."

A breath rattled in her throat. Her face was turned to one side, her left cheek pressed against the ground. She moaned, moved her head a little.

"Alive!" Catfish said. "You're still alive!"

He sat up straighter on his knees, pondering what to do.

He'd already shoved his neckerchief into the bullet wound, to try and staunch the blood flow, but it didn't appear to be doing much good. More blood was oozing out of the wound to glisten ominously in the starshine.

There was really only one thing he could do.

"Julia, my lady," Catfish said, leaning low to speak gently into her ear, "I'm gonna saddle Jasper and get you to town. Now, the way you're bleedin', the ride might kill you. It's gonna be mighty agonizin', fer sure, but I don't see no other way. I can't leave you an' fetch the doc alone. Not with them three jaspers an' Black Taggart on the lurk. If I go probin' around in that wound with my knife . . . well, it'll just make it worse, an' that's a fact. Your only chance, the way I see it—"

"Catfish." Julia's low, raspy voice cut him off.

"Yes, my lady," Catfish said, placing his gloved hand on the back of her head once more.

"Saddle Jasper an' take me to town," she said, keeping her eyes closed, barely moving her lips. "I'll take my chances with you an' Jasper."

Her lips played at a smile.

"You got it! I'll be right back!"

"I'm not going anywhere."

Chuckling dryly, Catfish leaped to his feet and went scrambling around heavily, breathing hard as he jogged away from the near-dead fire, jerked off a glove, stuck two fingers into his mouth, and whistled. He was weak from blood loss and pain, but was desperate to get Julia to town. He had to whistle several times, stopping and listening, stopping and listening, before he heard the distant rataplan of galloping hooves. The sounds grew louder until Catfish could make out the vague, shadowy outline of Jasper galloping toward him, the horse's silhouette growing larger and larger in the darkness.

Catfish ran over and grabbed his blanket and saddle roll, and when the horse rode up to him, blowing, stomping, and shaking his head against the smell of fresh blood, Catfish tossed the blanket and saddle up onto the bay's back. He tossed his saddlebags up behind the saddle, then hurried over to where Julia lay as before, on her belly; he hoped against hope she was still alive.

He placed his hand on her back, felt the weak flutter of her heart.

At least she was still breathing.

With both hands, he eased her over onto her back and said, "This ain't gonna feel one bit good, but here we go, milady . . ."

He snaked his arms beneath her neck and knees. As he hoisted himself up off the ground, the lady in his arms, she scrunched up her face and said, "Oh, Catfish, it hurts so bad!" She gave a coughing sob.

"I know, dear lady. I know it does."

"Was it . . . was it . . . ?"

"Your wretch of a husband?" Catfish said as he set her up on his saddle, then toed a stirrup and climbed up behind her. "I do believe it was. Him and his three hapless cutthroats. Came back to kill me. Prob'ly heard the shootin' between me an' Black Taggart. Came back, saw me, figured they'd kill me after dark."

He reined Jasper north and put the steel to the horse's flanks.

As the horse snorted loudly and lunged off his rear hooves, Catfish choked back a sob of his own and said, "Ah, milady, that bullet that you got was meant for me!"

"Oh, Catfish," she said, her arms around his neck, burying her face in his chest. "Better me than you!"

"Don't say that!"

"It's true!" She sobbed against his chest, soaking his shirt with her tears. "It's true!"

Suddenly she pulled her face away from his chest and frowned curiously up at him. "Who's Black Taggart?"

Catfish flared a nostril, hardened his jaws. "Just

an' old friend o' mine," he growled. "An' old friend I tend to meet up with again soon . . . kick him out with a cold shovel!" He clucked and touched spurs to Jasper's flanks once more. "Come on there, boy. I know you got more speed than this! Come on—let's get this lady to the sawbones!"

Jasper was surefooted and sharp-eyed. The terrain was uneven, but the horse faltered only a couple of times. Catfish slowed him every quarter mile or so, not wanting to kill him or cause him to go lame. Still, he saw the flickering light of the oil pots of Wolfwater after an hour's ride from the place at the base of the ridge where Julia had been shot. Most of the town was dark, but he was surprised to find that the Black Cat Saloon still appeared open—even now at nearly four thirty a.m.

What was the manager/proprietor Burt Whitaker doing, anyway? The curfew was one a.m., but glancing through the place's large plate glass window as he passed, Catfish saw more than a few customers scattered at the bar and at tables, a bowler-hatted man and a working girl dancing to the clattering of the Black Cat's mechanical piano. A good dozen horses were tethered to the hitchracks fronting the place.

Catfish gave the Black Cat only a passing thought. He had bigger fish to fry—namely, getting the shuddering woman in his arms help from the local medico.

He reined Jasper to a skidding stop out front of the Lone Star Outpost. As he did, he saw three men—two big and burly, one small and slender, all three clad in business suits, but their ties askew—rising from where they'd been sitting on the steps of the broad front veranda. Catfish recognized the smaller man as Julia's manager, Howard Dale. The other two were bouncers.

"Good God!" said Dale, tossing away his cigar and hurrying down the steps. "I was wondering where she was. Her horse returned without her to the livery barn!"

Catfish swung his right foot over his saddle horn and stepped to the ground.

Julia cried out, which she'd been doing during the long, rough run back to town. At least she was still alive.

"No time for explanations," Catfish said, quickly mounting the veranda steps. "She took a bullet in the back." He glanced at the two bouncers standing where they'd been sitting, looking down the steps at Catfish and their obviously ailing boss. "One of you, fetch Doc Overholser! I'll carry her up to her suite. Tell him Julia . . . uh, Miss Claire . . . took a bullet to the back and he's gonna have to dig it out of her!"

"Gotcha!" said one of the beefy men, who lurched into motion, hurrying down the steps and into the street.

"Right this way, Marshal!" Dale said, jogging up the steps ahead of Catfish and pulling open one of the heavy oak doors. "I wanted so desperately to send men out looking for her, but her horse returned after dark, and they had little hope of backtracking it!"

"Long story," Catfish said, moving through the open door.

Unlike the Black Cat, the Lone Star Outpost was following his and Brazos's curfew, he saw. The place was deserted, all the chairs overturned on the tables. Only a few ceiling lamps burned. The big clock on the wall above the doors ticked loudly, woodenly, highlighting the cavernlike, well-appointed saloon's funereal silence.

Breathlessly, Julia moaning in his arms, Catfish climbed the stairs to the third story and hurried down the hall lit by two bracket lamps to the door to Julia's suite.

"That will be locked," Dale said. "Miss Wilkes is in there."

"Still?" Catfish said. Guilt prodded him. He'd been so busy in recent days he'd failed to check on Beth.

"This room is empty, I believe." Dale twisted the knob of the door on the opposite side of the hall from Julia's, thrust the door wide. "Yes," he said.

Catfish brushed past Dale as he moved into the small room furnished sparingly with a bed, a dresser, a washstand, and little else. Velveteen curtains were drawn across the window over the bed.

"Here we go, honey," Catfish said as he eased Julia onto the bed. "The ol' sawbones . . . er, I mean *doctor* . . . is on the way."

Julia did not respond. She appeared unconscious, her eyelids fluttering just a little, hands spasming slightly as pain racked her.

"What happened?" Dale asked, moving tentatively into the room, lacing his hands together, the right one of which bore a gold onyx ring.

Dale was a strange, fussy, little man whose innate formality and neatness seemed in contrast to his profession, which was managing a saloon, gambling parlor, and brothel. Catfish didn't know him, hadn't exchanged more than a handful of words with him. He doubted anyone really knew him. Maybe Julia did. They seemed well suited to each other as business partners, Catfish vaguely thought, since both their pasts were shrouded in mystery.

At least Julia's had been shrouded in mystery. Now almost too much had come to light—at least for him.

Catfish was about to respond to Dale's query, but stopped when the door to Julia's suite *clicked*. Both men turned to watch the door draw open and Beth Wilkes step out, clad in a red velvet robe and elastic slippers—Julia's duds, most likely. The girl still appeared pale and drawn. She wore her unbrushed hair down. She blinked sleepily as she crossed the hall and stepped into the open doorway behind the saloon's manager, scowling with growing concern at the woman on the small bed.

"My God," she said in a voice hushed with awe. "What happened?"

"You'd best go back to your room," Catfish said. He'd drawn a chair up to the bed and had sagged into it. He held one of Julia's hands in his own. "You don't want to see this."

"Miss Julia," Beth said, moving slowly into the room, astonishment glazing her eyes. She looked at Catfish. "What happened?"

"She's been shot," Catfish said.

"Oh, my Lord!" Beth said, her eyes glistening now with sudden tears. She was on the brink of crying.

Catfish was about to rise from his chair and usher her back to Julia's suite when he heard two sets of footsteps on the stairs. Then they were in the hall and the town's doctor, as well as the bouncer who'd summoned him, were standing in the open doorway.

"Good God!" the middle-aged, gray-headed sawbones intoned, eyes widening behind his round little spectacles. Clutching his medical kit before him, Overholser stepped into the room. "Out! Everyone out!"

"You got it, Doc," Catfish said, rising from his chair.

Catfish touched Beth's shoulder, about to usher her out of the room, but then the doctor said,

"Except Beth. She can stay. I'm going to need help."
He looked at Beth still staring down in shock at Julia.
"A woman's help. Can you manage it—do you think
so, Beth?"

Beth turned to him, nodded resolutely. "I can
manage it."

Catfish liked the look in the girl's eye. Maybe helping the doctor with Julia, a woman Beth had come to
love, obviously, would help her dig herself out of the
black hole she'd been in ever since the Thorsons had
killed her father and kidnapped her.

Catfish went out and drew the door closed behind
him.

He turned to the bouncer who remained in the
hall, looking concerned, as the man said in a thick
Irish brogue, "Who in God's green fields would want
to shoot the boss ma'am? I can't imagine her havin' a
single enemy in the world!"

"Long story" was all Catfish said. Even if he wanted
to spill the beans of Julia's shooting, which would
mean spilling the beans about her past as well, he
wouldn't know where to begin. Hopefully, no one in
town would ever know about it. Besides him, that
was. He'd hunt the woman's husband and those
three raggedy-heeled henchmen of his and turn
them all toe-down before they could soil the lady's
reputation.

No telling what they'd do now, having shot her—
the target of their torment—instead of Catfish, whom
they'd apparently wanted out of their way and off
their trail.

He pinched his hat brim to the befuddled-looking
bouncer, who looked as though he were about to
burst the seams of his tailored three-piece suit, and
headed for the stairs. He was worried to death about

Julia, but another concern pushed its way into his mind.

He stopped at the end of the hall and turned back to the bouncer.

"Say, why's the Black Cat still open? Brazos and I spread the word far and wide that no saloons were to be open after one a.m."

"Ah," said the Irishman. "Word has it, he ran into a bit of resistance—in a dark alley."

"Ah, hellfire!"

The bouncer held up his big hand, palm out. "Not to worry. Someone seen him walk out of the alley and climb onto his horse, so he's all right. Probably rode home to rest up a bit."

"Yeah," Catfish said, ramming his clenched right fist into the palm of his left hand. "Who was part of this resistance?"

"That I can't tell ya, Marshal. You'll have to find that out on your own, I reckon." He grinned and pinched the brim of his hat.

No tattler, he.

Catfish grumbled out a curse and headed on down the staircase. He went outside, tied Jasper to a hitchrack, giving the horse's neck an affectionate pat. "Not to worry, you stalwart cuss. Your reward for a job well done ain't far away. I'll take you over to the livery barn"—he slid his Yellowboy from its saddle sheath—"after one more little errand."

Catfish racked a live round into the Winchester's action, off-cocked the hammer, and, holding the rifle down low against his right leg, tramped off in the direction of the Black Cat, spurs clanging angrily.

Chapter 28

The Black Cat was hopping even now after five in the morning, with the dawn showing a pale wash between the peaks of the Rawhide Buttes, east of Wolfwater.

The reason the humble, deep, narrow, mud brick hovel was still open was simple. Customers from the Black Cat had had the "discussion" with Brazos. Likely jumped him in the dark, had him outnumbered.

That was the only way to have a "discussion" with Brazos McQueen. Guilt raked Catfish. He should have been here to back his partner's play. On the other hand, they were both spread thin. Too thin. They needed an additional man or two. They needed two or three in addition to the two old former cowpunchers holding down the jailhouse after regular business hours.

Catfish would like to know just who the men who'd jumped his deputy were. Some were likely to still be in the Black Cat.

He stepped up to the batwing doors, peered over

them and into the light and shadows cast by a dozen
ceiling and bracket lamps. The mechanical piano
was still getting a workout. Two drunk doxies and
three drunk cowboys were dancing near the piano,
which abutted the watering hole's rear wall. Another
dozen were sitting at tables, drinking and playing
cards or bellied up to the bar. A conversational roar
echoed around the room.

There was a particularly lighthearted, jovial air
about the place. Sort of like the inside of a school-
house when the teacher was out back fetching fire-
wood, say.

When the cat was away. Or a maligned curfew was
lifted . . .

Two more doxies were just then coming down the
stairs running up the middle of the building's rear
wall. They were holding up a drunk cowpoke between them. The man's eyes were glassy, and he was
having a hard time keeping his chin from drooping
down against his chest. His hat hung down his back
by a chin thong. He was dragging his heels across the
risers, stumbling. The doxies regarded him and each
other with concern, giving starts each time the man
stumbled.

When the doxies—both very scantily clad, indeed,
their hair in disarray after what had obviously been a
long night of toil—and the cowboy reached the bottom of the stairs, they ushered him across the room,
weaving around tables. The other customers laughed
and made jokes as the pair headed for the batwings.
As they did, the others followed them with their smiling countenances. One by one, and two by two, the
other customers' gazes found Catfish staring in at
them, a hard angry expression on his fleshy mug.

When the girls saw Catfish, their eyes widened.

They slowed their pace, exchanged skeptical glances, then continued to the batwings. Catfish stepped to one side, giving them and the half-conscious cowpoke passage. Once outside, they set the man down on the bench. He promptly fell to one side and drew his legs up, raising his knees to his chest. He closed his eyes and immediately began snoring.

"Long night, ladies?" Catfish said.

They both regarded him sheepishly, then pushed through the batwings and hurried back across the room and up the stairs at the rear, casting cautious gazes back over their shoulders.

Catfish shouldered the Yellowboy as he pushed through the batwings, took one step into the saloon, and stopped two feet in front of the louvered doors clattering back into place behind him. He quickly surveyed the smoky den of iniquity. As he did, the dancers stopped dancing, one of the girls stumbling on a too-high heel and saying, "Ouch!" Catfish had heard her above the piano's maniacal, tinny, automatic playing. The conversational hush in the room had died, however.

Now all the customers stared at Catfish, their smiles and grins gone, replaced by stony, vaguely guilty expressions.

Catfish was glad when the piano wound down to a halt at the end of "Little Brown Jug."

He saw a hand move furtively beneath a tabletop roughly fifteen feet ahead, and to his right. The ringed hand of an obvious card sharp—a dandy with a pencil-thin mustache with curled and waxed ends—he brought the Yellowboy down quickly, drew the hammer back to full cock, and drilled a round into the table before the sharpie could, shattering a shot glass and causing pasteboards, coins, and green-backs to fly.

The man gave a yelp and jerked back in his chair. He turned to glare, red-faced, at Catfish.

"Hands above the table, *friends*!" Catfish barked out as the echoes of the Winchester's report dwindled to silence.

Catfish looked at the beefy bartender Burt Whitaker, who also owned the place. The man was leaning forward, ham-sized, red fists clenched atop his plankboard bar. Catfish narrowed one eye as he said, "What're you doin' open, Burt? You was supposed to close hours ago."

"Now, look here, Catfish!"

"No, you look here, you walleyed son of Satan!" Catfish barked. "Friends of yours might have had a *conversation* with my deputy, but that don't change the rules! Who are they?" He turned to the fifteen or twenty men standing or sitting around the room. He narrowed his eye again with menace. "They still here?"

"No, they ain't still here!"

"Names!"

"You know I can't give you names!" Whitaker barked back at Catfish, glancing cautiously around the room where his customers sat or stood, resembling wax statues. The only movement in the room was the tobacco smoke webbing under the gas lamps hanging from the ceiling, some attached to wagon wheels.

"Don't doubt it a bit," Catfish said. He had a feeling he knew who the culprits were. Likely, a couple of men known as the Logan brothers, who, along with their father, R.J. Logan, owned and operated the Logan Box L–Tumbling 8 Ranch, several miles south of Wolfwater, in butte and brush country. The other culprits were likely several men who rode with them and a couple of townsmen—no-accounts, all. All Black Cat regulars. The Logans and a few men came to town two or three times a week to gamble, carouse with the working girls, and get puking drunk. Catfish had had several in his lockup more times than he could count on both hands. They'd usually slept off their drunks, paid their fines for drunk and disorderly, fetched their horses from a livery barn, and galloped back to their ranch, casting sour looks over their shoulders at Catfish.

They were trouble.

They'd likely gotten drunk here, seen Brazos making his rounds, and decided to set a trap for him.

Catfish should have been here.

He clenched his teeth, barely controlling his rage. He felt like drilling a round through the jowly Whitaker's fat, red face. Barring that, however, he decided to do the next best thing.

"I know I can't make you give up their names," Catfish said, ejecting the spent round from the Yellowboy's breech. It *pinged* and rolled around on the floor near his boots as he stood with his feet spread a little more than a shoulder's width apart. "But I sure can blow off steam!"

"No—wait, now!" Whitaker said, his jaws suddenly hanging, eyes widening in fear. He straightened and, holding both big hands up, palms out, took one step back, saying, "Don't you do it, Catfish!"

As Catfish levered a fresh round into the Winchester's action, grinning devilishly, Whitaker squeezed his eyes shut and turned his head to one side, believing the next round fired here tonight would be through his head. Catfish raised the Yellowboy to his shoulder, aimed toward the bar, and squeezed the trigger.

Whitaker yelped as the .44 round went caroming over his thick, left shoulder to smash into the back bar mirror behind him. Shattered glass rained down over the shelves beneath the mirror, screeching like schoolgirls finding a snake in the privy.

Whitaker turned to gape at the first shattered panel of his beloved mirror. It was the only thing worth a crap in the otherwise rough-hewn establishment. He constantly polished all three wood-framed panels lovingly. BC for "Black Cat" was stenciled in gold leaf into the center of each panel.

Still grinning in ominous delight, Catfish racked a fresh round into the Yellowboy's action and raised the rifle to his shoulder.

"Oh, God, no!" Whitaker bellowed, throwing both hands up again toward Catfish, his dung-brown eyes cast in terror. "Don't you—not again!"

His plea was punctuated by the Yellowboy's roar, sending another round into the polished mirror's second panel, to the right of the terrified barman, whose thin, greasy gray-brown hair hung to his shoulders. The slug drilled into the stenciled monogram. More glass rained until there were only a few shards left in the panel.

Again, Catfish racked a fresh round.

Whitaker screamed girlishly, almost sobbing, as yet another round took out the third and final panel of his beloved mirror.

"Oh, you devil!" Whitaker howled into his beefy left forearm, which he held over his mouth, tears dribbling down his fleshy cheeks from his bereaved eyes. "Oh, you devil!"

As Catfish racked yet another round into the Winchester and turned the gun on the room, making sure none of the customers was taking advantage of his distraction with the mirror to drill one of their own rounds into his back, he said, "Thank you, Whitaker. Comin' from you, you copper-riveted spawn of a back-alley cur, I'll take that as a compliment. Now," he added, raising his voice, "everyone out!"

Everyone in the room scrambled to his feet or jerked into motion. While the remaining two girls in the room went running up the stairs, holding their skirts above their bare ankles, the men stampeded toward the batwings. Only a couple took the time to throw back the last of their drinks or to take finishing drags off their quirleys or cigars.

The gambler who'd been reaching for his pistol cast a flared-nostril glare at the lawman as he, too, headed for the doors.

"Hold on," Catfish said, grabbing the man's arm and turning him around to face him. He was tall and thin with the pale, washed-out pallor of a man who rarely saw the sun. He'd taken the time from his gambling, however, to buy himself a tailored checked suit and red foulard tie pierced by a diamond pin. He probably thought the tony duds impressed his opponents, and that the ladies liked the cut.

Catfish said, "I'll take that." He pulled the man's pistol from its holster. It was a brass-plated, cartridge-firing .38 LeMat, with a twenty-gauge barrel under the smaller one piggybacking it. The pearl grips shone in the gaslight that was now competing with the light of the rising sun. "Hmm," Catfish said. "That's right impressive. I'll hold on to it for you . . . for safekeeping."

"For how long?" the sharpie snapped.

"Till you're dead! Now, get your raggedy behind out of town an' don't you ever step foot in Wolfwater again!"

The gambler's mouth opened to give a retort. Apparently giving it further consideration, however, he closed his mouth, swung around, and hurried through the batwings. Gone.

Catfish turned to the last man left in the place. Whitaker stood behind his bar, hands to his face as he stared in grief and shock at his ruined mirror. "Staying open was a costly mistake. Second only to you letting those jackals rough up Brazos."

Catfish rested the Yellowboy on his shoulder and turned to the batwings. He knew he'd never get the names of the assailants out of the man.

"Who's going to pay for my bar?" Whitaker demanded.

"You are," Catfish growled, and went out.

He slid the Yellowboy into his saddle scabbard, mounted Jasper, and put the tired mount into a slow walk in the direction of the jailhouse. There was a little wagon traffic on the street, but not much. The sun still hadn't cleared the Rawhides. A few shopkeepers were sweeping their stoops and setting goods out on their boardwalks for display. Several nodded to Catfish; Catfish nodded back. He knew most of them, though in the years since he'd turned in his badge and holed up in his old shack with Hooligan Hank, there were several he didn't recognize.

As he and Jasper drew within a few yards of the jailhouse, he reined in sharply. He'd just seen a man draw his head suddenly back from the adobe brick building's far front corner. Catfish had glimpsed a red shirt and the gleam of a gun in the man's hand as well.

"Giddyup, boy," Catfish said, and clucked Jasper ahead.

He drew his bone-gripped .44 from its holster and clicked the hammer back with a weary sigh.

Would the trouble never end?

Chapter 29

Catfish rode to the far front corner of the jail-house, checked Jasper down, and extended his Colt straight out in front of him, aiming down the jailhouse's north side. The man he'd just seen ran around the rear corner, disappearing for a second before he reappeared. At least his right hand reappeared. So did the revolver in that hand, aimed toward Catfish, who could see the man's head now, as well as the front brim of a low-crowned black hat.

Catfish fired, blowing the hat off Juan Montana's head a quarter second before the kid's Colt spoke, flames lapping from the barrel, sending the bullet high and wide as the kid yelped and stumbled backward. He disappeared until Catfish gigged Jasper into a run down the side of the jailhouse. At the rear corner, he checked the horse down again and saw the kid on his butt, just then sitting up and reaching for the silver-chased Colt he'd dropped.

Catfish triggered another round into the ground an inch to the gun's right, and the kid drew his hand back with another yelp, clutching it to his chest and staring down at it worriedly, likely counting his fingers. As he did, Catfish swung down from Jasper's back, holstered his Colt, walked over, and slapped the kid's young, handsome mug, first with the palm of his hand and then with the back of it.

"What a little tinhorn demon," Catfish said. "What were you about to do—bust Skinny out of jail so you could take him out in the country and hang him?"

"It's better than he deserves!"

"Were you gonna shoot the jailer I hired, too?"

The kid didn't seem to know how to answer that. He let the question go, briefly looking sheepish, then glared up at Catfish and said, "He killed my sister. My own flesh and blood! He deserves to die! Raven deserves to be avenged!"

He let out a strangled sob, and his brown eyes glistened with emotion as he continued to glare up at Catfish.

"Look, kid," Catfish said, moderating his tone and hooking his thumbs behind his cartridge belt, "I can't let you do that. I know Skinny deserves rough justice, but I run things in this town. If you were to go in, shoot my jailer, and hang Skinny, you'd hang, too. Now, what would be the point of that?!"

"You don't understand, lawman! He killed my sister! She was all I had in this world! Now she's gone—because of *him*!"

"You don't think I know what it's like to lose somebody? Well, I do. I lost my entire family—Ma, Pa, two sisters, and an older brother to the Comanche up by Palo Duro Canyon, on our little shotgun spread. I was only seven years old. My ma sent me to hide in some shrubs, and from there, I watched the whole thing. Believe me, I saw every detail . . . remember every detail. I hear the screams of my family dang near every night, wake in a cold sweat dang near every night!"

Catfish paused, shook his head. "Don't tell me I don't know what it's like to lose someone. Most do. You've just joined the party, kid. And don't think I haven't seen you skulkin' around town, keepin' an eye on me an' Brazos, looking for your opportunity to bust into the jailhouse. I have just been too busy to slap you down about it. But now I am!"

He grabbed the kid's gun, slid it behind his cartridge belt; then, using the young man's collar, he jerked the kid to his feet.

"Hey, what do you think you're doin', you old scudder?"

"Chargin' you."

"For what?"

Catfish gave him a shove, sending him back around the jailhouse's rear corner. "You took a shot at me, ya tinhorn! That's the attempted murder of a lawman. And then you insulted me, to boot!"

Catfish gave the kid another shove, up along the side of the jailhouse. "Get your hands up!"

The kid did not comply, just kept walking straight ahead. He turned his head slightly to one side, stealing a look behind him. Catfish knew he was considering making a move on him. No sooner had the thought passed through Catfish's brain than the kid, indeed, whipped around, eyes glittering devilishly in the lemony light of the sun just then clearing the Rawhides.

Catfish rammed his right fist across Montana's left temple.

His prisoner grunted and dropped to a knee.

"That'll get you even more time." Catfish jerked him to his feet again, gave him a hard shove around the jailhouse's front corner. "You'll be spending plenty of time with Skinny, all right. Time right here until the judge comes—don't rightly know what's keeping old Hangin' Hiram—and time aboard the judge's jail wagon manned by two deputy U.S. marshals. You an' Skinny will have plenty of time to palaver about your fates!"

"I'll strangle him through the bars!"

"No, you won't." Catfish shoved him up the steps of the jailhouse's front stoop. "It's just that I'm startin' to see more similarities than differences in your characters. A pair of young tinhorns who can't mind your manners or your betters!"

Another hard shove sent Montana stumbling into the jailhouse; Catfish, tight on his heels, kicked the door shut behind him. Despite his rough tone, he felt sorry for the kid. He'd hold him for a few days, and when he thought Montana was no longer a threat, he'd let him go.

"What in holy blazes is goin' on, Catfish!" exclaimed Harold Simmons, one of the two jailers Catfish and Brazos had hired to keep an eye on their prisoners while the two lawmen tried to get the lid back on the town. "Heard the shots, an'—"

"We have another prisoner, Harold. You can go on home now. Tell Miriam hello." Miriam was the wife of the tall, elderly, stoop-shouldered gent wielding a double-barreled shotgun in front of Catfish's desk.

"Don't mind if I do."

While Catfish shoved his prisoner toward the four cells lined up at the room's rear—only two of which were now occupied, the other prisoners having paid their fines—Simmons set the shotgun on the desk, donned his hat, and headed for the door. Skinny glared through the bars of his cell on the far side of the block, and said, "*Him!* What'd you bring him here for? You know he wants me dead!"

The cell next to Skinny's held two bearded prospectors; they'd gone head-to-head in a back alley over a claim dispute, with each man wielding a pickax. They stared incredulously through the bars at Catfish and his new prisoner. Neither had money to pay their ten-dollar fines, so Catfish was still considering what to do with them. Probably send them out to muck out livery barn stalls or to sweep out saloons for a few days. He just hadn't gotten around to it yet.

"Shut up or I'll throw him in your cell and you two can work it out your ownselves," Catfish shot back at the thin killer. "It'll be cheap entertainment!"

"That would be just fine with me!" Montana barked over his shoulder at Catfish before casting an enraged look at Skinny.

Skinny blanched.

"Yes, I know it would; I know it would," Catfish said, opening the door of the cell on the opposite side of the block from Skinny. "Gotta admit I wouldn't mind seein' that. Better'n he deserves."

He shoved Montana into the cell and closed the door. He hung the ring of keys on a ceiling support post, then walked over to his desk and sagged into his chair. He gave a weary sigh and tossed his hat onto the desk, over the shotgun Simmons had left there.

He was blown out. Worn to death, felt like. But he had more to do, and he was on duty today, since Brazos was likely out for the day. Catfish wanted to check on Brazos, but first he had to stable Jasper. Then he wanted to go back over to the Lone Star Outpost and check on Miss Julia's condition. His eyes were heavy, however. Blurry with weariness. Exhaustion weighed like an anvil on his shoulders.

He glanced at Montana, glaring through his cell bars toward Skinny, who'd slumped onto his cot, ignoring the brother of the girl he'd killed. The two prospectors, standing in their own cell between Montana and Skinny, looked apprehensive as all get-out, as though they feared they might get caught in a cross fire.

Catfish chuckled at that. He opened a desk drawer, pulled out the bottle, and splashed a liberal shot of whiskey into his cracked stone mug. He returned the bottle to the drawer, then got up and walked over to the stove sitting in the middle of the room. Simmons had left a pot of gurgling coffee on the warming rack. He filled the cup with the coffee and took a few bracing swallows. Then he retrieved his hat, hitched up his pants and cartridge belt, told his prisoners to behave themselves, and went out.

As he led Jasper over to the livery barn in which he lodged the mount, he went over all his problems, which included his continued taming of Wolfwater, once more. He needed to find the men who'd stomped the stuffing out of Brazos, the men who'd shot Julia, including her vile and obviously poison-mean Russian husband. He also needed to find the mysterious Black Taggart, who'd apparently decided to snuff Catfish's wick once and for all.

Why?

Had he just ridden through town and seen that Catfish was back in commission? Maybe instead of letting Catfish get crossways with him for the back-shooting varmint having lodged a bullet up close to Catfish's spine, he'd decided to rid his back trail of him. Maybe he was paranoid, believing Catfish was looking for him, and he was tired of having to look over his shoulder.

Whatever the reason, Catfish was going to take the man out *before* Taggart could take Catfish out. If he was still in the area, that was. Maybe after last night, he'd decided to hightail it once more.

Probably not. Since he'd come after Catfish again, Catfish had to assume he'd stay to finish the job. That meant he, Catfish, would have to keep looking over his shoulder. Though he would be suspicious, even if Black Taggart wasn't after him—what, with all the hard cases looking to perforate his and Brazos's hides for whatever reason.

Walking back over to the Lone Star in the full flush of morning, he felt chicken flesh rise across his back, up high between his shoulders. It was as though some witch had drawn a target on his back with a cold finger. He looked around carefully, his still-keen gaze scouring all nooks and crannies along both sides of the street from which a would-be assassin might be drawing a bead on him.

He stepped over the newly laid, silver rails glistening brightly in the morning sun, and cursed once against the coming of the iron horse as he took one more look around. Something moved on a rooftop behind him. He saw a hatted head—a gunman hunkered down up there, ready to trigger a shot!

Catfish gave a grunt as he unsnapped the keeper thong from over his .44 and jerked the revolver out of its holster. Crouching, spreading his feet for better balance, he raised the piece up toward the roof of O'Malley's Gun Repair and started to tighten his right index finger on the trigger.

Just as suddenly, he drew his finger away from the trigger.

More of the hatted head had come into view. The head was moving, the man's face in profile, as the man was working a crowbar up under a shake. Nails bristled from between Gabriel Montoya's lips, beneath his flowing black mustache, as the man winced with effort as he jerked down on the crowbar's handle. The shake leaped up, out of the roof, and Montoya grabbed it before it could slide down the steeply pitched roof.

Catfish lowered the Colt with a relieved sigh.

The Mexican roofer was repairing some shakes on the establishment's roof.

Catfish's heart, which had started racing the moment he'd seen the hat, now slowed. The beefy lawman looked around, feeling the blood of embarrassment rise in his fleshy face. Several passersby, including two men in business suits and bowler hats, were regarding him sheepishly. Two bosomy old hens in flowered dresses, shawls, and big picture hats—two ladies from Widow Kotzwinkle's Women's Sobriety League—were just then passing on the boardwalk fronting the gun repair shop, arm in arm, woven baskets hooked over their free arms, regarding Catfish with incredulous scowls on their bloated, deeply lined faces.

As they continued their stroll, one turned to the other, tipped her head back, and raised her fist, thumb extended toward her lipless mouth in a jeering pantomime of a man taking a drink. A big drink, which Catfish suddenly needed. They laughed, then stepped off the boardwalk, paused to let a farm wagon pass on the cross street, and continued walking in the direction of the haberdashery on the street's other side.

Blood continuing to burn in Catfish's cheeks, he quickly pouched his pistol, removed his hat, ran his arm across his forehead, then returned the topper to his head and continued across the consarned rails to the other side of the street.

Was he losing his nerve?

Well, heck, who wouldn't get a little jumpy after all the lead that had been flung his way?

Silently cursing the judgmental, jeering SOB who lived in his head, he climbed the broad steps fronting the Lone Star Outpost, nodded to a couple of Julia's beefy bouncers standing on the stoop, talking in their Irish accents, smoking fat cigars, and . . . what? Were they regarding him with mocking derision?

Never mind them!

He pushed through the heavy oak doors and, a minute later, stopped on the steps rising to the saloon/brothel/gambling parlor's third story as Doc Overholser suddenly appeared on the steps before him, black leather medical kit in his hand. He had a grim expression on his pale face, his lips set in a straight line beneath his carefully trimmed gray mustache.

"Doc . . . ?" Catfish said, squeezing the varnished wooden rail on the right side of the carpeted stairs.

"She's alive," the medico said. He wagged his head gravely. "I couldn't get the bullet out. It's too close to her heart."

"Oh . . ."

The spare-framed doctor in his customary gray suit stopped on the riser just above Catfish. "She's lost a lot of blood. She's going to be weak for a good many days. I told Beth to try to get as much broth down her as she can. I'll stop by again this evening."

"Is she . . . gonna . . . ?"

The doctor, who'd started down the stairs again, stopped and glanced over his shoulder at the lawman. "Die? Only time will tell. She's conscious. You can go up and have a word with her, but only for a minute. What she needs now is sleep and food." The doctor's scowl deepened. "Who on God's green earth shot her? What was she *doing* out there?"

Catfish didn't know what to say, except "Later, Doc."

The doctor gave his head a single, slow wag, then continued down the stairs.

Heavy with worry, Catfish watched him cross the saloon's main drinking hall, sparsely populated this early hour of the day, and push out through the doors and become absorbed by the West Texas sun's lens-clear light.

Catfish gave the rail another frustrated squeeze, then continued on up the stairs and into the hall. He tapped lightly on the door.

"Who is it?" Beth Wilkes asked in her soft, low voice.

His hat in his hand, Catfish opened the door and poked his head into the room. "Me, honey."

Beth was sitting in the chair drawn up close to the bed. A water basin sat on the table beside the bed. Beth was just then wringing out a cloth in the basin. Running the cloth gently across Julia's forehead, she said, "Hello, Catfish."

Julia's open eyes regarded Catfish warmly, though there was the darkness of pain in them as well. Her mouth corners quirked up with an attempt at a smile, and she said even more softly than Beth, "Hello, Catfish. Come." She blinked slowly and tried to quirk another smile. She slid a pale hand out from under the bedcovers to gesture at Beth. "Meet my nurse."

Moving slowly into the room, Catfish regarded Beth and smiled.

He was surprised to see her not wearing the night-clothes of before. She wore what he assumed was one of Julia's dresses—a lime-green affair trimmed with white lace. She wore a gold brooch around her neck, and her dark brown hair, which shone with a recent, thorough brushing, was pulled back in a queue and tied with a ribbon that matched the dress.

The young woman's eyes were brighter than before, and she'd lost some of her deathly pallor. Her fingernails, formerly bitten to the nubs, were now touched with a healthy pink. Julia's ill health had apparently distracted Beth from her own. She had a purpose, albeit a grim one, in nursing her benefactor back to health.

Catfish returned his gaze to Julia, who looked frighteningly pale as she rested her head back against the pillow and her own brown hair, which made a thick, lovely nest for it. She slid her right leg close to the left one beneath the heavy covers and gently patted the bed beside her.

"Come," she said, "sit."

"Ah . . . I don't know if I should. Doc says you need your rest."

Julia tried another smile. A bemused light shone in her eyes, briefly. "I need my friends more." She glanced at Beth. "My only two in the world."

Chapter 30

"Ah, hell . . . er, I mean *heck* . . . Julia," Catfish said, inwardly condemning himself for his language once more—had he been raised by wolves?!—"everybody loves you."

She blinked, wrinkling the skin above the bridge of her nose. She shook her head, and, with a glance at Beth, who continued to swab her forehead with the cool cloth, and then at Catfish, said, "But you two are my only friends." She patted the bed again. "Sit down."

"Ah, heck," Catfish said, chuckling, holding his hat over his heart, his big fingers worrying the edges of the brim. "I might break it, send us both tumbling."

Beth looked up at him, smiling.

Julia chuckled, then frowned again. "Please . . . don't make me laugh, you lummox."

"All right, then; all right, then." Chuckling, Catfish eased his considerable weight down on the edge of the bed. It squawked and sagged deeply, but he didn't think it would break.

Julia looked seriously up at him and Beth. "I have something important I want to say."

Catfish shared a curious glance with Beth. Turning back to Julia, he said, "What's that, honey?"

"I've sent for an attorney. I've never had a will. Didn't see much need for one. But now . . ." She looked from Beth to Catfish, her eyes gravely serious. "If I go, and there's a good chance of that because the doctor wasn't able to dig the bullet out—"

"Oh, no!" Beth interrupted her. "Julia, no!" Tears glistened in her eyes.

"Please, Beth," Julia said commandingly.

Beth looked at her, sucking back tears.

"I want you both to have this place."

"Now, Julia," Catfish said, still worrying the brim of the hat in his lap.

"Catfish, please," she said, scowling at him. "Let me finish."

Catfish pursed his lips and nodded.

"I'm giving you each half. If you don't want it—I know you both have other lives—Beth, I know you'll want to get back to teaching soon, then sell it. But it's yours to do with as you please."

Beth sobbed and covered her mouth, choking back more cries.

Julia looked at Catfish. She was the one who appeared as the schoolteacher now, lecturing a pair of students who were testing her patience. "Will you do that for me? If I pass—and I'm not saying I will, but I might if that bullet shifts around—it will give me peace knowing that all I built here in Wolfwater will go to my only two friends."

Again, she looked at Beth before shuttling her gaze back to Catfish. "Two friends I love with all my heart."

Tears glazed her eyes.

She rested her head back against her pillow. "You haven't answered me," she said with that schoolmarm's crisp impatience.

Catfish was choking back sobs of his own. Staring down at the hat he was giving a workout, he nodded, then said, "Yes . . . of course, Julia. We'll do good by you, my lady. You deserve that much."

Beth sobbed again and nodded. "Yes, Julia . . . anything you want."

"Now, Beth, would you leave Catfish and me alone for a minute?"

Beth nodded. "Yes, of course." She rose, dropped the cloth in the water, and lifted the basin. Turning toward the door, she said, "I'll freshen the water." She stopped at the door and glanced over her shoulder at Julia. "I'm going to bring you some soup." It was her turn to put some schoolmarm's command in her voice.

Julia did not respond. She kept her gaze on Catfish. Her eyes were suddenly flat, dark, and stony.

Beth went out and clicked the door shut behind her.

Catfish frowned curiously down at Julia.

"Catfish?" she said.

"Yes, Julia."

"Kill Sergei for me, will you?" She wrinkled her fine nose with bitter disdain. "And those three henchmen of his. Find them and kill them."

"Planned to," Catfish said. "As soon as Brazos is back on the job, I'll ride out, find those devils' lair, and kick all three out with a cold shovel."

"Tell Sergei it's from me . . ." She quirked a frigid half smile. "Will you?"

Catfish smiled. "Be happy to." He leaned down and planted a tender kiss on her forehead. "Now I'll leave and let you get some rest."

He rose, the bed squawking as it lifted back into place.

He walked to the door.

Behind him, Julia said, "Make sure that shovel is really cold, will you?"

Catfish glanced over his shoulder at her. He smiled and set his hat on his head.

He winked, then opened the door and went out.

He took one step forward, and if he would have taken another one, he would have stepped right smack dab into Grant Dragoman. "Whoa, whoa, whoa, there, Catfish!" the rancher said, laughing.

He was dressed in a Western-cut suit, with a high-crowned cream Stetson and a turquoise-studded neck-piece. His double-breasted charcoal-gray wool jacket was lightly powdered with trail dust. His face was large and handsome, despite leaning toward the dissipation of too much drink and living boldly into his sixties. He even seemed to have most of his large yellowing ivory teeth, Catfish noted with some jealousy as the man stretched his lips in a patronizing smile. He chuckled patronizingly, too, and patted Catfish's shoulders twice.

More artificial fawning that slopped over into open mockery.

"You're back on the job, I see. Well, well, imagine that! At your age"—he dropped his gaze to Catfish's rounded belly—"and, uh, girth!" Again, he patted Catfish's shoulders twice, chuckling. "Good for you. Never give up, I say!"

His features clouded over suddenly. "Good God—

I heard about Julia. Uh . . . Miss Claire. I galloped to town with my foreman—got here as fast as I could." He tried to step around Catfish, reaching for the handle of Julia's door. "I'm going to look in on her."

Catfish didn't move.

Dragoman peevishly frowned at him. "Step aside, man. You heard me."

"She's resting."

The scowl on the rancher's face turned more severe. "What's that?"

"She's resting. Doesn't want to be disturbed. How 'bout you an' me go down an' drown us an egg in a beer? Now, that's my kind of breakfast." Catfish smiled and patted his belly. "I'm on a diet, you see."

"No, no, no. I want to check in on—" Again, he reached for the door.

Again, Catfish blocked his way.

"What on earth's gotten into you, Catfish?" the man said, wrinkling his nose with scorn.

"We're gonna go down an' have us"—Catfish patted the man's shoulders twice, firmly—"a little palaver." He grinned, knowing his teeth weren't as purty as the rancher's.

Dragoman studied him, deeply incredulous. Then he shook his head and threw his hands up in supplication. "All right, all right. Have it your way, Catfish." He gave a derisive laugh. "Let's go drown an egg and have us a palaver!"

The two men strode down the hall and then down the staircases. Catfish led the rancher to a table a good distance from the other few drinkers and breakfasters in the room. They moved away from where he saw Dragoman's foreman, Lon Caville, laying out a game of solitaire and nursing his own beer, with a glowing orange egg lolling at the bottom of a dimpled schooner. Caville, a tall, slender, sandy-haired man with a handlebar mustache, caught sight of his boss and Catfish, then scowled.

Dragoman gave the man a slight, dismissive wave as Catfish dragged a chair out from the table with his foot and sank into it. The rancher sat rather indignantly into a chair on the other side of the table, then leaned forward on his elbows, entwining his hands.

Catfish signaled the bartender, a scrawny, mannish-looking woman named Maud Cahill, who'd finally tired after twenty years of running a shotgun ranch south of Wolfwater, after her husband took an Apache arrow to the back of his neck, and moved to town. She'd needed a job to support herself, and Julia gave her one without hesitation. The salty little woman, always attired in a men's wool shirt, denim jeans, and worn stockmen's boots, and with a tightly rolled quirley always dangling from one side of her mouth, didn't exactly harmonize with the tony elegance of the Lone Star Outpost. The Lone Star boasted varnished wood, gleaming mirrors, a brass footrail running along the base of the long, elegant, zinc-topped bar, and deep green velveteen drapes. But Julia gave her the job because she needed one.

That was Julia.

Catfish had known Maud for years. He'd known her husband, too.

She brought the schooners, each with an egg at the bottom, and set one on the table before Dragoman. As she set the other in front of Catfish, she gave him a vaguely questioning look, then shrugged both her skinny shoulders beneath her dark blue wool shirt and, sucking the quirley and blowing the smoke out of her Indian-dark nostrils, headed back to the bar.

"Now, then," Dragoman said impatiently.

Catfish sat back in his chair, one hand wrapped around his schooner on the table, and thumbed his hat up on his forehead. "Why'd you hire a no-account shooter like Eldon Ring to kill Julia's husband?"

The man stared across the table at Catfish, with his eyes suddenly bewildered, his jaws loosening until Catfish thought his chin would strike his chest.

"I know all about it," Catfish said.

"How . . . ? How . . . ?"

"Never mind how. I found Ring dead in a wash after he followed Sergei Zhukovsky and his three henchmen out of Wolfwater. Everybody knows Ring lost his nerve up in Wyoming an' hasn't been worth a wrinkled buck bill in years, though he continued playing like he was a stone-cold killer for hire. Dumb as a plug, most likely, to boot." Catfish took a sip of his beer, licked the foam from his mustached upper lip. "Why'd you hire him?"

Suddenly nervous, Dragoman stared into his schooner, his red face turning even redder, until it was the deep purple of a West Texas sunset just before dark. The skin around his eyes was yellow. The man's reaction told Catfish he'd guessed right about the man's ploy.

"I . . . I don't know what you're talking about," the man said to the inch-thick foam at the top of his glass.

"You didn't want him to be successful, that's why," Catfish said, slowly turning his own schooner on the table before him. "You wanted Julia to know you'd hired her husband's killer, but you didn't really want him killed."

The rancher lifted his chin and bunched his purple cheeks until his eyes were slits. "Are you *mad?*"

"Boilin' mad. You wanted that crazy Russian to ruin Julia. Why, Dragoman?"

"That's absolutely insane. You know that, don't you?" Dragoman sagged back in his chair and slapped one big hand down on the table. "You're too old for the job, Catfish. Too old. Too much drink!"

"Everyone knows you asked for her hand many times. Just as many times, you offered to buy her out. She didn't want to marry you and she didn't want to sell to you. You're not a man who takes no for an answer. Especially not from a woman. She humiliated you. It's been eating at you. Finally, when she rode out to your ranch asking for help with her husband, who wants to ruin her, you saw your chance of getting her back. If Zhukovsky ruined her, you could easily buy her out. Maybe even marry her. Her name wouldn't be worth squat in town if the town found out about her past. She'd need you then, wouldn't she, Dragoman?"

Catfish grinned then. "The joke's on you, Dragoman. Julia doesn't need *any* man. Least of all, one like you." He shook his head slowly, his shrewd grin in place. "Doesn't matter how desperate she got, she'd never marry you. She wouldn't sell to you, either. No chance!"

Catfish slapped his own hand down on the table, causing the foam to wash up against the sides of his glass. "Oh, and there's one more joke. This one really puts the pie on your face, Dragoman. It was one of Zhukovsky's tinhorn henchmen who shot Julia."

"You're a fool," the rancher bit out, flaring his nostrils, miniature bayonets of raw fury hurling from his eyes.

"Maybe," Catfish said, leaning forward in his chair. "Just know this, Dragoman. If she dies"—he lifted his gaze to the ceiling above the table—"I'm gonna kill you. No amount of men will save you. I will hunt you down, get you alone, and drive a pill right here!"

He touched his right index finger to the middle of his forehead.

A muscle in the rancher's right cheek twitched.

"I won't listen to any more nonsense coming from a senile old man. Rest assured, I'll be having a chat with Mayor Booth about your future. I think he'll agree you need to spend your remaining years at your catfish hole!"

He thrust his schooner, which he hadn't taken a single sip from, away from him distastefully, rose from his chair, beckoned his foreman, and stomped toward the door.

Caville gave Catfish a threatening look as he walked past him, hurrying to catch up to his boss.

Catfish pinched his hat brim to him.

Chapter 31

Wanting to give Jasper the rest he himself could not afford, Catfish rented a horse from Russell McCormick at the Break O' Day Livery Barn and rode out to the east end of town, where Brazos rented a cabin from Hettie Rose. The Widow Rose, as she was known in town, rented the small log shack flanking her own to Brazos.

Both hovels were sun-splashed now as Catfish rode up out of a dry wash separating the two shacks from town. Clothes hung from a line strung between two scrub oaks to the right of the first shack, near a dying fire over which a large copper pot hung from an iron tripod. The clothes shone brightly—vivid reds, greens, blues, and yellows—in the sunlight, nudged a little by a breeze that was growing hotter by the minute.

Already, Mrs. Rose had done laundry. Now she was likely inside the shack with her quiet boy, Peter, darning clothes for the townsfolk who patronized her. Peter was likely practicing his letters and numbers. Or reading. Catfish had heard the boy liked to read.

Mrs. Rose herself had taught him, Catfish had heard, as, being Black, the boy wasn't allowed to go to the white school in Wolfwater.

That was a crying shame, to Catfish's way of thinking. For both the boy and his mother, who felt compelled to teach him to somehow survive in the white man's world while she worked herself to the bone, providing for them both.

Lonely dang life out here, Catfish thought as he pulled his rented horse around the widow's cabin and over to the one Brazos rented behind it. Brazos's shutters and door were closed. No sound or movement around the boxlike log place, save the hot, dry breeze rattling mesquite and willow leaves and the chirping of desert wrens in a cedar thicket off the cabin's right front corner.

Depressing place out here, Catfish thought as he halted the mount before the lone hitchrack fronting the small, shabby front stoop fronting the cabin. He didn't know how Brazos could take it out here. Probably because all he did was sleep here. In the weeks since he and Catfish had donned their badges again, they'd both mostly been working. Little time even for sleep. That fact was darn real as Catfish crawled heavily down from the saddle now, fatigue weighing heavy on his shoulders. In fact, his left foot slipped out of the stirrup and dropped to the ground, giving Catfish a start. He grunted and fell wearily against his saddle, blinking and shaking his head.

Come on, you old goat, he silently told himself. *You got a job to do. No time to sleep till Brazos is back on his . . .*

He let the thought trail off incomplete. He'd heard what sounded like a woman's muffled laugh beneath the scratching breeze, piping birds, and the squawk of the clay water pot, or olla, hanging from a nail in an awning support post on the cabin's front stoop. *Nah.* He shook his head, blinked his eyes several times, rapidly. *Couldn't be.*

Lack of sleep was making him hear things, just like it was making him conjure assassins where there were only roofers with nails bristling from between their lips . . .

Then it came again—a woman's muffled laugh. The thud of someone slapping a table echoed, which was next followed by the brief, bemused chortle of a young boy.

The voice of a man sounded from inside the cabin—resonant, but too low and quiet for Catfish to make out what the man was saying. What *Brazos* was saying. That was Brazos's voice, sure enough. Buoyant with subtle humor.

Catfish turned to the cabin, scowling.

What in tarnation?

He moved slowly to the two porch steps, climbed them slowly, one hand on his pistol grips. He looked around carefully, wondering if he was being led into a trap, maybe one that had already been set for his partner. After the *first* one that had been set for Brazos the previous night, that was. Maybe the killers had come to finish him off and then Catfish, to boot!

He winced as, crossing the porch, his right boot made a worn, age-silvered floorboard squawk faintly. Tightening his right hand around his gun handle, he moved up to the door and bent his head to listen. Sure enough, that was Brazos's voice inside the place, all right.

Now he could vaguely make out what the man was saying, ". . . had the stuffin' kicked out of one end before, but never both ends at once!"

Again, the woman laughed—a muffled sound as though she was holding her hand over her mouth.

The boy laughed loudly, delightedly.

Then Brazos laughed, too. Catfish hadn't heard his partner laugh in a long time. Surely, neither he nor Catfish had had anything to laugh about lately, not like they had in times past, but that was Brazos's voice, sure enough. Ripping loose with abandon, vaulting above the woman's and the boy's laughter.

Scowling his incredulity, Catfish lifted his left hand and lightly tapped his knuckles against the door comprised of vertical pine boards between which windblown seeds, cactus thorns, and sand had gathered over the long years since Samuel Rose had built both cabins out here on the edge of nowhere—one for him and his bride to live in, one to rent out to a fellow prospector. Catfish tripped the door's latch, and as the door shuddered open a few inches on its leather hinges, he cast his mystified gaze into the cabin.

As he did, Brazos, sitting at the small, square table just beyond the door, jerked his pistol up from his right hip, clicked the hammer back, and aimed it at the door. His molasses-dark eyes gazed threateningly down the barrel, until his black brows stitched and he lowered the gun slightly and said, "*Cha'les?* What in tarnation you doin', skulkin' around on my front porch?" He depressed his Colt's hammer with a click. "Lookin' to get yourself drilled a third eye—one you can't *see out of*?"

The woman and the boy turned to Catfish then as well, dark eyes widening in shock and sudden fear, the humor of only a second ago erased from their faces. All three sat at the table, which was fairly buried beneath the platters, plates, cups, and bowls of a hearty meal. The leavings of which—as well as the succulent aroma of which—spoke of nicely browned baking-powder biscuits, rich dark sausage gravy, scrambled eggs, fried potatoes, and a glass pitcher of creamy milk. The boy sat on the side of the table nearest the door, hipped around in his chair to regard the intruder, round-eyed. The Widow Rose sat at the end of the table, to the boy's right. Brazos sat across from the boy, studying Catfish incredulously as he slowly lowered his Colt, until it disappeared beneath the table.

Then there was nothing to impede Catfish's view of his partner's face, which was a swollen mask of cut, scraped, and otherwise badly abused tissues. Both eyes were nearly swollen shut so that the man's eyes were black slits in the center of two puffy mounds. His lips resembled raw beef, both bristling with sutures. Brazos wore a red longhandle top, the open V-neck of which revealed a thick white bandage wrapped around his chest and belly.

"Yep," Catfish said, "you had the stuffin' kicked out of both ends, all right." Suddenly, seeing all eyes on him, he felt as though he had intruded on a family having breakfast together. He glanced at the boy and the widow once more, then said to Brazos, "I was just checkin' on ya, pard. Heard about the, uh, incident. I see you're still kickin', though. Taken care of real good." He glanced at the Widow Rose, then stepped back and started to draw the door closed. "I'll come back later."

He'd almost latched the door, when Brazos said loudly, "Cha'les, get in here!"

"Yes, yes, yes," the Widow Rose said, rising quickly

from her chair, coffee-brown cheeks darkening as a flush rose into them. "Please, Marshal Tuttle. Come on in. Peter an' I were just leav—"

"No, no, no," Catfish said, shoving the door open again, keeping his hand on the knob. He wished he would have ridden off when he'd heard the woman's and the boy's laughter. He was intruding, indeed, and he felt sorry as heck about it. His curiosity had gotten the better of him. "You stay right there, ma'am. You too, Peter. I'll just . . ."

But she was already to the counter running along the kitchen's back wall, her arms full of plates and platters. "Peter and I have much work to do at our own place, Marshal," she said with a flush-faced glance over her shoulder, setting her load of dirty dishes into the wreck pan. "I just . . . we just . . . I mean . . . I saw Brazos—I mean, *Deputy McQueen* . . . ride home late, slumped over on his horse. I saw he needed assistance, so I only . . . well, I only . . ."

"She fixed me up right fine," Brazos said as Peter helped his mother clear the table. Brazos, too, seemed a little chagrined, embarrassed, as he dug into his tobacco pouch on the table for his makin's sack. "Don't know what I woulda done without her. Don't think no ribs are broke through, but they're bruised up good, an' this here bandage makes the pain right tolerable." He jerked his head back irritably. "Get in here, Cha'les. Stop standin' there like a calf caught in a thicket. Get in here!" He glanced at the widow clearing more cups and plates from the table. "You don't need to go, Het . . . er, I mean, uh, *Mrs. Rose.* You an' Cha'les here ever been properly introduced?"

He glanced up at Catfish, who took one more tentative step into the cabin, and then Brazos dribbled chopped tobacco onto the wheat paper troughed between his fingers.

"Uh," Catfish said. "Well, no, I reckon not prop—"

He stopped as the widow swung toward him, a little breathless, and self-consciously tucked her curly hair into the messy bun atop her head. "I just came back over this morning because I knew Braz—I mean"—she stomped her foot down in frustration, causing the boy to jerk with a start—"Mr. McQueen needed a proper meal in his belly. You know, so he can heal!"

Catfish stopped halfway between the door and the table and raised his hands, palms out. "Oh, you don't need to . . . you don't need to . . ."

"Sit down, Cha'les," Brazos said, slowly curling the paper into a cylinder. "The damage has been done," he added with a dry chuckle.

The table having been cleared, the widow turned to Brazos, smoothing her apron down flat against her thighs, and said, "Peter and I will leave you men to your business. I will come back later and finish cleaning up this mess I made."

"Oh, no nee—" Brazos said, but stopped when the breathless widow grabbed the boy by the arm and jerked him out the door, fumbling the door closed behind her.

"Mama," Catfish heard the boy say outside, "what's wrong with—"

"Shh," came her quick retort. "Never you mind. Come along. We have work to do, for pity's sake!"

Their quick footsteps dwindled to silence.

Catfish turned to Brazos. "Sorry, pard. I—"

"There ain't nothin' to be sorry about. The lady tended my injuries and was kind enough to make me breakfast. I insisted she didn't—by God, that woman has enough work to do, Lord knows—but she insisted, and in my condition, I couldn't do much to stop her."

Brazos flicked his thumbnail across a lucifer match; the flame hissed and leaped to life. He touched it to the quirley protruding from his stitched, puffy lips, which made Catfish wince to look at it.

Catfish moved up to the table, placed his hands on the back of the chair that the boy had been sitting in. "There's nothin' to be embarrassed about."

Brazos frowned as he blew a smoke plume toward the ceiling. "I'm not embarrassed about noth . . ." He let his voice trail off, frowning pensively at the chair the widow had been sitting in. He shrugged sheepishly, then said, "I don't know."

"You looked good together. All three of you."

Catfish dragged a tin cup down from a shelf above the dry sink and wreck pan, then filled it from the gurgling coffeepot on the small black range's warming rack.

"Did we?" Brazos said, frowning at him curiously, his ears turning a little darker as he blushed again.

"Why, sure you did." Catfish sat slowly down in the boy's chair, wincing at the popping and creaking in his old, battered knees and hips, not to mention his shoulders. He almost felt as bad as Brazos looked. "You like this lady . . . the Widow Rose?"

Brazos seemed to ponder the question as he stared self-consciously at the lit end of his cigarette. He pursed his lips, nodded slowly, then frowned and looked over at Catfish suddenly. "Enough on that. Cha'les, we got problems. Big problems."

"Don't I know!" Catfish exclaimed. He hadn't even begun to tell his end of things!

"Finish your coffee," Brazos said, sticking the quirley between his lips, then placing his hands on the table and rising with a painful grunt from his chair. "Take your time, gonna take me a few minutes to get my battered carcass dressed."

"You just stay right where you are, old son!" Catfish objected.

"Uh-uh, uh-uh," Brazos said. "You an' me is headin' over to the Yellow Rose. I got me a man to see about a hoss!"

He gave Catfish a sly wink. At least Catfish thought he winked. The flesh was so swollen around both eyes it was hard to tell. What was not hard to tell was that Brazos was not heading for the Yellow Rose to talk to any man about a horse . . .

No, he had a man to kill, or Catfish missed his guess.

Chapter 32

Catfish saddled Brazos's mount in the stall stable behind the deputy's cabin.

As he did, he filled the injured man in on what he'd been through earlier—following Julia out of town as she'd followed the raggedy-heeled regulator, Eldon Ring, who was following the tall, pale, odd-looking gent, who'd turned out to be Julia's husband, who was here in Wolfwater to blackmail her for former transgressions against him. Zhukovsky had been riding with his three henchmen.

Catfish told Brazos about finding Eldon Ring dead in the wash, about Catfish getting ambushed by none other than Black Taggart, and then Julia getting shot by one of Zhukovsky's men, just when she and Catfish had thought they were both out of the proverbial woods. Leaning against a stout ceiling support post, Brazos, whose battered face still made Catfish flinch, listened raptly.

When Catfish had told him about his recent conversation with Grant Dragoman in the Lone Star Outpost, both men mounted their horses and rode back into Wolfwater. As they rode, scanning the dusty streets around them for more would-be assassins, Brazos told Catfish about the conversation he'd overheard in the back room of the grocery store.

"So some of Wolfwater's saloon owners—all lesser lights—are plotting to take someone down, eh?" Catfish said, fingering the two days' worth of beard stubble on his chin. "I'll be hanged. Who could they be wantin' to take down . . . and why?"

"I haven't a clue, Cha'les."

"An enemy . . . or someone they see as an enemy. Likely, another saloon owner. Competition."

Brazos glanced at him. "Miss Claire? She's about the most powerful saloon owner in town."

Catfish thought it over. "Nah. She couldn't be that unlucky, could she? I mean, her husband's already tryin' to take her down, an' so far, he's done a purty good job." He shook his head. "Nah . . . can't be. None of the other saloons see her as competition. She's too far out of the league of *all* of 'em! Besides, Julia brings in business for everybody!"

"Yeah, yeah," Brazos said. "I suppose you're right."

They'd just swung their horses down a side street and were nearing the Yellow Rose Saloon, near the street's far southern edge—a long, low wood-framed building with a brush-roofed front gallery shaded by a dusty cottonwood. The building had once been painted yellow, but most of the paint had been worn away by the West Texas weather, leaving only bits of curling pieces and most of the weathered wood exposed.

The Yellow Rose was a favorite hangout for some of the rowdier card players and drinkers in the area. These were the types of men—mostly grub-line riders and border toughs, Mexicans and whites, and a few half-breeds or mestizos—who slunk off to squalid brothels after the saloons closed and were up at first light, ready to play more poker and drink more whiskey at the Yellow Rose. The squalid den practically defined the term "hole-in-the-wall." A Mexican named Willie Rodriguez owned the place, and he ran it with his pudgy, but pretty, daughter, Carlotta. She was small, but she kept the often-unruly customers in trim with a quick, south-of-the-border temper and a plump iron fist.

"Brazos?" Catfish said as he pulled his rented mount up to one of the three hitchracks fronting the place. The three rails had a total of maybe eight mounts tied to them. "What're we doin' here?"

Brazos was about to respond, but stopped when a man's agonized cry rose from the saloon's bunkhouse-style bowels. A woman's angry shriek followed the man's wail and then there was the clatter of a chair being scraped across the floor and then quick, heavy footsteps. Again, the man wailed above the thumping of the fast-moving feet and jangling spurs.

The wailing and the thumping grew louder, until a man burst through the batwings, followed by a short, wide, brown-skinned young woman in a low-cut, sleeveless white blouse, flowered skirt, and a red bandanna holding her thick dark brown curls back from her face. Carlotta had the man's right ear pinched between the thumb and index finger of her left hand, and was regaling the man in a chaotic stream of Spanish, spoken too quickly for Catfish to make out more than a few Spanish epithets, including "pig," "dirty dog," and "the spawn of curs." She ushered him across the dilapidated gallery fronting the doors and into the street. When the man had taken three whimpering steps, Carlotta released his ear suddenly and gave his backside a hard kick with her right foot, clad in a gold-buckled black ankle boot.

Her victim, a frequently out-of-work cowpuncher named J.W. Yates, flew forward and went sprawling in a cloud of dust. As he did, Catfish saw that his left ear was bloody. As the hapless fool lay moaning on his belly, sucking air like a landed fish, Carlotta stood before him, feet spread wide, and pointed a bloody obsidian-handled stiletto at him as she spat in English: "If you ever come around here again, spawn of a trash-eating sow, I will hack off your other ear, dry it, and hang it around my neck!"

She spat wickedly in the dirt between the man's boots, then leaned down to clean off her nasty-looking pigsticker on the man's left pant leg. She hiked up her skirt to return the stiletto to a small, slender leather sheath strapped to her comely left calf, then regarded the man again. She furiously said, "Teach you to keep your hands to home, cracker!"

She gave a punctuating, satisfied grunt, glanced at Catfish and Brazos sitting their mounts, eyeing her uncertainly, then smiled broadly and said, "Welcome, amigos! Come in and cut the trail dust!"

She swung around and flounced across the gallery and back through the batwings, which shuddered into place behind her.

Catfish returned his gaze to the sobbing J.W. Yates, who clamped his left hand over his left ear.

"Ouch," Catfish said, turning to Brazos. "That had to hurt!"

"You're tellin' me," Brazos said. "I thought *I* was in pain. At least I still have both ears."

"That makes you one up on J.W."

The two men laughed; then Brazos sobered suddenly, removed his deputy town marshal's star from his shirt behind his duster, and held it out to Catfish. "Hold that for me, will you, boss?"

Catfish glowered at him. "Who you callin' 'boss'?"

"You're my boss, whether it makes sense or not. You know that, Cha'les. Hold on to that for me."

Catfish uncertainly plucked the star from the man's gloved hand.

"For the next minute or so, I'm off the clock," Brazos said, and swung down from his saddle.

"What in tarnation . . . ?" Catfish eased his own battered bulk out of his own saddle, then tied the reins to a hitchrack and followed Brazos up onto the gallery.

He stopped when, four feet ahead of him, Brazos stopped to peer over the batwings into the Yellow Rose's thick shadows. From here, Catfish could smell the fetor of tobacco smoke, cheap perfume, and unwashed bodies emanating over the louvered doors. Brazos stood staring over the doors, his back straight. Catfish could see a tight muscle twitch in his neck, just beneath his left ear.

"Oh, oh . . ." Catfish had seen that twitch before.

What had followed hadn't been no square dance, either . . .

"Now, partner," Catfish said, squeezing the man's star in his left hand, leaving his right one free in case he found himself needing to back his partner's play.

Brazos raised his hands up before him, palms out, and thrust the doors wide. He stepped through them, taking several long strides inside. As he did, Catfish followed him in and then took several steps to the left, toward the bar that ran along the wall on that side of the rough-hewn shack, his right hand on the grips of his .44 . . . just in case.

Brazos strode slowly straight into the room.

At the room's far end was the faro layout. The faro dealer was the thuggish Duke Scallion—a big, lantern-jawed man, with a dark brown patch beard and a broad nose lumpy at the bridge, where it had been busted several times. The part-time mine guard was clad in a cheap three-piece suit, complete with a faded red ribbon tie and frayed-brimmed bowler hat. Two Mexicans in dusty trail garb and low-crowned straw sombreros stood before Scallion's table, staring down as Scallion turned over a card on his faro layout.

Scallion smiled up at the two Mexicans and chuckled jeeringly through his teeth, saying, "Sorry, Pancho, my boy. Better luck next . . ."

Scallion let his voice trail off when he slid his gaze around the two Mexicans to see Brazos striding toward him, stiff-backed, the deputy's hands clenched at his sides. Scallion studied Brazos for about three seconds, his jaws slowly unhinging, until fear glinted in his eyes, and he rose awkwardly from his chair, stumbling backward and knocking the chair over with a loud *bang*.

The two Mexicans turned to Brazos then, likely seeing the killing fury in the Black man's eyes, and sidled quickly away and around Brazos, then hurried outside through the batwings. As Brazos stopped ten feet from the faro table, Scallion raised an arm and pointing finger and said, "Now . . . you just hold on. You hold on now, blast you. You got no call . . ."

"I got no call to fill you so full of lead you'll rattle when you walk?" Brazos asked as Catfish raked his cautious gaze around the room, making sure none of the other customers were about to shoot him in the back. "Was it not you who led me into that trap last night?"

"What?" the faro dealer said, his voice cracking on his exasperation and fear. "*Trap?* What're you talkin' about? Trap!" He glanced around the room at the other customers, all watching intently. "I don't know what this boy's even talkin' about. Why, he's crazy. Look at him—he musta got drunk an' fell down. You know how *they* are!"

He gave a nervous chuckle and then went silent.

The rest of the room was silent, save for the ticking of a clock behind the bar, where Willie Rodriguez and Carlotta stood, regarding Brazos and the faro dealer intently. Carlotta broke the silence to bark out commandingly, "No trouble in here, gring—"

Her father, who couldn't have stood much over five feet six inches, a slump-shouldered fellow who wore his long hair in a queue down his back, and had a large wart protruding from the side of his nose, nudged her with an elbow. Carlotta looked at him, frowning, then returned her gaze to Brazos and the faro dealer. Likely seeing the direness of the situation and noting that Brazos's anger was even out of her control, Carlotta held her tongue.

Good idea. Brazos was wound up tighter than a coiled diamondback . . .

Scallion seemed to see that as well. He stumbled back against the plank wall behind him and raised both hands to his shoulders, palms out. "Now, see here . . . now, see here . . . I don't want no trouble."

"You bought yourself a whole pack o' trouble last night, Scallion. Now you can either claw iron or die like the worthless, cowering dog you are!" Brazos raised his hand to his chest, apparently showing his lack of a badge. "See there? I'm taking an hour off. Personal business to attend to, if you get my understandin'?"

Scallion pointed at Brazos again, narrowing one fear-bright eye. "You can't do this! You can't do this!" He slid his gaze to Catfish. "Tell him he can't do this!"

"Still got your badge, Brazos," Catfish said. "You can have it back when you want it. In the meantime, I got somethin' in my eye. Got somethin' in *both* eyes, it seems. Can't see a thing!"

To Scallion, Brazos said, "You gonna defend yourself, you gutless cur? Or you gonna die like the cowardly dog you are? *Your choice!*"

Scallion lowered his hands slowly, stretching his lips back from his teeth and groaning in deep frustration. Suddenly he gave an animal-like wail that sounded like a mother calf giving birth, and it filled the entire room. He thrust his right hand toward the Remington .44 slung low on his right hip. He got the hogleg out of its holster and half raised before Brazos's Colt bucked and roared, smoke and orange flames lapping from the barrel.

The bullet drilled a puckered blue hole in the dead center of the faro dealer's forehead, three inches above the bridge of that wedge-shaped, crooked nose. The man fired his own pistol into the floor and began to slide down the wall behind him, when Catfish, who'd been raking his cautious, protective gaze around the room, held that careful gaze on a man sitting at a table near the saloon's right wall, his back to it. Catfish had seen him when the lawman had first walked into the saloon, saw that he'd been laying out what appeared a game of solitaire. He hadn't seen the man's face, however, for he'd held his chin down so that his eyes and nose were hidden behind the broad black brim of his low-crowned hat.

The man had raised his chin now, however.

The black brim had come up to reveal the demonic amber eyes set too close together on either side of a pitted hatchet nose. Thin pink lips were stretched back from long, slender, crooked yellow teeth as the man grinned across the room at Catfish, eyes glinting like red stones at the bottom of a shallow, sunlit stream.

Black Taggart!

The man leaped to his feet as though he had springs in his ankles. He swept both flaps of his black Prince Albert coat back behind the handles of twin pearl-gripped Colts. His hands dropped in a blur of fast motion for both smoke wagons.

He had Catfish dead to rights.

Catfish threw his big, unwieldy body straight forward onto a table just as Black Taggart's hoglegs roared, making the whole room jump. Taggart's bullets cut through the air just over Catfish an eye blink before the lawman slid forward off the table, hit the floor on his left shoulder, and clawed his .44 from its holster.

He aimed hastily up and at a slant at Taggart, who was just then cocking his twin poppers.

Taggart saw Catfish's pistol aimed dead center on him and, knowing now that it was his opponent who had the upper hand, gave a girlish scream, opening his mouth with all those long, narrow, catlike teeth wide as Catfish's .44 spoke the language of sudden death.

Boom! Boom! Boom!

Boom!

Taggart stumbled back against the wall, teeth still clenched, amber eyes dropping in horror toward the four bullet holes leaking blood through his white shirt and paisley vest.

The man's spidery hands opened.

His pistols dropped with one thud and then another to the floor.

"*Ach!*" he wailed, and then dropped down to the floor and sat there, back against the wall, glaring down at Catfish still on the floor by the table he'd slid off of, smoking .44 still extended.

Catfish glanced toward Brazos, who stood in a crouch, his own Colt extended toward the fast-dying killer. Brazos glanced at Catfish and frowned his incredulity.

Catfish climbed heavily to his feet, ignoring the fresh aches and pains in every joint, not to mention his left shoulder. Brazos slid his pistol to cover the room, while Catfish limped over to the table behind which Black Taggart sat, back against the wall.

The dying killer's eyes rose to Catfish.

His lips stretched back once more from his catlike teeth.

Catfish frowned. The man seemed to be making a noise. It was sort of like a hiccupping sound.

Then he realized the man was laughing deep in his throat.

Taggart grinned up at Catfish, eyes bright with mockery.

"You're too late," the dying killer said in an ominously soft, raspy voice. He blinked. "You're too late . . . to *save her*!"

He opened his mouth and threw his head back, laughing.

Then his mouth and eyes closed, and he slid sideways down the wall to lay on one shoulder with a heavy sigh, dead.

Catfish's heart turned a somersault in his chest. He turned to Brazos.

"It's Julia, after all, partner!" he yelled. "Here, *catch!*"

He flung the badge at his deputy, who caught it out of the air with one hand.

Then Catfish ran as fast as a much younger man through the batwings, Brazos hot on his heels.

Chapter 33

Grant Dragoman pushed through the Lone Star's heavy oak doors.

He stepped to one side and looked carefully around the vast, cavelike room.

The old reprobate, Catfish Charlie Tuttle, was gone. Good.

It was almost noon, so there were plenty of diners and drinkers, serving girls hauling large trays of steaming food to men—mostly men, but a few women as well, for the Lone Star's dining room was deemed fitting for the fairer sex. Yes, the place was busy. Julia was really making a killing, though Dragoman himself preferred the grub over at the Chinese Lantern. He considered the food here bland, overpriced slop.

Of course, maybe his resentment had something to do with his bleak assessment.

Inwardly he chuckled.

The important thing was that the place was busy. The milling crowd would mostly cover him, render him less conspicuous as he made his way around the rear of the room and over toward the broad, carpeted stairs, as he did now, feeling his heart thud nervously. He'd left his foreman over at the Chinese Lantern. He'd told Caville he was returning to the Lone Star for a drink with his attorney. Caville didn't know what he was really up to. No one but a handful of others in town did.

Men he hoped he could trust. He was staking his reputation, as well as his freedom, on them. It certainly would have helped, had they sent the right men to get the town's two lawmen out of the way. He'd thought they'd be killing Abel Wilkes and Bushwhack Wilbur Aimes, but that was before Wilkes and Aimes were killed by Frank Thorson. It should have been easier to take out the aging and out-of-practice Catfish Tuttle and Brazos McQueen, but they'd flubbed the job. All the killers they'd hired, including an old nemesis of Catfish's—Black Taggart—had flubbed it good.

Dragoman was out of time, however. He couldn't wait any longer. He'd waited long enough. With Eldon Ring having met his Maker, which Dragoman had gambled he would do, the time was ripe now to finish Julia, once and for all.

He paused near a carved stone elephant, mounted on a carved stone column, near the bottom of the staircase in order to check his gold-washed timepiece. One minute after eleven. He snapped the lid closed and returned the piece to his coat pocket and started up the stairs.

His heart beat eagerly.

His man should be entering through the saloon's rear door—really, a very flimsy affair—locked with only a bracketed crossbar, which was too meager for an establishment that took in very impressive profits a day. Julia never posted any guards back there. You'd think she would know better. She probably thought she and her fine establishment were above being robbed. She didn't think anyone would dare.

Silly woman. She really had needed Dragoman in her camp. In her bed. Now she'd pay for her foolishness, and the Lone Star would be out of business, no longer around to mock him.

Her manager, Howard Dale, would be in her office, going over accounts and preparing cash drawers for the afternoon. He'd have most of the money from this morning in there, was probably counting it now. And he had a safe stuffed, likely to near brimming, with cash from the past week's business in there as well. Julia deposited the money in the bank only once a week.

Smiling and pinching his hat brim to a couple of *nymphs du pave* descending the stairs, chatting animatedly between themselves, likely too distracted to take much note of the rancher's presence—no, no one outside his tight circle of local conspirators must suspect he'd had any part in what was about to occur—he ascended the stairs to the third story. He was glad when he saw no one else in the long hall before he drew up to the door behind which he knew Julia lay, recuperating.

He lightly tapped with his knuckles, turned the knob, and poked his head into the room. She wasn't alone. The former marshal's daughter was with her. Beth Wilkes turned to Dragoman. She sat on a chair beside Julia's bed, spooning soup into Julia's mouth. Now she held the spoon just above the steaming bowl and frowned curiously at the rancher.

"Well, hello, there, young lady," he said, stepping

into the room and removing his hat. "How's our girl doing?"

Lying back against two pillows propped partway up against the bed's brass headboard, Julia stitched her brows in a scowl, croaking out, "Grant . . ."

She didn't appear all that happy to see him. Just self-conscious, Dragoman supposed. She'd looked far better.

Unless Catfish had shared his suspicions with her . . .

Dragoman took another couple of steps into the room, holding his hat low before him. "I came as soon as I heard," he said. "How are you doing, Jul"— he glanced at Beth gazing incredulously up at him, and amended—"er, I mean, Miss Claire?"

He smiled broadly, warmly. Julia, of course, saw no warmth in the smile. The man's eyes were flat and hard. Her heart quickened, the blood in her veins chilled. Beth could sense it as she shuttled her own troubled gaze between Julia and the tall, red-faced, handsome, but hard-eyed, man looming over them. His short, thin brown hair, combed straight back from a pronounced widow's peak, was laced with gray. Gray in his sideburns as well. He had a big, walnut-gripped pistol holstered high on his right hip. Beth could see it behind the lapel of his dust-sprinkled gray coat.

A well-known, successful man, he was an intimidating specter before them.

Standing over them, Dragoman was reflecting on what was likely happening in Julia's back-room office at that very moment—his man, a killer known as Hobarth, moving into her office, drawing down on Julia's manager, likely beating the man until he opened the safe teeming with all that raw cash . . .

Not that he needed the cash. No, that would go to

the men, his cohorts, and the killers they had working for them . . .

Dragoman would be satisfied with merely putting
Julia out of business, once and for all. Of course,
Zhukovsky might have done it. Though he'd never
met the man, the Russian had given Dragoman the
idea of going even further. He liked the idea of ruining her name, but Dragoman knew Wolfwater better
than the Russian did. The town would forgive her
trespasses, and she'd continue ignoring Dragoman's
pleas for a business partnership and marriage.

No, ruining her name in Wolfwater was impossible.

But he could destroy her. Utterly destroy her, as
well as her precious business, the Lone Star Outpost.

Anger burned in him, but he kept the smile on his
face as he turned to Beth Wilkes. "Miss Wilkes, would
you mind if Miss Claire and I had a private word?"

She frowned up at him, hesitant. She looked at
Julia. Julia slid her gaze to her. The two women looked
at each other in silence for about two seconds and
then Miss Wilkes set the bowl on the table beside the
bed, haltingly, her hands shaking a little, the spoon
rattling.

"Oh," she said, rising from her chair. "Of course."
She looked down at Julia, gave a stiff smile. They
seemed to be silently communicating something.
What was it? "I'll be back . . ."

Julia gave a slight nod, then returned her incredulous gaze to Dragoman.

Miss Wilkes glanced up at Dragoman, then moved
to the door. At the door, she stopped, glanced at
Dragoman and then Julia once more, then twisted
the knob and went out.

Dragoman slacked his tall frame into the chair Beth had abandoned; holding his hat on his lap, he reached forward to wrap his right hand around Julia's left one, atop the covers. "How are you doing, my dear? Does it hurt terribly? What did the doctor say?"

Julia turned to face him, smiling. "I'll be fine." She lifted her head slightly, lifted her pale hands as well, and fiddled with her messy hair. "Good Lord—I must look terrible."

"Oh, you couldn't if you tried!"

Julia grimaced, shook her head.

Dragoman took her hand in both of his, pulled it up to his mouth, and planted a repellent kiss on it. "This wouldn't have happened if you'd married me, you know? I would have protected you . . . from him."

Julia gazed up at him flatly.

"Have you met him, Grant? Zhukovsky? Did you throw in with him . . . to ruin me? Is that why you hired the inept fool Eldon Ring?"

Still holding her hand up close to his mouth, Dragoman shook his head. "No, no. I wasn't in cahoots with him. True, I hired Ring because I wanted Zhukovsky to continue bedeviling you. I thought he might drive you . . . and the Lone Star . . . to me at last." Again, he shook his head, regarded her somberly. "I didn't want this to happen, Julia. It must have been a mistake. I heard you were out with that fat fool of a town marshal. Zhukovsky likely wanted him killed and out of his way. Just as I've tried to."

The rancher chuckled dryly. "I swear the man must have nine lives. I've heard a good dozen men—tried-and-true killers, all—attempted to kill him and his deputy. Hasn't happened yet. But I heard the deputy was taken out of commission last night. That leaves only Catfish. He's likely dead drunk . . . dead asleep. If not"—he gave a deep sigh—"oh, well. He'll wish he was."

"Why?"

"Here's what's going to happen, my dear. I'm robbing you. I and several of the smaller saloon owners in town. You see, I convinced them that once we robbed you and burned down your establishment, you'd be ruined. Better than merely ruining your reputation could ever do. We've hired a gang of men."

Dragoman released her hand, pulled his timepiece from his pocket, and clicked open the lid. He smiled down at the watch, snapped it closed. "In about two minutes, they'll be here. Shooting up the place, robbing your barman, just as my other man, Hobart, is likely cleaning out your safe even as we speak." He returned the watch to his pocket and rose from his chair. "They and the other saloon men will split the plunder among themselves, and once I burn you out . . . burn the business to the ground . . . any inquiring authorities will chalk it all up to simple robbery. Nothing more, nothing less. The robbers have orders to head to Mexico just as soon as they meet the saloon men at a determined place in the desert and split the proceeds."

He'd walked over to a chest of drawers and scooped a hurricane lamp from its surface. He caressed it almost lovingly before him, the lit wicking aglow in the room's shadows relieved only by sunlight edging around the drawn curtains of the single window. The coal oil sloshed around inside the lamp's glass bowl. The flame flickered, dancing this way and that as the rancher gently rocked it.

Julia watched the flame, her heart quickening.

She chuckled to herself. She'd been so afraid of

Zhukovsky that she hadn't realized who her true enemy was. A man who'd professed to love her and wanted to spend the rest of his life with her. With her and the Lone Star Outpost, of course.

Men.

She should have known even before Catfish had put the thought in her head.

This was it, then. This was the end.

Unless . . .

Dragoman's face grew stony as he walked back to the bed, staring darkly down at Julia. He set the lamp on the night table, beside the bowl of half-eaten soup. He sat down in the chair and leaned forward, elbows on his knees.

"Don't worry—I won't let you burn, my dear. At least . . . not alive. I still love you, you see. You deserve better than that. I'll make it as quick as I can. All right?" He leaned farther forward, shoving his large hand out toward Julia, wrapping them around her neck almost tenderly.

"Grant," she said as he began to apply pressure. She tried to slide her fingers behind his hand, to pry them loose, but in her weakened condition, her strength was no match for his. She choked as more pressure was applied. "Grant!"

Dragoman smiled devilishly down at her as he tightened his grip.

As he cut off her breath, large, dark motes filled Julia's vision. Her head swelled, and she tried to gasp in vain for a breath.

Above the rushing in her ears, Julia heard the door latch move . . .

. . . saw the door open slowly . . .

Beth Wilkes stepped into the room, her brown

eyes large, round, and bright with terror. She held Julia's pearl-gripped pocket pistol in both hands. She stepped forward haltingly, and just as haltingly said, "M-Mr. D-Dragoman . . ."

Keeping his hands wrapped tightly around Julia's neck, Dragoman whipped his gaze toward Beth, anger flaring his nostrils. "Put that gun down! You're no match for me! Do you know who I am?"

"I know exactly who you are," Beth said, voice trembling. "And I'm going to shoot you if you don't take your hands away from Julia's neck."

"Put that gun down, I said!" Dragoman barked, keeping the pressure applied to Julia's neck.

Beth narrowed one eye as she aimed down the Merwin & Hulbert's barrel.

The gun popped. The bullet screeched past Dragoman's head to plunk into the wall behind him. He flinched and pulled his hands away from Julia's neck. Julia tipped her head back, gasping for air and placing her own hands on her bruised neck.

"You silly child!" Dragoman said, facing Beth, who was aiming the revolver at him from six feet away. "You're no match for me!"

"Oh, yes, I am!" Beth retorted, her voice quaking with fear, but laced with satisfaction as well.

Just then, a man's voice bellowed from the saloon's main drinking hall—"All right, this is a hold-up! Everybody on the floor!"

Another man shouted something unintelligible.

A gun roared. Then another.

Beth lowered the pistol and turned her head with a gasp.

"Beth!" Julia cried as Dragoman lunged toward the girl.

Beth swung back toward Dragoman and screamed as the .38 bucked and roared, knocking her backward.

Dragoman yelped and flew backward into the chair and night table. He rolled off the table, screaming as the lamp he'd just shattered with his body spilled burning coal oil on him. Instantly the floor on that side of the bed and table was in flames. The flames were crawling like flickering orange snakes up the drapes drawn over the window. They engulfed the writhing form of Grant Dragoman as he tried to fight them in vain, screaming.

They were slithering away from the burning rancher toward the bed.

"Julia!" Beth screamed.

Chapter 34

Catfish hadn't leaped into a saddle for a good twenty years.

But now he leaped onto the rented horse's back after ripping the reins from the hitchrack. He almost overshot the saddle and tumbled down the other side, but he grabbed the horn just in time and righted himself. Brazos leaped onto Abe's back and together they swung their mounts around and galloped back in the direction of the main drag, as though both horses had tin cans tied to their tails.

They hadn't made it to the corner of the side street they were on and the main drag when they started hearing muffled shooting and shouting. As they galloped around the corner, Catfish whipped a look at Brazos and yelled, "That's comin' from the Lone Star!"

"We better wait and talk about this, Cha'les!" Brazos yelled, keeping pace beside Catfish.

Catfish whipped his rein ends against the horse's backside, urging more speed. "We'll talk about it when it's over!"

As he and Brazos approached the impressive structure of the saloon, which sat on a corner of the main street's south side, Catfish saw flames dancing in a third-story window, burning the drapes closed over it. "That's Julia's room, gallblastit!" he bellowed as more shooting and yelling sounded from the Lone Star's ground floor, just behind the stout oak doors flanking the broad front porch.

"I said everybody down or we'll blow you to hell and gone!" came a man's shrill, commanding voice behind the doors.

"Gallblastit," Catfish shouted. "They're gonna rob the place, shoot it up, and burn it down. Dragoman's behind it. I know he is!"

"Cha'les, we don't know how many polecats we're up against!" Brazos said as they both checked their horses down near the dozen or so horses, along with two carriages and a ranch wagon, parked in front of the place.

Catfish leaped from the saddle, his Yellowboy in hand. "We'll know in two jangles of a doxie's bell, partner!"

"Law, law, law!" Brazos exclaimed as he leaped down from his own horse's back.

He followed Catfish up the porch steps and together they stopped at the doors leading to the main drinking hall. They heard more sporadic shooting and shouting from the other side of the doors.

Catfish racked a round into his Yellowboy's chamber and said to Brazos, "Ready?"

Brazos jacked a round into his Winchester's breech and said to Catfish, "No!"

"All right—let's go!" Catfish said, and shouldered the left door open.

Brazos shouldered the right door open and together they burst into the place, each dropping to a knee just inside the doors and pressing the rear stocks of their rifles to their shoulders. Catfish looked around quickly. There were a good ten robbers standing here and there about the room, which was hazy with tobacco and gun smoke. Each was wearing a flour sack mask with the eyes, nose, and mouth cut out. They all wore dusters and were wielding rifles. One of the robbers was at the bar, aiming a rifle at Maud Cahill, who was shoving greenbacks and handfuls of coins into a gunnysack laid out atop the bar.

When Catfish and Brazos had entered the saloon, Maud, whose head rose only a foot above the bar, had been hurling narrow-eyed curses at the man accosting her for the money. Now she and the man at the bar whipped startled looks toward the two lawmen down on their knees as they tracked their rifles around the room. In fact, everyone in the saloon had turned to regard the newcomers—all the masked, duster-clad robbers and all the customers lying belly-down on the floor of the large, carpeted room.

Catfish heard girls screaming on the establishment's second and third floors as he said, "A holdup, eh? Well, that's over. Drop those rifles, gentlemen—and I use that term *very lightly*—or prepare to be blown to Kingdom Come!"

"Ah, crap—it's them two local lawdogs!" bellowed one of the robbers.

"There's only two of 'em," barked the man at the bar, swinging around to face the lawmen and raising his own Yellowboy rifle to his shoulder. *"Kill 'em!"*

Before he could get a shot off, Maud grabbed a whiskey bottle standing atop the bar and smashed it over the robber's head, caving in his brown Stetson.

"Oh, no, you don't, vermin!" the little lady cried, her haggard face a mask of unadulterated fury. The bottle broke in her hand and the robber grunted and dropped like a fifty-pound sack of parched feed corn.

The bottle's crash and the robber's grunt signaled the start of the fusillade.

Catfish and Brazos quickly picked out targets and commenced firing before the robbers, most still squaring their shoulders and aiming their long guns at the two lawmen, could get off a shot. Catfish and Brazos's targets were blown back off their feet and onto a table and a chair, respectively, a second or two before the others commenced shouting and firing, orange flames and pale smoke lapping from their rifle barrels.

Knowing they were outnumbered and that the other robbers had them dead to rights as they ejected the spent shells from their rifles' breeches and pumped in fresh, Catfish and Brazos moved forward and spread out, hunkering down behind tables and chairs, picking out fresh targets and firing as the robbers fired at them, sending hot lead curling the air around and over their heads, plunking into tables and knocking over chairs.

Catfish shot another one of the robbers and dropped down behind an overturned chair. As he did, he locked eyes with none other than the Wolfwater mayor Derwood Booth, who was hunkered down with one other businessman under a table four feet beyond Catfish.

"Good Lord, Catfish!" the prim and proper mayor intoned, holding his hat on his head with one hand, "what in heaven's name is going on here?"

"Heaven don't have nothin' to do with it, Mayor,"

Catfish said as slivers were shot out of the chairback before him, the overturned chair giving insignificant cover from the bullets slicing the air around him. In fact, one bullet just then blew his Stetson off his head and tossed it back against the bar. Catfish raised his head and rifle and shot another robber, then said to Booth, "But if I was you, I'd try to make it out the doors. The third floor's on fire!"

As a bullet carved a hot line across Catfish's right cheek, he heard a catlike wail behind him: "Oh, you dirty devils—die, each an' every one of you yellow-livered curs!"

Lowering his head and pumping a fresh round into the Yellowboy's action, Catfish glanced over his shoulder to see Maud opening up on the robbers with an old-model Spencer repeating rifle she had propped across the top of the bar, her raisin face cheeked up against the rear stock.

"Thanks, Maud!" Catfish yelled as he knocked over a table to use as a shield.

"Don't mention it, Catfish!" Maud returned as her Spencer's maw blossomed smoke and flames. "Happy to clear the town of rats!"

One of the robbers bellowed miserably, while yet another—most were down now, firing on Catfish and Brazos from behind tables, chairs, and ceiling support posts—shouted, "Lord A'mighty—we're surrounded, boys!"

Brazos shot that one, who fell back against a table, then twisted around to hit the floor, crawling madly toward the room's rear wall, unsheathing a pistol on his hip. As he did, Catfish saw Brazos step out from behind a ceiling support post and shoot the crawling outlaw in the back of his head, laying the man out flat on his belly.

Catfish and Maud dropped two more.

Catfish tossed away his empty Winchester and slid his .44 from its holster, but held fire when he could locate no more targets behind the heavy fog of webbing and waving powder smoke. The only one left standing, it appeared—and he was only halfway standing—was one upon whom two of Julia's bouncers had descended and were hammering mercilessly with their fists against the wall up which the broad stairway climbed.

Catfish rose to his knees, looked around once more, and glanced at Brazos, who said, "Looks like they're all fresh meat, partner!"

Just then, a man screamed from the rear of the room, to the right of Julia's gambling layout. A second later, a thick-waisted and broad-shouldered man came through that door, wailing and dragging his boot toes. The tall man wore a brown duster and cream hat. He dropped six feet in front of the door, and Catfish saw a knife protruding from his back, blood welling up from the blade embedded between his shoulders.

Howard Dale came through the door next, his lips bloody, broken spectacles hanging off one ear. A shoulder of his frock coat was torn. He held a bulging burlap bag in his right hand. He stopped, looked down at the now-dead outlaw, then glanced at Catfish and said, "Never underestimate a quiet man! He was about to run out the back with the money from Julia's safe, but he didn't give me credit for having a knife!"

Meanwhile, smoke was roiling down the stairs, down which a good dozen doxies were running, screaming and crying as they ran.

"Good for you, Howard!" Catfish yelled, then turned to Brazos. "Julia and Beth!"

Catfish ran through the crowd of customers hurrying toward the doors while holding a handkerchief over their mouths and grimacing down at the dead men around them.

With Brazos hot on his heels, Catfish climbed the steps quickly, breathless and sweating, his bullet-creased noggin and his grazed cheek burning. He couldn't quite believe his old ticker was still beating, but it was not only beating, it was racing and knocking against the back side of his breastbone. He hoped he could reach Beth and Julia before it gave out.

He did.

Beth was leading Julia down the second-floor stairs, which were now engulfed with smoke, flames leaping like a dragon's breath through the stairwell above them.

"Oh, for pity's sake," Catfish said, reaching them. He picked Julia up in his arms. As he did, Brazos picked up Beth, yelling, "Hold on, honey!"

Both women were coughing and choking on the thick smoke, their eyes watering.

"The Lone Star," Julia said. "I have to save it. It's all I have!"

"Too late, darlin'," Catfish said, halfway down the stairs and descending quickly, his own eyes burning from the smoke. "Too much fire. They'll never get it out!"

He was hearing the bells calling for the bucket brigade outside, but he knew he was right. The townsmen forming the brigade would never get organized in time to save Julia's beloved business.

He ran across the smoky saloon hall. Howard Dale was waiting by the door beside Maud Cahill. Each held a gunnysack. Dale raised his and said, "We have all the cash!"

Then he and Maud waited until Catfish, Brazos, Julia, and Beth were outside and descending the porch steps, before following them out and into the crowd gathered in front of the Lone Star Outpost, eyes wide with shock. There seemed a haphazard attempt to form a bucket brigade from the town's well, but too few men had gathered, with too few buckets. By the expressions on the men's faces, Catfish could tell they knew all hope was gone. The town's beloved saloon, owned by the town's beloved proprietor, was as good as kindling.

Already, flames were licking up the side of the building, above the window of the room Julia lived in, toward the roof. There would be no getting water up there. Soon the roof would collapse and so would the rest of the place.

Catfish and Brazos carried the women across the railroad tracks, a good distance from the fire, and set them down on the boardwalk, on the opposite side of the street from the inferno. Julia stared at the burning building and sobbed. Brazos was down on one knee, beside Beth, rubbing her back, as she, too, stared in horror at the conflagration.

"Don't worry, honey," Catfish told Julia. "You'll rebuild. The town will hel—"

He stopped when he saw a tall, pale figure in a three-piece suit and a monocle dangling from a lapel of his black coat peering toward him from behind an awning support post half a block up the street to the west.

Zhukovsky!

His three henchmen stood in a doorway of a saloon to the Russian's left, also peering toward the fiery debacle. The Russian had a supreme look of satisfaction on his face. He raised a cigar to his lips, took a puff, then swung around. He and his three raggedy-heeled tough nuts strode into the saloon. Catfish didn't think the man had seen him. He'd been too busy enjoying Julia's misery.

He and the three others were likely waiting for the next train to take them out of Wolfwater.

Catfish looked at Brazos. "I'll be right back, partner!"

Frowning curiously at Catfish striding past him, Brazos said, "You look like you seen a ghost."

"I have," Catfish said, unholstering his .44. "The ghosts just don't know they're ghosts yet!"

Brazos watched Catfish disappear inside the saloon.

Shouts and wails followed. So did six thundering revolver shots.

Catfish emerged from the place thirty seconds later, grinning and striding back toward Brazos and the women.

"Now they do," he said, holstered his smoking .44. He looked at Julia staring at him questioningly and said, "Kicked out with a cold shovel, honey!"

He winked.

Julia smiled.

Catfish knew she was going to be just fine.

So was he, by gum. So was he . . .

TURN THE PAGE FOR AN EXCITING PREVIEW!

MONTANA

**Two Families. Six Generations. One Stretch
of Land.
A Bold New Saga Centuries in the Making.**

*An exciting new series from the bestselling Johnstones cele-
brates the hardworking residents of Cutthroat County: the
ranchers who staked their claims, the lawmen who risked
their lives, and the descendants who carried their dreams
into the twenty-first century.*

Bordered by the Blackfeet Reservation to the north
and mountain ranges to the east and west, Cutthroat
County is seven-hundred glorious square miles of
Big Sky grandeur. For generations, the Maddox and
Drew families have ruled the county—often at odds
with each other. Today, Ashton Maddox runs the
biggest Black Angus ranch in the country, while
County Sheriff John T. Drew upholds the law like his
forefathers did over a century ago. A lot has
changed since the county was established in 1891.
But some things feel straight out of the 1800s.
Especially when cows start disappearing from the
ranches. . . .

Intrigued, a local newsman digs up the gun-blazing
tale of the land-grabbing battles fought by Maddox's
and Drew's ancestors. Meanwhile, their present-day
descendants face a new kind of war that's every bit
as bloody. When a rival rancher's foreman is found
shot to death, Ashton Maddox is the prime suspect.

Sheriff Drew is pressured into arresting him, in spite of a lack of evidence. So the two families decide to do what their forefathers did so many years ago: join forces against a common enemy. Risk their skins against all odds. And keep the dream of Montana alive for generations to come . . .

National Bestselling Authors
William W. Johnstone and J.A. Johnstone

MONTANA

On sale wherever Pinnacle Books are sold.

Live Free. Read Hard.

www.williamjohnstone.net
Visit us at www.kensingtonbooks.com

Chapter 1

After opening the back door, Ashton Maddox stepped inside his ranch home in the foothills of the Always Winter Mountains. His boots echoed hollowly on the hardwood floors as he walked from the garage through the utility room, then the kitchen, and into the living room.

Someone had left the downstairs lights on for him, thank God, because he was exhausted after spending four days in Helena, mingling with a congressman and two lobbyists—even though the Legislature wouldn't meet till the first Monday in January—plus lobbyists and business associates, then leaving at the end of business this afternoon and driving to Great Falls—for another worthless but costly meeting with a private investigator—and crawling back into his Ford SUV, to spend two more hours driving, with only twelve on the interstate, then a little more than a hundred winding, rough, wind-buffeted miles with hardly any headlights or taillights to break up the darkness. And having to pay constant attention to avoid colliding with elk, deer, bear, Black-foot Indian, buffalo or even an occasional moose.

Somehow, the drive from Basin Creek to the ranch road always seemed to worst stretch of the haul. Because he knew what he would find when he got home.

An empty house.

He was nothing short of complete exhaustion.

But, since he was a Maddox, he found enough stamina to switch on more lights and climb the staircase, clomp, clomp, clomp to the second floor, where his right hand found another switch, pushed it up, and let the wagon wheel chandelier and wall sconces bathe the upper storm in unnatural radiance.

The grandfather clock, still running, said it was a quarter past midnight.

His father would have scolded him for leaving all those lights on downstairs, wasting electricity—not cheap in this part of Montana. His grandfather would have reminded both of them about how life was before electricity and television and gas-guzzling pickup trucks.

When he reached his office, he flicked another switch, hung his gray Stetson on the elkhorn on the wall, and pulled a heavy Waterford crystal tumbler off the bookshelf before making a beeline toward the closet. He opened the door, and stared at the mini-icemaker.

His father and grandfather had also rebuked him for years about building a house on the top of the hill. "This is Montana, boy," Grandpa had scolded time and again. "The wind up that high'll blow you clear down to Coloradie."

Per his nature, Ashton's father had put it bluntly:

"Putting on airs, boy. Just putting on airs."

What, Ashton wondered, would Grandpa and Daddy say about his having an icemaker in his closet? Waste of water *and* electricity!

Not that he cared a fig about what either of those hard rocks might have thought. They were six feet under now. Had been for years. But no matter how long he lived, no matter how many millions of dollars he earned, he would always hear their voices.

Grandpa: *The Maddoxes might as well just start birthin' girls.*

Daddy: *If you'd gone through Vietnam like I did, you might know a thing or two.*

He opened the icemaker's lid, scooped up the right number of cubes, and left the door open as he walked back to the desk, his boot heels pounding on the hardwood floor. Once he set the tumbler on last week's Sunday *Denver Post*, which he still had never gotten around to reading, he found the bottle of Blanton's Single Barrel, and poured until bourbon and iced reached the rim.

Grandpa would have suffered an apoplexy had he knew a Maddox paid close to two hundred bucks, including tax, for seven hundred and fifty milliliters of Kentucky bourbon. Both his grandpa and father would have given him grief about drinking bourbon anyway. As far back as anyone could recollect, Maddox men had been rye drinkers.

The cheaper the better.

"If it burns," his father had often said, "I yearns."

He sipped. Good whiskey was, he thought, worth every penny.

Now he crossed the room, glass still in his hand, till he reached the large window. The heavy drapes had already been pulled open—not that he could remember, but he probably had left them that way before driving down to the state capital.

They used to have a cleaning lady here. One of the hired men's wife, sweetheart, concubine, whatever. But that man had gotten a job in Wyoming, and she had followed him. And now. . . with Patricia gone . . . Ashton didn't see any need to have floors swept and furniture dusted.

He debated closing the drapes, but what was the point? He could step outside on the balcony. Get some fresh air. Close his eyes and just feel the coolness, the sereneness of a summer night in Montana. Years ago, he had loved that—even when the wind come a-sweepin' 'cross the high plains. Grandpa had not been fooling about that wind, but Ashton Maddox knew what he was doing, what the weather was like, when he told the man at M.R. Russell Construction Company exactly what he wanted, and exactly where, he wanted his house.

Well, rather, where Patricia wanted it.

Wherever she was now.

He stood there, sipping good bourbon and feeling rotten, making himself look into the night that never was night. Not like it used to be.

"You can see forever," Patricia had told him on their first night up here, before Russell's subcontractor had even gotten the electricity installed.

He could still see forever up here. Forever. Hades stretching on from here north to the Pole and east toward the Dakotas, forever and ever and ever, amen.

The door opened. Boots sounded heavy on the floor, closing, a grunt, the hitching of jeans, and sound of a hat dropping on Ashton's desk.

"How was Helena?" foreman Colter Norris asked in his gruff monotone.

"Waste of time." Ashton did not turn around. He lifted his tumbler and sipped more bourbon.

"You read that gal's hatchet job in that rag folks call the *Big Sky Monthly*?"

"Skimmed it. Heard some coffee rats talking about it at the Stirrup."

"Well, that gal sure made a hero out of our sheriff." Ashton saw Colter's reflection in the plate-glass window. He held a longneck beer in his left hand. "And made Garland Foster sound like some homespun hick hero, cacklin' out flapdoodle about cattle and sheep prices and how wind's gonna save us all." Colter lifted his dark beer bottle and took a long pull.

Ashton started to raise his tumbler, but lowered it, shook his head, and whispered: "'. . . while beef and wool prices fluctuate, the wind always blows in this country.'"

The bottle Colter held lowered rapidly. "What's that?"

"Nothing." Now Ashton took a good pull on bourbon, let some ice fall into his mouth, and crunched it, grinding it down, down, down.

"Thought you said you just skimmed that gal's exposé." The foreman frowned. Colter Norris never missed a thing: a sign, a clear shot with a .30-.30, a trout's strike, or a half-baked sentence someone mumbled.

Raising the tumbler again, Ashton held the Waterford toward the window. "He didn't put up those wind turbines," he said caustically, "because of any market concerns." He shook his head, and cursed his neighboring rancher softly. "He put those up to torment me. All day. All night."

A man couldn't see the spinning blades at this time of night. But no one could escape the flashing red warning lights. Blinking on. Blinking off. On and off. Red light. No light. Red light. No light. Red light. Red . . . red . . . red . . . red . . . all night long, all night long till dawn finally broke. There had to be more wind turbines on Foster's land than that skinflint had ever run cattle or sheep.

Ashton turned away and stared across the room. Colter Norris held the longneck, his face showing a few days' growth of white and black stubble and that bushy mustache with the ends twisted into a thin curl. The face, like his neck and wrists and the forearms as far as he could roll up the sleeves of his work shirts, were bronzed from wind and sun, and scarred from horse wrecks and bar fights. The nose had been busted so many times, Ashton often wondered how his foreman even managed to breathe.

"You didn't come up here to get some gossip about a college girl's story in some slick magazine," Ashton told him. "Certainly not after I've spent three hours driving in a night as dark as pitch from Helena to here by way of Great Falls."

"No, sir." The man set his beer next to the bottle of fine bourbon.

"Couldn't wait till breakfast, I take it." Ashton started to bring the crystal tumbler up again, but saw it now contained nothing but melting ice and his own saliva.

"I figured not." Few people could read Colter Norris's face. Ashton Maddox had given up years ago. But you didn't have to read a cowboy's face. The voice told him everything he needed to know.

This wasn't some hired hand wrecking a truck or ruining a good horse and had been paid off, then kicked off the ranch. It wasn't someone who got his innards gored by a steer's horn or kicked to pieces by a bull or widow-making horse.

Frowning, Ashton set the glass on a side table, walked to the window, found the pull and closed the drapes. At least he couldn't see those flashing red lights on wind turbines now.

He walked back and made those cold blue eyes meet Colter Norris's hard greens.

"Let's have it," Ashton said.

The foreman obeyed.

"We're short."

Ashton's head cocked just a fraction. No punch line came. But he had not expected one. Most cowboys Ashton knew had wickedly acerbic senses of humor—or thought they did—but Colter Norris had never cracked a joke, hardly even let a smile crack the grizzled façade of his face. Still, the rancher could not believe what he had heard.

"We're … *short?*"

That rugged head barely moved up and down once.

Ashton reached down, pulled the fancy cork out of the bottle, and splashed two fingers of amber beauty into the tumbler. He didn't care about ice. He drank half of that down and looked again at his foreman.

No question was needed.

"Sixteen head. Section Fifty-four at Dead Indian Pony Creek." He pronounced creek *crick*, as did many Westerners.

The map hung on the north-facing wall, underneath the bearskin, and Ashton took his glass and rising anger to the modern map hanging on the paneling. Colter Norris left his empty longneck on the desk and followed, but the foreman had to know better than point.

Ashton Maddox knew his ranch, leased and owned, better than anyone living. He found it quickly, pointed a finger wet from the tumbler, and then began circling around, slowly, reading the topography and the roads.

"You see any truck tracks?" he asked.

"No, sir. Even hard-pressed, a body'd never get a truck into that country 'cept on our roads. What passes for roads, I mean. Our boys don't even bring ATVs into that section. Shucks, we're even careful about what horses we ride when working up there."

Ashton nodded in agreement.

"Steers?" he asked. "Bull or . . . ?"

"Heifers."

"Who discovered they were missing?"

"Dante Crump."

The head bobbed again. Crump had been working for the Circle M for seven years. He was the only cowboy Ashton had ever known who went to church regularly on Sundays. Most of the others were sleeping off hangovers till Mondays. A rancher might question the honesty of many cowboys, but no one ever accused Dante Crump of anything except having a conscience and a soul.

Ashton kept studying the map. He even forgot he was holding a glass of expensive bourbon.

Colter Norris cleared his throat. "No bear tracks. No carcasses. The cattle just vanished."

"Horse tracks?" Ashton turned away from the big wall map.

The cowboy's head shook. "Some. But Dante had rode 'cross that country—me and Homer Cooper, too—before we even considered them cattle got stoled. So we couldn't tell if the tracks were ours or their'n's."

"Do we have any more cattle up that way?" Ashton asked.

"Not now. Dante went up there to bring them up to the summer pasture. We left fifty down there in September. Found bones and carcasses of three. About normal. Dante brought down thirty-one. So best I can figure is that sixteen got rustled."

"Rustled." Ashton chuckled without mirth. The word sounded like something straight out of an old Western movie or TV show.

"Yeah," the foreman said. "I don't even never recollect your daddy sayin' nothin' 'bout rustlers."

"Because," Ashton said, "it never happened." He let out another mirthless chuckle. "I don't even think my grandpa had to cope with rustlers, unless some starving Blackfoot cut out a calf or half-starved steer for his family. And Grandpa had his faults, but he wasn't one to begrudge any man with a hungry wife and kids." He sighed, shook his head, and stared at Colter Norris. "You're sure those heifers aren't just hiding in that rough country."

The man's eyes glared. "I said so," was all he said.

Which was good enough for Ashton Maddox now, just as it had been good enough for Ashton's father.

"Could they have just wandered to another pasture?"

"Homer Cooper rode the lines," the foreman said. "He said there was no fence down. Sure ain't goin' cross no cattle guards, and the gates was all shut and locked."

They studied one another, thinking the same thought. An inside job. A Circle M cowboy taking a few Black Angus for himself. But even that made no sense. No one could sneak sixteen head all the way from that pasture to the main road without being seen or leaving sign.

"How?" Ashton shook his head again. "How in heaven's name . . . ?"

Colter Norris shrugged. "Those hippies livin' 'cross the highway on Bonner Flats will say it was extra-terrestrials."

He said that without a smile, and it probably wasn't a joke. In fact, Ashton had to agree with the weathered cowboy.

The *Basin River Weekly Item* had reported cattle turning up missing at smaller ranches in the county, but Ashton had figured those animals had probably just wandered off because the ranchers weren't really ranchers, just folks wealthy enough to buy land and lease a pasture from the feds for grazing and have themselves a quiet place to come to and get a good tax break on top of that. Like that TV director or producer or company executive who ran buffalo on his place and had his own private helicopter. There were only two real ranchers in Cutthroat County now, though Ashton would never publicly admit that Garland Foster was a real rancher. He'd been a mostly a sheepman since arriving in Cutthroat County, and now he was hardly even that.

He looked at the curtains that kept him from seeing those flashing red lights all across Foster's spread.

"How did someone manage to get sixteen Black

Angus of our herd out of there? That's what per-
plexes me." He moved back to the map, reached his
left hand up to the crooked line marked in blue type
Dead Indian Pony Creek, and traced it down to the
nearest two-track, then followed that to the ranch
road, then down the eleven miles to the main highway.

"Without a truck or trucks. Without being seen?"

Colter Norris moved closer to the map. Those
hard eyes narrows as he memorized the topography,
the roads, paths, streams, canyons, everything. Then
he seemed to dismiss the map and remember the
country from personal experience, riding a half-
broke cowpony in that rough, hard, impenetrable
country in the spring, the summer, the fall. Probably
not the winter, though. Not in northern Montana.
Not unless a man was desperate or suicidal.

The head shook after thirty seconds.

"I can take some boys up, see if we can find a trail,"
Colter Norris suggested.

Ashton's head shook. He had forgotten about a
wife who had left him. He had dismissed a fruitless
trip to the state capital and then for an even more
unproductive meeting in a Great Falls coffeeshop
with a high-priced private dick.

"No point in that," Ashton said. "They stole sixteen head of prime Black Angus because we were
sleeping. Anyone who has lived in Montana for a
month knows you might catch Ashton Maddox
asleep once, and only once, because I'll never make
that mistake again. They won't be back there. Any
missing head elsewhere?"

"Nothin' yet," Colter Norris replied. "But I ain't
got all the tallies yet."

He remembered the bourbon, and raised the tumbler as he gave his foreman that look that needed no re-interpretation.

"I want those tallies done right quick. Because there's one thing in my book that sure hasn't changed since the eighteen hundreds. Nobody steals Circle M beef and gets away with it."

Visit our website at
KensingtonBooks.com
to sign up for our newsletters, read
more from your favorite authors, see
books by series, view reading group
guides, and more!

BOOK **CLUB**

BETWEEN THE CHAPTERS

Become a Part of Our
Between the Chapters Book Club
Community and Join the Conversation

Betweenthechapters.net